CW00972125

Falcon Warrior

Falcon Warrior

The Swordswoman Book III

Malcolm Archibald

Copyright (C) 2017 Malcolm Archibald
Layout design and Copyright (C) 2017 Creativia
Published 2017 by Creativia (www.creativia.org)
Cover art by Cover Mint
Edited by Lorna Read
This book is a work of fiction. Names, characters, places, and incidents are the product of the author's imagination or are used fictitiously. Any resemblance to actual events, locales, or persons, living or dead, is purely coincidental.
All rights reserved. No part of this book may be reproduced or transmitted in any form or by any means, electronic or mechanical, including photocopying, recording, or by any information storage and retrieval system, without the author's permission.

For Cathy

Venient annis saeula seris
Quibus oceanus vincula rerum
Laxet, et ingens pateat tellus,
Tethysque novus detegat orbes:
Nec sit terries ultima Thule

In later years the age shall come
When the Ocean will unloose the bonds of nature
And the vast earth will stretch out,
And the sea will disclose new worlds:
Nor will the globe be utmost bound by Thule
Seneca: Medea, Act II, v. 371

Chapter One

The wind came from the south and east, driving *Catriona* onward into a never-ending waste of sea, as it had done for days past and probably would do for days to come.

'How long has this storm lasted?' Bradan shook water from his hair, only for another wave to crash against *Catriona*'s high prow and splatter him with a fresh supply of spindrift.

Sitting in the stern with her right hand fixed on the tiller, Melcorka shrugged. 'I do not know. Does it matter? If we were not here, we would be somewhere else.'

'I would prefer to be somewhere else rather than in a small boat in the middle of the Western Ocean.'

Melcorka glanced around. 'It is better to journey with hope than to arrive at disappointment,' she said. 'And as long as we are miserable in *Catriona*, we are alive.' She grinned. 'Would you prefer we were under the water than on top of it?'

'I would rather I had my feet on solid land,' Bradan said. 'We have seen nothing but waves for weeks now.'

Melcorka smiled. 'Oh, Bradan the Wanderer! It was you who wanted to venture out of Alba. It was you who wished to find the lands where grow the strange fruits that wash up on Alba's western coasts.'

'I know that,' Bradan agreed.

'And here we are, sailing to find your exotic lands.'

Bradan gave a rueful grin. 'Indeed. I'll keep quiet now and allow you to enjoy our pleasure cruise in the endless ocean and when we fall over the end of the earth, you will remind me that this was entirely my fault.'

'Of course I will,' Melcorka told him. She shook her head, so the hood of her travelling cloak flicked off and her long black hair tossed around madly in the gale. 'I wonder what it will be like to fall off the end of the world?'

'I spoke to a very wise old druid about that very matter once,' Bradan said seriously.

'I remember,' Melcorka said. 'That caused us all sorts of trouble.'

'There is no trouble that you cannot handle,' Bradan said. 'This druid, Abaris, told me all the wonders of the world, but alas, my mind could only retain a fraction of the information.'

'Minds are like that,' Melcorka said.

'But there is one thing I do remember,' Bradan said. He lowered his voice, but she could still hear him despite the howling of the storm. 'The world is not flat, it is round, so if a man...'

'Or a woman,' Melcorka interrupted.

'Or a woman – I was about to say that. If a man or a woman keeps going in any direction, he or she will eventually end up back where they started.'

Melcorka laughed. 'I can't see the point in that,' she said. 'What is the sense in going for a long journey, just to arrive back at your starting place?'

'For the adventure,' Bradan said, 'and for the experiences... the places you see, the different people you meet, the strange lands and cultures!'

'So why are you complaining?' Melcorka asked sweetly. She looked around. 'Here, we are surrounded by strange... water.' She laughed again. 'At least we have the adventure of the voyage.'

'What's that?' Bradan pointed ahead. 'I think we have another sort of adventure about to start.'

Melcorka peered into the storm, where great, grey-green waves rose higher than their spiralling mast, with the tops curling, spewing silver-white spindrift and then swooping down toward *Catriona* like some roaring monster from the deep. 'I can only see waves ... No, wait... You're right, Bradan. There is something there.'

There was something behind the waves, something vast and shining; something so strange that Melcorka could not believe what she saw. 'It's a mountain of glass, right in the middle of the ocean.'

'It's moving,' Bradan said. 'It's a floating island of glass.'

'We'll try and go round it.' Melcorka struggled to push the tiller to the left, fighting the power of the wind and waves. *Catriona* protested against the alteration of course; with her stern no longer directly in the wind and waves, water poured in over her port quarter to rush knee-high, the length of the boat.

'She doesn't like this,' Bradan said.

'It's either this or ram into that.' Melcorka nodded toward the great island of ice that was rapidly approaching them. She pushed the tiller harder, so *Catriona* heeled further over and shipped even more water, which swirled around their legs.

'I don't know about us ramming into it,' Bradan said. 'I do know that *it* is trying to ram *us*. Look at the thing! It's going against the wind. I've never seen the like.'

Melcorka nodded. The massive mountain of glass was ignoring the wind as it surged toward them, its great pinnacles thrusting aside the waves in great white spumes of foam and spindrift. 'Nor have I. Maybe there is somebody on board it. It could be a type of ship up here.'

The glass mountain was closer now and much taller than *Catriona*'s mast. It soared two hundred, three hundred feet high, whitely translucent with jagged peaks on top and a base of green-blue embedded with small pebbles.

'That's not glass,' Bradan said. 'It's ice! That is a floating mountain of ice!'

'I've never heard of that before.' Melcorka stared at the thing that came toward them. 'I did not know the sea could get that cold.'

'Nor did I.' Bradan stared at the thing. 'And it's still coming toward us at great speed.'

Waves splintered against the base of the ice mountain, sending spray and spindrift high in the air, to blow back against *Catriona*, splattering against the wooden hull and into the faces of Bradan and Melcorka.

'We're going to hit it!' Bradan shouted.

A wave lifted *Catriona* high in the air, just as the ice mountain dipped into the trough of the swell, so when the sea threw them, they landed thirty feet up the sheer ice wall.

'Hold on!' Bradan grabbed Melcorka as *Catriona* crashed against the solid ice. 'Careful, Mel!' They ducked as the ship heeled violently to larboard and began to slide slowly toward the sea.

'We're going back down!' Melcorka yelled. *Catriona* scraped down the edge of the ice, losing slices of her outer planking and landing with a mighty bang on a ledge barely broad enough to accommodate the hull. The boat swayed, nearly toppled over and righted herself, to sit precariously on the narrow shelf above the churning sea with her mast at an acute angle.

'What happens now?' Melcorka looked over the side of *Catriona*, shrugged and smiled at Bradan. 'I've never been in quite this position before, stuck on an ice mountain in the middle of the sea.'

'I doubt that many people have,' Bradan said. 'I've never heard of such a thing.' He returned Melcorka's smile. 'Well, we wanted new experiences, and here we are. At least we're safe here.'

'And stuck. We could stay here until this mountain melts, I suppose.'

'Or until the storm subsides. We're not too far from the surface of the sea. We can just slide *Catriona* down. She is the most stable ship I have ever sailed in.'

'Just settle down then,' Melcorka said. 'And wait.'

She smoothed a hand along the tiller and watched the mighty waves rise and fall. Patience was not typically one of her strongest virtues, but travelling with Bradan had matured her. Now, she sat back in the stern and allowed herself to relax amidst the howling wind and the crash of waves against the floating mountain of ice.

'We are not alone, you know,' Bradan said, some time later. 'We are being watched.'

Melcorka scanned what she could see of the horizon. 'Either you are talking about a whale under the water or a bird above, but I can see neither.' She looked at Defender, the large sword that accompanied her everywhere. 'I hope you are not referring to seals. I have seen enough seals to last me forever.' She recalled her battles with seals and selkies before they had left Scotland.

'No,' Bradan said, 'I am not referring to a seal, a whale or a bird. I am referring to a full-grown woman.'

'Oh?' Melcorka frowned. 'I can't see a ship, either.'

'She is not in a ship,' Bradan said quietly, 'she is only a few feet from you right at this minute, and she is watching everything that you do.'

This time, Melcorka's hand stroked the hilt of Defender, savouring the thrill of power that the sword always gave her. 'Where is this woman?' she asked quietly.

'Look to your left,' Bradan said.

'There is nothing there but ice.' Melcorka looked to her left and smiled again. 'And that woman sitting inside the ice.'

'I think she is dead,' Bradan said. 'At least, she looks dead to me.'

Entombed within her prison of ice, the woman sat on a carved wooden stool with her elbow on her knee and her chin cupped in her hand. Her face was a tawny copper colour, and she wore a bright green tunic decorated with the likeness of a black falcon, with a beaded band around her forehead.

Melcorka pressed her face against the ice so she could see better. The woman's eyes were open and her headband was decorated with the same engraved falcon in the centre of a white circlet. Melcorka looked directly into her eyes and knew there had been profound wisdom there once, and some deep power that she could not understand. 'Now, where did she come from, I wonder?' Melcorka mused.

'We could ask her,' Bradan suggested.

'I doubt she would tell us much. I wonder who she was and how she got inside the ice mountain?'

'I doubt we will ever know,' Bradan said. 'Perhaps there is a race of people that live inside the ice?'

'You should know. You are the man who got all the wisdom of the druids.' Melcorka looked upward as a chunk of ice the size of a human head slid down the exterior of the mountain and landed in the sea. The resulting splash showered *Catriona* with cold water.

'Aye, it's already beginning to melt,' Bradan said. Leaning over the gunwale, he ran his hand across the surface of the ice and showed it to Melcorka. 'See? It's wet. I think there must be a lot of ice in the north, where it is colder than here. The further south this mountain drifts, the warmer it gets and the more it will melt.'

'We may go north sometime and see your ice,' Melcorka said, 'but at present, this ocean current is taking us south and west.' She settled down. 'I am going to sleep until something happens. Good night, Bradan.' She faced the woman in the ice. 'Good night, strange woman.'

Next morning brought the sun, stronger than it had been for some days. Melcorka watched as water droplets oozed down the outside of the ice mountain, merging to form a constant stream that poured into the sea from the lip of the ledge where *Catriona* sat.

'Our ice island is getting smaller by the minute,' Bradan said. 'If this continues, we'll soon be back on the waves again.' He nodded to the woman in the ice. 'All three of us.'

'I still wonder who she was,' Melcorka said, 'and where she came from. I have never seen a woman of her colouring before.'

Bradan nodded. 'I have heard that there are black people and brown people and people of all sorts of colours in this world.'

Melcorka pondered that information for a moment before she replied. 'So there are green people and red people and blue people?' She shook her head. 'I don't believe a word of it. I am more interested in finding out how this woman got to be within the ice and in making sure that we don't end up the same way.'

Bradan ducked as a large chunk of ice detached itself from the side of the mountain and crashed into the sea. It floated alongside for a few moments, clunking and clinking until it spun away on some sub-current.

'This thing is melting away,' Bradan said. 'I don't think we have to worry about being frozen in.' He pushed at the ice beside him. 'We'll be able to shake hands with this lady soon.'

'Let's do just that.' Melcorka unsheathed her dirk, the long fighting knife of the Gael, and hacked into the ice. 'We might find out more about her if we meet her properly.'

'If you have a little patience, the ice will melt itself,' Bradan said.

'I've had enough of being patient.' Melcorka prised free a chunk of ice and forced a crack that extended across the face of the frozen woman. 'Stand back.' She levered the ice away and kicked the shattered remnants into the sea.

The woman fell into Melcorka's arms. Stiff and cold, she stared into nothing through almond-shaped eyes that still retained that aura of power and knowledge. Even although she was long dead, it was evident that at one time she had been an important personage.

'Who are you?' Melcorka bent to search the woman. She had a small leather pouch on a belt around her waist, which Melcorka lifted and emptied on to her rowing bench. A handful of copper trinkets clattered onto the wood, each one in the shape of a falcon with extended wings and a sharp-pointed beak. 'I am taking these,' she said. 'I don't like robbing the dead, but these might help identify you if we ever come across your family.'

'Take that circlet from her head as well,' Bradan said. 'It may help.' He viewed the corpse. 'She looks as if she was important.'

'I thought that as well.' Melcorka could not escape the power of those almond-shaped eyes.

'I wonder if she was some sort of ice-princess?' Bradan frowned. 'She must not have felt the cold at all.'

'She must have been a very hardy woman,' Melcorka said. 'I wonder how long she has been trapped in this ice mountain for?'

'We have no way of knowing,' Bradan said. 'It could have been weeks, or even months.'

'Somebody will be waiting for her to come home,' Melcorka said. 'Should we carry her in *Catriona?*'

'Carry her where? And for how long?' Bradan asked. 'She will smell once she thaws. We'll bury her at sea.'

'That might be best,' Melcorka agreed. 'Do you know the proper words to say?'

'I will say what I think is best,' Bradan said. 'I'm sure she won't mind what the words are.'

The woman was small in height and stocky in stature. They wrapped her in her simple tunic and then in a swathe of sailcloth, weighed at the feet with a couple of heavy boulders from their ballast.

'Goodbye, ice woman,' Melcorka said quietly. 'May you find peace.'

'May our God and your God protect you on your journey to the next world,' Bradan said, as they watched the body sink into the water. There was barely a swirl, with an escaped strand of dark hair the last thing they saw.

'We will never know who she was or where she was from.' Melcorka secreted the headband and the small bag of small copper falcons inside her cloak. 'Now, we will wait until the ice melts and then continue our journey to nothingness. Unless you have decided that you've seen enough of the ocean?'

'We're not going back. There is too much of the world to explore.' Bradan's smile lightened the mood. 'That is the end of that small adventure.'

The sudden wind ruffled Melcorka's hair and raised goose-pimples along her back. It died as soon as it had begun, leaving her slightly unsettled, although she could not say why. She shrugged, looking to the sea where the corpse had sunk. Somehow, she doubted if that small adventure had indeed finished.

'Come on, Bradan,' she said. 'Sing something cheerful to me. Sing a song of the sea or a bawdy drinking song from Fidach of the Picts.'

'I can't sing,' Bradan said. 'I've no voice at all.'

'Oh, come on. You know how much I love music.'

'You asked for it,' Bradan said and began a loud Pictish song. The ancient words swept across the waves of the cold northern sea as Melcorka thought of that mysterious woman, so lonely in her ice mountain. Yet to Melcorka, she was not quite dead; something of the expression of her eyes lingered even as the ice mountain drifted southward in the current and somewhere close by, a whale called mournfully.

They settled down in *Catriona*, watching the dull grey seas rising and falling beneath the light grey sky. Twice they ate and twice they slept without the sky darkening, for in these northern latitudes there was neither night nor day at that time of year. And still, the water wept from the great mountain of ice, shrinking it hour by hour.

'I wonder which will happen first,' Melcorka said. 'Will the ice mountain melt or will they reach us?' She nodded toward the flotilla of sails that thrust from the southern horizon.

'Ships.' Bradan had not noticed them.

'I wonder who they could be, so far away from the world?' Melcorka said.

'Or so far away from *our* world,' Bradan said. 'They might be close to their own. Like the woman we buried at sea.'

'They are Norsemen.' Melcorka said flatly. 'They have the striped sails and the bearing of those savages. Five ships full of Norsemen.' She glanced toward Defender. 'What are they doing out here? There are no priests for them to plunder, no women to rape, no farmers to murder and nobody to take for slaves.'

'We'll soon find out why they're here,' Bradan said. 'They're altering course toward us.'

The square, striped sails became more distinct as they came closer and then the ships' hulls gradually rose over the horizon. Melcorka watched as they came closer; watched the familiar dragon figureheads grow more distinct, with their staring eyes and gaping jaws.

'The first time I saw a dragon ship close up,' she said quietly, 'I was in the Firth of Forth. We were crossing in a fleet of small fishing boats and coracles. I was separated from the rest and Egil was the master.'

She closed her fist around the hilt of Defender. 'He slaughtered all my family that day.'

'Egil is dead now,' Bradan reminded her gently. 'These ships are not his. You cannot hate all Norsemen because of the actions of one man.'

'I do not hate all Norsemen.' Melcorka's knuckles whitened on the hilt of Defender. 'I am just telling you what happened.'

The leading dragon ship was much closer now, so Melcorka could see the sun glinting on the iron bosses of the round shields that lined the gunwales, and the serried spears waiting around the single pine mast. She saw the steersman in the stern with his long blonde hair waving gently, and the crew crowding to stare at this incredible mountain of ice carrying a strange vessel in the middle of the ocean. There were pointing fingers and men buckling on swords, a brace of archers fitting arrows to their bows and a handsome, stern-faced woman standing on a raised platform in the stern, with a tall and younger man at her side.

'This is no raiding fleet,' Bradan said. 'Look at the second ship.'

'Horses,' Melcorka said. 'They give the Norsemen greater mobility.'

'Not only horses. There are also cattle – listen.'

A slant of wind brought the sounds to Melcorka; the lowing of cattle, neighing of horses and, high above, the high-pitched crowing of a cockerel.

'Perhaps these Norse are returning from a raid.' Melcorka defended her corner.

'Have you ever known a Norse war party to bring home cattle and poultry?' Bradan shook his head. 'I have not. These are settlers, not warriors. They are heading somewhere to make a new life.'

'We'll soon find out,' Melcorka said, 'but I won't trust them until I have more proof that they are settlers – and even then I won't trust them.' She adjusted her sword belt so that Defender was within easy reach.

'Take it calmly, Mel, take it calmly. They might be peaceful.'

Melcorka grunted. 'They are Norsemen. They don't know the meaning of the word *peace*.' She glared across the water as if the intensity of her gaze could sink the entire Norse fleet.

The ships came closer, with the sails furling and the oars lifting as they glided alongside.

'Who are you?' the tall young gallant in the first ship called out cheerfully. 'I see you have found a nice iceberg to take along with you.'

'We are Melcorka of Alba and Bradan the Wanderer,' Bradan shouted across the gap between the ships. 'The ice mountain – berg, as you call it – found us, rather than us finding it. Who are you?'

'I am Erik Farseeker, and this is my mother, the lady Frakkok.' He indicated the handsome woman. 'And these are our followers.'

'Well met, Erik Farseeker, and the lady Frakkok!' Bradan shouted. 'You are far from home, Norseman. Your mother, I believe, has a name from the Picts?'

'I am of the province of Cet, once Pictish and now part of the Norse Jarldom of Orkney.' Frakkok's voice was strong and as clear as the eyes that surveyed *Catriona* and all on board her. 'Do you know my people?'

'We know Prince Aharn of the Picts of Fidach well,' Bradan said.

'He is my nephew, as was his brother Loarn,' Frakkok confirmed, unsmiling. 'Where are you bound?'

'Wherever the sea road leads,' Bradan shouted. 'Or wherever this great ice mountain takes us. Where are you going with your cattle?'

'Greenland.' Erik grinned as he spoke. 'There is land for the taking there. Fertile land, sweet water, seas full of fish and no fierce Pictish warriors or Scots spearmen waiting to cut your throat.'

'Where is Greenland?' Bradan asked. 'I don't know the name.'

Erik's grin widened even further. 'Come with us and find out, if you can bear to be parted from your icy companion.'

Bradan glanced at Melcorka, who shrugged and nodded. 'I have never seen Greenland. It will be a new experience.'

'If you don't mind us coming along, we will visit this Greenland of yours,' Bradan said.

'Come along and welcome,' Erik said. 'The more, the better and who knows? You might like it well enough to settle.' Standing at his side, Frakkok nodded once, although her eyes were hard as she scanned Melcorka.

She will know me next time we meet, Melcorka thought and laughed. 'We are not the settling type, but we will come along and bid a happy good-day to Greenland.'

'You will need to come off your iceberg first.' Erik's smile did not waver.

Erik had scarcely uttered the words when a crack appeared along the entire side of the berg, accompanied by an ear-battering creaking.

'We're moving,' Bradan warned, as the ledge and the ice on either side began to slide down toward the sea. 'Hold on!'

Catriona veered first to larboard, then starboard, as she slithered down the side of the berg to splash into the sea in the midst of a cascade of ice and chilled water. Melcorka ducked as a chunk of ice crashed past her head to shatter on the gunwale and then they were merely rocking, with water splashing inboard and surging up to their knees.

'That was fortunate.' Erik had flinched at the avalanche of ice. 'Welcome to my fleet.'

Frakkok stood unmoving in the stern of the dragon-ship as if she saw a disintegrating iceberg every day of her life. Her gaze remained on Melcorka for a long minute before it slid away. A gust of wind spread graying, once-dark hair across her face so for an instant, she appeared to be looking through a curtain, and when it flicked clear, her eyes were once again on Melcorka, thoughtful and brooding.

'That Pictish woman is still examining me,' Melcorka said.

'The Picts are like that,' Bradan said. 'They are a thorough, careful people, as you know.'

Melcorka nodded. 'I remember that.'

Catriona joined the flotilla, raising her sail and sliding alongside the rearmost two ships. They were observed by a trio of curious cows and half a dozen Saxon slaves as they surged through the grey-green seas.

'I've never sailed with cattle before.' Melcorka adjusted the tiller slightly as the wind altered. 'It is already a new experience.' She looked forward, where the dragon ship of Erik and Frakkok ploughed the sea-road. With the sails set, she eased through the long swells, a masterpiece of the shipbuilders' art, as was only to be expected from a Norse vessel.

'Greenland,' Bradan said. 'I wonder if it is green and if your green people live there?'

Melcorka altered her grip on the tiller. 'If there are black and yellow people like you say, there may well be green people in Greenland.'

'I look forward to meeting them,' Bradan said.

The Norse ships, much larger than *Catriona*, were surging through the sea on either side of them with Erik's ship a length in front, the point of the arrow-head formation. In the stern of her vessel, Frakkok turned, placed her hands on the rail and stared at them.

'Frakkok still does not like us,' Melcorka said. 'However friendly Erik appears to be, that woman is watching us all the time.'

'I noticed,' Bradan said. 'I did not know that Pictish women willingly married Norsemen. She must have done so to be so readily accepted.' He looked over the fleet. 'There are about forty Norse women here, and twice that many men, plus slaves. They are undoubtedly settlers rather than raiders.'

'Brave men and women.' Melcorka gave grudging approval. 'Any brash young fool can carry a sword and kill monks or unsuspecting farmers or villagers. It takes real courage to collect your family and possessions and create a new life in an unknown land.'

'That was very profound,' Bradan said. 'Is this the same ferocious woman who single-handedly chased the Norse out of Alba?'

'That never happened,' Melcorka said. 'As you know full well. And Frakkok is still studying us. Don't look.'

'I am not looking.' Bradan continued to stare at the cattle in the nearest dragon ship. 'These are not the best beasts. The Norse may be great warriors, but their livestock skills leave much to be desired. Look at that one.' He pointed to a ragged dun cow. 'She won't last the winter.' He lowered his voice. 'I can feel Frakkok's eyes burning through us. That woman means us no goodwill and, as she is the matriarch of this fleet, she could turn them all against us.'

'We'll see what this Greenland place is like first,' Melcorka said. 'I am intrigued by the name!' She looked up, smiling. 'I would love to see your green men in Greenland.'

'They are your green men, not mine,' Bradan said mildly. 'And are the Norse safe with you? Or will you look for an excuse to kill them all?'

Melcorka touched the hilt of her sword. 'Let me deal with the Norse,' she said.

Bradan glanced at her. There had been something chilling in her words. 'You are a warrior, Mel but you don't kill merely because you don't like somebody. If you're looking for trouble, we'd best turn around and steer back into the storm. These are settlers, remember, Melcorka, not Vikings.'

'The Norse murdered my mother, they killed all my friends, they wiped out the entire population of my island and they tried to kill you at Callanish.'

'I know all that,' Bradan said quietly. 'I also know that you killed Egil, the Norseman who murdered your mother.'

'There are others,' Melcorka said. 'There are plenty of others.'

'Forget them,' Bradan said. 'You have killed the murderer. Now, you must put all that behind you, Melcorka. Egil was a vicious killer but most Norsemen are no different from the Scots or Picts. Some are bad and some are good.'

'And none are to be trusted,' Melcorka said grimly.

'Frakkok is not Norse,' Bradan reminded her. 'She is a Pict, and we have many Pictish friends.'

Melcorka stroked the scabbard of Defender and said nothing.

Chapter Two

They saw the mountains the next day, seemingly floating above the horizon, white with snow, as serrated as a broken saw and taller than any they had seen in Alba.

'So Greenland has white mountains,' Bradan said.

'Green and white land, then.' Melcorka watched the Norse flotilla tighten around them as they sailed closer to this new land. Erik waved to them until Frakkok snapped something to him and he turned rapidly away. 'Erik is scared of her.'

'I've never seen a scared Norseman before,' Bradan said.

'Nor have I.' Melcorka watched the young Norseman as he made minute adjustments to the sail. 'Nor have I,' she repeated thoughtfully.

They pushed on toward Greenland with the sea calm and the wind light. Patches of mist drifted across the sea, dissipating, reforming, altering Melcorka's perception, so she was unsure of distances and objects until a faint sun burned the sea clear, revealing Greenland.

The mountains were in the background, how far away Melcorka could not tell; white and sharply serrated, they rose as a backdrop to a land that was otherwise drab brown with patches of lovat-green and as many rocks as any island in the Outer Hebrides.

'I can't see much green here,' Bradan said.

'There are no green men, then.' Melcorka sat at the tiller, steering to make the best of the fluky wind. 'That is a pity. I was quite looking forward to seeing a green man.'

They sailed up a small inlet, with tumbled, lichen-stained rocks on both sides and clear water speckled with floating ice beneath their hull, until they came to the inlet's head, where the ground levelled out. There was brown moorland scattered with rocks, looking very similar to the landscape of North West Alba, a handful of scrubby trees and a scattered settlement backed by square fields. A score of cattle grazed in the fields, watched by a few young boys, while men in baggy trousers worked at digging out the moorland to create more arable land.

'It is very peaceful, this Greenland.' Bradan looked around. 'These men are not carrying swords, and their spears are all piled at the end of the fields, a two-minute run away. It's also a bit far for raiding Vikings to sail, or even Caterans.'

'It is peaceful,' Melcorka agreed. 'But there is smoke coming over that ridge there.'

'I can't see it.'

'Nor can I. Smell the air.' Melcorka said. 'And look at the ridge. Everywhere else is clear while it is hazy. There is smoke there.'

The Norse fleet sailed in as if they knew the place intimately and drew up on a shallow shingle beach a few yards below the settlement. Within a few moments, the men splashed into the water as they began to unload the livestock. There was the sound of lowing cattle and neighing horses, laughing men and the high-pitched screech of excited children. Some women greeted the men with hugs; others were more passionate while a few watched with disappointment or anticipation. Erik stood alone and slightly forlorn as Frakkok snapped rapid orders.

'They've been here before,' Melcorka said. 'This is a return visit.' She steered *Catriona* toward the beach, close to the Norse vessels but not alongside them. 'I still don't trust these people,' she said, as Bradan looked questioningly at her.

'Aye.' Bradan nodded. 'It's sensible to keep some distance until we're sure.'

They crunched onto the pebbly beach, where small wavelets softly splashed and the sound of seabirds competed with the lowing of cattle. A man lifted a hand in quiet greeting to them before helping unload the larger Norse ships. Melcorka stepped ashore and staggered. After weeks at sea, the land seemed to sway underneath her.

'Come along, you two.' With nobody apparently willing to greet him, Erik strode toward them, hand outstretched in welcome and sword at his hip. 'I'll show you around our little settlement of Frakkoksfjord.'

'That would be kind of you.' Bradan placed a hand on Melcorka's shoulder before she opened her mouth to refuse. 'We'd like to see this place. I thought Tir nan Og was over the sea, not this Greenland.'

Erik's laugh sounded genuine. 'Do you like the name? My name-sake Erik the Red called it Greenland to encourage settlers here.'

'I like the name,' Bradan said.

'Are you burning the heather to make new fields?' Melcorka was more direct than Bradan.

Erik frowned. 'Not to my knowledge...' He looked around.

'There is fire over there.' Melcorka pointed to the ridge on the north. She touched the hilt of Defender and immediately felt the heightening of her senses. 'And somebody is shouting.'

'I'll have a look.' Erik said. 'If you will excuse me?' He strode toward the ridge.

Melcorka watched him curiously.

'He seems friendly enough,' Bradan said. 'He's invited us to his settlement and showed no hostility at all.'

'Not yet,' Melcorka said. 'He's too polite for a Norseman.'

Erik was three hundred paces away and moving fast. Melcorka did not see why he hesitated and looked back over his shoulder. 'Skrael-ings!' His voice was louder than Melcorka had expected. 'The Skrael-ings are attacking us!'

'What in the name of God is a Skraeling?' Bradan lifted the rowan-wood staff that was the only weapon he carried.

'I don't know,' Melcorka said, 'but I think we're about to find out.'

Erik's words were spread from man to man and woman to woman, so that nearly all the adults in the settlement grabbed a weapon and rushed to join him. While warriors carried sword, spear or axe, slaves and women hefted staffs or even brooms.

'We are guests here,' Bradan reminded. 'We must follow the rules of hospitality.'

'I know.' Melcorka was already hurrying after Erik. 'Our hosts' fight is our fight, his enemies are our enemies and his friends are our friends. Whoever these Skraelings are, by tradition, they are now our enemies.'

'I am no fighting man,' Bradan reminded her.

'And I am no lover of the Norse,' Melcorka said. 'Yet I will join them in this fight. Stay behind if you must, Bradan. I will think no worse of you.'

'I know that.' Bradan matched her step for step as she hurried to the ridge.

Of the hundred or so people in Frakkoksfjord, nearly all surged forward. Only when she neared the summit of the ridge did Melcorka unsheathe Defender and, as always, the surge of power made her tingle and gasp. She savoured that feeling for only a second.

'Come on, Skraelings!' Melcorka shouted. 'Come on and die!'

From the crest of the ridge, they viewed an undulating, slowly rising plain of heather and scrub, scattered with rectangular, stone-built houses in the manner of the Norse and with small fields that the Norse had newly hacked from the surrounding ground.

Three of the houses were on fire, with smoke belching from the rough thatch and orange flames flickering from the small, square windows. Three people lay on the ground, with others running toward them, screaming in fear. Melcorka remembered the villages in Scotland that had been attacked by the Norse, and she wondered how these people liked being on the receiving end for a change. Only then did she look at the attackers. They were unlike anything that she had seen before.

Dressed in a mixture of furs, they were smallish in stature, with bulky bodies and tanned faces with slitted eyes. They moved fast and fired arrows from small bows, or carried long spears with barbed points.

'This is not your fight!' Erik said quickly. 'You are our guest.'

'In my culture,' Melcorka said calmly, 'guests adopt the enemies of their hosts. Your enemies are now my enemies.' She felt the smile stretch across her face. 'Come, Norseman – let's kill these Skraelings together!'

Erik's smile matched that of Melcorka. 'I wondered if you could use that sword,' he said. 'Come, then.' He advanced without another word, stepping sideways to ensure that both had sufficient space in which to fight.

Melcorka counted over two hundred Skraelings. They advanced in a semi-circle that outflanked the ragged ranks of the Norse and fired a constant stream of arrows as they moved. To Melcorka's right, a man yelled as an arrow sliced into his face. He grabbed at the shaft and shouted again as another slammed into his arm. Staggering, he dropped his sword, and more arrows landed on him, thudding into his chest and kidneys. He screamed again and fell, writhing on the ground.

Melcorka spared him one glance and looked toward the Skraelings. 'Do you have a strategy, Erik?'

'I haven't had time,' Erik said.

'So we just kill as many of them as we can,' Melcorka said.

'That sounds like a good plan,' Erik agreed.

'So be it.' Melcorka hefted her sword and faced the oncoming Skraelings.

Feeling the power and skill of Defender's previous owners surging through her, Melcorka ran toward the centre of the Skraeling ranks. She saw the first arrow whistling toward her and sliced it from the air, watching the two halves fall harmlessly to the ground.

A Skraeling fitted another arrow to his bow but before he could draw, Melcorka reached him. She swung Defender in a short arc that ended with the blade hacking at the man's neck. Propelled by jets of blood, the Skraeling's head sprang up, only to fall, bounce on the ground and roll over and over until it ended up in a shallow indentation.

Deflecting another arrow that zipped toward her, Melcorka hacked downward at the next Skraeling, neatly removing his arm, altered the angle of her blade to chop at another man's legs and then stepped over the screaming casualties to charge into a group of archers, scattering them left and right before her blood-smeared blade.

'Odin! Odin owns you! Odin!' The Norse battle-cry erupted around her as the Norsemen charged forward to roll up the left flank of the Skraelings. There were a few moments of frantic chopping with swords and thrusting with spears, and then the Skraelings broke and ran. There was no attempt at defence; one minute they were there and the next they were gone, fleeing northward with the more forward of the Norse pursuing them and a few arrows chasing them in their retreat.

Melcorka watched, frowning. 'These Skraelings were no warriors,' she said. 'They ran the minute we attacked them.'

'Thank you for your help.' Erik was panting as he cleaned blood from the blade of his sword.

'It was my duty as a guest.' Melcorka glanced around. Bradan was safe, leaning on his staff as he surveyed the scene of the one-sided skirmish.

Erik nodded. 'You fight well.'

'Who are these people?' Melcorka gestured to the bodies of the men she had killed. The Norse were busily engaged in disposing of the wounded with neither compassion nor relish. They killed each man quickly.

'Skraelings.' Erik shrugged. 'They sometimes come from the north and attack our farms. Sometimes we kill them, sometimes they kill us, but I've never known them to come in such numbers before.'

'Maybe they have a reason.' Bradan put his staff across the writhing body of the nearest still-living Skraeling, defending him from a squat and ugly Norseman. 'Rather than kill all these men who are no longer a threat to you, we could ask why they attacked the settlement.'

'Why do we care?' Erik seemed surprised at the idea. 'If they come, they come. If they don't, then they don't. What does it matter?'

'If there is a reason,' Bradan said patiently, 'you and the Skraelings might work out a way of living in peace together.'

'Why?' Erik asked. 'We are Norsemen. We are used to war.'

'There are only a handful of you,' Melcorka explained patiently. 'If you lose a few people with each encounter, soon there will not be enough of you remaining to defend yourselves against a larger number of attackers.'

Erik shrugged. 'We could do that. Bring him back to Frakkoksfjord and we'll ask him. We can kill him later.'

His callousness did not surprise Melcorka. 'Or you could let him live and send him back to his people as proof that you are peace-loving Norsemen.' She tried to keep the irony out of her voice.

'Why?' Erik sounded genuinely surprised.

'For the same reason. So that your people will not be killed as they care for their animals.' Bradan indicated the dead Norse farmers. 'There is more to being a leader than possessing a bloody sword.'

Erik shrugged again. 'Bring him to Frakkoksfjord then, although Fate decides who lives and dies, not you and I.'

Melcorka threw Bradan a 'told-you-so' look and ensured the Norse were relatively gentle with their prisoner as they carried him back to the settlement.

Frakkok looked surprised when the Norsemen brought back a live Skraeling. 'What do you intend doing with that? First, you take in strays from the sea, and now you keep Skraelings alive.' She poked at the wounded man with her foot. 'Burn it.'

Erik nodded. 'We will, Mother. After we have asked it why the Skraelings attacked the settlement.'

'It would be better to ask where the Skraeling village is, so you can destroy it and grab their lands.'

Erik glanced from Bradan to Frakkok and back. 'I'll do that,' he said.

'No.' Frakkok's voice was soft and sinister. 'I'll do that.' Lifting the wounded Skraeling by the hair, she snapped an order that saw two men run forward and rip off the man's clothes. Melcorka watched dispassionately; she had no love for cruelty but had seen too much to worry unduly about it.

Stripped of his furs, the Skraeling was stocky, with shining, tawny skin and a bleeding sword-slash across his ribs. Bradan reached into the small pack he carried over his shoulder, took out a pad of moss and pressed it against the wound. 'That will stop the bleeding,' he said, 'and make sure the devil does not get in to poison you.'

'Bring fire,' Frakkok said quietly. She watched as the Norsemen made a small fire within a circle of boulders. They piled up driftwood and brought smouldering rushes over. Within a few moments, flames were licking knee-high. The Skraeling coughed as smoke curled around his face. He did not look scared as Frakkok ordered him to be brought closer, although it was evident that she intended something unpleasant.

'Why did you attack us?' Frakkok asked bluntly. 'If you tell me, I will have you killed quickly. If you don't, I will straddle you across the fire and ask again as you burn.'

The Skraeling looked at the fire and then at Frakkok. He decided that she was in earnest. 'The Ice King,' he said.

'The Ice King,' Bradan repeated. 'Who or what is the Ice King?'

'He rules the North,' the Skraeling said. 'He's guarded by fierce animals and cannibals from the other world.'

'I see.' Bradan glanced at Melcorka. 'Why do we always end up with monsters?'

She shook her head. 'That seems to be our fate.'

'It is not a fate I like.' Bradan grunted and spoke to the Skraeling again. 'Did the Ice King order you to attack the Norse?'

The Skraeling looked at the fire again. Now, it was larger, with flames that leapt waist-high. 'Will you let me live?'

'I have no intention of killing you,' Bradan said. 'I hope that Frakkok will show the same mercy if you help us.' He turned to face Frakkok. 'Will you allow this man to live?'

Frakkok grunted. 'He may live,' she said. 'I won't kill him.'

'There you are, Master Skraeling. You have your life,' Bradan said.

The Skraeling stepped back slightly from the fire. 'The Ice King did not order us to attack the strangers. The Ice King is pushing on our hunting territories. We need the land where the pale strangers are.'

'What is this Ice King like?' Frakkok seemed to be interested at last.

'I don't know,' the Skraeling said. 'Nobody has ever seen him. We only know that he lives in the North with his animals and foreign man-eaters.'

'You have told us all that you know, then?' Frakkok asked.

The Skraeling nodded.

'He has fulfilled his part,' Bradan said. 'Now you must keep yours.'

'Why in Odin's name would I do that?' Frakkok sounded surprised. She raised her voice. 'Throw him in the fire!'

'You gave your word!' Bradan stepped forward.

Frakkok turned aside and walked away. Three Norsemen grabbed hold of the Skraeling, lifted him high and dumped him in the middle of the fire. Sparks and fragments of burning wood sputtered past the containing boulders and sizzled on the coarse grass.

'No! Let the man live!' Bradan stepped forward, to see half a dozen Norsemen slide their swords free of their scabbards.

Melcorka put a hand on Bradan's arm. 'No, Bradan. This is not our concern. We don't know how this settlement works.'

'I told that man he would live!' Bradan shivered as the Skraeling began to scream.

'Frakkok decided otherwise,' Melcorka said. 'And she rules this settlement. Frakkok has more power in her village than Erik has.' She had to raise her voice above the shrieks of the Skraeling. The Norse-

Falcon Warrior

men were prodding at him with their swords, keeping him inside the flames.

Melcorka watched for a moment. 'Killing one's enemies is one thing,' she said. 'But torture is something I dislike.' Drawing Defender, she thrust it through the Skraeling's heart. When the Norsemen voiced their anger at this end to their entertainment, she faced them, sword in hand and they backed off.

'Don't you wish to fight me?' Melcorka challenged. 'Come on now! There are scores of you, and I am a lone woman.'

They withdrew, shouting, with their swords pointing at her. Not a single man stepped forward.

'Come on, Bradan.' Melcorka said. 'There are no warriors here.' Returning Defender to her scabbard, she turned her back and stalked back to the settlement. The behaviour of the Norse worried her; she had never in her life met Norsemen who were afraid to fight, whatever the odds. Something was wrong with these men.

Chapter Three

They sat inside the stone-built hall that was the largest building in the village, with the mist creeping outside and a great fire roaring at the head of the room. Smoke coiled from the open fire to the rush thatches far above, while uneven beams of driftwood spanned the breadth of the hall, some decorated with elaborate carvings, others still as rough and crude as they were the day they were lifted from the shore. Shaggy-haired dogs lay on the floor, or watched the men and women who shared the long table that stretched the full length of the building; a table spread with horns of ale and great hunks of meat piled on wooden platters. There was the occasional burst of song and rough northern voices roaring their opinion on every subject that came up.

Frakkok and Erik sat at the head of the table as befitted their status.

'We'll sit tight in Frakkoksfjord,' Erik said, 'and put out sentries to warn of any Skraeling inroads.'

Melcorka exchanged glances with Bradan and said nothing.

Frakkok was not as kind. 'If I knew you wanted to live forever, I would have raised you in my wool basket.'

'What does that mean?' Erik looked bemused.

'I think your mother is suggesting that you should do something more aggressive,' Melcorka hinted.

'What should I do?' Erik wondered, smiling as always.

Frakkok leaned forward and pressed a long finger into his ribs. 'Have I taught you nothing? If you have an enemy, you destroy them. You don't wait for them to come to you!'

'You think I should attack the Skraelings then?' Erik sounded a little disappointed that his mother had not praised his idea.

'You can do that, Erik.' It was clear that Frakkok had difficulty controlling her temper. 'But then you will have this Ice King on our border.'

'It may be better to attack him as well,' Erik said.

Frakkok raised her eyebrows. 'That would be best.'

'If I may speak?' Melcorka asked.

'Indeed you may!' Erik was all amiability. 'You are an honoured guest, and you fought well against the Skraeling army.'

'Thank you.' Melcorka tried to avoid Frakkok's pointed glare. 'Did you have any trouble with the Skraelings before this Ice King appeared?'

'Not really,' Erik said at once. 'A few skirmishes between our herders and hunters and theirs. They never attacked us like that before.'

'Then the Ice King is the problem,' Melcorka said. 'Remove him, and the Skraelings will not bother you unduly.'

'Will you come along?' Erik asked eagerly.

'You are my host,' Melcorka said. 'Your enemies are my enemies.'

Erik's smile showed his pleasure, until he realised that Frakkok was frowning. He looked away, his face reddening.

'It's not our fight,' Bradan said later, as they squeezed into their quarters, a corner of the great hall shared with a courting couple and two slavering hounds.

Melcorka glanced at their companions. The dogs were more intent in scratching fleas than anything else, while the young lovers had far more interesting things on their minds than the words of a pair of foreign travellers. 'We are guests. It is tradition to embrace the friends and fight the enemies of our host.'

'It is a foolish tradition,' Bradan said. 'What if Erik's enemy was the Lord of the Isles, your half-brother? Or the Queen of Alba?'

'Then he would not have invited us,' Melcorka said. 'It is the way of the world, and it is best never to make a tradition or break a tradition.'

'We are not in Alba now,' Bradan said.

'There are some traditions that I will carry with me wherever I go,' Melcorka said. 'It is only good manners to help your host.'

'Even if he is a Norseman and you have no love for the Norse? They slaughtered your family, remember!'

'I remember,' Melcorka said. 'I will never forget. But Erik did not slaughter them. He is quite entertaining. He is the most vulnerable and personable Norseman I have ever met.'

'You are beginning to like that Norseman.' Bradan sounded amused.

'I am,' Melcorka agreed, shaking her head. 'There is something about him that I cannot fathom. He is not like any other Norseman I have ever met. He is rather cute, I think.'

'Oh.' Bradan looked away. 'Rather cute.'

'He is like a puppy dog,' Melcorka continued, only slightly aware of the impact her words were making. 'He's all wagging tail and big eyes. He is the sort of man who would do anything for anybody. Even you, Master Cynical, must admit that he is friendly.'

'Oh, he is friendly enough and to spare,' Bradan agreed.

'It's his mother I am wary of,' Melcorka said. 'Frakkok is the real power here. She orders poor Erik around and manipulates him as if he was still a child.'

'Then by siding with your host, you are supporting her,' Bradan pointed out. 'For all you know, the Ice King is a peaceful man who has been here forever, and the Norse have provoked him. Don't forget what they did to Alba before you kicked them out.'

'I won't forget,' Melcorka said. 'But, as you said, Egil is dead now. Erik is nothing like him.'

'No. He is cute,' Bradan said.

'Exactly.' Melcorka did not register the sarcasm. 'I will accompany him to face this Ice King.' She smiled. 'He was brave enough against the Skraelings, but I don't think he is a natural warrior. He may need help.'

'In other words, you'll put our lives at risk fighting a Norseman's battles,' Bradan said.

'Our hosts' quarrels are our quarrels,' Melcorka reminded him. 'Besides, you don't have to come. You're not a warrior.'

'I am coming!' Bradan said fiercely. 'Do you think I would let you go alone?'

Melcorka took a deep breath. 'No. I don't think you would ever do that.' She put a hand on his arm. 'We have done too much together.' Her smile was one of pure mischief. She watched the courting couple for a moment. Both were now stark naked and indulging in a very energetic bout of love-making. 'Erik is very cute, though.' Placing her hands under the hips of the girl at her side, she shoved the lovers aside and spoke sharply to them.

'Go and do that elsewhere. We need the space.' She watched them roll away without either of them breaking contact with the other, shook her head and smiled. 'Young love, eh?'

Bradan nodded. 'Melcorka, they are only a year or so younger than you.'

'I know,' Melcorka said. 'It's just that sometimes...' she hesitated, 'sometimes I feel so very much older than my years.'

'It's the kind of life you lead,' Bradan said. 'Perhaps it might be better for you if you settled down somewhere. You should find a good, steady man and build a life together, rather than wandering the highways, byways and oceans with a wastrel like me.'

'Perhaps sometime,' Melcorka said. 'Not yet, though. I rather enjoy the company of a sour-faced wastrel like you. I think...' Reaching over to him, she demonstrated what she was thinking.

Next morning was bright and cold, with a hint of mist lying close to the ground. Leaving Bradan to sleep, Melcorka left the hall to walk around the settlement, ignoring the scurrying slaves who tended the livestock and did the menial tasks.

'Well met, Melcorka,' Erik's cheerful voice greeted her. 'You are up early!'

'As are you, Erik.'

'I like the mornings,' Erik said. 'I noticed that you always carry that sword.'

'I do,' Melcorka said.

'It is unusual for a woman.' Erik was smiling as always.

'So I am told.'

'May I see it?' Erik held out his hand. 'Please?'

She pondered for a moment. Could she trust this Norseman with Defender? Without it, she was no more than an island girl; all her power and skill was invested in that blade. Over three years ago, she had made her choice between luxury and the way of the warrior. She had chosen the warrior's path, and Defender had been presented to her on that lonely island off the west coast of Scotland. At first, she had thought it only a sword, until Ceridwen of the People of Peace, the fairy folk, explained to her how Defender had been made.

'Derwen made this sword,' Ceridwen had said. 'It came from long ago, long back, and Derwen made it for Caractacus, who was betrayed by a woman. It was the blade of Calgacus, the swordsman who faced the iron legions of the south in the long-ago days of heroes.' She ran her hand the length of the scabbard, without touching the steel of the blade. 'It was the sword of Arthur, who faced the Saxon and now it is the sword of Melcorka.

'It was a sword well made,' Ceridwen had said, 'in Derwen's forge. It was made with rich red ore with Derwen tramping on bellows of ox-hide to blow the charcoal hot as hell ever is. The ore sank down, down through the charcoal to the lowest depth of the furnace, to form a shapeless mass the weight of a well- grown child.

'Derwen carried the metal to the anvil and chose the best of the best to reheat and form into a bar. He had the bar blessed by the druids of his

time, and by the holy man who came from the East, a young fugitive from Judea who fled the wrath of the Romans.

'Derwen cut his choice of steel into short lengths, laid them end on end in water blessed by the holy one and the chief druid of Caractacus, and drew them long and long before welding them together with the skill that only Derwen had. These operations working together equalised the temper of the steel, making it hard throughout, and sufficiently pliable to bend in half and spring together. Derwen tested and re-tested the blade, then hardened and sharpened it with his touch and his magic. In the end, in the final forging, Derwen sprinkled his own white powder of the dust of diamonds and rubies into the red-hot steel, to keep it free of rust and protect the edge.'

'May I see it?' Erik repeated. He was still smiling, his eyes wide and blue and far too friendly for a Norseman. 'Look...' Unfastening his sword belt, he handed it to her openly. 'You see? Now I am defenceless before you. You have your sword and mine.'

Melcorka took his sword. She could not help her smile; nor could she help liking this man, despite his nationality. Could she trust him? There was undoubtedly something about him that appealed to her.

Unfastening her sword belt, Melcorka handed over Defender. She doubted that Erik had the skill to use it, anyway.

'Shall we go inside out of the cold and mist?' Erik indicated a house nearby. 'It's not a day to linger outside.'

Melcorka smiled; she had never met a Norseman, or any warrior, who admitted feeling cold. 'If you wish.' She felt exposed without Defender, even if Erik seemed as innocent as a baby.

The house was empty and not much warmer than the outside, with very little light penetrating the small windows and the wind rustling the rough thatch above. Erik slid Defender from her scabbard. 'That is a beautiful sword.' He ran his fingers over the hilt. 'The craftsmanship is superb. Who was the swordsmith?'

'A man named Derwen,' Melcorka said, 'a very long time ago.'

'The balance is excellent.' Erik took a practise swing. 'Even I could be a warrior with a blade such as this.'

'Are you not a warrior now?' Melcorka asked.

'Not a proper one.' Erik was surprisingly honest. 'I have little skill and no experience.' His smile wrapped around her. 'I hope for the opportunity soon, but there is nobody to fight here except the Skraelings, and they are not formidable.'

'You can't forge a reputation unless you face known warriors,' Melcorka agreed. 'Were you not involved in the late war in Alba?'

'I was not,' Erik said.

For some reason, Melcorka was glad of that answer. She did not want to think that she had opposed this man. 'It was a bloody campaign,' she said.

'So I heard.' Erik ran his hand up the length of the blade. 'I have never seen craftsmanship like this before.' He smiled at her. 'You will have to send this Derwen to me. I could use such a man.'

'He is long dead.' Melcorka unsheathed Erik's blade. About half the weight of Defender, it was decorated with spiral patterns and had a runic script running above the guard. 'What do these letters mean?' She smiled. 'I never learned to read.'

'Thor and Odin own you,' Erik said. 'May I try your belt on?' Before Melcorka could reply, Erik shrugged off his ornate light blue cloak and fastened Melcorka's sword belt around him, so the hilt of Defender protruded above his left shoulder. 'It's very heavy,' he said.

'You get used to it. The balance makes up for the weight.' Melcorka watched as Erik stalked the length of the house, shouted 'Thor' and drew Defender as if to strike.

'Would you part with your sword?'

'I would not,' Melcorka said. She tightened her grip on Erik's sword, wondering if he was going to attack her.

'Nor would I, if it was mine.' Erik stepped toward the door, still holding Defender.

Melcorka followed. 'She had served me well in the past, and will do so in the future.'

Erik stepped outside and shivered. 'Thank you.' He handed Defender back.

It was the first time Melcorka had ever been thanked by a Norseman.

'We've left something in the house. I'll get them.' Diving back inside, Erik returned with both cloaks and a grin on his face.

'Thank you, Erik.' Melcorka touched his arm, just as Bradan came out of the great hall. He looked from one to the other and then down at the ground. 'Bradan!' Melcorka shouted. Without a word, Bradan walked away, tapping his staff on the hard ground.

'He did not hear you,' Erik said. 'The air here does that sometimes. It takes sounds and twists them.'

'That must be it,' Melcorka said. She did not like to see Bradan turn his back on her.

They gathered at the Thing-mound, the small hillock where every adult male of Frakkoksfjord met to discuss events. Melcorka counted them: one hundred and fifteen men armed for war. Being Norsemen, they were mainly tall, muscular and confident in their ability to confront and defeat any enemy, even though many had not a suggestion of facial hair yet. Others had beards of iron-grey or silver. It was a mixture of youth and creaking experience. All carried a weapon, from short spears to the full set of sword, shield, and axe, although the latter was in the minority.

'They look an unusual collection of old men and children.' Bradan leaned on his staff. 'They are more farmers than warriors, yet they think they know what they are doing.'

Melcorka nodded. 'They are Norsemen – part farmer, part seaman and always ready to fight.'

'Well, if this Ice King has pushed the Skraelings southward, he must be quite a warrior himself. These Norsemen will get their chance to fight. Even those fresh from their mother's arms.'

'You don't have to come with us,' Melcorka said.

'Yes I do,' Bradan said quietly, glancing at Erik.

Intercepting his glance, Melcorka shook her head. She did not know if she was pleased about his jealousy, or annoyed. Either way, it was showing a new side of Bradan.

'Men!' Erik stood on top of the Thing-mound and raised his arms high. 'We are heading north into the unknown.'

They gathered around, nodding and murmuring agreement. One youth raised a spear and shook it.

'We have travelled further than any other Norseman. We have braved the Western Ocean and found this new land. We have broken it in and settled farms here. We have faced and overcome the Skraelings. Now, we are going into even more new lands. We will find this Ice King, whoever he is, and we will kill him.'

The men cheered this time, with most of them waving swords or spears in the air. They began to chant. 'Odin! Odin!', or 'Thor! Thor!'

'Last time we heard that slogan, we were opposing their armies on the banks of the Tummel,' Melcorka said. 'I never thought to be fighting alongside the Norse rather than opposing them.'

'Nor did I.' Bradan tapped his staff on the ground and eyed the Norsemen. 'They don't look terribly different from the way the Scots did when they marched to war. Maybe people are much the same the world over.'

'Maybe they are,' Melcorka said. 'Yet I can't remember the Scots or Picts sending fleets over to conquer the Norse, or to conquer anybody else, for that matter.'

The women waved them goodbye and immediately returned to their work. Only a few turned to watch their men advance to battle. Melcorka caught Bradan's eye, shrugged, hitched Defender higher up her back and walked on. Although she was a guest, she moved to the front of the small army; she refused to follow in the wake of a bunch of Norsemen, allies or not.

They marched northward, one hundred and fifteen armed Norsemen, one female warrior woman and one wandering man with a staff and a laconic, musing face.

'This is very familiar.' Bradan tapped his staff on the near-frozen ground. 'You and I, marching with a band of warriors, not sure what is ahead of us.'

'I remember,' Melcorka said. 'Last time we were on the island of Lewis searching for Abaris and the Shining One.'

'I remember. And this time we are in Greenland, hunting for the Ice King.' Bradan looked around at the unfamiliar landscape. It was not dissimilar to western Scotland, except that here, jagged, icy-white mountains replaced the grey-blue mountains of Scotland.

'He's not much of a war captain.' Melcorka nodded towards Erik. 'His men are in no formation at all.'

The Norse moved in a straggling mob, with every man choosing his own path. They talked in loud voices, wandered where they liked and appeared more casual than Melcorka would have allowed.

'Erik is very young,' Bradan said. 'And I think the old men have spent their lives farming, not raiding. They do not have the appearance of Vikings. There are no scars, and their muscles are bunched, not smooth.'

'I'll talk to him.' Melcorka stepped to Erik's side. 'Erik, have you thought about sending out scouts, so you know what is ahead?'

The smile was expected. The answer was not. 'We don't need scouts for the Skraelings. They are only savages with no knowledge of war.'

'What if they attack us just now? You are not in any formation. They could pick off the stragglers without any difficulty.'

'We are Vikings!' Erik said. 'We have conquered half of Europe and travelled to Miklagard and the lands of the Caliphs. We rule most of the English kingdoms...'

'... but were defeated in Scotland,' Melcorka could not resist adding.

'We haven't given up there.' Erik showed some spirit for the first time. 'We'll be back.'

'Were you involved in that campaign?' Bradan asked.

'No.' Erik shook his head. He looked like a young boy, guilty about being caught skipping his lessons or forgetting some chore.

'Have you ever fought in a battle?' Melcorka watched as a dozen Norsemen wandered off to the left, singing some song she did not know.

'You know I have!' Drawing his sword, Erik took a practice swing to prove his ferocity as a warrior. 'You saw me fight the Skraelings.'

Melcorka nodded. 'I saw you fight the Skraelings,' she echoed.

'I am a Viking warrior.' Erik was apparently boasting for the benefit of his men, or to boost his own courage. 'My men will sweep the Skraelings aside and deal with this Ice King. He will be just another Skraeling, a fur-clad savage.' Still smiling, he ran to the front of his men.

'Erik has no experience in war,' Melcorka remarked to Bradan. 'If he had fought in a real war, he would have bragged about it. He has only been in that one tiny skirmish with the Skraelings. I think Frakkok is trying to blood him by ordering him against this Ice King.'

'Not the best man to lead this mob toward an unknown enemy.' Bradan tapped his staff on the ground again. 'Maybe you'd be best take charge.'

'I am a guest of Erik. I have no right to control his army.' Melcorka glanced around the Norsemen. 'If you can call this an army.'

'It is a group of armed farmers.' Bradan looked around. 'Compared to them, Hector's Hebrideans were as disciplined as the Romans.'

'You keep close to me,' Melcorka said. 'This may not end well for Erik's men.'

The further they walked inland, the rougher the terrain became. Within a few miles, there were patches of snow on the ground, which increased in size as they headed north.

'Look!' Bradan nodded to the west.

At first, Melcorka thought it was a collection of sticks and rags, but as she looked, she realised that it was a collection of huts. Made of driftwood covered in sealskin, they would have merged with the landscape save for the group of children that played around the doorways and the old woman who sat with them, chewing on something that looked like seal fat.

'Erik!' Melcorka drew his attention to the village. 'Down there.'

'Skraelings!' Erik's roar sounded like a rutting stag. 'Come to me, men, and we'll slaughter them!'

'Oh, dear God.' Melcorka shook her head. 'Is that what the Norse are reduced to?'

At the warning, the Norse drew their weapons and clustered around their leader, shouting to Odin and Thor.

'I can't let them massacre these people,' Melcorka said to Bradan. She stepped forward. 'Erik,' she said. 'Do you know anything about this Ice King?'

Erik frowned. 'No,' he said. 'I did not know he existed until that Skraeling told us.'

'It might be better to get some information about your enemy before you fight him,' Melcorka said.

'How?' Erik hefted his sword, eager to prove himself.

'Ask the Skraelings.' Melcorka allowed him a few moments for the idea to sink in before she continued. 'They have more reason to dislike the Ice King than you have, so far, and they know more about him.'

'We will capture another one,' Erik said.

'Why?' Melcorka asked bluntly. 'You have a mutual enemy. Why not combine against him?'

Erik frowned. 'We could slaughter them,' he said.

'Or they could slaughter you,' Melcorka said. 'Look around.' She had been watching the surroundings, seeing movement among the ragged rocks and drifts of deep snow. 'I suspect that they are watching us right now. It would be best if we appeared friendly.'

'What?' Erik turned around, waving his sword. Bradan put a hand on his arm.

'If Melcorka warns you about an enemy,' Bradan said softly, 'it's best to listen.'

'She is only a woman!' a tall, bearded Norseman shouted. 'What does she know about war?'

'The lady Frakkok is only a woman, too,' Bradan reminded him.

'Attack the Skraelings!' the bearded man shouted. 'Kill them all!'

'Look around you,' Melcorka said.

The Skraelings seemed to rise from the ground, bows strung and spears ready. They surrounded the band of Norsemen without a word being spoken.

'We come in peace!' Melcorka took the initiative. 'We seek an alliance.' Hoping that no hothead among the Norse would launch an abortive attack, she stepped toward the centre of the Skraeling ranks. She guessed there were more than two hundred of them, stocky men, wary of eye and with a score of arrows following her. 'Where is your leader?'

'I am here.' The man who spoke was no different in appearance from his colleagues. Short in stature, with slightly slanted eyes and a tawny complexion, he held a small but powerful bow with the arrow pointed directly at Melcorka's throat.

'I am Melcorka of Alba. I am staying with the Norse of Frakkoksfjord.'

'I am Almick.' The man said no more. His beard was small and neatly trimmed, his eyes unwavering.

'Are you the leader, the headman here?' Melcorka asked.

'I am.'

'We are going to attack the Ice King,' Melcorka said bluntly. 'We have no quarrel with you or your people.'

'You killed some of my people,' Almick said. 'And you are carrying weapons.'

'Your people attacked the Norse settlers.' Melcorka was very aware of the Norse behind her. With their reputation for extreme violence, she was not sure if they would suddenly charge at the Skraelings. If that happened, whoever won the battle, there would be casualties on both sides and their position would be weaker.

Melcorka took a deep breath. 'Look, Almick. I will show you my peaceful intention.' Unstrapping Defender, she placed it on the ground. Without the magic of her sword, Melcorka knew that she was as vulnerable as any other woman in these circumstances. All her power lay in that weapon.

She stepped forward, fighting her fear. If the Norse were correct, then her fate had been decided long before she was born, so it should make no difference if she was armed or not.

Almick did not lower his bow.

Melcorka took the dirk from its sheath and placed it beside Defender. 'You see?' she said. 'I am helpless before you. We seek friendship and an alliance against the Ice King.'

'What do you know of the Ice King?' Almick asked.

'Nothing,' Melcorka admitted. 'Nobody of Frakkoksfjord had heard of him until one of your people told us.'

'That was Ulmock, my brother,' Almick said.

Suddenly, Melcorka felt extremely vulnerable. 'I did not know.'

'You put him in a fire.' Almick pulled back his bowstring.

'Melcorka saved him from torture.' Bradan stepped beside Melcorka. 'She made his death easier.'

Melcorka could nearly taste the tension as the Skraelings and the Norse faced each other, one side holding drawn bows, the other renowned for their skill with axe and sword.

Almick's laughter was unexpected. 'I was going to kill him myself!' he bellowed, dropping his aim. 'You saved me the trouble!'

The other Skraelings began to laugh, too, and soon the Norse joined in, although Melcorka doubted whether one in ten of them understood why they were laughing. Within a few moments, the Skraelings had surged forward and were talking to the Norse in a strange mixture of both languages, accompanied by signs and facial expressions.

Within a few moments, what had nearly been a battle became a party, as Norse and Skraelings combined in a friendship cemented by drinking, singing, and women.

'This is not what I had imagined when we left Frakkoksfjord.' Melcorka stepped over a copulating couple.

'They are getting closer.' Bradan smiled as a young Norseman was dragged happily into one of the Skraeling huts by two stocky, smiling Skraeling women. 'They will either be the best of friends tomorrow, or sworn enemies.'

The celebrations continued for two days and two nights before settling down into a drunken slumber. Melcorka surveyed the village, where sundry Norse and Skraelings in various stages of dress and undress and in myriad positions occupied every corner, nook and hollow.

Almick and Erik joined her, the former looking as satisfied as any cream-licking cat and the latter white-faced, drained and weak. The Skraeling woman who clung to Erik was grinning until Almick pushed her away.

'That is one of my wives,' he said. 'I told her to make sure you were cared for, Erik. If she failed, you may beat her.'

'She did not fail.' Erik did not meet Almick's gaze.

'Now that we are all friends together,' Melcorka said, 'tell us about the Ice King, Almick.'

Almick chewed on a chunk of seal blubber. 'I don't know much about him. He appeared when my grandfather's grandfather was a boy and bothered nobody until a few years ago, when he began to send out his great creatures. They attack our kayaks at sea and attack our hunting parties on land, so we have been forced further and further south.'

'What is he like?' Bradan asked.

'Nobody has ever seen him,' Almick admitted.

'You said he sends his creatures. What are these creatures?' Melcorka touched the hilt of Defender, feeling the thrill of contact.

'He sends bears on land, and walruses at sea,' Almick said. 'Yet they are much fiercer than any I have ever seen.' He hesitated for a second. 'It is said that he also controls the amoraks.'

'The what?' Melcorka asked. 'I do not know the term.'

Almick looked around fearfully. He lowered his voice. 'They are creatures from the deep ice,' he said. 'Terrible things, like wolves but ten times fiercer. They have not been seen in living memory.'

Melcorka touched the hilt of Defender. 'I will watch out for them,' she said. 'As for bears, well, we have bears in Alba,' Melcorka said. 'We hunt them for sport.'

'These bears hunt *us* for sport,' Almick said grimly.

'By Odin! I'd like to see the bear that could hunt a Norseman!' Erik shouted, then glanced at Almick's wife and looked away again.

'When you gather your men together,' Melcorka said, ignoring Erik's outburst, 'we can march north. Do you know where this Ice King lives?'

Almick shook his head. 'We only know he is in the north beyond the river of ice.'

'What is the river of ice?' Bradan asked.

'A river of ice is ice moving in a river.' Almick's explanation did not help in the slightest.

'We'll see it when we see it,' Melcorka said. 'Let's head north, and hope to entice this Ice King away from his throne.'

Erik produced a twisted smile. 'We are Norsemen,' he said, without conviction. 'We will melt him.'

After prising the men from their new female friends, Erik marched the army north at noon that day. Melcorka, Erik and Almick were in front, with the combined army of Skraelings and Norsemen at their back. After the first natural suspicions had been paid to rest, there was no disagreement between the groups. Norse and Skraelings merged happily together. The combined group moved on as the terrain grew wilder and the snow deeper and more extensive.

'They should call him the Snow King rather than the Ice King.' Bradan looked ahead. They had only been walking for a full day and were already trudging through deep snow, with magnificent white mountains ahead and occasional flurries of snow blasting into their faces.

Melcorka flicked snow off the hood of her cloak. 'I wonder if he even exists?' she said. 'There are no people here, no buildings. There is nothing for a man to rule over except wilderness.'

'There are giants.' One of the younger Norsemen pointed to the right. 'There are giants there!'

'Now, that's different.' Bradan hefted his staff. 'I've never seen a real giant before. Where are they, boy?'

'Over there!' The Norseman gesticulated wildly into a blizzard of snow. 'I saw them moving in there.'

Chapter Four

Melcorka saw the shadows first, stretching dark and sinister along the snow. Each was as long as a Norse dragon ship and as wide as a Hebridean broch.

'I've heard of giants,' she said, 'but I never expected to meet one.'

'We are travelling to have new experiences and see all the different cultures of the world,' Bradan said. 'I suppose that giants must be a culture, just like everybody else.'

'You sound very calm about meeting giants.'

Bradan shrugged. 'What is there to worry about? We have met Picts, Islesmen, Norsemen, People of Peace, the Shining One, the Morrigan and now the Skraelings. Giants are just one more culture.'

'They are a very large culture.' Melcorka nodded to the shadows that loomed out of the blizzard toward them. 'I hope they are friendly.'

'So do I.' Bradan tapped his staff on the ice. 'They have no reason to attack us. We are no threat to them.' His grin was slightly sardonic. 'If they are anything like as big as they appear, then we are definitely no threat to them!'

'In our experience, creatures don't need a reason to attack,' Melcorka said. 'We'll soon see.'

The shadows increased, growing longer and darker until the younger Norsemen either spoke louder to show they were not afraid, or edged behind their companions and proved that they were. The low, deep roar echoed across the ice, louder than any human voice, making even the bravest of the Norse, scions of a people who had spread terror across half of Europe, stop dead and reach for their weapons.

'Odin save us!' a tall man named Leif said. 'They have loud voices.' He hefted his axe and grinned nervously, hoping for support.

The Skraelings knelt on the ground, fitting arrows to their bows. Some looked at the Norse while others stared into the clearing blizzard.

'This could be interesting.' Melcorka stepped forward, with Bradan one step behind her and slightly to her left. 'Let's talk to these giants.'

'It may be best to wait and see what they are like.' Erik had a hand on the hilt of his sword.

'Wait if you like,' Melcorka called out. She strode ahead, feeling the power of Defender surge through her. 'I'm sure the giants will be a lot friendlier by the time they reach you.'

'I think you're looking forward to this,' Bradan said.

'I look forward to anything that unsettles the Norsemen,' Melcorka told him.

'Even when you think they are cute?'

Melcorka looked at him. 'That has nothing to do with it.'

The shadows lengthened; that deep roar sounded again, and then the giants appeared. At first, there were six of them, and then seven, eight and with others following close behind. Massive and shaggy, they gleamed white against a background of snow.

'They're not giants,' Bradan said. 'They're some sort of bear. Ice bears!'

The bears were much larger than any Melcorka had seen before, at least half as large again as the tallest man, and they alternated between running on all fours, to standing on their hind legs as they approached these intruders in their territory.

'Can we talk to these giants?' Bradan placed his staff in front of him as if to prevent these monsters from tearing him to pieces.

'I've known bears to fight in self-defence,' Melcorka said. 'They never attack people without reason.'

'These bears don't appear to know that,' Bradan said.

They attacked from all sides, roaring as they came closer, with their massive, clawed paws hooking at the humans and their jaws lined with teeth as large as a man's thumb. One of the young Norsemen turned to run and slipped on the ice. Two of the bears immediately dropped to all fours and buried their heads in his body. The man's screams rose shrilly and died away slowly.

'Stupid boy,' Bradan said. 'Animals are always attracted by weakness.'

'They're coming at us now.' Melcorka slid Defender from her scabbard. 'I don't like killing animals.'

'I like them killing us even less,' Bradan said.

The first bear dropped from two legs to four as it ran directly at Melcorka, and then rose to its hind legs as it closed. Pushing Bradan behind her, Melcorka lifted Defender high and swept it to the right. The huge blade sang as it hissed through the air, immediately killing the bear. The blade stuck in the muscular flesh, so she had to tug it out.

'They are tough animals,' she said.

A flight of arrows passed Melcorka; each one landed on the body of the next bear. It stopped for only a second, bit at the arrows and continued.

'Its fur is too thick for the arrows to penetrate,' Bradan said, as he stepped beside Melcorka and lowered his staff. The stout length of wood looked a puny defence compared to the bears. 'I've never seen bears as aggressive as these are.'

'Something has stirred them up,' Melcorka guessed.

The Norsemen were formed into a ragged clump, all facing outward with their weapons ready.

'I've never known Norsemen as hesitant as this before, either,' Melcorka said. 'Egil and his boys would have charged into the bears to prove themselves better than anybody else.'

Bradan nodded. 'They are cute, though.'

Melcorka grunted. That throwaway comment had hurt him more than she had realised. 'Only one of them,' she said. 'The old greybeards are not.'

'Here they come again,' Bradan warned. The bears dropped to all fours and advanced in a white-furred phalanx. The Skraelings fired their arrows again, with the same result as on the previous occasion. Erik glanced at Melcorka as if seeking her permission, and then he stepped forward, swinging his sword.

'Come on then, bears!' he shouted out. 'Come and face Erik Farseeker.' He moved sideways until he was alongside Melcorka.

'Get back, Bradan!' Melcorka snapped. 'You're not a fighting man!' She pushed him behind her.

The bears rose one by one until they all stood on their hind legs, towering above the humans. They opened their mouths and roared, with the sound echoing over the stark landscape. They seemed to rise from every dip in the landscape; shaggy, huge, with pink tongues lolling from gaping mouths and predatory eyes fixed on the ragged band of humans that stood in front of them. Melcorka felt herself shiver as many pairs of dark, menacing eyes fixed on her as if wondering what her flesh would taste like.

'There are hundreds of them.' Tall Leif sounded nervous.

'Plenty for all of us,' Melcorka agreed, sounding more positive than she felt. She tightened her grip on Defender and shuffled forward in a half-crouch, waiting. Melcorka knew that as long as she held Defender, she could cope with whatever attacked her, but she also had to ensure that Bradan was safe. She glanced behind her. 'Keep back, Bradan. This will get bloody.'

Bradan leaned on his staff, watching the bears advance. 'It always does,' he said.

'Now they'll charge.' Erik sounded nervous; he looked at Melcorka and copied her stance.

'Listen,' Melcorka said.

Something sounded in the distance, long and low, the tone cutting through the rough roaring of the bears. It sounded again, sonorous, echoing over the wild terrain.

'That's a horn,' Erik and Bradan said simultaneously.

'That means there are people out there,' Melcorka said.

The bears stopped, turned around and loped away slowly, jostling one another as they vanished into the distance. The snow started to fall again, lightly coating the deep prints of the bears.

'So whoever blew that horn controlled the bears.' Melcorka sheathed Defender. 'It may be the Ice King or somebody else. I wonder who he is and what else he controls...' she stared forward into the glaring white waste and the hypnotically whirling snow, 'and why he is luring us out here.'

'Luring us?' Erik asked. 'What do you mean?'

'We are being drawn to meet somebody.' Bradan tapped his staff on the ice. 'Or perhaps something.'

Chapter Five

'I've never seen anything like that before,' Melcorka said. 'What is it?'

'It's like a river,' Bradan said. 'Except that it's made of ice. It's a river of ice. Truly we have seen wonders since we left Alba.'

The allied force halted at the side of the river.

'We call it a glacier,' Erik said. 'It is the ice flowing toward the sea.'

Bradan surveyed the glacier; he could see it moving infinitely slowly, with chunks of ice grinding and shifting on top. 'It will not be easy to cross.'

'The Ice King is on the other side, so they say,' Almick said. 'My people have never been over there.'

'So you don't know if the Ice King is there, or even if he exists at all,' Bradan said. 'All we know is that somebody blew the horn that controlled the bears and somebody is putting pressure on your herders and hunters.'

Almick nodded. 'We have never been across there,' he repeated.

'If you do not go, you will never know.' Melcorka put a foot against the glacier. She could sense a very slight trembling. 'It does not seem too dangerous.'

The Norse and the Skraelings clustered at the side of the glacier, peering across at the north side where the ground rose in a series of steep ridges toward the blue-white range of mountains that had been their destination since they started out.

'Who will be first to cross?' Almick was more nervous than Melcorka had ever seen him. His Skraelings pulled back at once.

'I will be first!' Bjorn, a young, swaggering Norseman looked around to ensure that everybody appreciated his bravery.

'Perhaps I should go...' Melcorka began, but Bradan took hold of her arm.

'No. Let the Norse go first. This is their war.'

Straight-backed, Bjorn took one step onto the glacier. 'It's all right,' he shouted. 'I will lead the way, and you can all follow me!'

He walked on, occasionally jumping over unseen obstacles and stopped in the centre of the glacier. He looked back at them, waved, turned, stepped onto a large rock and disappeared.

'Where is he?' Erik asked. 'Bjorn! Where are you?'

'Give him a minute,' Bradan said. 'He may have slipped, or found something.'

A minute passed. And another. Bjorn did not appear.

'He's vanished,' Bradan said.

'I'll find him.' Erik stepped onto the ice.

'Your men need you.' Bradan seized his arm. 'If you disappear like Bjorn did, who will lead this troop?'

'I'll go.' Thorfinn was blond and tall, with a neat beard and bright blue eyes. He stepped onto the glacier without hesitation and strode forward in the wake of Bjorn.

'Can you see Bjorn?' Erik shouted, after a few moments.

'He's not here,' Thorfinn said. 'There is no sign of him at all. It was here that he vanished.' He clambered onto the rock.

'Where in Odin's name can he be?' Erik shouted.

'There is a ...' Thorfinn said no more. He slid into the ice without another word.

The Skraelings began to murmur, facing each other and talking in high-pitched tones. One or two stepped further back from the glacier.

'They're getting scared,' Melcorka said.

'So am I,' Bradan admitted.

'Unless somebody finds out what's happening, the Skraelings will go no further,' Melcorka said.

'You are not that somebody.' Bradan stepped in front of her. 'This is not our war, Mel!'

Melcorka warmed to him all over again. 'I have to be that somebody. Erik is too young and inexperienced, and I doubt that any of the Norse is a true warrior. They are farmers, explorers, settlers... brave men, yes, but not men like the Norse we fought in Scotland.' She touched his arm. 'I did not come along to stand and watch.'

'Mel...' Bradan reached out a second too late as Melcorka stepped onto the glacier.

She had expected it to be slippery, but a thousand years of movement had added a thick carpet of small stones to the surface, so she walked as smoothly as on a made-up track.

'Take care...'

She heard Bradan's concerned voice. The ice was firm beneath her feet, undulating slightly and rising to a ridge on which stood a single isolated rock that the ice must have carried for scores, perhaps hundreds of years.

That must be the rock that Thorfinn and Bjorn stood on, Melcorka told herself. *I won't make that mistake.* Instead, she walked to the far side. 'There's nothing here,' she shouted and then stopped.

Beyond the prominent rock was a chasm extending downward as far as she could see. The sides were of glistening ice, so smooth that there was not a single irregularity.

'There is something strange here,' Melcorka said. 'This does not seem natural.'

'Is Thorfinn there?' Erik shouted.

'I can't see him.' Melcorka stared downward, trying to see into the depths. A shaft of sunlight magnified the natural shine of the ice and reflected it from side to side until the deep interior of the chasm was a blaze of silver.

So where do you lead? And where are the missing men? Melcorka wondered. She had two choices; either she could explore this new phenomenon, or press on across the glacier and continue the journey to the Ice King.

Walk on, she decided. The Norsemen were warriors who had taken their chances.

The remainder of the glacier stretched ahead. Melcorka skirted the chasm and walked to the far bank. There were no obstacles in her path, nothing but rough ice embedded with pebbles. She turned around to wave on the others. 'Come on over. Just watch for the chasm and avoid that rock!'

She was speaking to nobody. All the Norse and the Skraelings and even Bradan had gone. In their place, she could see nothing except a white glare so dazzling that it hurt her eyes. Then it faded, and she saw the castle.

Where did that come from?

It was like nothing she had ever seen before. Towers soared skyward behind high walls, with castellated battlements and a gatehouse guarded by an intricately worked portcullis. That was all astonishing enough in this barren land, but what was more surprising was that it was built entirely of ice.

'I wonder who lives here?' Melcorka said quietly. 'I will guess that it is the Ice King.' She raised her voice. 'Bradan! Erik! Almick! Can anybody hear me?'

Only the echo of her voice came in mocking reply. She tried again. 'Hello! You in the ice castle! Can you hear me?'

There was still no reply.

She was alone on this bitter, white waste with no sign of Bradan and the allied army, and the ice castle seemingly deserted. 'Hello!' she repeated, 'Is anybody inside?'

Again, there was no reply. Watery sunlight reflected achingly from the tall towers.

'I'm coming in!' Melcorka walked to the gateway, crossing an ice-drawbridge over another deep chasm. The portcullis was down; each bar was of ice as thick as Melcorka's forearm, interlocking with each other in an intricate pattern that forbade any intruder from entering.

Above the door was a symbol carved into the ice, white on silver-white and as sharp as if it had been made that very day. Melcorka looked at it, knowing it was familiar but unable to say where she had seen it before.

'I'm coming in!' Melcorka shouted again. 'Either open the portcullis, or I'll break my way through.'

There was still no reply. The portcullis remained down. There were no birds, no insects, no animals and no wind; there was nothing to relieve the unbroken silence of that castle in the middle of the Greenland ice.

Drawing Defender, Melcorka slashed right and left, slicing through the ice to make a hole in the portcullis. The ice broke with a musical tinkle, falling to the ground in a million slivers that rattled and slithered and finally rested still. Silence returned. Melcorka peered through the hole into a vast outer courtyard, beyond which tall towers of shining ice stretched to a sky that was altering colour from grey to blue.

Melcorka stepped cautiously in, holding Defender in front of her, all her senses on high alert.

The outer courtyard was empty. Tall walls of ice stretched around her, pierced by round-headed windows. Four towers funnelled toward the sky, silver-white thrusting to bright blue. Two nailed down the front corners of the castle; two secured the rear.

'Hello!' Melcorka called once more. 'Is there anybody here?'

Balancing Defender on her right shoulder, Melcorka stepped on, through an arched doorway that led to the inner courtyard. Her footsteps echoed from the ice; her voice pealed around her.

'Hello!'

The inner courtyard was as empty as the outer had been. Square and smooth, it was surrounded by walls of ice, pierced with windows that glared blankly at Melcorka as if at a mortal enemy.

'Is anybody here?' Melcorka heard her words echo and re-echo around the confined space until they died to a whisper. 'Well, this is strange,' she said. 'I have an entire castle and nobody to share it with.'

Four doors opened from this courtyard; one into each of the rearmost towers, one back to the outer courtyard and one into a large building that sat between the two towers. That doorway was more ornate, arched like the others but decorated with carved polar bears and walruses. It was open, revealing a tantalising glimpse of stairs that led upward. Above the door was the same coat-of-arms that had been above the main gate. A bird in flight, wings extended, talons ready to pounce and beak thrusting forward.

'Hello! I am Melcorka of Alba!'

Her voice echoed again.

'You are not very welcoming to a guest!'

Her words bounced around, distorted by their surroundings.

'I am coming in!'

She stepped through the doorway. To her right was an empty chamber; to her left, its twin. In front, a flight of stairs swept upward. Grasping Defender firmly, Melcorka moved on, one step at a time.

'Bjorn! Thorfinn! Are you up there?'

She heard the sound first, a soft, regular thumping that she could not place. She waited, Defender ready.

The thing rolled down the stairs, one step at a time and nudged her left foot. She glanced down and met Bjorn's eyes. They were wide open, light blue and terrified. The young man had died in fear.

'Hello again, Bjorn,' she said softly. 'You will be in Valhalla now, welcomed into the Hall of Heroes.'

'Who's up there?' Melcorka called. 'Is Thorfinn still alive?'

She heard a whispering, like the wings of a flock of geese, and then nothing. The renewed silence was intense.

'Thorfinn?'

The noise was like nothing she had heard before; a gurgling, snarling sound that raised the hairs on the back of her neck. The scream came a second later, long and shocking: the cry of a man in mortal fear.

'Enough of this.' Rather than wait to see what would come down the stairs, Melcorka ran upwards, two steps at a time, with the point of Defender thrust out in front of her like a lance.

The scream ended abruptly. The snarl altered to a bubbling laugh that seemed to come from the depths of hell, and then Thorfinn appeared. He slithered down the stairs on top of a wash of his blood, except his body had been torn open and his insides were missing. Melcorka leapt over him as Thorfinn rolled past her and downwards; she slipped on his blood and continued upward.

'I am Melcorka of Alba!'

The doorway was arched, with that same flying-bird symbol above it. Melcorka pushed through and saw the creatures.

There were four of them, creatures larger than any wolf she had ever seen, with long snouts and mouths armed with a double row of inward-curving teeth. Their claws left ragged indentations on the ice and their tails ended in balls of spikes.

'Now, what the devil are you?' Melcorka asked and answered her question. 'Of course! You are the amoraks that Almick told us of. I thought you were a myth and yet here you are.'

The amoraks waited for her in a semi-circle, each one with a leather collar around its neck, ringed with spikes of ice. Blood-tinged spittle drooled from their mouths, and when their tongues extended, they were serrated and long.

'Come on if you dare.' Melcorka stood in a half-crouch, holding Defender before her. Only then did she see the cords that held the amoraks secure. Each cord was of strands of silk, twisted into a finger-wide leash that extended from the back of the brute's collar to an ice post that stood at the far end of the room. The blood that pooled on the floor showed how Bjorn and Thorfinn had died. There was no sign of Bjorn's body.

'So who put you here?' Melcorka asked. 'And why?' She raised her voice. 'I'm coming through,' she shouted. 'Your amoraks are in my way. If they attack me, I will kill them!'

As soon as the words were said, the ice post melted as if it had never existed and all four amoraks leapt at her, mouths gaping wide, exposing cruel, sharp teeth.

Thrusting Defender into the chest of the first, Melcorka was surprised at the sheer weight of the creature. She tried to withdraw her blade, gasped as she realised it had stuck in the amorak's ribcage, slid it sideways and yelled as a second amorak fastened its teeth onto her left thigh. Despite the enhanced strength and skill that flowed through her from Defender, the pain was sickening. The third amorak came from the right with its mouth fully extended and its teeth still bloody from Bjorn or Thorfinn. Melcorka could not see the fourth.

Despite all Melcorka's efforts, Defender was still sticking in the first amorak's ribs. Rather than try to slide the blade again, Melcorka pushed harder, until the point protruded out the amorak's back. As the creature squealed in agony, Melcorka ignored the pain of her thigh, lifted the amorak clean in the air, swung it around her head and crashed it on top of the creature that was gnawing at her leg.

The sudden impact dislodged the chewing beast, which turned to bite at this unexpected attack. Putting her foot on the now dead first amorak, Melcorka finally yanked Defender free, ducked low and sliced the blade sideways. She had learned that the creatures were too well muscled and boned for even Defender to penetrate with ease, so she aimed for the legs of the third amorak. She felt the shock of contact and the creature howled. With three of its legs immediately amputated, it fell, gushing out scarlet blood. Melcorka left it there, killed the second with a simple thrust to the back of its neck, stepped back and searched for the fourth. The whole affair had taken less than a minute.

The ice chamber was empty save for the two dead amoraks and the one that was quickly bleeding to death.

'Who are you?'

The voice came from nowhere, echoing around the ice, low, booming and with an accent that Melcorka had never heard before.

'I am Melcorka of the Cenel Bearnas in Alba!' She gave her name and clan proudly. 'Some call me the Swordswoman!'

She waited for a reply. There was none.

'Show yourself, Ice King – if that is who you are!'

Pushing the dead amoraks aside, Melcorka saw a small door on the opposite wall, where the pillar of ice had been. Thrusting Defender forward like a spear once again, she pushed into the doorway. There were more ice steps, slippery as wet glass, coiling around a central pillar and heading upward as far as she could see.

I must be in one of the towers, Melcorka told herself and climbed on. 'Are you there, Ice King?' she challenged. 'I am coming for you.'

The laughter surrounded her, echoing from the ice, battering at her ears, nearly deafening her with the sheer volume of sound.

'You are my enemy!' Melcorka shouted. 'You attacked the Skraelings and you killed Thorfinn and Bjorn. I will kill you!'

The laughter increased, peal after peal of it, so loud it was painful as it entered Melcorka's head, making it hard to concentrate or even think. She climbed on, step by step, each one taking her higher towards... she did not know what they took her towards. She only knew she had to climb, to fight this mysterious king with his command over wild beasts and a voice like the peal of thunder.

Thunder? That was Thor's province. Was she going to have to fight Thor and his mighty hammer? She smiled; why not? She had already defeated Bel, the sun-god of the Celts. Why not Thor, too? Let him come! Limping, aware she was losing blood from the deep wound in her left thigh, Melcorka pushed on, gasping with effort and pain, but unrelenting.

'I'm coming, Ice King! Wait for me! I am going to kill you!'

The laughter ended abruptly. The silence was so acute, it was painful. The steps continued. Melcorka hurried, climbing, counting each step, wondering if she would reach the moon or heaven first. She shouted for the Ice King to show himself.

'Ice King! Face me! I am Melcorka of Alba!'

And then she was running through a small door and onto the battlements of the corner tower, with all of Greenland stretched before her.

'Where are you?'

The floor was of ice, the battlements of ice. The view was immense. She could see the white ice-cap that covered most of this vast land, with the serrated mountain peaks to north and west; while away, far away in the south, was the tiny patch of green and brown that marked the cultivated settlement of Frakkoksfjord.

There was a group of specks down there, so small that Melcorka could barely make them out. They were moving, some this way, some that, and she knew that she was looking down on the allied Skraeling-Norse army that had come to battle the Ice King. But of the king, there was no sign.

'Now what?' Melcorka asked. 'Fight me, Ice King!'

The laughter surrounded her. Emanating from nowhere, it once again disturbed her ability to think and seared agonisingly into her brain, so she clenched her eyes, dropped Defender and covered her ears with her hands. The sound battered at her, sending her to her knees amidst the chill water and ice.

Melcorka swore; there was no water here a moment before. Forcing open her eyes, she saw she was in a puddle of water, a puddle that was rapidly expanding and deepening as the ice melted.

'Oh, dear God!' Melcorka looked around her. The nearest battlements were nearly gone as they dissolved away, and the steps she had come up were no longer clear-cut and pristine; their edges were blurred and soft. They were melting; the whole castle was returning to water under her feet. If she remained here, she would have nothing underneath her except liquid and a very long fall to ground level; she had to get back down.

Climbing up ice stairs with an injured leg had been bad enough. Trying to hurry down when the stairs were inches deep in water and liable to disappear beneath her feet, was ten times worse. With each second, the castle became more precarious, the steps more slippery and the walls thinner as they quickly dissolved.

Ice became sludge, and Melcorka felt herself falling through bitterly cold water, turning around, trying vainly to slow her passage. She saw the missing amorak beside her, its paws and tail flailing frantically and then she was in the midst of a river of rushing cold water, surging onward. Melcorka lifted her head and saw the crevasse ahead, with its terrifying drop to nowhere. The melting castle was propelling her toward her death with shocking speed.

The amorak was beside her, trying to bite her with its massive jaws. She kicked out, felt the shock of contact, saw the white teeth flashing and then it was gone, falling into the crevasse with its tail lashing around, knocking chunks of ice from the smooth sides. And then Melcorka was at the edge and plunging into the unimaginable depths. The amorak's harsh, barking howl continued for minutes until it faded away.

'No!' Melcorka shouted. 'I'm not going down there.'

Unsheathing Defender, she thrust sideways so the blade rammed into the ice side of the crevasse. It held firm; she felt the sword quiver as hundreds of tons of water crashed on top of them, nearly forcing her to release her grip on the hilt. The flow of ice-bitter water continued for what seemed like hours as the remains of the castle plummeted on top of her and down, down to the depths below.

The water slowed and then stopped. Melcorka shook a million droplets from her head and body and looked around. She was about three hundred feet below the lip of the crevasse, with Defender her only support and the chasm clutching at her with its invitation to fall down and down forever. Melcorka hung for a moment, holding onto the hilt of Defender as she assessed her situation.

She looked down, seeing the light fading as the crevasse plummeted to the unknown. There was no escape that way. She looked up, seeing the sheer ice walls ascending toward the surface. She had to climb up there, or she would die. There was no choice. She was so far down that nobody could see her, and even if they did, they could not rescue her. She had to rely on herself and nobody else.

It was fortunate that she had grown up on a small Scottish island where clambering down cliffs to rob bird's nests for eggs had been a regular chore. It had been a choice between climbing or starving, so Melcorka was no novice at rock-climbing. However, these walls were of glass-smooth ice and offered no grip. She reached up with her left hand and found only smoothness.

I will have to make my own handholds, Melcorka realised.

Pulling herself upward with great difficulty, she leaned her upper body across Defender, hoping that she had thrust it far enough into the ice to hold her weight. Sliding her hand inside her cloak, she pulled out the dirk she kept under her armpit, reached up as far as she could and began to hack at the ice. She needed a hand-hold deep enough to support her while she leaned down for Defender. Anything less and she would be falling into the abyss.

In such a cramped position, the work was hard and perspiration soon beaded on her face and trickled uncomfortably down her back. Gasping, she hacked at the ice, wondering how many centuries it had been there and ignoring the chips and chunks that cascaded past her and down into the terrible depths.

That will do, she told herself. *I've made it deep enough and angled it inward, so I have something to grip.*

She glanced down into nothingness and contemplated letting go and falling forever and ever toward the unfathomable blackness.

No! That way of thinking brings only madness. Upward and onward! she told herself sternly.

Sliding her hand into the first hole, Melcorka tested it, found it held her weight and began a second. It was harder as her muscles tired, but each handhold brought her a little closer to the top. Taking a deep breath, she stepped clear of Defender into the new holes, reached down and released the sword, to jam it into the ice a few feet above her head.

That's one small step, she told herself. *Only a couple of hundred more and I will be on the surface.*

'You will die down there!' The voice boomed and echoed around the chasm, thundering in Melcorka's head so she winced.

'Is that you, Ice King?' Melcorka called. 'Your melting castle failed to kill me, and I chopped your amoraks to pieces. What will you try next?'

'This!' The voice sounded again, even louder, and ended in that now familiar laugh.

'What?' Melcorka asked.

She did not have to wait long. The crevasse wall opposite her shifted, easing an inch closer to her. She looked up, seeing the rectangle of sky far above shrink slightly.

'I will close the walls slowly, Melcorka of Alba, so you are crushed to death a fraction at a time. You will die in exquisite agony, over hours.'

'I'm not dead yet!' Melcorka said, hacking another handhold in the ice and lifting herself another two feet higher.

'Soon,' that voice said, and the crevasse walls creaked closer to her.

'Coward!' Melcorka shouted. 'You are afraid to face me in battle. You kill from a distance. You are a coward!'

The wall closed another finger's width. Melcorka knew that her insults would not work. The Ice King would not be taunted into facing her.

Melcorka stabbed her dirk into the ice, knowing that she could not carve out handholds fast enough to reach the top before the walls closed in. She had to try something else. Holding the dirk in her left hand, she grabbed Defender by the hilt and thrust it, right-handed, into the ice wall. With one blade in each hand and her feet scrabbling desperately to find minuscule indentations in the ice, she moved up hand over fist, inch by painful, muscle-tearing inch. This way was much riskier. If she slipped... She dared not think of that drop beneath her.

The rectangle of sky was closing above her. The wall opposite was only a few feet away. Melcorka knew she would not manage to reach the top before she was crushed. 'I'm not going to die under the ice in Greenland,' she said. 'I refuse to die like this.'

The ice wall opposite shifted another inch closer.

'No, Ice King, you won't defeat me. I can turn your attack against you.' Reaching across, Melcorka wedged herself between the two walls and pushed upward. She swore as her feet slipped and for a moment she was held in place only by pressure and a sliver of Defender's blade. Gritting her teeth, she pressed harder and slid another few inches, and then another.

The gap at the top was closer than before, but the crevasse was pressing shut. Melcorka felt the sides squeezing her. She looked up, stretched and swore.

'Mel!'

The voice penetrated the Ice King's noise within her head.

'Mel!'

Only one man ever called her that.

'Bradan!' She shouted the name. 'Bradan! Down here!'

The staff was in front of her, a lifeline to the top. Melcorka grabbed hold of it with her left hand, still gripping Defender in her right, gave a final push with her feet and felt herself lifted upward. She reached the surface of the ice just as the crevasse closed with a hard slam. Lying face down, Melcorka gasped for breath as her muscles screamed in pain.

'I thought you were dead,' Bradan said.

'Not yet,' Melcorka gasped. 'If you had not been there, I would have been.'

'You're hurt.' His hands were on the wound in her thigh.

'It'll heal,' Melcorka said. The pain she had forgotten returned now, throbbing with each beat of her heart.

'Oh, dear God! What's that?' Bradan asked.

Melcorka struggled to her feet, gasped at the pain and straightened up. Erik was watching her, smiling as always, with Almick at his side and the combined Norse-Skraeling force scattered around them. At Bradan's words, every man looked upward and most backed away, swearing. Only Erik and two other Norsemen drew their swords and stepped forward.

The thing rose from the ice. Three times the height of the tallest man, it was composed entirely of ice, with the shape of a human and eyes deep and black and featureless.

'You must be the Ice King.' Melcorka forced any fear from her voice. 'It is about time you showed yourself.' She ignored the group of men that clustered around the thing. Whoever they were, they could wait. She had come to fight the Ice King, and that was what she would do.

The great voice boomed out again, the sheer volume of sound sending Skraelings and Norsemen cringing backwards. 'I control all this land. I was here before man, and I will be here long after man has gone.'

'I am not man.' Melcorka held herself erect. 'I am woman!'

She spared a glance at the five men who stood around the Ice King. They were nearly as tall as the Norsemen and dressed in clothes the like of which Melcorka had never seen. Each man wore a surcoat emblazoned with the same coat of arms that had been displayed above the doors of the ice castle. The pouncing falcon looked even more predatory, given its present company.

'Kill her,' one of the men ordered. He shared the same tawny colouring as his companions but was even taller, with handsome features. 'Kill her and then kill all the others.'

'You may not find that so easy,' Melcorka warned.

Stepping forward, she replaced her dirk under her arm and hefted Defender two-handed. The Ice King swept an arm toward her in a sideways motion that would have knocked her flat if she had not jumped back. She sliced with Defender, heard a crunch and saw two of the Ice King's fingers fall off.

'I'll kill you piece by piece,' Melcorka said, as the Ice King roared and staggered back, looking at his injured hand.

'Kill her. Kill her now!' the men ordered.

The Ice King stepped forward, lifted his right foot and stomped downward, missing Melcorka by a bare yard. She thrust Defender into his foot and pulled it out quickly as he bellowed in pain and jumped back, shaking his foot. In place of blood, clear water gushed out to promptly freeze in the cold air.

'Why do you wish to kill me?' Melcorka asked.

'You are my enemy!' The Ice King tried another clumsy stomp. Again, Melcorka avoided his foot. She stabbed Defender into his ankle.

'We are not your enemy!' Melcorka retrieved Defender and withdrew a step. She heard the hiss of arrows as the Skraelings and Norsemen unleashed a volley. Some stuck into the Ice King; others bounced harmlessly off his body to clatter onto the ice around him.

'You are going to melt all my ice and make my land green!' The Ice King lifted his hand, and a column of ice appeared beside Melcorka. He blew, and it toppled toward her. She jumped aside as it smashed into a thousand jagged pieces.

'We are not going to do that!' Melcorka said. 'We have no intention of taking your ice!'

Another ice column formed beside her, and then an entire wall of ice surrounded her. Melcorka hacked into it with Defender.

'You called my land Greenland!' The Ice King said. 'You want to make it green.'

'Kill her!' the men at his side ordered. 'Kill them all before they take away your ice and make everything warm and green, so you have no home.'

'It was them!' Melcorka said. 'These men told you these lies!'

The five with the colourful coats of arms emblazoned on their clothes all pointed to Melcorka. 'Kill that woman,' they ordered. 'She is your enemy!'

The Ice King looked down at her and caressed the stumps of his fingers. 'I will kill you,' he said.

'I don't want to hurt you, Ice King,' Melcorka said. 'These men are causing trouble between you and us. You lived in peace with your neighbours for years before they came. Who are they?'

'Torngit!' Almick's voice floated toward her. 'They are the torngit!'

'What is the torngit?' Melcorka asked.

'The foreign men! The torngit are men from abroad that live in the ice hills. They do not belong here.'

Melcorka nodded. 'Ice King! We wish you no harm!' She ducked as the king threw a huge block of ice at her. The Skraelings replied with another volley of arrows. One of the Norsemen shouted and ran forward with his axe, only for the Ice King to stand on him. A red smear spread across the frozen ground.

'Enough!' Melcorka yelled. 'There has been enough senseless killing!' Charging forward, she leapt over a sudden chasm that the Ice King created and landed in the midst of the tawny-skinned men. 'Who are you, torngit?' Grabbing the first by the throat, she shoved him backwards. 'Why are you spreading these lies about the Norsemen?'

'Kill her!' the other torngit men shouted in unison. One lifted a short spear with a stone head and thrust it at her. Melcorka parried the blow with ease, cut the man's arm off and killed him with a back-handed swing.

'Who are you?' she asked again.

'Don't kill me! Don't kill me!' the torngit she held squealed, trying to prise her grip free.

Another of the torngit threw his spear at Melcorka. She twisted aside, so the spear hit her captive instead. He screamed, squirming and trying to pluck the weapon from his back. Dropping him, Melcorka killed the spear thrower with a simple slash to his throat. The only torngit that was still standing drew a short dagger, but Erik knocked it out of his hand and lifted his sword.

'Don't kill him!' Melcorka's shout was too late as half a dozen Norse swords plunged into the man. Only the wounded torngit was left, moaning as he held the protruding spear.

'Ice King!' Melcorka yelled. 'We will not hurt you! You have my word, and I am Melcorka of Alba!'

The Ice King stood static, still nursing his injured hand.

Kneeling beside the wounded torngit, Melcorka took hold of the spear. 'You are going to die,' she told him. 'If I take the spear out, your blood with gush out and you will die quickly. If I leave it in, you will die more slowly, but you will still die and in infinitely more pain. If you tell me who you are and why you turned the Ice King against us, then your gods will be pleased that you told the truth and you will go to your heaven. If you lie, you will go to a place of eternal torment. The choice is yours.'

The man pointed upward, where the sun was easing aside a cloud. 'My god is watching me now.'

'Bel,' Melcorka said. 'The sun god. Do you worship the sun god?'

'The sun,' the man said softly. 'The sun is waiting for me.'

'Then please him,' Melcorka said. 'Tell me the truth, so you do not go to him with a lie upon your soul. Where are you from and why turn the Ice King against us?'

'I am from the Empire of Dhegia!' the torngit said proudly. Pushing Melcorka's hand away, he struggled to stand. 'My people are going to expand over the entire world. I am just preparing the way.' Temporarily ignoring the spear in his back, he lifted both hands. 'We came from the west and the south and will take over this whole land and then go onward!'

The Ice King's deep voice thundered. 'This is my land. I am king of the ice. Nobody will take my kingdom from me.'

'My king commands vaster armies than you can ever imagine,' the torngit said. 'He wants you as an ally. If you turn against him, he will destroy you.'

'I will turn the sea to ice and freeze his armies,' the Ice King boomed.

'My sun god will melt you, ice man!' the torngit boasted, until the Ice King lifted him in one hand.

'I die to serve you, Wamblee!' the torngit shouted, and then the Ice King pulled his head from his body and tossed both parts in opposite directions.

'We won't get any more from him, then,' Melcorka remarked. 'Well, Ice King, now you know that your friends were not friends at all, will you believe me that neither the Norse nor the Skraelings intend melting your ice to turn this land green?'

'I need assurance,' the Ice King said.

'I am Erik of Frakkoksfjord,' Erik said. 'I give you my word that we are not going to melt your ice and turn your land green.'

'If you do,' the great voice boomed, 'I will send my amoraks to kill your livestock and turn your streams to ice. I will freeze you out. I will have my bears hunt your men, and my walruses sink your boats.'

'That is agreed,' Erik said.

'We have a bargain then,' Melcorka said. 'The Norse will not turn the land green, and the Ice King will not destroy their settlement.'

'We have a bargain,' the Ice King affirmed. He looked at Melcorka through those deep, dark eyes and slowly merged with the ice all around him, leaving nothing to show that he had ever been there. Melcorka looked around. The bodies of the men from Dhegia lay side by side with the Norseman, staining the ice with their blood.

'Well, now we know where our iceberg woman came from.' Bradan pointed at the falcon symbol on the Dhegians' clothes. 'That's the same one as she wore.'

Melcorka wondered how she could have been so stupid. 'I thought I recognised it, but I could not remember where I had seen it.'

'The Empire of Dhegia,' Bradan said. 'And they want to take over the world.'

'I wonder where it is, and what it is like?' Melcorka said. 'An empire that can control an Ice King and has women travelling inside icebergs must be worth visiting.'

'An empire that wants to control the entire world may be best avoided,' Bradan said quietly. 'They don't seem to be the friendliest of people.'

Melcorka produced the headband that the woman from the iceberg had worn. She did not know what compelled her to wrap it around her forehead and allow the fringed ends to fall to her shoulders, but she did. She smiled at Bradan and then gasped.

She was in a city so large she could not see the end, with great, sloping pyramids of grassy earth rising in every direction, surmounted with tall buildings. Other buildings were smaller, beautifully thatched and neat as anything she had ever seen. Bare-chested people walked all around, bowing when they came to her. There were tradesmen, craftsmen, and warriors with elaborate costumes. Some carried spears, others clubs with heavy stone heads, elaborately carved. She belonged here. She was wanted here. She was important here. This city was her home.

'Melcorka?' Bradan was looking at her curiously. 'Are you all right?'

She snatched the headband off. 'Of course,' she said, wondering what had happened.

Bradan raised his eyebrows. 'I'm glad to hear it,' he said. 'We'd best get back to Frakkoksfjord.'

Chapter Six

It was their second feast in the central hall of Frakkoksfjord. With Frakkok and Erik at the head of the table, the Norsemen lined up on either side and Melcorka and Bradan at the foot. Melcorka listened to the rough Norse voices singing their songs of battle and wondered how this had happened. Not long before, she had fought a Norse invasion of Scotland, sword to sword against thousands of these pagan warriors and now she was fighting and eating side by side with them.

'I hear that rather than fight the Skraelings, you joined up with them, and you allowed this Ice King to live as well.' Frakkok's voice was as carping and unpleasant as ever.

'We did not need to fight the Skraelings,' Erik said. 'Melcorka arranged an alliance with them instead. The Ice King thought we were a threat to him. These men from the Empire of Dhegia had told him lies about us.'

Frakkok shook her head. 'So you decided to avoid yet another fight. Your father chose the warrior's path and died a man. You seem destined to live forever and die swaddled in soft wool in front of a nice, warm fire.'

'There was no opportunity to fight, Mother.' Erik said. 'The men from the Empire of Dhegia were killed.'

Frakkok stopped with a forkful of food halfway to her mouth. 'How many of them did your sword taste?'

'I was there.' Erik avoided the question.

'How many did you kill?' Frakkok repeated.

'None,' Erik admitted.

'*None?*' Frakkok repeated scornfully. 'As I thought. You are no warrior, and I doubt if you are even a man. Shall I find some little boys to warm your bed before you enter? Some nice, smooth little boys that won't task you too much?'

Melcorka looked away. She did not wish to witness this ritual humiliation.

'Your cute friend is not looking very happy,' Bradan said quietly. 'Frakkok is baiting him for some other reason. She is playing with him for her own ends, whatever those ends are.'

Melcorka nodded. 'She is manipulative,' she said. 'She is a witch in her way. Hush now, and listen.'

'I am not inclined toward boys, Mother.' Erik's face was as red as the most brilliant sunset.

'I am not sure about that,' Frakkok said. 'You avoid enemies and do not even recognise when they appear.'

'Your cute friend is thinking.' Bradan chewed on a mouthful of fish. 'He is wondering how to get his mother's approval. Ah! He has had a thought. He is talking now.'

'If this Empire of Dhegia wants to take over the world, then it will be a threat to us here,' Erik said slowly. 'We will have to defend ourselves against it.'

Frakkok's grunt was audible around the whole hall. 'So you intend to wait for these mysterious Dhegians to attack us, do you?'

'What else can we do?'

Frakkok leaned forward. 'What would your father do?' Her voice cut like a steel blade.

Erik looked away, unable to meet his mother's eyes. It would have taken a sharp sword to slice through the thick silence at that table as everybody waited for Erik to reply.

'Father would have attacked the Dhegian Empire,' he said, with a sudden smile of inspiration.

There was something like a collective sigh from the men. Melcorka knew that Erik had just cast the dice of his fate. Now, it depended on the numbers that rolled out.

'Does his son have something of his father inside him?' Frakkok's voice was quiet, yet audible to everybody in that hall. 'Or will it be toast beside his fire and pondering what luxuries he should fill his house with?'

There could only be one answer to that. To Erik's credit, he did not hesitate. 'I will follow Father's path,' he said, still smiling. 'Wherever it leads.'

'That's the answer I hoped for.' For the first time since Melcorka had met her, Frakkok seemed proud of her son.

'I am also going,' Melcorka said softly. 'I must see this Empire of Dhegia. Are you with me, Bradan?'

'Do you need to ask?' Bradan sounded slightly wistful.

'No.' Melcorka shook her head.

'You must make arrangements,' Frakkok said. 'How many men are you taking? How will you find this place? What will you do when you get there...?'

There was a sudden babble of noise as all the men at the table gave their advice in loud voices, accompanied by raised knives and much banging of fists.

'Wait!' Erik stood up. 'Listen to me!'

The noise continued, growing in volume as each man sought to make his point heard. Lifting a tankard, Erik crashed it down on the table, shaking the platters and nearly breaking the fingers of the unfortunate man who sat on his right.

'I am in charge here!' That statement rolled around the hall. 'I will decide what we will do.'

The noise subsided, save for a few murmured comments and a single laugh.

'What's amusing you?' Erik asked.

'You have no experience in war.' The speaker stroked his grey beard. 'You have had one small skirmish with the Skraelings, who are a despicable enemy, and now you intend leading an army against what may be a vast empire? Now, that is amusing. You need men of valour, men who have seen battle.'

'Do you mean men like you?' Erik asked.

'I mean men like me,' the greybeard answered.

Erik glanced at Frakkok, who held his gaze and said nothing. She was allowing Erik to make his own decisions.

There was another silence. The grey-bearded man laughed again, with two of his companions joining in, shaking their heads.

Melcorka watched, wondering how Erik would cope with this first challenge to his authority. She did not dislike the young Norseman; quite the reverse, indeed.

'Come on, Erik,' she said, so softly that only Bradan could hear. 'You're in charge here. Prove it.' She felt Frakkok's gaze on her and looked up. The Pictish woman was staring at her, dark eyes vicious.

'Well, Ragnog,' Erik dropped his eyes, 'you do have a point there.'

Melcorka was not alone in feeling disappointment as Erik sat back down.

'I do lack experience in major battles.' Erik continued to speak from his seat.

Ragnog the greybeard laughed again and belched coarsely.

'But I have something that you lack,' Erik said, and the smile was back. 'I have the sense not to challenge the leader of Frakkoksfjord!' He roared out the last phrase, and the hall came alive again.

Melcorka put a hand on Bradan's arm and squeezed, encouraging Erik with her thoughts. 'Go on, Erik,' she said softly. 'Show that you are a leader, or Ragnog and his ilk will always be contemptuous of you.' She looked around, searching the faces. The hall was divided between those who supported Erik and those who openly jeered at him. It was not quite an even split, but most of the older men supported Ragnog. while the younger ones, the youths and those who could not yet shave, were in Erik's camp.

Lifting his tankard, Erik threw it directly at Ragnog, who caught it one-handed and placed it back on the table.

'I will accept that challenge,' Ragnog said. 'And I will kill you like a dog!' He leered at Frakkok. 'If I have your ladyship's permission?'

Frakkok lifted her hand. 'You do not need my permission to kill,' she said. 'Or to be killed.'

Melcorka could nearly taste the tension as the Norsemen waited for Erik's response.

'Then we fight,' he said at length.

An outburst of noise filled the great hall as men and women shouted in anticipation and pounded the tables with fists, knife-hilts, and tankards. As soon as the words left Erik's mouth, the men began to roar about who they believed would win, with the younger warriors yelling for Erik and the older men claiming that Ragnog's experience would win the day.

'Without Erik,' Bradan murmured, 'there will be no heir apparent in this settlement. There will be a civil war to decide who will be the next leader.'

'That is the Norse way,' Melcorka said.

'We should leave if that happens.'

'If Ragnog kills Erik, we will be on *Catriona* within the hour,' Melcorka agreed.

'When shall I kill you?' Ragnog asked casually. 'I would like to finish my meal first. I prefer to fight on a full belly.'

'I can fight at any time.' Erik stood up and took hold of his sword hilt. 'I can finish my meal when your head is lying in the dirt.'

'So be it.'

They stormed out of the hall side by side, with neither man giving space to the other, so their shoulders bumped in the doorway. Being heavier, Ragnog knocked Erik aside, much to the glee of his supporters, who shouted anew at this example of their champion's superior strength.

'Ragnog will gut the young pup!' a one-eyed man shouted.

'I wager two slave girls that he kills Erik quickly.' The speaker was middle-aged, with a short sword at his belt and the beginnings of a paunch.

'I'll take that bet,' said a dapper young blond named Sigurd. 'Erik is too fast for the old man.'

'Do you have two slave girls?' the paunchy man asked.

'I have three!' Sigurd boasted.

'Then wager them all – if you have faith!' The paunchy man looked for support from his peers and then roared with laughter as Sigurd stuttered that he had to keep one for himself.

'Outside then, and let's watch the boastful young pup cut down to size,' the paunchy man roared, and led the rush to the door.

With the men at the forefront of the ring that quickly formed, the Norsemen bayed for their favourite as Erik and Ragnog stood a few paces apart. Erik drew his sword and threw away the scabbard in a gesture so dramatic, his supporters cheered anew.

'I have thrown away my scabbard,' he shouted. 'I won't pick it up until Ragnog welters in his own intestines.'

'In that case, it will lie useless forever.' Ragnog lifted a huge axe, took a practice swing and faced Erik. 'I will kill you quickly, Erik, not for your sake, but to spare your mother the grief of watching her son suffer.'

'Now, watch and learn,' Bradan murmured. 'You may have to fight either of these men at some time. Observe their strengths and weaknesses.'

'Thank you, Bradan, for your advice.' Melcorka did not mean to sound sarcastic.

There was no finesse in Ragnog's attack. He charged with a roar, swinging his axe as if he was trying to chop wood. Erik withdrew rapidly, dodging the blade and poking ineffectually with his sword. Neither man made contact.

'My slave girls are safe,' the paunchy man shouted. 'Erik does not have the stomach for a fight.'

'You have too much stomach for a warrior,' Sigurd said. 'Be careful that nobody cuts it off.'

Erik lifted his sword again and stepped into the middle of the ring. He looked worried.

'Breath deep, boy.' Ragnog balanced his axe across his shoulders. 'For these breaths will be your last!' He stepped forward slowly, before unleashing a mighty downward swing. Rather than waiting for the blow, Erik backed hurriedly away with his sword raised to parry. The elder half of the crowd cheered while the younger looked sulky.

'Sigurd, do you not wish to increase that bet to three slave girls?' the paunchy man yelled. 'Or I will take that handsome young boy you have as well – except you would miss him too much!'

Sigurd said nothing. He grabbed hold of the hilt of his knife and glared at the paunchy man, who laughed loudly.

'If you dare, boy, if you dare.'

'That stroke would have cut Erik in half,' Bradan said. 'If it had landed.'

'It did not land,' Melcorka looked away. 'There is little to learn here. It is a duel between an old brawler and a boy with no will to fight.'

'It is not finished yet,' Bradan said. 'We may be surprised.'

Ragnog charged again, this time swinging his axe from side to side in a succession of controlled sweeps that would have gutted Erik had he not dropped to the ground and rolled away. The older man turned with a surprising show of speed, lunged at Erik and missed, so the axe thudded into the soil. For a second, he struggled to free it while the younger men yelled for Erik to strike while Ragnog was helpless. Instead, Erik stepped back with his sword held upright.

'Kill him!' Sigurd shouted. 'He would kill you!'

'I will not kill a helpless man,' Erik said.

'You are a fool!' the younger men responded, while Melcorka nodded.

'He is a statesman,' she said. 'If he killed Ragnog when he was unable to retaliate, the older men would say it was a foul blow.'

'You like him, I think,' Bradan said.

'I am growing to dislike him less,' Melcorka agreed. She could feel Bradan's gaze on her.

'Some may think him cute,' Bradan reminded her.

'And others may take offence at a word with no meaning.'

Ragnog freed his axe and stepped back. 'You are indeed a fool, Erik,' he said. 'In war, only a fool does not take advantage of his enemy's weakness.'

For the first time, Erik advanced. He stepped forward, slowly at first and then with increasing speed, thrusting with his sword. Ragnog swung his axe so the two blades clattered together, and then the men closed. Knowing he was the lighter by some distance, Erik slid his left foot at the back of Ragnog's knee and then pushed. It was not a hard push but enough to unbalance Ragnog. With Erik's foot behind his knee, he fell and sprawled on his back. The look on his face was comical as he dropped his axe and lay there, swearing mightily.

'That was a clever move,' Melcorka said, as the crowd roared for Ragnog's blood.

Then Erik hesitated. Rather than finish Ragnog off, he looked upward to his mother, eyebrows raised as if he was asking her permission to kill his opponent. Seeing his weakness, Ragnog kicked upward mightily, catching Erik on the thigh, the force of the blow twisting him sideways.

Rolling to his feet, Ragnog swung sideways with his axe, only to find that Erik was not there. Either the pain of the kick had angered him, or Erik had finally decided that he had to win this contest, for he fell to the ground, rolled once and lunged upward with his sword.

The blade plunged into Ragnog's belly. Erik sliced it sideways, so the older man's intestines slipped out in a pink and white mess. Standing, and with his sword still inside Ragnog, Erik slid the blade upward.

'At last, you have learned how to fight!' Ragnog said, with his insides piling onto the ground at his feet. 'You are a man after all. Make your father proud, Erik!' He crumpled and died without another word.

Frakkok nodded once. 'You took your time to defeat an old man,' she said. 'Next time, don't be so slow. You did not deserve that victory.' She turned away and returned to the great hall.

'Aye. Nothing will shake a mother's love,' Bradan said.

Melcorka nodded. 'Erik tried to show compassion. I respect that.'

Chapter Seven

'We will take one ship,' Erik said. 'And thirty men. That is a large enough party to fight, but small enough not to starve. We will carry food enough for three months.'

The men at the table nodded. Since his victory over Ragnog, Erik had earned the respect of even some of the elders, while the younger men followed him without question.

'I want volunteers,' Erik said. 'And I will choose those I think best fitted for the journey. I want only one old man, one with experience of voyaging and skill in battle tactics. The rest will be young, fit and eager.'

'And loyal to himself,' Melcorka murmured to Bradan. 'Erik is no fool. He does not want some old warrior who was a friend of Ragnog to stab him in the back.'

Bradan tapped his staff on the floor and said nothing.

'This will be a hard journey. We do not know where it will end,' Erik said. 'I want only the best. Everybody will carry a sword or an axe, plus a shield and spear. Every third man will be an archer, with at least five-score arrows.'

The men nodded without hesitation.

'I want two tarpaulins for foul weather and clothes against the ice. I want dried meat for the journey and a lodestone for navigation.'

'You want a lot,' Frakkok interrupted. 'You are making more preparations for the voyage of one ship than your father made when he led a whole fleet to attack Northumberland!'

For a second Erik fell silent and Melcorka thought he would crumble before his mother's criticism, but instead, he retaliated. 'Father was only fighting one minor English kingdom. We are going against an entire Empire.'

Melcorka saw the slight gleam of satisfaction in Frakkok's dark eyes as she leaned back in her seat.

Erik looked up. 'Bradan... Melcorka. Are you coming with us? Or do you have another star to follow?'

'I am coming,' Bradan said. 'They call me Bradan the Wanderer, and this is as good a direction in which to wander as any other.' His smile was slow. 'I wish to see this empire that sends out emissaries to Ice Kings yet ignores settlements such as yours.'

'And you, Melcorka?'

'I am coming.' Melcorka did not mention the vision that still haunted her from the time she had donned the headband. 'Bradan and I have our own boat.'

'You call her *Catriona*.' Arne, young and eager to prove himself, scoffed. 'That is no name for a warship! We are in *Sea Serpent*!' His laugh found some support from his colleagues.

'*Catriona* has carried us to strange seas and dangerous waters,' Melcorka said. 'She has never let us down.' She did not mention that she had been built by a man who was half-selkie. Such information was best kept to herself.

'I am sure *Catriona* is a fine vessel,' Erik said, with a smile. 'But will you be able to keep level with *Sea Serpent*? She is a fast ship, and we may sail into wild seas.'

'When you reach the Empire of Dhegia,' Melcorka said, 'we will be there.'

'You don't know where it is,' a young Norseman named Thorkil scoffed. 'Only the Vikings can sail these seas.'

'It is to the west and south of here,' Melcorka said.

'We Norsemen call it Vinland,' Thorkil said. 'Only Norsemen know the sea-road.'

'The Dhegians also seem to know it,' Melcorka said.

'We will destroy them,' Thorkil boasted.

'We will see.' Melcorka thought of the confidence of the wounded Dhegian before the Ice King killed him. 'They may be a tough enemy to destroy.'

'We are Vikings,' Thorkil said. 'We defeat everybody.'

Melcorka looked at him, her eyes darkening with memories as she recalled the scenes of slaughter when the Norse had ravaged Dunedin, and the piles of bodies at the battle by the Tummel when the combined forces of Alba, Fidach and the Lord of the Isles had finally defeated the Norse invasion. 'Not everybody,' she said quietly. 'Not everybody.'

The Norseman grabbed for the hilt of his sword and was rising from his seat, until Erik pushed him back down. 'Easy, Thorkil, I need you alive. Melcorka is the best warrior I have ever seen.'

'She has not met me yet,' Thorkil said.

'That is why you are still alive,' Erik said, with his characteristic smile. 'Now, sit back down and continue living.'

'I can kill her,' Thorkil protested.

'That is possible,' Melcorka agreed. 'If you and ten of your friends crept up on me while I was asleep.' She smiled across at him, daring him to draw sword, willing him to fight her, desperate to kill him.

'Mel...' Bradan placed a hand on her arm. 'This is not like you.'

'Back off, Bradan.' Melcorka shook his hand off.

'We should all back off a little,' Erik said. 'We have a greater enemy to fight than our own reputations.'

'That is true,' Bradan said. 'Melcorka does not need to kill a beardless puppy to prove herself, while Thorkil here had better learn to control his tongue if he hopes to exercise it before the Dhegians.'

There was a celebration that night, with much drinking, singing and boasting. Melcorka watched the Norsemen carousing, seeing them pair off with the women, to stagger away into the dark, or simply find an unoccupied corner of the great hall to engage in coupling that was more animal than amorous.

She saw Arne kick a young slave girl, grab her by the hair and drag her, screaming, to the wall.

'I wonder if they acted like this before they attacked Alba?' she said.

'Quite possibly,' Bradan said. 'It seems to be their way.' He drank from a horn of ale. 'You're not yourself just now, Melcorka. Something is on your mind.'

'I *am* myself,' Melcorka protested.

'Are you sure you wish to journey with the Norse?' Bradan gestured to Arne. 'They are upsetting you.'

'If they upset me too much, I will kill them.'

'That's exactly what I mean, Mel. I've never heard you talk that way before.'

'I am fine.' Melcorka leaned closer to him. 'Leave me alone, Bradan.'

Bradan lifted his hands, palms toward her. 'You're alone, Melcorka. Just remember that you don't have to be alone. I am here if you need me.'

The slave girl screamed shrilly as Arne pushed her onto the ground and ripped up her dress. She was about ten, skinny and underdeveloped. Dropping his trousers, he prepared to enter her.

'She's a bit young for you.' Erik hauled Arne away. 'You'd be much better off coupling with a woman, rather than a child.'

'I like them young,' Arne protested. 'And she's only a slave.'

'She's *my* slave.' Erik lifted up the child. 'Off you go. Frakkok needs help with something.' He pushed her toward the door and crooked his finger to a dark-haired woman in her late twenties. 'You! Arne needs a woman.'

The slave woman came forward, apparently less than reluctant. Extending her right hand, she took hold of Arne and pulled him close.

Melcorka nodded to Erik. 'That was well done,' she said.

'Hilda likes men,' Erik said. 'Any men. Even Arne. Other women reject him. That is why he has to find a child.'

'You have goodness in you.' Melcorka was aware of Bradan watching her. 'You will make an excellent leader, once you earn the respect of your men.'

Erik's smile broadened. 'I will earn it.' He touched her on the arm. 'And I will earn yours.'

Bradan looked away, his eyes troubled.

Melcorka shrugged and left the hall. Finding a secluded corner, she slid a hand inside her cloak, removed the headband and slipped it over her forehead. Within seconds, she was back in that strange city of tall, earthen mounds and stone pyramids, where polite people treated her with respect and bowed as she approached. She leaned back and smiled, allowing herself to drift away into this new world.

Chapter Eight

They sailed on the morning tide, with the mist hugging close to the sea and hiding the high white mountains of Greenland. There were two vessels, the dragon ship *Sea Serpent* and the much smaller *Catriona*, both under muscle-power alone.

'It's good to be back at sea.' Melcorka hauled at her oar.

Bradan nodded, unspeaking.

'Now it's you who is not himself.' Melcorka glanced across at him. 'You have hardly said a word since last night.'

'From what I heard, this Vinland is a fair distance away.' Bradan did not explain his silence. 'This could be a long row.'

'I hope that Erik knows what he is doing,' Melcorka said.

'If not,' Bradan said, 'we'll leave him to do what he wishes and head out on our own.'

Melcorka tossed back her hood so that her dark hair hung free. 'You don't like Erik, do you?'

'I don't trust him,' Bradan said.

'When we first met these Northmen, you warned me not to judge them all like Egil. Now it is you who is doing the judging.'

Bradan grunted and nodded. 'That could be.'

'Perhaps you need to find some trust.' Melcorka replaced her hood.

They rowed on, with the silence broken only by the ripple of water under *Catriona*'s counter and the soft surge of the sea against their prow. Twice, whales surfaced nearby, surveyed them and submerged again. A flight of birds passed close overhead and Melcorka looked up in the hope that there was an oystercatcher, her totem bird, among them. There was not. They heard the melancholic call of geese, unseen in the mist, a reminder of home. They rowed on in the wake of *Sea Serpent* until a breeze whispered from the south and they could hoist the sail.

'That's better now,' Bradan said.

Melcorka did not answer.

At night, they furled the sail and put out a sea anchor so they would not lose touch with *Sea Serpent*. They heard the rough Norse voices drift across to them and watched small icebergs bob past, wary in case of a collision. None came close. They slept, though twice Melcorka woke to find Bradan watching her through concerned eyes. Turning her back, she went back to sleep, wishing she had the peace and solitude to don her headband.

They moved on at dawn, heading south and west for the land that Erik called Vinland and with the wind bellying their sail as *Sea Serpent* pulled further ahead.

'We might lose them,' Melcorka warned.

'That could be a blessing,' Bradan said.

'What does that mean?' Melcorka rounded on him, instantly angry.

'Exactly what the words said. I think that losing *Sea Serpent* might be a blessing.'

'We are going to find a huge empire that wants to take over the world!' she blazed at him, eyes hot. 'Do you not think that the more swords we have, the better chance we have of success?'

'And do you think that another thirty untried blades will be of any use if this is an empire of thousands?' Bradan faced her with anger every bit as intense.

'This is not about numbers, is it?' Melcorka said. 'You have something else on your mind. Something is bothering you.'

'You know full well what it is!' Bradan shouted.

'You'd better tell me, Bradan!' Leaving her oar, Melcorka stood up and stepped toward him.

'Or what, Melcorka? Or you'll draw your big sword and cut my head off?' Bradan held her gaze, unblinking and unafraid. 'Where are you, Mel?'

Her slap took him by surprise, so he staggered back and nearly fell over the thwart.

'Sail-ho!' The hail came from *Sea Serpent*. 'Sail astern!'

'These seas are getting far too crowded.' Bradan smoothed a hand over his face.

'Get back to your oar,' Melcorka ordered. 'It might be one of the Emperor's ships.'

'It's a Norse dragon ship,' Bradan said. 'Unless the Dhegians have the same design.'

'And look who is standing in the bows?' Melcorka said.

Neither of them mentioned the slap.

'Erik!' Frakkok called across, ignoring *Catriona* completely as she balanced easily in the bows of her ship. 'The Dhegians have burned Frakkoksfjord and slaughtered our people. We are all that is left.'

There was instant pandemonium in *Sea Serpent* as the crew lined the sides, asking questions, making comments, drawing their swords in a fury.

'We must go back!' one red-haired man named Gunnar said. 'We'll go back and find them! We'll slaughter them!'

'No, Gunnar,' Frakkok said. 'They've long gone. They'll be on their way back to Dhegia. We go on. They burned our home, we will burn theirs!'

'We did not see any ships,' Gunnar said.

'They came out of the fog and disappeared in the fog,' Frakkok told him. 'They may have passed you the same way, or sailed an entirely different route.'

'That is a lot of explanation from Frakkok,' Bradan said. 'She is usually close-mouthed.'

'She could be guilty that the enemy caught her so easily,' Melcorka said.

Bradan nodded. 'That could be so,' he said.

'How many did we lose?' Erik shouted across to Frakkok.

'Everyone except those on my ship. I have only twenty men and five women. No more questions now. Head west.'

Melcorka raised her eyebrows. 'We have a new leader, it seems. I wonder what Erik thinks about that!'

'Something cute, no doubt,' Bradan said. He sat at his oar and pulled.

Now three ships strong, the small flotilla surged westward, with *Catriona* between the two dragon ships and the grey sea rising and falling all around.

'Where are we headed now?' Melcorka shouted across to Erik.

'Still Vinland!' Erik yelled back. 'And watch for the icebergs.'

There were days of clear sailing. There were days when the fog was so thick that the mariners placed lighted fir torches on stern and stem posts, so their neighbours could see them. There were days when the wind came from dead ahead, so the crews spent sweat-laden hours labouring at the oars merely to maintain their position. There were days when storms hurled mountain-high waves at the small flotilla, with the wind howling through the rigging and the sea breaking creamy green against the hulls. There were days when the sun was as bright and hot as midsummer, baking them at the oars.

Then there was the day of the iceberg...

'Look at that!' Bradan gestured to the north. 'It's like a floating island.'

'It must be half a mile long, at least,' Melcorka said.

The thing floated majestic and serene, with pinnacles of ice higher than any cathedral and an aura of cold that chilled even across the hundreds of yards that separated them.

By now used to the smaller bergs that they cautiously passed, the Norsemen also lined the sides of their vessels to point and stare at this island of ice that floated silently past them. As they watched, the northern edge of the berg sheared off, creating a massive wave that roared toward the flotilla.

'Steer toward the wave,' Bradan ordered.

'I already am.' Melcorka was at the tiller, pointing the bow toward the fast-approaching wall of green water. It gathered strength as it came nearer, with the water speckled with fragments and chunks of ice.

Catriona's bow lifted, higher and higher until the ship was suspended at an acute angle and the stores rumbled and rolled along the deck planking toward the stern where Melcorka clung to the tiller. 'Hold on!'

Grasping the mast with both arms, Bradan nodded. 'You too, Mel.'

They watched the bow lift until it was nearly vertical, twisting to starboard as if *Catriona* was about to capsize. Melcorka kept her eyes open, hoping that the magic that protected *Catriona*'s crew from drowning in Scottish waters would work this far west. And then they were levelling out, cruising on the summit of that massive green-and-silver wave with the iceberg still floating in front and the smaller chunks of ice clattering and clinking all around.

Melcorka stole a glance right and left. *Sea-Serpent* was there, missing her mast but upright. There was no sign of Frakkok's ship. And then they were descending the other side of the wave, with *Catriona*'s bow plunging down, down and down forever and the sea roaring and howling around them.

Catriona smashed into the swelling sea, taking on scores of gallons of water, as waves surged and crashed around the hull, white and green and roaring with rage.

'Bradan!' Melcorka yelled. She looked forward – he was no longer at the mast. 'Bradan!' The sick horror was worse than anything she had felt since she had lost her mother. '*Bradan!*'

'Here, Melcorka.' The voice came from the flooded bows. 'I'm here.' He stood up, holding his staff and shaking off the water that cascaded from him.

'I thought...' She bit off the end of her sentence.

'My staff was nearly overboard,' Bradan said. 'I had to go after it.'

'What?' Sudden anger washed away Melcorka's relief. 'You could have been washed overboard and drowned. You fool!'

'This staff is important to me.' Bradan held it up.

'Did you not think that other things may matter more?' Melcorka closed her mouth. She was not yet ready to say what was on her mind. He should know, anyway.

'We've lost a ship,' Bradan said.

'I'd rather lose a hundred ships than lose you,' Melcorka said, but so softly that Bradan could not hear her.

Sea-Serpent rolled in the sea alongside them. Of Frakkok's ship there was no sign, although a few heads bobbed with a scattering of wreckage among the waves. Melcorka saw Erik's men throwing lines into the sea and Frakkok clambering nimbly over the stern. For one second, Frakkok's gaze locked with hers; there was nothing there but hatred. Melcorka lifted a hand to acknowledge her rescue. She did not know why Frakkok harboured this animosity. She only knew that it was deep and corrosive and when it eventually came into the open, one of them would be badly hurt. That time was not yet here.

There was the day of the sea monsters...

'What in God's name is that?' Bradan pointed to larboard. 'It is a sea monster!'

The Norse apparently thought so, too as they clustered in the stern of *Sea-Serpent*, staring at the things that swam alongside.

Enormous and dark, the monsters rose from the green depths of the sea and stared back at the men who gawped at them. Massive in size, they had long, curved fangs on either side of their heads, were more than twice the size of a man yet swam with the grace of a seal.

'It's a dragon!' Arne shouted.

'No, it's a Kraken,' Gunnar contradicted.

'It's a walrus,' Erik said. 'They are quite common.'

'Kill them!' Frakkok ordered.

Arrows and spears whizzed from *Sea Serpent*, most to miss, some to bounce harmlessly from the thick hide of the walruses, and a few, a very few, to stick in. Then the walruses dived and were gone forever.

'We killed them!' Arne yelled.

'You did not,' Melcorka said softly. She remembered the Ice King mentioning his power over the walruses and wondered if he had sent them to spy on them. With their great fangs, they would have been a formidable foe.

'You should have jumped over the side to fight them,' Frakkok chided Erik.

Erik looked away, saying nothing. Melcorka slipped a hand inside her cloak and stroked her headband. When she looked back at *Sea Serpent*, Erik was watching her. He returned her smile of encouragement, and for a long minute, she held his gaze.

The ships sailed on.

'If those were an example of the sort of creatures this new world of Vinland has,' Bradan said, 'this expedition will bring many hard knocks and very little glory.'

Melcorka nodded. 'There are many wonders ahead,' she said. She did not mention that splendid city she had seen in her visions, or the men who walked at her side. One of them had been Erik. She had not seen Bradan there.

There was the time of the shallow seas...

The fog was thick again, clinging to the ship as they eased along, with the oars shushing into calm water and the sound of their voices echoing hollowly, eerily to one another. Melcorka looked to starboard, where strands of mist wisped from the newly repaired mast of *Sea Serpent* and trailed behind her like the ragged remains of a tattered flag.

'Look down,' Erik shouted to her. 'Look at the sea. It's alive!'

'Alive?' For a moment, Melcorka thought that Llyr, the sea god, was about to clutch at them. Instead, she saw that only a few feet under *Catriona*'s keel, the sea was one huge mass of fish. Silver cod by the million, the fish formed a shoal so large that they sailed over it for days and it never ended.

'It is a fishing bank like no other I have ever seen before,' Bradan said. Reaching over the side with his staff, he hooked it under a large cod and tossed it on board. It lay there, wriggling and silver. He added another, and another. 'Breakfast, dinner and tea,' he said, 'with no effort at all.'

'Truly this New World is a land of wonders,' Melcorka said.

'And look!' Bradan shouted. 'I can touch the bottom of the sea!' Leaning over the side, he thrust down with his staff. 'There is sand beneath the fish.'

'We are lucky we are of shallow draught,' Melcorka said. '*Sea Serpent* had better be careful.'

Her words were prophetic, for twice that day the Norse dragon ship ran aground and the crew had to disembark and walk through the sea. With the water lapping up to their chins, they pushed their ship along, cursing, stumbling and supremely unhappy with life.

'We will tow you,' Bradan shouted.

'We don't need your help!' Frakkok said.

'We want to help!' Bradan insisted and threw a line across. Erik tied it around the mouth of the dragon figurehead and sent two of his men to *Catriona* to give extra power to the oars.

Despite Frakkok's frown, the little extra pull helped. Each time they hauled on the oars, *Sea Serpent* eased a little closer to deeper water.

'Don't get drowned now,' Melcorka shouted cheerfully to the men who still trudged through the water.

Frakkok said nothing as *Sea Serpent* floated free at last and the two oarsmen boarded again.

They sailed on, cautiously.

'Thank you!' Erik waved, and Melcorka replied, happy to have the Norseman's company in this strange new world of monsters, shallow seas and vast mountains of floating ice.

That night, as Bradan slept on the deck, she fingered the headband. Even that slight touch brought a shiver to her. She held it up high, examining the workmanship and the strange falcon design.

'Who made you,' she said quietly, 'and where are you from? What strange nations lie ahead?'

On an impulse, she once more placed the band around the head and again experienced that strange vision.

There were thousands of people around her, men and women, some bare-chested, others elaborately clothed but all with that same attractive, copper-coloured skin and all treating her with tremendous respect, even awe.

She walked along a broad street with great green mounds rising on both sides and a massive square-based pyramid in front, surrounded by a high wall. Beside her was a tall, very handsome man who walked with great dignity. Ahead of them, there was an elaborate gateway guarded by men with beautifully fashioned clubs and headdresses of bright feathers. They stepped aside as she approached. The sky above was brilliant blue, cloudless as it stretched forever upward. Colourful birds sang among scattered trees, and she was at peace.

'Melcorka.' Bradan's voice penetrated her mind, awakening her. She shook him away, desperate to return to that beautiful place where she was wanted and admired. That place where she belonged. Instead, she opened her eyes to the wet, cold deck of *Catriona* and drizzling rain that wept from an overcast sky.

'Time you were awake. There is land ahead.' Bradan's smile was slow. 'A land neither of us knows.'

Without any order given, the Norsemen on *Sea Serpent* furled their sail and rested on their oars. Melcorka and Bradan did the same, staring ahead at the coast of this new world.

'So there it is,' Bradan said. 'The land that the Norse call Vinland.'

'I wonder what adventures lie ahead?' Melcorka mused. 'What strange peoples, what creatures, what buildings and ideas.' She felt interest surge within her. It was as if she was meant to be here...

as if some manifest destiny had brought her here, so far from her tiny island across the sea.

'We will soon find out.' Bradan tapped his staff on the deck. 'God help us, we will soon find out.'

Melcorka nodded, slid her hand inside her cloak and fingered the headband again.

They skirted the coast for three days, seeking some inlet to guide them inland. Instead, they saw dense green forests of tall pine trees and rough rocks, with high hills further inland.

'This is a huge land,' Melcorka said.

'It is bigger than Alba, I think,' Bradan agreed. 'And it's fertile with forests.'

'Where are the people?' Melcorka asked. 'Where are the fishing boats and the coastal villages? Has some enemy destroyed them? Have the Norsemen harried and pillaged this coast as they did to Alba and Northumberland and Ireland?'

'Perhaps not the Norse,' Bradan said. 'Perhaps it was this Empire of Dhegia.'

It was another day before they saw their first native of Vinland. They continued to cruise, with the heavily timbered coast so close that they could smell the sweet scent of pine and hear the music of the birds.

'Over there – what's that?' Bradan shouted. 'It's a boat.'

The vessel was small, narrow and close to the shore, with two half-naked men kneeling inside. As soon as they saw *Catriona* and *Sea Serpent*, the paddlers turned their vessel and sped for the shore faster than even *Catriona* could follow.

'They are only Skraelings,' Erik shouted from *Sea Serpent*. 'They are not like the warriors of Dhegia. Let them go.'

Melcorka nodded and lifted her hand in acknowledgement. That was their first contact with men from this new world. She thought of her visions, of the streets and civilisation, of the city that was larger than anything she had ever seen before. These semi-naked Skraelings could not have built such a place. There was more inside this new world than these men, however fast their boat had been.

'Are you all right, Melcorka?' Bradan was at the tiller, guiding *Catriona* past a headland where the sea surged and splintered. Seagulls circled them, squawking loudly.

Melcorka nodded, wordless. For some reason she could not explain, she could not tell Bradan what she had seen, and what she thought.

'Do you want to tell me?'

'There is nothing to tell,' Melcorka said.

He watched her for a long minute and glanced across at *Sea Serpent,* where Erik stood in the stern beside Frakkok. 'When you want to tell me the truth, I am willing to listen.'

Melcorka said nothing. She was not sure what truth Bradan wanted to hear. How could she tell him about her visions, when he was not part of them and another man was? Yet how could she continue to lie to Bradan? Turning away, she stared at the coast of Vinland, more miserable than she had been for many months.

For the next week, they hugged the coast and probed into inlets where more Skraeling boats slipped away from them, and river mouths that led to nowhere except dark forests tainted with the slight drift of wood-smoke. Finally, *Sea Serpent* turned a headland into what was undoubtedly the estuary of a major river, or even the end of Vinland.

'This is a beautiful place,' Melcorka said, as they cruised past a large island, so close they could smell sweet grass and hear the chatter of a thousand birds. Ignoring the constant stare of Frakkok, Melcorka acknowledged Erik's cheerful wave and steered them onward, with the wind pushing them against the current of a powerful river.

'We are heading deep into Vinland,' Melcorka said. 'I wonder if the Norsemen have explored this part already, or if we are the first?'

'I don't know,' Bradan said. 'I can't see any sign of the Empire, anyway.'

'Nor can I,' Melcorka said.

They sailed on, tacking back and forth against the current, occasionally resorting to the oars when the wind died. On the third day, Bradan sniffed the air.

'I smell smoke,' he said. 'Wood smoke.'

'There will be a village ahead,' Melcorka predicted, scanning the wooded shores for signs of life. She was the first to see the boat, another of the small, light, double-prowed vessels favoured by the local Skraelings.

'Erik!' she shouted and gestured to the boat. 'I am going to follow it!'

As she expected, at the sight of *Sea Serpent* and *Catriona,* the Skraeling boat turned around and sped for the shore.

'Follow her,' Melcorka ordered and watched in case the Skraeling vessel vanished into some hidden creek in the forest. It was fast and manoeuverable, with the paddlers pushing her forward with a skill that Melcorka could only admire.

'They're not running from us,' Melcorka said. 'They're bringing news of our arrival to their village – and there it is now.' She pointed as the Skraeling boat eased onto a muddy beach.

'I see it,' Bradan said and furled the sail.

Catriona eased to a halt in the river, close to the Skraeling village.

Composed of about thirty huts, some conical, others rounded or rectangular, the village was surrounded by a simple palisade and had a dozen of the light, narrow boats drawn up from the river. The inhabitants gathered to watch this strange vessel, so unlike their native craft, and the larger *Sea Serpent* that waited in deeper water. Dressed mainly in furs, men and women mingled together, some with elaborate winged hats of a style Melcorka found quite attractive, others bare-headed with long hair down to their shoulders. The men carried bows and arrows, or short spears.

'They are not firing at us,' she said.

'I don't think they are unfriendly,' Bradan said. 'Let's say hello.'

The Skraelings stepped back as Melcorka and Bradan splashed ashore. Some pointed arrows at them or lifted their spears, although most just looked curious. One elderly woman took a pace forward, speaking in a low, clear voice.

'I don't know what you are saying,' Bradan said, smiling. 'I am Bradan the Wanderer.' He jabbed a finger on his chest. 'Bradan!'

The woman waved her hand to indicate the entire village. 'Lnu'k' she said, as if that settled all arguments.

Bradan touched Melcorka. 'Melcorka,' he said. 'Melcorka.'

'Tomah.' The woman pointed to herself. 'Tomah.'

Unsure what to do, Melcorka smiled as widely as she could, bent, and kissed Tomah on the forehead. That seemed to work. More of the Lnu'k people surged forward and for the next few minutes, Bradan and Melcorka were at the centre of a crowd, all engaged in mutual pointing, name-giving and kissing, with much smiling and laughter for good measure.

'They are friendly!'

Arne led the first of the Norsemen ashore, sword drawn and shield up as protection. As some of the Lnu'k men lifted their spears and bows in natural retaliation, Bradan stepped forward and knocked Arne's shield aside with his staff.

'These people are friendly!' Bradan said.

'You will die for that!' Arne lifted his sword high, only for Melcorka to disarm him with a single swing of Defender.

'Nobody will die today,' she said.

'Melcorka is right, Arne.' Erik lifted Arne's sword and replaced it in its scabbard. 'These people are no threat to us.'

Now that both sides had guaranteed peace, the Lnu'k and the voyagers mixed in harmony, exchanging gifts of furs and dried fish for lengths of rope and pieces of dried seal meat.

Tomah attached herself to Melcorka and dragged her around the village, showing her the pointed huts which she called wigwams, with their framework of poles covered with birch bark and their entrances pointing eastward, toward the rising sun. She called the rectangular huts 'lodges', while in the centre of the village was a cleared area around a central carved pole. Melcorka understood this to be a ceremonial or sacred area, although she had no idea which god, or gods, these Lnu'k people worshipped.

Taking hold of Melcorka's sleeve, Tomah pulled her inside what must have been her own wigwam and led her to the place of honour at the centre back. In seconds, Tomah's entire family squeezed in around the central fire, and a smiling woman produced a meal of fish.

'Bradan.' When Melcorka indicated that she wanted him with her, two of the youngest Skraelings ran outside and ushered him in, laughing at the whiteness of his skin under his clothes and touching his hands. They spent the night on supremely comfortable mat beds made of spruce boughs and reeds, so similar to the heather beds of Alba that Melcorka wondered if there was some relationship between the two peoples.

Next morning, they emerged into the village to see the Norsemen emerging from various lodges and wigwams, some alone, others with Lnu'k women. Children swarmed everywhere, of all ages and stages of dress and undress, with much tolerance and laughter.

'How old are you?' Melcorka asked Tomah, using sign language and smiles to convey her question.

The old woman lifted her hand and spread her fingers, again and again, counting the years slowly. When she reached a hundred and ten, she stopped and gave a toothless smile.

'That is impressive,' Melcorka said. 'I've never met anybody as old as you.'

Tomah smiled again, rubbed her belly, then pointed to some of the younger children and back at Melcorka.

'I think she wants to know how many children you have,' Bradan said.

'None.' Melcorka shook her head. 'None. I have no children.'

Tomah raised her hands high.

'She is wondering how a beautiful woman such as you can be childless,' Bradan tried to translate.

Melcorka smiled. 'I may have children some time,' she said. 'I have much to do first.'

Tomah laughed and touched Bradan in a very intimate spot. He shook his head, pushing her hand away as she laughed all the more, with other women gathering around to share in the fun.

'Tomah,' Melcorka asked, as they sat around the fire with the smoke seeping through the hole at the apex of the wigwam, 'do you know of the Empire of Dhegia?'

Tomah flinched at the name and looked away, raising both hands in the air.

'She knows the name,' Bradan said. Leaning forward, he used his finger to draw on the ground, reproducing the symbol that had been on the clothes of the iceberg woman and the men around the Ice King. 'Do you know that sign, Tomah? It is like a bird, a falcon...'

Still with her hands held high, Tomah backed away, shaking her head violently. Quickly erasing his drawing, Bradan took hold of her.

'It's all right, Tomah. We are not from Dhegia. We mean you no harm.'

'She's not happy,' Melcorka said. 'Tomah, Dhegia is our enemy. How can we find them? Where is this place?' She was unsure if the old woman understood her words, so she repeated them, pointing in every direction.

Grabbing hold of Melcorka, Tomah led her out of the wigwam and across the village to a small, oblong lodge made of wood, near to which a fire was burning inside a triangular fireplace. The man who tended the fire looked every bit as old as Tomah. Unsmiling, he listened as Tomah spoke to him and then pointed to the building.

'You want me to go in there?' Melcorka asked.

There was a rocky path between the fire and the building, and a small, low entrance. The roof was of spruce boughs, piled high.

'I think she does,' Bradan had followed them. 'Maybe there is somebody inside who can give you directions to Dhegia – a chief or a priest or the like.'

Melcorka crouched down to look inside. The entrance was too narrow to walk through and too dark for her to see the interior. 'I'll go in,' she said.

Taking hold of Melcorka's cloak, Tomah pulled it firmly and tried to drag it away, shaking her head.

'You have to take your cloak off,' Bradan said, 'and everything else, I think,' he continued, as Tomah pulled at Melcorka's leine.

'Take care of Defender.' Melcorka handed Bradan the sword. 'If any Norseman tries to take it from you, kill him.'

'I am no killer...' Bradan began.

Melcorka stood proud, tall and stark naked as Tomah hauled out some small clay pots from the shelter of the fire and dabbed her with the contents.

'Some sort of herb concoction,' Melcorka said. She glanced at the fire-tender, who was watching with no interest. 'I can smell sage and sweet grass,' she said and widened her eyes as Tomah put something in her mouth, chewed vigorously and dabbed the semi-masticated mess on her belly.

'That must be important,' Bradan said.

Speaking all the time, Tomah guided Melcorka down to her hands and knees and pushed her to the entrance of the small lodge. Melcorka had a final glance around, suddenly aware that most of the Norse were watching her and Erik's eyes were roving around her body, as hungry as those of any adolescent youth. She allowed him a moment and then crawled inside the hut. Tomah followed.

There was nobody else inside; there was no seer to predict her future, no wise man ready with advice. Tomah pushed her into a sitting position on the ground, beside a sizeable hole. Retreating quickly, the old woman returned with a wooden pot, from which she took seven heated granite stones and placed them in the hole, one at a time. She returned four times with a further seven stones, so there were twenty-eight ready-heated stones in the central hole. The small space in the lodge was as hot as anywhere Melcorka had been in her life.

'What are you doing?' Melcorka asked.

Ignoring her, Tomah scurried away again and returned with a pot of water. Using a cedar branch, she flicked the water onto the stones, so a hissing cloud of steam filled the interior of the lodge.

'What is this for?' Melcorka asked, before she realised that it was a religious ceremony. Closing her mouth, she leaned back and waited to see what would happen.

Steam surrounded her, thick and hot. She struggled to breathe, gasping for air in that dark, hot place. She lay back against the log wall, mouth open, feeling the sweat bead on her face and trickle down her perspiring body to form little pools where she was sitting. Her mind drifted, back to her island childhood and onto her first sighting of Defender. Then she was in Alba, seeing the slaughter of Dunedin and the battle of the plains of Lothian, and on to that strange Castle Gloom and the road north, where the People of Peace intercepted them. In her mind, she revisited Fidach with the painted, carved stones and then she was at the battle by the banks of the Tummel. She moved on, to the rule of Queen Maelona of Alba and the struggle against the Shining One at the Callanish Stones.

Then there was Bradan, always there, ready with advice and support, with his laconic statements and dependability.

Melcorka's head swirled with the steam. She could not tell where she was or what she was thinking. She was outside her body, looking down on that small lodge in the village, with the great river running past. She could see the silver streak of the river probing inland, further than she had ever traveled, in a land so vast that she could not comprehend distance, where travel was measured in weeks and months, not hours and days.

The river thrust westward, through endless dense dark forests, with spectacular waterfalls greater than anything Melcorka could have imagined; and then there were inland seas, appearing one after another in a mighty succession of fresh water. Melcorka could only wonder at the sights, and soon there was even more to take her attention. There was a river even mightier than the previous one, flowing south through the wooded countryside near plains so vast, they stretched forever. And then, after an uncountable length of time, she saw the city she visited whenever she donned the ice-woman's headband.

'Is that Dhegia?' Melcorka asked. 'Is that the evil empire?'

She did not know. Melcorka only knew that if it was, then she belonged among that evil, for she felt even more at home with these unknown peoples than she had ever done in Alba. And that was a disturbing realisation.

Tomah was grinning at her, hauling her, naked and slippery with sweat, out of the hut and shocking her with a deluge of cold water. Melcorka shook herself dry, realised that she was the centre of a hundred male eyes and grabbed the clothes that Bradan held out for her.

'I know where we are going,' she announced. 'I know where the Empire of Dhegia is.'

'Is it far?' Erik's eyes were hungry yet somehow nervous, as if he had never seen a naked woman before.

'It will be a long and an arduous journey,' Melcorka said. 'I don't think we will all survive, but I am going to try.' She raised her voice. 'Who is with me?'

The response was not as enthusiastic as she had hoped.

'Who is with me?' she shouted again.

Most of the Norsemen roared or raised their hands. Two did not. One grey-bearded man shook his head, and a young man who could not have been more than sixteen backed away. The chubby Lnu'k girl at his side provided ample justification for the young man's decision to remain behind.

'We will sail tomorrow,' Erik said, 'and this Dhegian Empire had better take care. The Norsemen are coming for them!'

That got the loudest roar of the day.

Melcorka sought out Bradan. 'I did not hear you respond,' she said.

'I did not think you would need to,' he said.

She nodded, no longer quite so sure of her man. Or of herself. 'I am glad you are still with me.' She smiled as Erik began a rousing speech to his men, and stopped to listen. Bradan walked away with his staff tapping on the ground.

Chapter Nine

Leaving the two Norsemen behind, the remainder sailed on up that mighty waterway with Frakkok beside Erik in the stern of *Sea Serpent* and Melcorka trying to ease her troubled mind through constant work. The land on either side was fertile and well-forested, with the occasional Skraeling village on the banks. They passed the small native boats, known as canoes, and sometimes traded with them, asking for information about the Dhegian Empire. On one occasion there was a skirmish, when a whole fleet of canoes swarmed out of a waterway and fired arrows at them. The Norse lifted their shields and shot back, glorying in this opportunity to show their prowess. Their arrows were longer than those of the Skraelings and landed with more power so, after a few moments, the canoes backed off. Three or four men floated in the water, punctured with Norse arrows.

'They're coming for us!' Bradan said, as the Skraeling fleet steered away from *Sea Serpent* and headed for the much smaller *Catriona*. There were around twenty of the light birch-bark canoes, each holding between two and eight Skraeling warriors resplendent with painted faces, bows and stone-headed war clubs.

'We can't outrun them,' Melcorka said. 'We must fight.'

The first arrows were well-directed. Standing tall, Melcorka drew Defender and chopped them out of the sky. The second flight was aimed entirely at her. Allowing the skill of Defender to flow through her, she sidestepped them all.

'Is that your best, Skraelings? I am Melcorka the Swordswoman of Alba! Fight me if you dare.'

They dared. The first canoe ran alongside, and half a dozen finely-muscled warriors swarmed out, clubs raised high. Melcorka met them with her swinging sword, chopped off the heads of the leading men, dodged the downstroke of a club, sliced sideways to gut the owner and thrust the point of Defender into the chest of the next man.

She saw Bradan jab the end of his staff into the groin of a Skraeling, and the last man jumped back into his canoe. By that time, the Norse had rowed over and ended the contest. Erik aimed *Sea Serpent* at the bulk of the canoes, ramming three in one mighty crash, capsizing them so his men could fire arrows and throw spears as the Skraelings struggled in the river. The chants of the Norsemen echoed to the forest around.

'Odin owns you! Odin owns you!'

'Thor and Odin!'

The remaining Skraelings retreated. Within a minute, the woods were quiet again and the upturned canoes, floating bodies and the greasy swirl of blood were all that remained as reminders of the short skirmish. A hush descended over the trees, with even the birds falling silent.

'Look.' Bradan pointed with his staff. On the bows of one of the upturned canoes, the figure of a falcon-headed warrior gleamed brightly. 'The sign of the Dhegia Empire.'

'These men know of the Dhegians then,' Melcorka said. 'Or they are part of them.' She lifted a hand in gratitude to Erik, who waved his sword at her. 'We'll stop at the next friendly village and see if they can tell us anything.'

The current strengthened as they moved upstream, but when another canoe came up to them, the Skraeling crew were friendly and they pulled up both vessels on a sand-spit and disembarked amidst a crowd of curious Skraelings.

After her visit to the sweat-lodge, Melcorka had a strange feeling that she understood these people. When she listened to them talking, she could follow the gist of the conversation, if not all the details.

'We are friends,' she said, hoping that her words would be understood.

They gathered around the communal village fire – Scots, Norsemen and the Skraeling chief, a man named Donnaconna.

'We are seeking the Empire of Dhegia.' Melcorka had appointed herself as the spokeswoman.

Donnaconna nodded. 'I know,' he said. 'News of your coming has already reached us.'

'Do you know of this city of Dhegia?' Melcorka asked.

'We call it Saguenay,' Donnaconna said. 'It is a rich land of gold and furs, with corn for everybody, but ruled by an evil king.'

'Will this river take us to the great inland seas?' Melcorka was satisfied with Donnaconna's answers so far.

'This is the great river of Hochelaga. Upstream is the great roaring and beyond that are the seas.' Donnaconna looked at *Sea Serpent* and *Catriona*. 'Can your boats fly?'

'They cannot fly,' Melcorka said.

'Then you cannot go beyond the great roaring. You cannot sail the inland seas. Even if you did, the oniare would capsize your ships and eat you all.' Donnaconna leaned back as if his words had settled the matter beyond question.

'The oniare?'

Donnaconna looked serious. 'The oniare is a great snake with a horn in the middle of its head. It lives in the inland seas and attacks canoes.' He puffed on a long pipe, blowing foul-smelling smoke into the lodge. 'Few have survived its attack.'

'It's a dragon! At last, a dragon!' Bradan exclaimed. 'I've always wanted to meet one.'

'Between the great roaring and the oniare and the hostile tribes, you will never reach Saguenay.' Donnaconna passed over his pipe.

'We will try our best.' Melcorka took a puff of the pipe and coughed. 'Thank you for the warning.'

'Then,' Donnaconna said, 'if you do reach Saguenay, the evil king will kill you all on his mound.'

'We are Norsemen.' Erik did not try the pipe. 'We are not so easily killed.'

Donnaconna puffed fiercely at his pipe, eyed Erik's sword, said a few words to a warrior who stood behind him and relapsed into silence.

They sailed the next day, ignoring the three medicine men with horns fixed to their heads and blackened faces, who paddled around their ships, shouting.

'They are trying to warn us off,' Erik called, from the deck of *Sea Serpent*. 'They want the treasures of Saguenay, or Dhegia, or whatever they call it, for themselves.'

'They won't get them!' Gunnar shouted. He drew his sword and thrust it in the air. 'The treasure of Dhegia is ours, and what a tale to tell when we get back!'

'*If* we get back,' a gaunt-faced man named Knut said grimly.

'When we get back,' Erik said quietly. He glanced at Frakkok, who grunted and looked away.

The two ships pushed on, day after day, sailing or rowing upriver, until they came to a stretch of rapids so vast and so turbulent that not even *Catriona* could sail up them.

'So now what do we do?' Erik stared at the raging white water that extended as far as they could see.

'We must go back,' Knut said. 'We've already explored further than anybody else in the world.'

'If the Dhegians can pass this, then so can we,' Melcorka said. 'Is there another channel?'

Erik nodded. 'That will be it. We'll go back downstream and search.'

They wasted two days in fruitless exploration, hacking through woodland, exploring small rivers that led nowhere, sweltering and sweating and plagued by insects. There was no other channel; there were only the rapids, growling and thundering before them.

Frakkok took charge as Erik hesitated once more. 'Then we either portage, or we leave the ships here and march to this Dhegia.'

'We'll need the ships later,' Melcorka said. 'There are inland seas ahead.'

'What makes you think that?' Frakkok turned poisonous eyes on her.

'Trust me – I know,' Melcorka said.

'Why should I trust you?' Frakkok asked.

Erik looked at his mother and then to Melcorka and back. 'Please don't squabble.' He raised his voice to a shout. 'Portage!'

Melcorka had never been involved in a portage before and could only follow Erik's lead as the Norse removed all the contents of the ships, chopped down trees and cleared a passage along the side of the river. Using the felled trees as rollers, the Norse pushed and hauled *Sea Serpent* along the cleared path.

Following in their wake, Melcorka and Bradan did the same with the much lighter *Catriona*, keeping close and learning this new skill by observation.

'You won't manage that alone,' Erik said. 'I'll lend you some men.'

'Leave them,' Frakkok said.

'Please, Mother,' Erik said and gave a weak grin when Frakkok grunted and turned away. 'She doesn't mean it,' he said. Melcorka raised her eyebrows in disbelief and Erik's grin faded and he looked away.

Within a few moments, three disgruntled Norsemen slouched back to help with *Catriona*'s progress. They used a simple method of rolling the ship along the felled logs, with the men lifting each log as *Catriona* passed over it, carrying it to the front of the ship and replacing it on the ground. They made steady if slow progress alongside the rapids. With the Norse in front desperate to show their superiority and the Norsemen with *Catriona* equally keen to demonstrate their strength and skill, they shoved and hauled and gasped the vessels beside the disturbed water.

'I sent Ulf ahead to scout,' Erik called back cheerfully. 'He'll find out how far these rapids stretch.'

'The Skraelings called them the great roaring,' Melcorka said.

At his best when working, Erik gave a huge grin and wiped the sweat from the forehead with the back of his hand, leaving a dirty streak. 'The Skraelings were right,' he said. 'The water is nothing if not roaring.'

Ulf did not come back. They heard his screams first, pitched high above the noise of the waters. Then there was an abrupt silence. Frakkok raised her eyebrows at Erik.

'Arne, Gunnar, Harald, go and see what's happened,' Erik ordered. 'The rest, keep pushing. We need this boat back afloat.'

The first arrow hit the hull of *Sea Serpent* a moment later. It stuck out, quivering, as the Norsemen stared at it.

'Skraelings!' Melcorka touched the hilt of Defender.

The war cry rose high and loud, a discordant shrieking that outmatched that of Ulf and was followed by a volley of arrows. Melcorka had a nightmare vision of multi-coloured faces and near-naked bodies among the dense forest, and then the Skraelings charged out, scores strong, with stone-tipped spears and stone-headed axes.

'They're not friendly.' Melcorka slipped Defender out of the scabbard and stepped forward. She saw the Norsemen draw swords and axes, with Frakkok passing out shields as calmly as if she were feeding livestock on her family farm.

'Come on, boys,' Frakkok said. 'They're only savages.'

'Shield wall!' Erik shouted, and the Norse instantly came together. The shields interlocked, circular, each one decorated at the owner's whim and with the sun reflecting from the iron bosses. Spears thrust out to hamper the Skraeling attack, while swords and axes were poised, waiting.

'Make room for three more!' Arne, Gunnar, and Harald ran to join them. 'The woods are thick with Skraeling,' Gunnar said, as he slid beside Erik.

The last time Melcorka had seen a shield wall, she had been on the opposing side. It was professionally interesting to watch it from a different perspective. It was also a little disturbing that she and Bradan were on the outside, alone and therefore vulnerable.

The Skraelings came in a screaming rush. The Norse met them in a stubborn, slashing wall and then Melcorka had other things to do rather than watch the Norse at play. Six Skraelings came at her, axes lifted and mouths open in high-pitched war cries. Feeling the surging power of Defender, Melcorka weaved a figure of eight in front of her, slicing the first two attackers nearly in half and taking the arm off the third. The fourth altered his attack to Bradan, who swung wildly with his staff, missed and nearly overbalanced. The Skraeling poised above him and lifted his stone axe, screaming some cry of triumph. Melcorka thrust Defender into his groin, ripped upward and sidestepped the next man before she ducked, swept her sword sideways and cut off his leg. The remaining Skraeling took one look at his dead and dying colleagues, decided he preferred his limbs and head attached to his body and fled back to the sanctuary of the forest.

The Norse had also repelled the Skraeling attack and stood, gasping, behind a mound of dead and dying bodies.

'You fought well!' Erik shouted.

Melcorka gestured towards the casualties. 'So did you.'

Then the arrows began again. Sigurd dropped with an arrow in his leg. He stood up, swore once, hauled the arrow out and stepped toward *Sea Serpent*. A Skraeling axe had shattered his shield, and he took another from Frakkok and re-joined the wall.

'There is no doubting that man's bravery,' Bradan said.

Erik surveyed the forest from whence the noise came. He ignored the arrow that thrummed into the hull of *Sea Serpent* a hand's-breadth from his face. 'Four men, act as the escort. Use your shields to deflect the arrows. The rest, push the ships.'

They began again, shoving at the ships alongside the rapids, moving them inch by inch, log by log, working in a haze of sweat and effort while arrows whistled past them to thump into the hull or the logs.

'Here's Ulf waiting for us,' Erne said.

Ulf was not dead, but he probably wished he was. Stripped naked, he had been castrated, and his eyelids and fingers cut off. The Skraelings had cut out his tongue and nailed him to a tree with wooden pegs. Now, he stared forward, making small mewing noises.

'We'll take care of you, Ulf,' Erik promised. 'You'll be all right.'

'He's better dead,' Frakkok said. 'He is no longer a warrior and no longer a man. You are his leader, Erik. Give him a merciful death.'

Erik glanced around, seeking support. Melcorka met his eyes and nodded. 'Ulf will die slowly, so a quick death would be a blessing for him.' She paused as Erik hesitated. 'It is what a Viking should do for his men.'

Closing his eyes, Erik nodded in obvious torment. Drawing his sword, he placed the point against Ulf's chest. 'May Odin welcome you to Valhalla,' he said, closed his eyes and thrust. 'Bury this Norse warrior.'

'We have no time,' Frakkok said. 'The Skraelings may return. We push on until we can get back into the river.'

'We will make the time.' Erik's voice was harder than Melcorka had ever heard it. 'Bury our friend Ulf.'

The Norse hesitated, torn between loyalty to Erik, fear of Frakkok and their desire to respect their colleague. Only when Frakkok turned away did they begin to hack out a hole in the root-tangled ground.

Melcorka nodded her approval as the Norse buried their colleague and only then did the tortuous portage begin again.

'I wonder why that tribe attacked us,' Melcorka asked, as she pushed at *Catriona*. The ship grated forward another couple of inches.

'We will never know,' Bradan said. 'Some peoples are naturally friendly, and others are aggressive. That is the way of the world.' He glanced around. 'Although I do think that the Empire of Dhegia is having an unsettling effect on the people around here.'

'That is certain.' Melcorka bent to *Catriona* again as the Norse replaced a roller in front. 'Ready... push!'

'Clear water ahead!' Erik's shout was more than welcome.

The rapids had extended for a full three miles of muscle-tearing effort, but the river stretched clear ahead. Melcorka looked at Erik; he was turning into a man. He had added maturity to that aura of cute hesitancy that still surrounded him.

Chapter Ten

As Melcorka had seen in the sweat-lodge, the rivers flowed from a succession of lakes, each large enough to be termed inland seas. When they reached the first, they looked around in wonder, for nobody had ever seen a lake this size before.

'It is a sea,' Gunnar said. 'We have reached the sea beyond Vinland. This sea will stretch to the end of the world.'

'It's only a lake,' Melcorka said. 'The water is fresh.'

It was a relief to place the ships onto such a broad stretch of water and sail westward, with the wind pushing them happily and the men relaxing.

'Hopefully, there will be no more portages,' Bradan said. 'I have had more than enough of pushing a ship that should be carrying me.'

Melcorka recalled her vision from the sweat-lodge. 'I fear there is worse to come,' she said. 'We have more work to do before we reach Dhegia.' And then her questions would be answered, Melcorka thought; then she would find out if she did belong with these friendly, respectful men and women of that strange city, and who the man was who accompanied her. And, she thought, where Bradan fitted in.

'Melcorka.' She became aware that Bradan had been talking to her for some minutes.

'Bradan?' She leaned on the tiller and smiled across at him.

'Have we taken the wrong route?' Bradan asked hopefully. 'I can hear a tremendous roaring ahead, as if we were entering the domain of a hundred dragons.'

'I was told there would be roaring water.' Melcorka had to raise her voice above the ever-increasing noise. 'I thought it must be the sounds we heard during that portage we did, but perhaps I was wrong.'

Furling the sail, Bradan moved to the bow of *Catriona* and peered ahead. 'There is a sort of white mist ahead,' he shouted, 'and that roaring sound must be more rapids.'

'The local Skraelings warned us that there was danger on this river.' Melcorka shifted the tiller so that *Catriona* moved closer to *Sea Serpent*. She shouted across to Erik. 'There is something ahead! It may be more rapids, or it may be a dragon.'

Frakkok stared at her from the stern of *Sea Serpent*. 'We can hear it,' she said coldly.

'We're going ahead to check,' Melcorka said.

Erik waved. 'Let me know if it's a dragon!' His eyes were bright blue in a face reddened by wind and weather. Once again, he looked like a young boy in a man's body.

'I'll do that.' Melcorka waved back and adjusted the tiller so that the current took *Catriona* away from *Sea Serpent* and towards that curtain of white mist.

'Back water!' Bradan shouted urgently. 'Mel! Grab the oars and row back for your life! It is a waterfall, a huge waterfall!'

It took both of them all their skill to haul *Catriona* back from the edge of what was undoubtedly the largest and most powerful waterfall they had ever seen.

'Dear God in heaven,' Melcorka breathed. 'How are we going to get past that?'

Bradan stared at the water that thundered vertically down a drop that must have been three hundred feet at least. 'I do not know,' he said. 'I do not know at all.'

'It's a waterfall,' Melcorka reported to *Sea Serpent*. 'It's the largest waterfall I have ever seen.'

'We have massive waterfalls in Norway,' Arne boasted.

'Can you sail down them?' Bradan asked. 'I will watch while you do.' He winced as Melcorka dug her elbow into his ribs. 'Melcorka and I will moor *Catriona* and see if it's possible to portage around the fall.'

'Erik and Arne will come with you,' Frakkok decided.

Melcorka wondered if Erik and Arne really wanted to leave the security of *Sea Serpent* to wander through the wilds of this new world, with its savage Skraelings and unknown hazards.

'It must be hard for a proud Norseman to have a woman managing his life,' Bradan said.

Melcorka nodded. 'It is high time he stepped out of Frakkok's shadow and became his own man.'

They tied *Catriona* to a convenient tree at a spot where the current was weak, and stepped ashore into a tangle of woodland and singing birds. The air smelled fresh and free, while the ground underfoot was a soft carpet of leaf mould.

'This is a wonderful place.' Bradan pointed to the track of a deer. 'The wildlife is prolific, the ground is fertile, and the trees are huge. The local people must think they live in paradise.'

'They are Skraelings,' Arne said. 'Naked savages.' He grinned and rubbed his hand along the hilt of his sword. 'They know nothing of the world.'

'They know how to live in it,' Bradan said.

Arne pushed ahead, hacking at the undergrowth with his sword, swearing when he stumbled, laughing when he scared a deer that ran, startled, to lower ground. Erik followed in the path Arne had carved, occasionally glancing back to where Melcorka and Bradan stepped lightly through the forest.

'Somebody is watching us,' Bradan said.

'There are three of them,' Melcorka murmured. 'Two men and a woman on the left.'

'That's how many I see.' Bradan tapped his staff on the soft ground. 'If there are three, there will be more.'

'Then let us hope that they are friendly,' Melcorka said. 'I do not wish to fight our way through every inch of this new land.'

They moved closer to the waterfall, eventually stopping when they came to a rock that afforded them a clear view.

'Oh, dear God,' Melcorka said. 'There are three waterfalls, not just one.'

Three waterfalls, each one larger than she had ever imagined, and each one throwing millions of gallons of water down to the continuation of the river far below. The sight took her breath away with its beauty, while simultaneously shocking her with the difficulty of manoeuvring *Catriona* past this new obstacle.

'So that's that.' Arne gaped at the trio of waterfalls, each creating a curtain of spray that rose high until dissipated by the wind. 'We can't get past that.'

Erik said nothing. He stared at the view, fiddling with the hilt of his sword with his mouth moving as if in silent prayer.

'This will be some portage.' Bradan leaned on his staff. 'We'll have to negotiate a steep drop as well as walking past these falls.'

'We'll need more than logs,' Melcorka agreed.

They stood in silence for some time as the incessant crash of the waterfalls echoed and re-echoed around them in a portrait of terrifying wild beauty.

'Once we are past this point,' Bradan said, 'there is no return. We must go on, wherever the road or the river takes us.'

'That is true,' Melcorka said. 'We might bring the ships down here, but we could not lift them back up.'

'This is where we decide.' Bradan leaned on his staff, staring at the majestic waterfalls. Blown on a breeze, the spray from the falls soaked them.

'We decided a long time back.' Melcorka stood up and spoke over her shoulder as she walked away. 'My decision will not alter because of a falling river.'

'Where are you going?' Erik called after them.

'Back to *Catriona*,' Melcorka said. 'We have to portage past the falls.'

'You are mad!' Arne shouted. 'You can't carry the ships past all this, and if you do, we will be stuck here forever.'

'I know.' Melcorka did not have to force her smile. 'We must go on and see what the world reveals to us.'

'You are mad!' Arne repeated.

'Are you going to try it?' Erik scrambled beside them, his face eager, enthusiastic. 'Are you really going to portage past these waterfalls?'

'We are going to portage *Catriona* past these falls,' Melcorka said, 'and then we are going to sail on into the next inland sea, and then the one after that and the one after that, until we come to the end. Eventually, we will find a great river, the mightiest river the world has ever seen, and we will follow it southward until we find this evil empire that is sending out its agents to spread death and destruction.'

'And then what?' Erik asked. 'What will you do once you find it?'

'That, we do not yet know,' Bradan said solemnly. 'We will see what we can do once we are there, and not before.' He stepped on, tapping his stick on the soft ground.

'Erik,' Melcorka turned around, 'if you accompany us, you will be Erik Farseeker indeed, the furthest travelling Norseman of them all. And if you turn back... Well, you already know the way to Greenland. The river current is in your favour so you will not find it a hard passage.' She waited a moment before adding, 'You had better ask your mother what to do.'

'I don't need her to tell me!' There was anger in Erik's voice, as Melcorka had intended. 'I make the decisions in my own household.'

'Then make one,' Melcorka said and turned away.

'That was a bit cruel,' Bradan said.

'It was necessary.' Melcorka glanced to the side. 'The Skraelings are still watching us. Move slowly so Erik and Arne can catch up.' She shouted a warning that saw Erik scurry to them and Arne follow with less speed and more dignity.

'Where are they?' Arne whipped out his sword as if ready for instant battle.

'They've been among the trees ever since we came on land,' Melcorka said. 'If they were going to attack, they would have done it when we were sliding down the slope.'

Arne laughed. 'They know we are Norsemen!'

'Aye,' Bradan said. 'That must be it. Ten thousand Skraelings are afraid of two Norsemen, a woman and a man with a stick.' He ignored Arne's glower.

Melcorka surveyed the route. 'We can slide *Catriona* down most of the way. The trees are quite far apart.'

'We won't need to fell trees,' Bradan agreed. 'Not for the first stage, anyway.' He pondered for a long moment. 'We can spread the spare sails under the keel and pull her along the downward slope on that, so long as we ensure she does not slide too fast.'

With her mast unshipped and securely tied on top and the canvas pad easing her passage, Melcorka and Bradan hauled *Catriona* onto the land and pushed her onwards and downward through the trees. Much smaller and lighter than *Sea Serpent,* she moved smoothly and was easier to negotiate than she had been on the log rollers, until they arrived at a steep, twenty-foot, near vertical drop.

'How do we do this?' Melcorka scratched her head.

'We use ropes and lower her.' Bradan looked behind them, where ten Norse were cutting trees for rollers as the others pulled and pushed the much larger *Sea Serpent* through the woods. 'We may have to ask the Norsemen for some muscle-power.'

Melcorka twisted her mouth in a frown. 'I'd rather not,' she said. 'We'll try this alone.' Wiping the sweat from her face, she first pushed and then tied back her hair with the headband she had retrieved from the woman in the ice. 'I can see better now,' she said. Removing a rope from the stern locker of *Catriona*, Melcorka looped it around the central thwarts and then around two of the trees that overhung the cliff. 'Take the tension, Bradan.'

'I doubt we're strong enough alone,' Bradan said.

'Take the tension, Bradan!' Melcorka put steel in her voice, and Bradan joined her. They slid *Catriona* gently toward the slope, using the trees as levers to reduce the strain as the ship gradually toppled over, bows first.

'Hold her!' Melcorka said, and then louder: 'Hold her!' as *Catriona* increased speed and began to fall.

'She's going!' Bradan shouted.

'Bradan!'

The rush of Skraelings from the woodland distracted her and she reached for Defender, but rather than attack, some of the newcomers took hold of the ropes, and others stood beneath *Catriona* and eased her down to the thick vegetation at the bottom of the cliff.

'Thank you!' Melcorka smiled at the bare-chested men who had joined her. They bowed deeply and spoke in a quiet language that she understood, although she had never heard it before in her life.

'It is our honour, Eyota,' they said.

'I am Melcorka of Alba, and this is Bradan the Wanderer,' Melcorka said.

'You are Eyota,' the men said, scrambling down the cliff to *Catriona*. Melcorka joined them, with Bradan a few yards behind. The Skraelings spoke quietly among themselves, then gathered around *Catriona* and hauled her through the trees at three times the speed that Melcorka and Bradan had managed.

'I don't know who you are or why you are helping,' Melcorka said, 'but I am glad to see you.'

'It's the headband,' Bradan said. 'They keep looking at your headband and calling you Eyota.'

'Maybe that means something in their language,' Melcorka said.

'It's a name,' Bradan said. 'They think you are somebody called Eyota.'

Melcorka ran the name around her mouth. 'Eyota.' It was strangely familiar. 'Eyota.' To her knowledge, she had never heard it until a few moments before, yet she knew it from somewhere. She shook the idea away and smiled. 'I hope they don't expect me to do anything smart.'

'Where are you going?' one of the Skraelings asked. 'Where are you going with the canoe?'

'To the big river,' Melcorka said. 'We are going past the great seas and down the big river to Dhegia.'

At the name, the man raised his hands. 'That is what the prophecy says, Eyota.' He smiled as if sharing some secret. 'You are here to fulfil the prophecy.'

'I am Melcorka of Alba... I know nothing about a prophecy.'

The men looked at each other and smiled. 'As you say, Eyota.'

'Do you know Dhegia?' Melcorka asked. 'Are you from Dhegia?'

The Skraelings smiled again. 'We are not from Cahokia or Dhegia,' they said. 'You know that, Eyota.'

Bowing again, the Skraelings backed away, and then turned and fled into the woods, leaving *Catriona* safe at the side of the river with the waterfalls behind them and the Norsemen nowhere in sight.

'They were a helpful bunch,' Bradan said. 'Even if they ran away.'

'They knew about this place Dhegia,' Melcorka said. 'I wonder what this prophecy is that they spoke about?'

'We might see when we get there, Mel,' Bradan said. 'Or should I call you Eyota?'

Melcorka touched her headband. 'This little piece of fabric seems very important,' she said.

Out of the blue, the vision returned and she saw that massive city with the pyramids and neat buildings. That was Dhegia. It could be nowhere else. And she was Eyota.

No, she was Melcorka.

Bradan reached out and touched the headband. 'It doesn't feel anything special. It must be that falcon design.'

Don't let him touch it.

Where had these words come from? Melcorka pulled back, frowning, and slipped the headband off. 'Yes, it must be the design,' she agreed. 'I wonder who Eyota is?'

'We may find out sometime,' Bradan said. 'Now that we're past the waterfalls, let's hope that the rest of the journey is easier than the first part has been.'

With a massive inland sea ahead of them, Melcorka and Bradan settled to wait for the Norse. They moored *Catriona* in the shelter of a dense copse of trees hidden from land and water, lay in the dappled sunlight and dozed.

They heard the noise before they saw the Norse. Frakkok worked with the rest and urged the men on with her acid tongue and occasional blows, as the Norsemen pushed *Sea Serpent* before them, swearing and shouting as they made progress. Then Erik gave a great whoop of joy. 'We are past them all!' He jumped up like a young boy, ripped off his clothes and ran into the water. 'Come on!'

The younger Norse followed, with the older men looking on with expressions that could have been of envy or amusement, Melcorka was not sure which. For a few moments, she watched the naked young Norsemen splashing in the water, wondering how warriors with such a reputation for ferocity could look so much like other men.

'You are smiling.' Bradan was lying on his back, ignoring the Norse as he watched Melcorka.

'I know.' She realised that she had been concentrating on Erik alone and looked hurriedly away. She was a fraction too late. Erik looked up and caught her gaze. He looked down at himself and grinned, just as Bradan looked over.

'We'd better be on our way.' Bradan rose abruptly, pulling Melcorka behind him. She looked over her shoulder and Erik waved to her, still obviously pleased with himself.

Maybe, Eyota's voice said in Melcorka's head. *Maybe so.*

'Is this the third of these great inland seas, or is it the fourth?' Melcorka wondered. 'I have lost count.'

'Does it matter?' Bradan adjusted the set of the sail so *Catriona* heeled slightly to larboard. This freshwater sea was choppy, with high clouds scudding across a sky of brilliant blue and *Sea Serpent* was two cables-lengths astern, with her striped sail now showing signs of wear and tear.

'If it's four, then we are on the last inland sea.' Melcorka recalled the map that had been imprinted into her mind in the sweat-lodge.

'I won't be sorry to leave them behind. The weather is as fickle as anything back home.' Bradan tugged on a line, which had no effect at all to *Catriona*. She powered on, throwing the waves aside in spumes of silver-white foam.

'There's another vessel coming,' Melcorka said quietly. 'To the north.'

Bradan ducked under the boom, shaded his eyes and looked north. 'I can't see anything,' he said.

'It's gone now,' Melcorka said. 'I'm sure it was there a minute ago.'

Bradan took a deep breath. 'I hope they're friendly, whoever they are.'

'So do I,' Melcorka said. After so long with only the two vessels on the water, she was used to their own company. Whatever she thought about Norsemen, it was reassuring having *Sea Serpent* with her crew close by when they were so far from home. Despite their lack of experience, they were still doughty warriors compared to most in the world.

'There it is again,' Melcorka said.

'That's no ship,' Bradan said. 'It's rising from the water and submerging again. It's only a fish.'

'It's too big for a fish,' Melcorka said. 'Remember what Donnaconna said? He told us there were monsters in these waters.'

'Dragons,' Bradan said.

'He called them oniares,' Melcorka said. 'Huge water snakes with a horned head and they attack canoes.'

'The Norsemen have also seen it now,' Bradan said.

Sea Serpent altered course with a flurry of spray and a flash of raised oars. 'Melcorka!' Erik's voice floated over to them. 'It's a dragon!'

'Best leave it alone!' Bradan shouted.

'They want to be remembered in the sagas,' Melcorka said.

'There's no need to seek trouble – it will find them when it's ready.' Bradan watched the Norse dip in their oars and haul mightily, so that *Sea Serpent* powered through the waves with her dragon figurehead lifting with every stroke.

'It's submerged again,' Melcorka said.

Sea Serpent passed over the stretch of water where the oniare had been, circled and backed water. The Norsemen lined the sides, staring at the disturbed water. 'Did you see where it went?' Erik shouted.

Frakkok pointed silently to the water.

'There it is again,' Bradan murmured, as the oniare rose a hundred yards astern.

It was smaller than Melcorka had thought, perhaps twenty feet long and more green than blue, with a broad, flat head adorned with a single spike the length of a man's arm.

'It's more like a large eel,' Melcorka said calmly. 'I thought dragons were huge, scaly things with wings and fiery breath.'

'That what everybody thinks,' Bradan nodded wisely, 'until they see one.'

Frakkok stepped onto the bulwark and shouted directions so that *Sea Serpent* steered straight for the oniare. Rather than wait until they closed, the Norse unleashed a volley of arrows. Two penetrated the creature's head, so it reared up and let out a high-pitched squeal.

'It sounds like a wounded pig!' Bradan said.

Laughing in triumph, the Norse fired another volley of arrows as the oniare writhed on the surface of the water. It squealed again, lashing its tail against the hull of *Sea Serpent* with a sound like the beating of a drum.

'It's calling for help!' Bradan said. 'Erik! Take care!'

'We'll finish it off.' Erik sounded as cheerful as ever. 'This dragon is easier to kill than those polar bears were.'

'Melcorka!' Bradan shouted. 'Here's the help coming!'

A second oniare rose from the water on the larboard side of *Sea Serpent*, ducked its head and thrust its horn into the back of one of the Norse archers. The man's sudden scream alerted his companions.

'There's another one!' Arne yelled.

'There's another two.' A squat man named Knut fired a wild arrow as a third oniare curled around the dragon figurehead and slithered inside the Norse ship.

'And here is Father,' Bradan shouted, as the water erupted at *Sea Serpent's* stern and a huge oniare, at least five times larger than the first, emerged into view.

'We'd best give them a hand.' Melcorka watched as the giant oniare stretched toward *Sea Serpent*. It opened its mouth to reveal a triple row of backwards-slanting white teeth and let out a squeal so loud that every Norseman winced. Erik covered his ears.

'Go to them, Bradan!' Melcorka yelled, drawing Defender.

'If only they had left the first beast alone,' Bradan muttered. He steered *Catriona* toward the dragon ship. 'I don't like killing things that have done us no harm. Erik Farseeker should mind what he does.'

'I think he is trying to prove himself to Frakkok,' Melcorka said.

'And to you.' Bradan's voice was so quiet that Melcorka barely made out his words.

The largest of the onioares swept its head sideways, knocking a bald Norseman into the water, where one of the smaller creatures wrapped its coils around the unfortunate man and dived under the surface. Another Norseman lunged at the huge creature with his spear, only for the oniare to bite him clean in two.

'That thing's evil!' Melcorka said.

'I think that *thing* is a mother protecting her babies,' Bradan said. 'Look!'

The largest oniare gave that tremendous bellow again, and one of the smaller oniare slipped away from *Sea Serpent* and returned into the water.

'So it is,' Melcorka said. 'It did not even appear until the first oniare was hurt.' She sighed. 'I don't wish to hurt a creature that is only looking after its young.'

Standing in the stern of *Sea Serpent*, Frakkok took an axe from one of her men and pushed Erik toward the oniare.

'Be a man!' she screamed. 'Go and kill that dragon, or at leat die trying to be a man!'

'There's another example of a mother's love.' Bradan said. 'I'd be happier if you left the Norse to fight their own battles, Melcorka.'

'You know I can't do that.'

Bradan nodded. 'I know. I wish you could.'

'Bring *Catriona* alongside,' Melcorka held Defender in a two-handed grip, 'and watch for the children.'

Bradan gave a small smile. 'The children are twenty feet long,' he reminded her, easing *Catriona* close to the Norse vessel.

'I noticed.' Melcorka vaulted onto *Sea Serpent*.

The huge oniare lifted its head and screamed again. Holding Defender in front of her, Melcorka stopped. 'I don't want to kill you,' she shouted. 'And I don't want you to kill me.'

'She's talking to it!' Arne shouted. 'That fool of an Alban is trying to talk to a dragon.'

'We killed one of yours,' Melcorka continued, and you have killed two of ours. Shall we call the bargain fair and end this here?'

The oniare opened its mouth wide, with the triple row of teeth gleaming and a forked, snake-like tongue darting out. Melcorka stood still as the tongue flicked toward her.

'Stop fighting!' Melcorka shouted to the Norsemen. 'Don't kill the little ones!'

'Who are you to give orders?' one man shouted and plunged his spear into the body of an oniare. The creature writhed and screamed, and the mother oniare lunged forward, its great jaws snapping. The Norseman backed away, lifting his bloodied spear.

'Help me!' he shouted. 'The dragon has me!'

The mother closed its mouth on the man, cutting him clean in half, and used its tongue to push the two halves into the water, where more of the smaller oniares appeared, gnawing on this fresh meat.

'Kill it!' Frakkok screamed. 'Erik! Kill that monster.'

'No!' Bradan shouted. 'It's not a monster, it's only looking after its children. Let the little ones alone and it will leave. If we don't attack them, they won't attack us.'

'Kill the dragons!' Another middle- aged Norseman lifted an axe and aimed at the nearest oniare.

Melcorka parried his blow with Defender. 'Bradan's right!'

The huge oniare swirled toward Melcorka. Replacing Defender in her scabbard, she stood still, trusting to Bradan's words. The oniare pressed its face close to hers, with its massive eyes unblinking as it surveyed her. Its tongue flicked out, probing at her neck and face and then withdrawing.

It screamed again, coiled around Melcorka with its head close to hers and much of its body still in the water. Its weight pulled *Sea Serpent* onto her side, so water lapped over the bulwarks and began to fill the interior.

'It'll have us over,' Arne said. 'We'll capsize!'

'Stand still!' Bradan shouted. 'If you attack, it will sink you, and you'll all die.'

One by one, the smaller oniares slipped off *Sea Serpent* and vanished under the surface. Only when they were safe did the mother also leave. She crawled from the bow to the stern, looking at each member of the crew in turn before flicking her tail in farewell. The disturbed water settled down as if the oniares had never been.

'You cowards!' Frakkok screamed. 'You are not fit to be Norsemen. Not one of you is fit to be a Norseman!'

Erik looked away. 'We could not kill it...' he began.

'You did not try,' Frakkok said. 'Oh, I wish I could meet a real man again. I want to meet a man like your father!'

'This is a family dispute,' Bradan said quietly. 'And, as such, is best left to the family to work out.'

'I am glad that woman is not in my family.' Melcorka stepped on board *Catriona*.

Bradan nodded. 'You did well, Melcorka. You always do well.'

Melcorka smiled. She glanced back at Erik. 'Some day that boy will have to stand up to his mother. Until then, he will never be a man.'

'That is also a family matter,' Bradan said.

Chapter Eleven

The great seas stretched ahead, limitless, pulling them onward as Melcorka followed the map she had in her head. She remembered that there was a small outlet from the last of the inland seas; a small river that led to one infinitely greater.

'Bradan,' she pointed to a break in the coast, 'that is where we must go.'

They looked at it together.

'It's not very impressive,' Bradan said. 'It could be any river in Scotland.'

'Do you trust me?' Melcorka asked.

'I do trust you,' Bradan replied immediately.

'Then follow,' Melcorka said.

Neither of them mentioned Erik, yet the smiling Norseman was in the forefront of Melcorka's thoughts as she steered for the small opening where twin trees marked the river-road south. She pointed to the carved falcon on both trees.

'You are right again,' Bradan said.

'Dhegia lies ahead.' Melcorka signalled to *Sea Serpent*, and they eased into this new waterway. 'Now, we head southward into the unknown.'

'And may God and the gods be with us,' Bradan said.

Every night as Bradan slept, Melcorka slipped on the headband, closed her eyes and experienced the visions until she could walk the streets of the city as if it were home. She could nearly smell the food cooking and hear the murmur of deep, musical voices. Each time Melcorka wore the headband, it was harder to take it off so she spent each day counting the hours until she could return to a city she had begun to think of as her own. She began to resent Bradan keeping her away from it.

They smelled the smoke a day before they reached the village.

'There is something ahead,' Bradan said.

Melcorka nodded. 'Best tell the Norse.' She touched the hilt of Defender.

'We can ignore it,' Erik began, then glanced at Frakkok and said, 'but we are Norsemen! We will investigate.'

'It may help us find Dhegia,' Melcorka agreed. 'Although we are still many miles to the north of the city.'

'I will lead,' Erik roared.

Melcorka nodded. 'As you wish.'

They advanced through the open woodland with swords drawn and arrows fitted to bows, one careful step at a time, with the noise of birds around them and an increasingly unpleasant smell in their nostrils.

'I know that stink,' Melcorka said. 'It is the smell of death.'

'Oh, sweet aroma of battle,' Arne said. 'It is welcoming heroes to Valhalla.'

'Oh, dear God preserve me from fools with big mouths,' Bradan said quietly, tapping his staff on the ground.

'You older men,' Erik said. 'Return to the ship. The rest, come with me.'

Arne pushed in front. 'I will lead,' he said.

'I should lead,' Erik said, stepping aside.

'I am the stronger,' Arne told him.

Melcorka watched and said nothing. Bradan sighed and looked down at the leaf-mould that covered the ground. 'There have been many people here,' he said quietly, 'walking in single file. See how deep their impression is on the leaves? No single man depresses the surface so far.'

Melcorka loosened Defender in her scabbard. 'Warriors?'

'I would say so,' Bradan said. 'Villagers do not need to hide their numbers.'

'A raiding party then,' Melcorka said.

They found the first body a minute later. A thousand flies rose as they approached, buzzing around their heads in a persistent blue-black cloud.

They stood around the corpse. 'His head has been crushed,' Erik said.

'He died easy.' Arne pretended to be unaffected by the sight. Erik stepped back slightly.

The next body was a few steps further on, equally furred with flies. 'He has been killed the same way,' Arne said.

After the first two, there was a steady stream of dead bodies, men, women, and children, all with the same fatal injury.

'They have all been clubbed to death,' Melcorka said. 'There are no puncture wounds from a spear or sword.'

'And they are all facing the same direction,' Bradan added. 'They were all running away. Nobody even tried to fight back.'

'What could scare an entire village to run?' Erik wondered.

'We do!' Arne said. 'When we raided Alba three summers ago, they ran like sheep before a wolf.' He stared at Melcorka, hoping for a reaction.

'Were you there?' Bradan asked quietly.

'I was in the first boat!' Arne boasted.

'You must have been all of fifteen years old.' Bradan tapped his staff on the ground. 'I cannot recall you at the battle by the Tummel.' He held Arne's gaze. 'Perhaps I only saw the back of your head as you turned to run.'

'You...' Arne stepped forward, his face twisted in rage.

'Enough,' Erik said. 'He is just teasing you, Arne. He means nothing by it.'

Arne's expression could have shaken a lesser man than Bradan as he turned away. 'You'll feel the edge of my blade later, Alban.'

'Only if I am asleep, or my back is turned,' Bradan said.

The village lay ahead of them. The slender palisade, which was all it boasted by way of defences, had been flattened in two places and all the lodges within were black, scorched and smouldering. Melcorka stood outside, remembering the carnage caused by the Norse at Dunedin. She said nothing as Erik led his men forward.

'They came from the south and the west,' Bradan said, 'and pushed the palisade flat.'

'The palisade was not meant to defend the village against men,' Melcorka added. 'It was only to keep the wild animals out and the domestic animals in.'

'There is where the fugitives fled.' Bradan showed where some of the stakes of the palisade had been pushed over from the inside, and where the trail of bodies began. 'And there,' he pointed to a passage of flattened grass, 'is where the attackers dragged the prisoners away.'

'Prisoners?' Erik asked. 'Why take prisoners?'

'Why do the Norse take prisoners?' Melcorka asked flatly.

'For slaves,' Erik answered.

'There is your answer then,' Bradan said. 'This was a slave raid.'

'The people in the village panicked. They were not expecting anybody to attack them, and they were not used to that sort of warfare.' Melcorka lifted one of the palings. 'They had flimsy defences, and I cannot see any casualties among the raiders. There are no warriors among the dead, and no fresh graves dug.'

'Unless the attackers took the dead with them,' Erik said.

'That is possible,' Melcorka said. 'We had better be prepared in case the raiders are still in the area.'

'This attack was three days back,' Bradan said. 'And when they left, they headed south.'

'Which is where we are heading.' Erik sheathed his sword. 'Do you think these slavers may be the very people we are seeking?'

'I do not know,' Bradan said. 'I only know that they are out there,' he nodded south, 'somewhere.'

Melcorka looked to the south. She stood on the trail of flattened grass where the slave-raiding column had passed and imagined the fear and the horror, the cruelty and the worry, the heartache and the tears. Putting a hand within her cloak, she touched the headband she had taken from the woman in the iceberg.

There were sturdy warriors with painted faces and headdresses of falcon feathers. They carried long-handled maces with stone heads, each one carved with slightly different patterns but each with a falcon carved onto the back. The warriors moved with grace, gliding between the trees with their maces balanced over their right shoulder; some had a small, circular hide shield on their left arm, decorated with the image of a flying falcon, its beak poised to strike.

Shuffling between the ranks of warriors were the slaves. They moved slowly, with bowed shoulders and downturned faces. None were over thirty and none under twelve years of age, male or female.

She looked down at them, unsure whether to be sad or happy. The man at her shoulder said something in his deep voice, and she laughed. He said something else, and she turned toward him and pressed closer.

These slaves would be useful in the days to come.

'Melcorka?' Bradan's voice penetrated the vision. 'Are you all right?'

'Of course, I am.' Melcorka controlled her irritation at Bradan's interruption. 'The Empire of Dhegia is in the south on the banks of a great river. These slavers are of the empire.'

'How do you know that?' Arne was prepared to jeer until Melcorka fastened her gaze on him.

'I know.' She turned away and walked back to *Catriona* with her mind in turmoil.

'Melcorka?' Bradan followed.

'Not just now, Bradan.'

'What's bothering you?'

'Nothing,' she snapped. 'Just leave me alone!'

What *was* bothering her? She did not know. She only knew that something had changed and was still changing. The man in her vision had meant a lot to her, and that man had not been Bradan. Who was he? And, more importantly, who was *she*?

There were other broken villages as they moved south, other places with smoke pressing on destroyed lodges and dead bodies lying under their covering of feasting flies. In every case, the dead had their heads smashed and only once did they find the corpse of a warrior.

The Norse surrounded him, discussing the body with professional interest. Frakkok looked down on him. 'He has the body of a warrior,' she said, 'and the scars of battle.' She crouched at the man's side, running her hand down the painted face. 'A young man still, yet see this?' She pointed to the healed cut across his ribs and the deep gash in his hip. 'He has seen battle more than once.' She stood up. 'He was a man to be proud of; a true warrior who will now be in Valhalla or wherever his people go.' Frakkok walked away without another word.

Bradan waited until she had gone before turning over a tuft of grass. 'Did you see this?'

The fabric had been trampled by careless feet and torn by some sharp object, yet the design was still recognisable. Melcorka lifted it carefully. The pouncing falcon sat on its bed of tiny white sea-shells, its claws outstretched and jaws ready to strike.

'That falcon seems to fly everywhere,' she said.

'It must be the symbol of this empire,' Bradan agreed.

Melcorka ran her thumb over the shells, feeling the care and devotion that had gone into creating such a vibrant image. 'Somebody spent a lot of time over this,' she looked southward as she felt the touch of a hand on her shoulder. 'Bradan...'

Bradan was two long steps away, out of reach. 'Yes?'

'Nothing,' she said. 'Nothing that matters. It is all right.' Dropping the cloth, she pushed it under the grass with her foot and skiffed dirt over the top. She did not wish Frakkok to see this sort of thing yet. That hand on her shoulder had been disturbing yet very welcome. It had not been Bradan.

'Let's continue.' She touched the hilt of Defender. As long as she had her sword, the world could throw anything it liked at her and she would be safe. She was Melcorka the Swordswoman; she must remember that. She was nobody else.

Then who was that other woman who shared her body and whose thoughts coursed through her mind and whose emotions and ideas clashed with her own?

Eyota.

Chapter Twelve

'Here we are.' Melcorka wiped the sweat from her forehead as she eased *Catriona* onto the broad river. It flowed southward through a land so endless, it seemed infinite. The banks were sometimes wooded and sometimes bare, but always dotted with villages that had once held a thriving population and were now smoking ruins.

'Look.' Bradan pointed to the bank of the river where scuff marks, footprints and a single corpse marred the beauty. 'This is where the slavers moored their boats. You can see the posts where the mooring ropes were tied and the marks where the people boarded them.'

'We are following their trail,' Melcorka said. She could nearly feel their presence, smell their sweat, hear their deep, sombre voices, taste the sweetness of their food and see the dark glint of their eyes.

Suddenly, she had a hankering to be home, where the pyramids rose against the clear skies and the tree-dotted plains, and cool forests extended forever; where the great river shushed beside the city, and the falcons presided over all.

But that was not home. She was an Alban, a woman from the Scottish Isles. Where was this place that intruded on her thoughts? She knew; of course she knew. She pushed away the knowledge, with all its memories and delights for the future.

Why?

Who am I?

'How long have we travelled for?' Erik asked.

'Months,' Melcorka said. 'I don't know. It feels as if we have been sailing and rowing and portaging forever.'

'By the look of this river, we have not finished yet,' Bradan said. 'I don't know where this empire of Dhegia is, but we are travelling a very long way to get to it. The possibility of it attacking Alba, or even the Norse in Greenland, seems remote.'

'The slaves who once lived in the burned villages may have thought the same,' Erik said.

'Come on! Stop wasting time!' Frakkok urged them on. 'Get *Sea Serpent* back on the water.'

With the current of the great river helping them, sailing at least was easy. Melcorka followed the wake of *Sea Serpent*, allowing the Norse ship, with her greater draught and larger crew, to find the best passage through the shoals and shallows. At night, they camped on whichever bank was most suitable, or on the occasional wooded island, with both vessels beached and sentries posted in case of attack.

It was four more days before they found built evidence of the empire. Bradan saw it first, and they steered *Catriona* across the width of the river to the small building on the bank. It was conical, with a flat roof, and built of earth rather than stone. A pole thrust from the roof and held a small square of embroidered cloth. The symbol was of a pouncing falcon.

'I think we are now in the territory of Dhegia,' Bradan said.

'That pole may even mark the border,' Melcorka said.

Sea Serpent had followed them, and the Norse splashed into the water to examine the flag.

'It's the same design as we saw earlier,' a slender man named Leif said.

Melcorka looked to the south and west, where tall grass whispered on a vast plain. 'So we've reached the Empire of Dhegia at last.'

She had never been here before, yet she did not feel like a stranger, yet alone an intruder. Crouching down, she knifed her fingers into the ground and lifted a handful of soil. It felt rich and moist and fertile.

'This will be good land to farm,' she said. 'It will raise a good crop of maize.'

'A good crop of what?' Bradan asked. 'Maize? I have never heard the term before.'

Melcorka frowned. 'Did I say that? I have no idea what it is. I must have heard the word from the Skraelings.'

'That must be it.' Bradan sounded sceptical. 'Now that we are inside Dhegia, we'd best be ready. If they are hostile...'

Melcorka stared southward into the distance. Somewhere down there, she knew, was the city she had seen in her visions. Somewhere down there was a familiar lifestyle she had never experienced before. 'Some may be hostile,' she said, 'and some will be very welcoming.'

'You could be right, Melcorka,' Bradan said.

'I am right,' Melcorka said. 'You'll see that I am right.' She felt utter certainty as she spoke, yet she had no idea why she should feel so sure. It was puzzling, and disturbing.

They sailed on, cautiously now, keeping to mid-channel whenever they could and watching for movement on the shores. There was the occasional wisp of smoke smudging the air, but too far from the river for them to leave the ships. Once, after a heavy shower of rain, a dead animal swept past.

'It's like a bull,' Bradan said, 'but far larger than any bull I have ever seen.'

Melcorka watched as the current carried the massive creature past them to the south. 'I wonder what that thing was, and if there are more like it?' She knew there were. Somehow, she knew that there were tens of thousands more, out there on the vast prairies that stretched to infinity.

'We'll see the Dhegians soon,' she said. Although she was thousands of miles and months of journeying away from Alba, she felt as if she was coming home. This great land with the mighty abyss of the sky above, resplendent with a million stars, was as familiar to her as the winds and mists of Alba. It was a place like no other, and she was quite content here; whatever the future held, she knew she could cope with it.

'Melcorka?' Bradan's voice penetrated her mind. 'Are you all right?'

'Of course.'

'Then could you steer the boat clear of that sandbank before we end our voyage right now?'

Melcorka started as she saw the water surging around a shingle bank ahead. She swung the tiller and *Catriona* edged clear. Melcorka watched their wake wash over the long grass of the islet, thinking how familiar this all was. But how could it be, when she had never been within three thousand miles of this place before?

The band of warriors could have been anybody as they trotted through the open woodland. Melcorka saw them from a distance and, handing the helm to Bradan, she ascended the mast for a better look.

'We have company,' she said to Bradan. 'From the Empire.'

'Are you sure?'

There was no doubt in Melcorka's mind. She had seen such men before, in her mind. 'Quite sure, Bradan.'

Bradan did not question her a second time. 'Best tell the Norse,' he said.

'There is quite a large party of men approaching,' she reported. 'They are in a column, four deep and about twenty strong.'

'That sounds like warriors!' Erik shouted back.

'That's what they are.' Melcorka remained at the crosstrees of the mast, with the sail barely rippling in a following breeze and only the current gliding them slowly downstream.

The warriors soon came up to them and trotted tirelessly along the bank of the river at their side, with only the leader turning his head to watch them. The rest, copper-coloured men with bare chests, small kilts and great stone-headed clubs or spears, looked ahead in rigid self-discipline. After a few moments, the leader barked an order and the first four men increased their pace and sped forward, keeping side by side. Within ten minutes, they were out of sight.

'They've gone to warn somebody that we are here.' Melcorka remained at the cross-trees. 'Yet there is some fortification up ahead.' She pointed to a small, slope-walled mound with a wooden stockade on top. As they watched, a flag was raised bearing the now familiar falcon symbol.

'It may be a border post or something similar,' Bradan said. 'It would be polite to stop there and announce ourselves.'

'The Norse are not here to be polite, they are more likely to land and wipe the garrison out.' Melcorka touched the hilt of Defender. 'I think the war is about to start.'

'The rest of the Dhegian warriors are waiting for us to land,' Bradan said quietly, 'and then they will either attack or ask us who we are.'

Melcorka nodded. 'They will not attack,' she said. 'They know something we don't know.' She watched the warriors closely; they were so familiar, yet something was very wrong.

Erik gave a sudden order and the Norsemen scurried to their rowing benches. *Sea Serpent* surged ahead of *Catriona*.

'They want to be first into Dhegia,' Bradan said. 'Let them. It matters not.'

Already four ship-lengths ahead, *Sea Serpent* came to a sudden, sickening halt. Her mast shuddered, and most of her crew fell forward, with Erik sprawling face down and even Frakkok staggering and clutching hold of the steering oar to maintain her balance.

'They've hit something!' Melcorka shouted. 'Take the sail in! Get on the oars!' She was on a rowing bench as she spoke, grabbing a set of oars and rowing astern as fast as she could. Bradan had the sail furled within a few seconds and thumped down at the oars.

'There's something in the water. *Sea Serpent* has run aground!'

'It's a boom.' Melcorka knew what had happened without looking. 'The Dhegians have put a barricade across the river to control traffic.'

Forewarned, lighter in the water and easier to handle than *Sea Serpent*, *Catriona* swung around before reaching the boom.

The Norse struggled to recover as *Catriona* surged the length of the boom, a simple affair of huge tree-trunks linked together to form a barrier across the width of the river and just under the surface, so it was nearly impossible to see until they were right on top of it.

The shouts of the Norse were plain above the surge of the river.

'Get the oars out!'

'Back water! Get out of this!'

'By Odin, they've got us!'

'Here they come! Here come the Dhegians!'

The instant that *Sea Serpent* struck the boom, a score of Dhegian warriors emerged from the stockade on the mound and swarmed across the top of the boom toward the Norse vessel, wielding spears and stone-headed clubs.

'Do we fight them?' Bradan asked. 'Or are they peaceful?'

The Dhegians answered that question in seconds. The leading man leapt on board *Sea Serpent*, swung his axe and smashed the skull of a gaping young Norseman.

'They are not peaceful,' Bradan said.

'We fight!' Melcorka steered *Catriona,* so her bow faced down-stream. She drew Defender, savouring the immediate surge of power that swept through her body. 'You stay here, Bradan. This is not a place for you!'

Initially taken by surprise, the Norse recoiled before the force of the Dhegian attack and another man fell. Half a dozen Dhegian spears thrust down into him.

'Alba!' Melcorka yelled, leaping from the deck of *Catriona* onto *Sea Serpent.* Two Dhegians turned toward her, clubs lifted. She swept Defender in a sideways swipe that removed the head from one and sliced into the upper left arm of the second. He screamed, spouting blood, and she thrust Defender through his throat, stepped over his writhing body and moved on.

'Odin owns you all!' Erik led the Norse counter-attack. The other Norsemen followed in a frantic rush that saw them crash into the still advancing mass of Dhegians. For a moment, the deck of *Sea Serpent* was a turmoil of blades and clubs, thrusting spears and gasping, roaring men, and then the sheer aggression of the Norse began to tell against the discipline of the Dhegians.

'We're pushing them back!' Erik shouted, gutting a Dhegian with his sword.

'Destroy them!' Frakkok shouted from the stern. 'Don't let any get away to warn their friends.'

Her men obliged. Now that they had recovered from the initial shock, they were responding like true Norse warriors, hacking and slicing with sword and axe, using their shield-bosses to crash into the Dhegians and the wooden shields to counter the swinging clubs and lunging spears.

For a short while, the contest seemed evenly balanced, and then Frakkok lifted a bow and fired an arrow that killed the leader of the Dhegian patrol. The rest wavered for a crucial second that Melcorka exploited.

'Alba!' she yelled, and stepped forward, killing.

The Dhegians broke. One second they were a disciplined fighting force; the next, they were a panicking, leaderless mob frantic to escape the iron swords of the Norse.

Running along the half-submerged boom, the Dhegians fled to land with the Norse following them. Erik was in the lead, his sword slicing at the rearmost of the Dhegians. One fell into the river and then the others were on land, running to the security of the small fortification. But the Norse blood was up; a wooden palisade was no barricade to their fury, and they followed the Dhegians up the steep slope, baying their war cries.

'Thor and Odin!'

'Odin owns you all!'

There was a brief flurry at the palisade when the Dhegians turned to fight, and then the Norse swarmed over the top of them, swords and axes busy. Within a few moments, there were only dead Dhegians and a slow flow of blood from the palisade down toward the river. Arne ripped down the flag and wrapped it around him as the Norse celebrated with loud cheers and a raising of swords and spears.

'Thor and Odin! Thor and Odin!'

Melcorka cleaned the blood from Defender and watched the Norse. 'Now you are heroes,' she said, 'fit to take your place in the halls of Valhalla.'

Erik caught the sarcasm in Melcorka's tone. 'We defeated a Dhegian war party,' he said. 'We have reason to celebrate.'

'We wiped out a border guard and a body of warriors,' Melcorka agreed. 'We do not know how many more warriors are ahead, or how large is the army of the empire upon whom we have just declared war.' She sheathed Defender and looked around. 'Yet here we are, thousands of miles from home, in a river that flows into their territory, with twenty-five Norsemen, one Pictish matriarch, and two Albans.'

'They outnumbered us, and we slaughtered them,' Arne boasted.

'These were border guards. Do you know any country that puts their best warriors on the border? No.' Melcorka answered her own question. 'They put their old and sick on the outposts – those who have fallen out of favour, those who are not wanted.' She nodded downstream, where the mighty river flowed on through the neverending landscape. 'Out there, somewhere, are the true warriors of Dhegia, perhaps thousands of them, and we are alone.'

'How do you know there are thousands?' Arne mocked. 'You know as little about them as we do!'

Melcorka held his gaze until he dropped his eyes. 'I know,' she said, as the images returned. She could see the vast city, the great mounds and the bare-chested warriors with the falcon headdresses and carved stone maces.

'Let's free the passage to this empire,' Bradan said. 'If we are sure we're going there.'

A series of stout ropes attached the boom to both banks of the river. Erik lifted his sword and chopped through the lines at the nearest bank. The boom parted, and they had free passage downstream.

Both vessels hoisted their sails and, for the first time since they entered Vinland, Melcorka saw Erik post watchmen on *Sea Serpent*.

'Melcorka!' Erik called across. 'We must speak.'

'Then do so,' Melcorka replied.

The land on either side was unchanged; there was mixed grassland or dense forest with no sign of human habitation and only an occasional animal.

'We will moor mid-river tonight. I don't trust these Dhegians not to attack us.'

Melcorka glanced at Bradan, who nodded. 'That makes sense,' she said.

'We'd better take watches,' Bradan suggested.

'You take the first.' Melcorka looked downstream. She could sense the presence of the great city; she was nearly home.

Night brought a display of spectacular beauty, an orange sky that stretched from horizon to horizon and reflected in rippling splendour across the wide river. Lying on her back, Melcorka stared upward, thinking that it was a long time since she had last seen such a sky, so similar to, yet so different from the lighter, more austere skies of Scotland's Hebrides. As so often before, she shook her head: that was a strange thought, she reasoned, considering she had never been here before. The lapping of the river was reassuringly familiar as she closed her eyes, listening to the deep breathing of Bradan and knowing that Erik and his Norsemen were so close on *Sea Serpent*. Yet it was neither Bradan nor Erik who stood at her side and whispered in her ear.

'Not long now. We'll be together again soon, Eyota. Not long now.'

Chapter Thirteen

Melcorka woke to something sharp pricking her under the chin. She brushed it away. 'Don't bother me now, Bradan.'

It returned, sharper and more insistent than before. Something banged into Melcorka's ribs; hard.

'What?' Opening her eyes, Melcorka stared around her. *Catriona* was filled with copper-coloured, bare-chested men with their faces painted half red and half white. Melcorka struggled up, reaching for Defender, only for one man to stand on her wrist and another to tap her ungently on the head with his stone club.

The pain was acute. Melcorka cringed, clasping both hands to her head. 'Bradan?'

Bradan was lying on the bottom of *Catriona* with a gaggle of Dhegians around him. 'Melcorka!' Bradan shouted and rose, throwing off one of the Dhegians. The man staggered back. 'Fight them, Mel!'

The second of the Dhegians lifted his club and crashed it against Bradan's head. He swore and put both hands to his head, and another Dhegian lifted a flint-bladed knife and slashed it across his chest.

'Mel...' Bradan spoke just that one word as the blood flowed from his new wound, and then he crumpled to his knees. He stared at Melcorka with the light fading from his eyes. Another Dhegian slammed a mace hard against his head, and Bradan fell face-first into the bottom of *Catriona*.

The Dhegians lifted his body and threw it overboard. The fast current whisked him away.

'No!' Melcorka yelled as three men took hold of her. 'Bradan!' She saw his body turn end over end and then sink beneath the surface.

'*Bradan!*'

Screaming, Melcorka thrust a sharp nail into the eye of one of her attackers, reeled as a hard fist crashed into the side of her head and kicked out wildly. She struggled, feeling her strength fade as the muscular warriors pressed down on her. One wrapped a cord tightly around her ankles, stopping the flow of blood as the others held her secure. They were quiet, professional, men who knew what they were doing and who had probably done this sort of thing before. She tried to kick, tried to punch, but against three strong men she was powerless. Within minutes she lay supine, tied tightly and with a rag stuffed into her mouth. The men stared at her; one traced the tattoo that decorated the left side of her face. He pointed to it and said something to his companions. They laughed, and all touched the design as if they found it highly amusing. One slapped her across the head and laughed again.

'Bradan!' Melcorka tried to shout, but the gag stopped any words from escaping. Helpless, she could only glare her hatred and anger and sick despair as the Dhegians crowded around, touching her face, running hard hands over her body, squeezing and prodding at her. She did not care. They could do whatever they liked, it did not matter. All that mattered was that Bradan was dead. That quiet, determined, intelligent man was gone and her world, all the world, was the poorer for his loss.

Bradan was dead, killed by these painted savages in this land far from home. Her Bradan. The words ran through her mind, again and again, depriving her of any will to fight. Sick, hopeless, she stopped struggling and looked up through eyes blank with despair.

The Dhegians lifted Melcorka as if she were a dead sheep, slipped her over a long pole by her bonds and stepped clear of *Catriona*.

Dazed, she saw that a whole fleet of canoes surrounded *Catriona* and *Sea Serpent*, with the Norse ship similarly filled with Dhegians.

Thrown into the bottom of a canoe, Melcorka could see nothing but the birch bark interior of the hull as the Dhegians paddled ashore. Two hefty warriors lifted her again, with the pole placed on their shoulders as they carried her into the interior. She swung painfully; suspended by her hands and feet, Melcorka soon felt the strain as the cords bit into her ankles and wrists. She moaned, twisting, hoping for relief but her physical pain was nothing compared to the mental and emotional agony of Bradan's death.

Night eased into day, and the Dhegians did not stop walking. They moved in single file at a steady pace, not quite a trot but faster than a walk. The constant motion made Melcorka feel sick, and her view was restricted to the back, loin-cloth and muscular legs of the man in front, a small arc of sky and the tall trees and grassland on either side of the path.

When the sun was at its apex, they stopped. The warriors formed a circle and ate some dried meat and porridge, talking in a language that Melcorka did not find hard to understand. She listened, picking out a word here and there. As far as she could tell, they were talking about the length they had to travel and what they would do to the prisoners. Melcorka heard the words 'slave' and 'sacrifice' mentioned; neither sounded inviting, but neither mattered compared to the loss of Bradan. Through her agony, Melcorka's subconscious heard one word repeated again and again: 'Wamblee'. The manner in which the warriors said it made Melcorka think it was somebody's name and the hushed tones suggested that Wamblee was important.

It did not matter. Nothing mattered.

The road led onto another, and soon they were passing neatly-tended fields of some high, yellow crop that Melcorka knew was maize. Few people were working on the outside fields, but there were more as they moved closer to a large settlement. Soon, they were among rows of small huts, all neatly thatched with grass. Men, women and children came to watch them pass, clustering in small groups and pointing. By twisting her neck, Melcorka could see she was only one of a number of prisoners, all tied to poles and carried in a similar manner. She could not make out faces; she did not care who they were. She wanted Bradan.

She tried to fight her despair. Without Defender, Melcorka knew she was even more helpless than any of the others, for she lacked the Norsemen's strength and fighting skill. She was only a young woman from the islands, entirely at the mercy of these brawny men in their alien culture. That did not matter compared to the death of Bradan. Nothing mattered besides that. Let them kill her; that did not matter, either.

The pain in her ankles and wrists was becoming intolerable. She heard herself moaning and fought the tears that were forcing their way through her closed eyelids. Heroes did not cry, she told herself. She was Melcorka the Swordswoman, Melcorka of the Cenel Bearnas, Melcorka of Alba. No! She shook her head. She was only Melcorka the island girl, alone and lost amidst a sea of pain and strangers.

The houses were closer together now, and grander, some two stories high, and then they came to the first of the mounts, steep-sided earth pyramids surmounted by a stockade with a building inside. Without stopping, the Dhegians marched toward one of the mounds, spoke to one of the guards at the surrounding palisade and entered through a tall gate. Only a few moments later, they were in a building that was too dark for Melcorka to make out any features, and then her bearers dropped her in an unceremonious heap and left her.

She was alone. She had nobody. Bradan was dead. Her mother was dead. All her family was dead. She looked around, hoping her captors had been foolish enough to leave Defender nearby. They had not. She was alone in a dark building somewhere in this unknown empire, in this new, mysterious land.

The darkness pressed down on her, dense and heavy, squeezing her into the ground, reminding her there was no hope. Without Defender she was nothing, and with Bradan gone she had no potential rescuer.

In Scotland and the seas round about, she could hope for an oyster-catcher, her totem bird. Over here, there was no such hope.

'Mother!' For the first time in years, Melcorka asked her mother for help, muffling the word through her gag. Bearnas was long dead, killed by the Norseman Egil, but still, Melcorka said her name. 'Mother, please don't neglect me in my time of need.'

The high-pitched piping came to her, penetrating the dark, probing the miles from the Hebridean seas to this far-distant land. It was so nostalgic that Melcorka felt the sting of tears in her eyes and the warm dampness as they coursed down her cheeks. It was the call of an oystercatcher, the black-and-white bird of the shore that she had known all her life.

'Well, now Melcorka.' Bearnas glided into the chamber, shaking her head. 'This is a pretty mess you have got yourself into, isn't it?'

It was the same sequence of words she had used when Melcorka was a little girl and had done something silly.

'Yes, Mother,' Melcorka said.

'You know that I won't neglect you.' Bearnas looked tall, elegant and completely in control. 'All you need is patience.' She knelt beside Melcorka. 'If I had a physical body, I would cut you free.'

'Are you really here, Mother?'

'No. I am dead,' Bearnas said. 'I am only here in spirit. You are calling on your memories of me.' Her smile was exactly as Melcorka remembered. 'Now you must ask questions of me, and I will answer.'

'Has Bradan really gone?'

'Bradan is with me, Melcorka.'

Melcorka looked away. She did not even wish her mother to see the depth of her despair. If Bradan was with Bearnas, then he was dead and in Tir-nan-Og, or whatever the equivalent was in this strange new world.

'How can I get out of this?'

'You have three weapons, Melcorka. You have Defender, you have your life experience and skills, and you have your brains. You must choose which one is best suited to which task and utilise it to the full.'

'When will I see Bradan again?' Melcorka had not expected that question to come next. She was asking when she would die.

'That depends on your will,' Bearnas said. 'How much do you want to see him as he is now?'

'That is answering a question with a question.'

'Only you know the answer,' Bearnas said.

'Why do I feel as if I have been here before?'

'Melcorka has not been here before,' Bearnas said, 'but one of you is returning.'

'One of me? What do you mean? I am only one.'

'Are you? When you hold Defender, you inherit all the skill and courage and knowledge of her previous owners. Do you think that all those personalities simply vanish back into the sword, the instant you return her to her scabbard? A small part of them remains in you, as a small part of you remains in Defender.'

'Was Arthur here? Or Calgacus?'

'You are not thinking straight, Melcorka. Defender was only an example. She is not the only magical thing you have touched recently.'

'I have not touched anything magical,' Melcorka said.

'Think, girl. Think.'

Melcorka screwed up her face. What had she touched that had given her strength? Nothing. But one thing had given her those strange visions. 'The headband? Was it the headband?'

Bearnas smiled. 'You know the answer, Melcorka. Be yourself, and remember how I brought you up.'

'Mother...' But Bearnas was gone. Melcorka was alone in that dark chamber with only her troubled thoughts for company. And the scratching of rats at the door.

Lying on her back, she tried to rub her bonds against the ground, hoping to wear away the cords. It was a slim hope but better than lying in black despair. That scratching continued, growing louder.

There are too many rats in the world, she told herself.

'Eyota?'

She had heard that name before. The voice was disembodied, seeming to come from nowhere. 'Eyota?'

Somebody laid hard hands on her arm. She struggled, trying to push them away. She refused to be taken to be executed, or whatever the Dhegians had in mind. Her mother had given her hope.

'It's all right. We are friends.' Although Melcorka had never spoken the language before, she now understood the meaning of the words. Somebody pressed close to her, eased the gag gently from her mouth and sliced through her bonds with a sharp blade.

Vaguely through the dark, she saw bodies around her. Somebody helped her to her feet.

'Keep quiet, Wamblee's men are all around.'

Melcorka kept quiet. She remembered her captors using that same name. Wamblee; she would remember that.

Somebody took her to a corner of the room, where hands guided her to a knotted rope and encouraged her to climb. There was a man above her and somebody beneath, a woman, she thought, with small hands, placing her feet on the knots and pushing at her buttocks.

'Climb, Eyota, please climb.'

'I am not Eyota,' Melcorka began but was quickly hushed to silence. The newcomers shoved and pulled her up the swaying rope to the roof of the building. Despite the urgency of her rescuers, she stopped for a moment to see where she was. A city stretched around her, visible under the moon and stars of an immense sky. She saw scores of the mounds topped with stockade buildings similar to the one in which she had been held, with a central mound larger than all the others, and then her rescuers were guiding her to another rope that hung on the outside of the building.

'Don't dawdle, Eyota and keep quiet for Inyan's sake.'

Melcorka did not question who or what Inyan was. She could see Dhegian warriors at the front entrance to the building and without Defender, she knew she could not fight them.

'This way, Eyota.' The female took her hand and led her away, with five men forming around them as if in protection. 'Can you walk? It will be hard after being tied up.'

'I can walk,' Melcorka said. The return of circulation after such a prolonged period of constriction was painful, but she revelled in the freedom of movement. She remembered a saying of her mother's: 'Pain is temporary, failure is forever.' Stretching her legs, she matched her rescuers stride for stride as they jogged through the quiet streets of the largest city that Melcorka had ever seen in her life. She remembered Dunedin, with its royal castle in which the King of Alba had lived; that was nothing compared to the size of this immense city.

Threading between a hundred houses and beneath a score of the tremendous steep-sloped mounds, they left the city and moved on into the whispering grassland of the plains.

After an hour, they stopped. The woman whispered, 'It's Chumani and her boys,' and a deep voice grunted: 'Enter.'

Within a simple stockade, a dozen lodges clustered around a central space and a score of copper-skinned men and women waited.

'Did you find her, Chumani?' the same deep voice asked.

'We have Eyota here, Chaytan,' the woman said.

'Bring her in,' Chaytan ordered.

In the growing light, Melcorka had her first opportunity to study her rescuers. Chumani, the woman, was even younger than Melcorka, a smooth-faced, almond-eyed beauty with sleek black hair and a slender body. The men who surrounded her were older, wiry rather than muscular, more graceful than any group of men Melcorka had ever seen before.

'Let me see her,' Chaytan said, and strong hands guided Melcorka to the central space. She looked up into a face that might have been carved from stone.

Chaytan was a warrior. He could be nothing else, with that face and build. He was walking muscle, with an incredible breadth of shoulders and chest, arms that were smooth and brawny and wrists as thick as most men's forearms. For all his impressive physique, it was his broad face that caught and held Melcorka's attention. He shared the almond-shaped eyes that were common to all in this gathering, but Chaytan's were deeper, darker and more knowing. He was so obviously a man of intense intelligence that Melcorka could forgive him the tight slash of his mouth and the out-thrusting chin that she took to denote stubbornness, or perhaps absolute determination.

'My daughter says that you are Eyota.' Chaytan spoke in a voice so deep that it reminded Melcorka of the grumble of distant thunder. 'Is that so?'

'My name is Melcorka, of the Cenel Bearnas tribe in Alba,' Melcorka had been raised to tell the truth, whatever the consequences and it was only a few hours ago since Bearnas had reminded her to be herself. 'I know nothing of this Eyota of whom you speak.'

'Tcha!' Chaytan said. 'I knew it was a waste of time! This stranger is only some foreign woman who only talks gibberish. Melcorka... Cenel Bearnas... what sort of rubbish is that?'

A tall man stepped forward, holding one of the ubiquitous stone-headed clubs. 'She is not Eyota. Enslave her or kill her.'

'No, Akecheta,' Chumani said. 'She is mine.' Despite her age, it was clear that Chumani had some power among these people. 'I will decide what to do with her.'

Chaytan gave a great roar of laughter. 'You and your boys have gone to a lot of trouble in rescuing this foreign woman from Wamblee. It is up to you to decide if she lives or dies.'

'She will live.' Chumani decided Melcorka's fate as casually as she would a mouse or a spider. 'I think she is Eyota.'

'She would surely know if she was,' Chaytan said.

'Eyota was the greatest woman ever to walk the land,' Akecheta said. 'She would not have to be rescued from Wamblee. The stories say that she will return one day and bring the people to peace and greatness.' He prodded Melcorka with his carved stone mace. 'This is only a foreign woman.'

'What does the prophecy say?' Chumani asked. 'It says that Eyota travelled to the north to get help. It says she will return from the north as a mighty warrior, with a band of warriors who will cleanse the land of a great evil and bring an era of peace and prosperity.'

'Mighty warriors do not get captured,' Akecheta said. 'This is only a woman.'

'She has the mark of Eyota.' Chumani pointed to the tattoo on Melcorka's face.

'A handful of sand will scrub that off,' Akecheta said. 'Look.' stepping forward, he grabbed hold of Melcorka's hair with his left hand and tilted her head back. Without thinking, Melcorka slipped her right leg behind his, lifted her right arm against his throat and pushed. It was the same simple move that Erik had used against Ragnog, yet it took Akecheta by surprise. He overbalanced and fell face-up on the ground, feet apart and loincloth flapping. Following up her advantage, Melcorka quickly lifted his club.

'I may not be your Eyota,' she said, 'but in my land, men do not treat women so, unless they wish to have this crushed.' She tapped the club against his exposed manhood and winked at Chumani. 'Do you wish me to continue?'

'No.' Chumani did not seem to object to Akecheta's discomfiture. 'That would be a waste.'

Melcorka looked and exchanged a secret smile with Chumani. 'That is true,' she said, easing Akecheta's injured pride. 'It is quite impressive.' She extended her hand to help him up and handed back the club. 'You might need this for a real enemy.'

Chaytan had watched and said nothing. Now, he spoke again with that deep bass rumble. 'Now that you have proved yourself a warrior,' he said, 'you can tell us where you are from and why you came to our land.'

They sat around the central space, with others joining them so there were upward of a hundred people gathered, men, women and a few children. The men all appeared to be warriors, whatever their age, while the women were lithe and handsome and not at all shy.

'Is this Eyota?' The question was asked a dozen times before Chaytan managed to impose order on the gathering.

'I am not Eyota,' Melcorka said.

'She is Eyota,' the women murmured, 'the great woman warrior come to save Dhegia from the curse of Wamblee. There is some reason she is not telling us.'

'She is only a woman,' the men replied, until Akecheta held up his hands and stood in the midst of them.

'You all know me,' he said, in a voice that nearly rivalled Chaytan for depth and timbre. 'I am Akecheta, a warrior.'

Men and women nodded their agreement.

'This woman, who calls herself Melcorka, knocked me down and could have killed me.'

'Or worse!' Chumani shouted cheerfully, as the women laughed and applauded.

'Or worse,' Akecheta agreed, without malice. 'She may or may not be Eyota, I do not know. But I do know that she is a redoubtable warrior who carries the mark of Eyota.'

Standing in front of the gathering, Melcorka told them that she was a woman from far away. 'I was travelling with my man, Bradan the Wanderer,' she said, 'but the warriors of Wamblee killed him.' Even as she said the words, Melcorka felt herself choke. Bradan was dead – that wise, patient, capable man with whom she had travelled so many thousands of miles. Bradan who had helped her expel the Norse from Alba; Bradan who had stood at her side as she fought the Shining One; Bradan who had defeated the Morrigan with his staff of rowan wood, was dead.

The gathering was silent, respecting her grief.

'He is with his ancestors in the spirit world,' Chaytan said. 'He will be happy there.'

The emotion was so intense that Melcorka could not hold it back. It was a terrible outpouring of grief, followed by the deepest anger that she had ever felt. Losing her mother had been bad, but Bearnas had chosen the warrior's path and had known that violent death was the nearly inevitable result. Losing Bradan was worse. Despite their disputes and disagreements, she had chosen him for her man, and he was dead. He had never been a fighting man but a seeker after knowledge. Now he was dead, dead, dead; murdered in a raid by the warriors of this Wamblee and the empire of Dhegia.

She felt herself shaking and realised she had been openly weeping in front of these Skraelings.

'Who is Wamblee?' She took a deep breath to control her breathing. 'What is he?'

There was a silence that lasted for a good thirty seconds before Chumani glanced at her father.

'He is the enemy,' she said simply. 'He is the most evil man ever to disfigure the world. Even Inyan and Wi have cursed him.'

'I see.' Melcorka had herself under control now. 'You don't like him. I understand that he is the ruler of the Dhegian Empire?'

There was another prolonged silence, followed by a low growl.

'He is the usurper,' Chumani said softly. 'He murdered the king and took control. Now, he seeks to extend his control over all the peoples as far as the northern seas and beyond.'

Melcorka nodded. 'We have such kings where I come from as well. Norse kings and Saxon kings and the like.'

'Wamblee wants to rule the world.'

'The world is a big place,' Melcorka said. 'Far bigger than I ever realised.'

Chumani screwed up her face. 'I don't know how big it is. All I know is that Wamblee captured the true king, killed him and is extending his rule over all the tribes and peoples of the world.'

'What do the people think about that?' Melcorka asked.

'His tribe, the Dhegians, follow him. They form most of his army and have subjugated the other tribes. Those of us who are free, live outside the city in scattered villages and small communities.'

'How many different tribes are there?'

Chumani looked at her father, who screwed up his face. 'I don't know. There are dozens, maybe scores. We are the Lakota. There are Oglala, Santee, Wahpeon, Yankton, Shawnee, Creek, Pawnees, Mohawk, Seneca, Oneida... far too many to name them all. Some are already enslaved, others are free in the forests or on the fringes of the prairies, or are scattered like us.'

'If there are so many tribes, why not rise against this Wamblee and kill him?' Melcorka looked for the most direct solution to the problem. She nodded to Chaytan and Akecheta. 'If all the men are as formidable as these two, then you have a good band of warriors to help you.'

'There are two reasons. One is that the tribes are not always friendly with each other,' Chumani said.

Melcorka nodded. 'It is the same in my land. The tribes – clans, as we call them – fight each other, rather than combining to fight the common enemy.'

'There is another reason,' Chumani said. 'Wamblee sacrifices the chiefs of each tribe. Their blood is given to Inyan and Wi...'

'Your gods?' Melcorka guessed.

'Inyan is the Rock – he is eternal. Wi is the Sun.' Chumani held up a small hand to stop Melcorka from interrupting again. 'Once the chiefs are sacrificed to Inyan and Wi, their power goes to the priests, and the priests are all from the Dhegia, so they do as Wamblee tells them. The people of the leaderless tribes must follow the priests, or their ancestors will be cast out of the spirit world to wander homeless and lost, suffering for all eternity.'

Melcorka nodded. 'I see,' she said. She understood the power of that damnation. She would not like to think of Bearnas' spirit suffering. 'Is there any way of getting rid of these priests?' She tapped Chaytan's stone mace. 'Like cracking them over the head with one of these?'

Chumani sighed. 'The prophecy told us that these dark days were coming... days when the tribes would be subject to an evil tyrant who would enslave them to build his monuments and who would try and extend his dominion all across the world.' The gathering sighed, nodded and made small sounds of assent.

'Did the prophecy also tell you how he could be removed?' Melcorka asked, expecting the answer that she received.

'The prophecy says that Eyota will return from the far north. She will have a mark on her face and will bring a band of fierce warriors who will defeat Wamblee. Only Eyota has the power to defeat Wamblee and his priests.' Chumani looked steadily at Melcorka. 'I thought you were Eyota. When I saw you with that band of warriors, destroying the border post, I thought you were the prophecy coming to life.'

'I am Melcorka, not Eyota,' Melcorka said. She thought for a moment. 'The men I came with are warriors. They will help you fight Wamblee.' She shook away the thought of Bradan. 'I had a sword when I came. I would like to have it back.' She explained what a sword was to these warriors who only knew war clubs, spears and bows. 'It is like a large knife, with a steel blade.'

'I have never seen such a thing.' Chumani said. 'Steel?'

Melcorka realised these people did not have steel. The only metal she had seen was copper. 'It is a very hard metal,' she said. 'Harder than copper, more supple than stone.'

'Where will this steel weapon be?' Akecheta asked.

'My sword is on board *Catriona*. That is the name of our ship, the canoe on which I arrived.'

Akecheta's grin was cheerful enough to gladden the heart. 'Let's see if your weapon is still on board.'

'Do you know where *Catriona* is?'

'I do. Your canoe is in Cahokia, the central city of the Dhegia Empire.'

The name was familiar. Melcorka ran the word through her mind as if it was an old friend. 'Is that where I was held? The city where I was a captive?'

Chaytan looked amused. 'You were on the outskirts. Cahokia is the largest city in the world.'

Melcorka tried to rise. 'When can we go there?'

'Soon,' Chaytan said. 'Once you have rested.'

Melcorka settled back. *I am going home soon.*

Chapter Fourteen

They left at dusk the next day, with Chaytan leading them in single file, Chumani at his heels and half a dozen Lakota warriors in single file. Melcorka was next to last, with Akecheta at the rear.

The night was clear and crisp, with the wind murmuring through the long grass and the boughs of the occasional tree swishing quietly. Stars glittered above them, stretching into infinity from horizon to horizon, with a three-quarters moon glossing the ground beneath and casting shifting shadows as the war-party passed. It was a surreal oxymoron, to be trotting across a familiar yet unknown land in the company of strangers she already felt she knew.

Keeping pace with the Lakota, Melcorka thought of the other expeditions she had been on, fighting the Norse and facing the Shining One, but always then she had Bradan at her side. Here, she was alone save for these copper-coloured warriors that she did not know.

I want Defender back, she said to herself, *I want Defender back*. The mantra gave her strength through that lonely night as they trotted across the vast prairie. Twice, animals howled in the distance, raising the hairs on the back of her neck. The Lakota ignored the sound and ran on tirelessly through the night.

The moon was at its peak when Chaytan raised his right hand in the air. The Lakotas halted at once, with Akecheta putting a heavy hand on Melcorka's shoulder.

'Cahokia,' Chaytan said.

Melcorka immediately recognised the city as if it was a familiar home. Surmounted by palisaded buildings, the great pyramid-shaped mounds dominated the quiet streets of smaller houses. The scattering of mature trees gave shade in hot days and shelter from the wind;, while the broad avenues led to the taller pyramids and the immense central space where public events occurred.

'It is the largest city I have ever seen.' Melcorka felt the atmosphere, the majesty, the vitality, yet it was not at all as she remembered, or as somebody else remembered for her. The undercurrent of fear was evident.

'Stay close,' Chumani said. 'Wamblee's patrols are everywhere.'

The Lakota warriors trotted again, keeping to the shadows of the buildings, their sandaled feet so quiet that even Melcorka hardly heard them. 'Stop!' Chaytan held up his hand again. They stopped immediately, hugging the shadowed side of a building as a Dhegia patrol padded past. There were ten warriors, half of them armed with stone-headed clubs, the others with short spears and every man parading a flint dagger at his belt.

The patrol padded on. Chaytan gave them a full minute before he moved, with the Lakotas behind him.

After twenty minutes, they stopped between two small, low buildings in the shadow of a high mound. There was a stone pyramid on top, with steps leading from the ground to a terrace, and then more steps flanked by stone carvings.

'That is the sacred temple,' Chumani explained. 'That is where the priests sacrifice the chiefs.'

Melcorka stared up at the dominant stone pyramid. She remembered the sacrificial fires at Hector's broch in Alba, and how she had rescued Bradan. Now she did not have Bradan to rescue. 'I don't like human sacrifice,' she said.

'Blood is sacred to Wi.' Chumani spoke as if it was a known fact.

They moved on, sombre now as the memory of the evil that infested this place seeped through them. When clouds obscured the moon, they moved in gloom.

'And that is the Citadel.' Chumani pointed to the largest mound of all. 'It took hundreds of slaves to build that, including many from tribes that no longer exist.'

Four muscular Dhegian warriors guarded the single great gateway that pierced a high wall encircling the base of the mound. Behind them, the pyramid rose in a series of vast terraces, with each of the four sides bisected by a central stone staircase. Near the summit was another wall, and beyond that, the roofs and upper stories of unknown buildings.

'That is the palace where Wamblee lives.' There was venom in Chumani's voice. 'That is where the evil snake rules.'

'His time will come.' Melcorka spoke more in hope than expectation. 'But what did you mean by tribes that no longer exist?'

'They are all dead,' Chumani said. 'Wamblee and his men worked them to death.'

'Perhaps it is time that somebody removed this Wamblee,' Melcorka said softly.

It was another quarter mile to the riverside, and then Melcorka stopped. Upstream, the river had been broad, but here it was colossal. Two rivers merged, creating a stretch of moving water unlike anything she had seen before.

'What is this river called?'

'We call it the Big River,' Chumani said, 'but the name Mississippi is being used. That is an Algonkian word, yet it has spread.'

'Mississippi,' Melcorka repeated. 'That is a lovely name. It sounds like the kiss of the water against the grass.' She nodded. 'I like it.'

Akecheta smiled. 'We'll make you one of the People yet,' he said. 'Despite your decorated face and strange accent.'

'I am Melcorka of Alba,' Melcorka began and then she stopped. What had she left in Alba? She had memories of her mother and memories of Bradan, both now dead. Wherever she travelled, those memories would remain. 'I would be honoured to be Melcorka of the Lakota.'

'We will have to give you a new name,' Akecheta said.

'She already has a name,' Chumani said. 'She is Eyota, the great one.'

'Look.' Chaytan pointed. 'Is that your canoe?'

Sea Serpent lay on her side on the shore, with her mast unshipped and her oars neatly piled a short distance away. *Catriona* was in the river, tied up and bobbing gently to the current. Two bored Dhegians guarded each ship.

'If my sword is on board,' Melcorka said, 'then I will be a warrior again, able to help you in your fight.' She did not like to think of the alternative. If the Dhegians had taken Defender, then Melcorka knew that she was no good to anybody. The rock-climbing skills of an Islander were useless in this land of forests and endless prairie.

Chumani touched her arm. 'You are Eyota,' she said quietly.

'Wait,' Chaytan said and signalled to Akecheta. The two of them crawled forward, hugging the ground until they came to the guards. They rose as one man, placed a hand over the mouth of their target, crashed the war-clubs on their heads and caught the bodies as they fell. The whole affair took less than two minutes.

'Come on,' Chumani said, and Melcorka followed her to the side of the great river. *Catriona* looked empty and forlorn, a seagoing ship outside her element. Melcorka jumped on board, with Chumani close behind her. The Lakota warriors strung out along the banks of the river, looking outward in complete silence.

'Find your sword,' Chumani whispered, 'before the Dhegians return.'

Dropping to a crouch, Melcorka searched for Defender. She looked under the thwarts, in the small lockers in bow and stern and between the benches. The sword was not there. The flicker of hope that had buoyed her vanished, to be replaced by sick depression. She had lost Defender; she was nothing. Doubtless one of the Dhegian warriors now possessed her sword.

The depth of her loss was crippling. The sword that Calgacus had carried against the Romans, that Arthur had wielded against the pagan Saxons and that Bridei had taken to defeat the Angles at Nechtansmere – gone. It had been entrusted to her care, and she had allowed the followers of Wamblee to take it and kill her man.

'It's not here.' Melcorka heard the catch in her voice. She was near breaking point. She had nothing left to offer.

There was no future. There was no present; there was only a past.

'Eyota,' Chumani sounded shocked. 'Eyota.'

'No, only Melcorka,' Melcorka said quietly. She took a deep breath. She was Melcorka of the Cenel Bearnas. She did not need a sword to make her way in the world, however illustrious its history. She had to remind herself that she had existed before she met Bradan and before Defender came into her life. 'I am Melcorka.'

'No, you are Eyota.'

Melcorka realised that Chumani was trembling. 'Are you all right, Chumani?'

The Lakota girl fell to her knees and handed something to Melcorka. It was the headband from the ice woman and the small bag of falcon trinkets that she had removed from the body.

'I found these,' Melcorka began and clamped her mouth shut. These people expected a deliverer to come from the north. They expected the deliverer to be a woman. She knew that when she donned that headband, she gained an insight into this place and these people. It now seemed obvious that the dead woman they had found had been Eyota – dead God alone knew how long ago and now buried at sea. Well then; the Lakota had helped her so now she must return the favour, and if that meant wearing the mantle of a dead woman, then that is what she would do.

'Eyota...' Chumani proffered the headband and bag again. She did not raise her head.

'Thank you, Chumani.' Melcorka said. Reaching forward, she took the bag of trinkets and placed them inside her now sadly battered cloak. The headband was next. She lifted it, feeling the quality of the cloth, the smooth falcon design, and nothing else. The design was not embroidered as she had at first thought, but was composed of hundreds of seashells, some coloured, others white.

Melcorka fastened the band around her head as she had done before. All at once, she could see more clearly. She felt a surge of confidence similar to that which she experienced when she unsheathed Defender; a new vitality, and definite authority.

'Eyota...' Chumani was down on all fours, her forehead touching the planking.

Reaching out, Melcorka lifted her up. 'There is no need for that sort of thing between friends.' The words came fluently, and Melcorka heard the timbre of her voice. It was deeper, more musical than the Gaelic with which she usually communicated.

'You are Eyota.'

'And you are Chumani, my friend.' Melcorka held her upper arms. 'Come on, Chumani. We did not find my sword.'

Suddenly, the loss of Defender was less critical. Out here in this wild western land of limitless prairies, vast forests, broad rivers and lakes as large as the sea, Melcorka's priorities altered. This headband with its intricate design seemed to give her some authority. But why her? Was it because she retained some of the residual magic of Defender and the force within the headband, whatever it was, recognised that magic and transferred its power to her? Melcorka shook her head. She did not know. She only knew that there was something here... something that affected her. She stepped clear of *Catriona* and onto the bank of the Mississippi River.

Chaytan stared at her, open-mouthed. 'So it's true,' he said. 'You are Eyota. Chumani was right all along. Well, don't expect me to grovel at your feet.'

'I would not wish that,' Melcorka said. The Lakota warriors were watching her, some openly staring, others shy, as if afraid to catch her eye. She raised her voice. 'I am Melcorka of Alba,' she said. 'I am also Eyota of Dhegia.'

They nodded, accepting her words as fact. Their eyes were filled with respect.

'Now we can rid ourselves of the plague of Wamblee.' There was great satisfaction in Chumani's voice. 'Eyota is back.'

'We'll return to your village,' Melcorka said, 'and plan how best to do this.'

'As you say, Eyota,' Chumani agreed at once.

Cahokia was awake. Melcorka frowned at the sound of a cracking whip and the shouts of the slave drivers. Chaytan's mighty hands unceremoniously pushed her into the shadow of a wall as the Dhegians passed. There were three of them, and all held a long whip with which they belaboured the long file of naked prisoners that walked in front.

'Why don't they fight back?' Melcorka asked.

'They are slaves,' Chumani explained. 'If they rebel against the legal ruler in any way, their ancestors will be cast out of the Spirit World.'

'We will have to do something about that.' Melcorka felt the spirit of Eyota surging through her, lending her knowledge and authority. She was no longer the young girl from the islands, but Eyota of Cahokia. She watched as the slaves left the centre of the town to descend into a huge pit where they worked with primitive spades, filling baskets of earth. They were joined by more and more, until there were hundreds of them, mostly men but also women, digging into the ground and carrying baskets of earth to add to an already large pile.

'They are building another mound,' Akecheta said. 'Wamblee wants this one to be the largest pyramid in the world, a tribute to his greatness. He will sacrifice two chiefs today to gain the approval of Wi.'

Melcorka nodded slowly, understanding Wamblee's need for blood sacrifice in this culture. 'I want those to be the last sacrifices that Wamblee ever makes.'

'Wait.' Chaytan said. 'Somebody is coming.'

The Dhegian patrol was fifty men strong, trotting in unison as they moved toward the Citadel. Armed with heavy, carved maces and small wickerwork shields, they checked the identity of every man and woman they passed.

'You!' The leader pointed to a man who had tried to slip away from them. 'Where are you going?

'N-nowhere,' the man stuttered.

'Nobody leaves when we sacrifice to Wi.' The captain took hold of the man's arm.

'I wasn't going anywhere,' the man said.

'You are now.' The captain snapped an order, and two of his warriors grabbed the man. 'Take him to the compound.'

'No!' The man looked around in sudden panic. 'You can't do that.' Suddenly jerking his arm free, he dashed up the nearest alleyway, with the warriors in close pursuit.

'We could help him,' Melcorka said.

Chaytan held her arm. 'Watch and learn, Eyota,' he said. 'It is better that you see what happens here.'

Caught by the warriors, the terrified man was dragged to the nearest open space. 'Kill him,' the captain said laconically.

'No!' The man screamed once before the maces rose and crashed sickeningly on his head. Pushing the body to the side of the road, the warriors moved on.

'Stay here, Eyota,' Chaytan said. 'Things have altered a lot since you were last here. You should know about the evil that you have come to cleanse.'

Within a minute, a tall man arrived and supervised a group of slaves who lifted the dead body and carried it away, with one slave sprinkling river sand over the mess of blood.

'That man mentioned a compound,' Melcorka said. 'What did he mean?'

Chaytan and Chumani exchanged glances. 'Come with us,' Chaytan said. 'It is not a pretty sight.'

'We'll have to climb one of the pyramids,' Akecheta said.

'Then that is what we shall do,' Chumani said. 'Eyota wishes it.'

There were many pyramids in the city. Some were mere mounds of soil surmounted by the house of a wealthy merchant or chief and others were taller, with public buildings on top. Chaytan brought them to one of the latter.

'This place is empty today,' he said. 'The officials are all going to the public square for the sacrifice.' A flight of stone stairs led upward to the palisade that encircled the summit of the mound and enclosed a squat building. Akecheta led them to the palisade and peered over. 'You can see from here, Eyota.'

The compound lay on the outskirts of the city. There was a twenty-foot-high wall of beaten earth topped by a stout stockade of pointed stakes. A dozen Dhegian warriors guarded the open doorway, while inside, some two hundred men and women were huddled together under the open sky.

'Why are they there?' Melcorka asked.

'They are now slaves,' Chaytan said soberly. 'Whoever needs a slave or two will come to the compound and select who or what they want, man or woman, for whatever reason they want.'

Melcorka eyed the guards. 'I am not surprised there is an aura of fear in this city.'

'We are waiting for your leadership,' Chumani said. 'We need some-body to unite the tribes. No tribe will follow the chief of another. Only someone that can command the respect of all the tribes will be successful.'

That sounds very much like Scotland, Melcorka thought, as the weight of responsibility pressed down on her. *I am an island girl, not a diplomat! Yet there is nobody else. There are wrongs to be righted and evils to remove. I have lost Defender; without my sword what can I do?*

'You can do your best.' Bearnas' voice sounded clear as the piping of an oystercatcher within her head. 'You are my daughter. I did not bring you up to shirk responsibility. You led the Albans against the Norse. Now lead these people against Wamblee and the Dhegians. That is your clear duty.'

Melcorka touched Eyota's headband. *This strip of cloth is what I have. This band is the symbol of power that these people seem to understand. Let's hope it is enough.*

She choked on a sudden wave of depression. *Oh, God, I wish I had Bradan here.*

There are other men.

That thought came unbidden to her mind. She blinked. Other men? Did she want other men? She looked around. Chaytan was too old; Akecheta was undoubtedly not too old. Without conscious thought, her eyes drifted over his body from his feet to his head and back. He was a well-made, muscular man, of that there was no doubt.

No! Melcorka told herself. That was not her way. From where had that thought come? From where had those desires come?

'How is the sacrifice conducted?' She tried to alter the direction of her thoughts.

'You'll see soon,' Chaytan said. 'The city is closed off so nobody can enter or leave. Everybody must attend, or they'll end up in the compound.'

Melcorka nodded. 'Then I will see the evil that we must eradicate.' She studied the city. 'How many warriors does Dhegia have?' She watched as a seemingly unending procession of armed men poured into the central square, with the immense sacred pyramid at one end and the Royal Citadel at the other.

'Dhegia is the largest tribe in our world,' Chaytan said. 'And every man is a warrior. Slaves do all the farming work and labouring work, and they can also be called up to fight.'

'Hundreds? Thousands?' Melcorka hazarded.

'As many as you can see,' Chaytan said, 'and there are more guarding and patrolling the borders. The ones you have to watch for are the Guards.'

The vast public space gradually filled up. Disciplined warriors lined the outside, with the outer ranks facing outward and the inner facing inward, where the civilian population of women, old men, children and slaves stood in their thousands. The warriors pushed through the centre of the crowd, forcing a passage that they quickly lined with armed men. Every second man faced the crowd, holding their clubs and spears, unsmiling, unemotional and professional.

'Here they come,' Akecheta said.

Wishing she had Defender in her hands, Melcorka could only watch as the procession entered the public square. Five tall men dressed in feathered headdresses and white furs were in front. Dignified and aloof, they carried an aura of sinister menace.

'The priests,' Chaytan said. 'They will perform the sacrifice. They are monsters without compassion, without mercy, without humanity, without pity, without a soul.'

'I see them,' Melcorka said.

The priests moved sedately, followed by two burly, broad-shouldered men carrying the largest war-clubs that Melcorka had ever seen. Each club had a stone head ornately carved into the shape of a pouncing falcon. Diagonally across their backs, each man carried a short, broad-headed stabbing spear.

'Those two are Wamblee's bodyguards,' Chaytan said. 'They kill on order. They are as fast as a falcon, as strong as a buffalo. They don't care who they kill. If Wamblee tells them to kill, then they obey without question. They crush skulls with ease and stab their spears into man, woman or child.'

'I see them,' Melcorka said.

Behind the bodyguard was a collection of men dressed in feathers, with rattles attached to their legs and carrying drums, rattles and whistles.

'Wamblee's musicians,' Chaytan said. 'They play only for the king and nobody else. Their music is sacred and can transport a man or woman into the next world.'

'I see them,' Melcorka said.

A huge man was next. He was the tallest man that Melcorka had ever seen, a full head and shoulders above even the two bodyguards, with a breadth of shoulders that was twice that of any ordinary man. His long tunic reached the ground and rippled with the coloured seashells that seemed to be valued by the Dhegians. The design on his chest and back was a falcon, and on his head, he wore a headdress made from falcon feathers.

'That is Wamblee.' Chaytan spoke with venom in his voice. 'He has never been bested in battle and has the power of Wi within him. He is evil on two legs. He kills on a whim, orders death as easily as he draws breath and drinks the blood of his victims to gain their strength.'

'I see him,' Melcorka said. She eyed the man who dominated this empire; the king who had made this city feared the length and breadth of this new world and whose power even extended to Greenland.

Behind Wamblee marched a hundred warriors, each one bearing a falcon's headdress and carrying a spear and a carved stone-headed club.

'They are Wamblee's Citadel Guard,' Chaytan said. 'They are the best warriors the world has ever seen or ever will see. They fight as one man, welcome death in honour of Wamblee and revere him as their god. They get the pick of the female slaves and the best of the crops. They train nine hours a day and have never been defeated in battle. To get to Wamblee, any enemy would have to kill every one of them. That is how loyal they are.'

'I see them,' Melcorka said.

Behind the Citadel Guard were a hundred young warriors with their faces painted half black, half white. They carried spears and a small shield. All were young men, lithe and handsome.

'They are the Wall Guard,' Chaytan said. 'Their job is to guard the wall of the Citadel. They have the best eyesight in Dhegia and practise with shield and spear seven hours a day. When they reach twenty-eight summers, the best of them fight each other and the victors are trained to become Citadel Guards. They are tested every full moon, and if any of them cannot hit a designated mark with his spear at fifty paces, ten times out of ten, he is put to death.'

'I see them,' Melcorka said.

Behind the Wall Guard came two tall men, as naked as the day they were born. Despite the ropes that tethered their legs and allowed them only a step of six inches, they walked straight and proud, ignoring the taunts of the guards they passed and the prods and insults of the men who pushed them onward to the steps of the sacrifice pyramid.

'They are the chiefs of the Kahows and the Hunoigs,' Chaytan said. 'A Dhegian raiding party captured them, and now they will be sacrificed. Their old women and children were put to death, and their young women handed to the Citadel Guard as gifts. Their men will be enslaved to build the great pyramid. All hope is gone from them.'

'I see them,' Melcorka said. She watched the two chiefs, wishing she could help but knowing that without Defender, she could not stand against even one of Dhegia's muscular warriors.

At the back of the procession marched fifty more warriors. They were older and wore furs while carrying shields and clubs.

'They are the Veterans. They have served their time as Citadel Guards and are now waiting to be told if they can marry, or if they will be sacrificed. Wamblee will decide. If they are permitted to take a wife, they may choose from any woman, slave or free, even those that the Citadel Guard have already chosen. If they are selected for sacrifice, then they will die willingly, knowing that their blood will merge with that of Wamblee, their king, and god.'

The tail of the procession was still entering the central square when the head was mounting the steps of the great sacrificial pyramid. There was a complete hush as the priests reached the summit, and then the priests began to chant. At first, Melcorka could not make out the words, although she recognised that the priests were talking to their god. They circled a curious table with sides that sloped to a narrow top ridge.

Only the priests spoke. Even Wamblee was silent as he reached the summit of the pyramid and took his place in a massive armed chair, surmounted with the carved figure of a falcon and with falcon feathers arrayed all around. He sat there in silence as the priests continued their chanting around the table. Melcorka started as she realised that it was not a table: it was an altar.

Somebody coughed. The sound echoed around the packed square as if it were a roll of drums. Immediately, all the guards turned inward, searching for the culprit. There was a surge of movement within the audience, leaving one man standing terribly alone amidst a circle of accusing faces.

Four guards closed on him, grim-faced and with clubs upraised. The man did not protest, merely closed his eyes as they dragged him through the crowd to the central path and crashed their clubs on him, again and again, until he was a bloody paste on the ground. Leaving his broken body, the guards returned to their posts, and the priests continued with their ceremony. Birds landed to peck at the still warm body. Nobody moved, nobody objected. Fear, acceptance or agreement kept them rigidly in place.

The priests continued with their ceremony, chanting, raising their hands to the rising sun and spreading their arms to include the entire crowd. They stopped abruptly, and the musicians took centre stage, circling the slope-sided altar. They moved slowly, raising their legs high and shaking them, so the sound of the rattles dominated the square. After four circuits, they began to beat their drums in a persistent rhythm that entered Melcorka's head, thrumming around her mind with its monotonous, insistent beat. She found herself nodding to the rhythm as one of the musicians played his whistle. The high notes rose skyward, imitating the sound of a falcon.

Melcorka realised that everybody in the audience was humming. The drone rose and fell in time with the music, and then rose higher and higher, speeding up as the dancers increased their pace and the volume of their words. The sound was hypnotic, spreading around the city and reaching even to the pyramid where the Lakotas stood. They also began to hum, with their throats vibrating to the insistent sound.

The musicians stepped into the background, with only the humming and drumming continuing, slow and sombre, as the chiefs of the Kahows and the Hunoigs were brought forward. The crowd continued with its drone, although Melcorka detected an air of desperation in the tone.

The first chief was led forward. He came quietly, but had a look of despair on his face as the priests lifted him high and placed him face-up on the table. Despite Melcorka's horror, she watched in sick fascination as the priests surrounded the naked man. Cutting through his bonds, they spread-eagled him on the narrow table, with one priest holding each limb. The fifth raised a small, leaf-bladed flint knife so the crowd could see it and slowly, carefully, pushed it into the chief's belly, deep enough to penetrate the skin but not deep enough to cause serious damage. The chief writhed in silent agony as the priest very slowly ripped the knife upward to his throat, then peeled back his skin, so the internal organs were on display.

Only then did the priest dig deeper, cutting out the heart and lifting it, still pumping, above his head. Slow blood dripped through the priest's fingers to land on the body of the chief. The drone of the crowd was high-pitched now, with undertones of panic. The priest handed the heart to Wamblee, who lifted it and thrust it into his mouth, so the chief's blood dribbled down his chin and onto his clothes.

'Oh, sweet Jesus in heaven,' Melcorka said, as Wamblee chewed mightily, swallowed and bit off another chunk of warm human heart.

With the chief now dead, the priests tossed his body down the stairs. It rolled slowly, one bloody step at a time. Before it reached halfway, a cluster of huge birds had descended, beaks probing, and the second chief was lifted and splayed on the table top.

'Time to go,' Melcorka said, 'while everybody's attention is on the sacrifice.'

'Now you have seen some of the evil,' Chumani said, 'will you fulfil the prophecy, Eyota?'

Still shocked by what she had seen, Melcorka nodded. 'I will do my best,' she said. She felt the approval of that insistent voice within her that she knew was Eyota, even as that other woman's eyes strayed over Akecheta's body.

Chapter Fifteen

A sudden storm had swept across the city, screaming from the prairie to the west to batter at the palisades and lift thatch from the rooftops. Men and women had sheltered from the fury, while the slaves in the compound cowered without shelter or compassion. Some had died, and their bodies had been left to rot among their less fortunate companions. Nobody cared in that place where hope was a stranger.

Chaytan used the distraction provided by the weather to return to Cahokia, bringing Melcorka and a chosen few in his train.

'The veterans are in charge now,' Chaytan said. 'They are going to pick their wives. It is their time.'

'I am more interested in the Citadel Guard.' Melcorka watched as the veterans lined up outside the Guard's barracks. They were laughing, nudging each other, obviously in high spirits. 'How will they react to these men stealing their women?'

'They have no choice.' Chumani spoke for her father. 'Wamblee has given the order, and they must obey. The Guards swear obedience from boyhood. Wamblee is their god as well as their king.'

Melcorka nodded. 'I would like to watch how these trained warriors allow their women to be taken away so easily.'

'It is true, Eyota,' Chumani said.

The Veterans filed into the barracks. Melcorka heard laughter and shouting, a scream or two and more laughter. After a few moments, the first of the Veterans emerged with a struggling young woman in each hand. Another followed, then another, each with a woman grasped by the hand, or wriggling and kicking under his arm.

'Don't the Citadel Guards object?' Melcorka tried to imagine what would happen if some group of Picts or Scots attempted to rob another of their women. There would be mass slaughter.

The Citadel Guards did object. They followed the Veterans out of the barracks, shouting and waving their hands. The Veterans looked back over their shoulders.

'It's our right,' they said. 'If you live to be Veterans, you will do the same.'

The last of the Veterans had a weeping young girl balanced over his right shoulder. He turned around. 'If you don't like the system, complain to Wamblee. I'm sure he will listen.' He laughed, held his trophy even tighter and walked casually away.

Melcorka raised her eyebrows to Chumani. 'That was interesting.' She lowered her voice. 'I do not like to see women used as commodities, as if we were not every bit as valuable as men.'

Chumani nodded slowly. 'If I were you, Eyota, I would hope to change that.'

Chapter Sixteen

'Wamblee has a formidable military force.' Melcorka had donned Eyota's headband to add authority to her words. 'His bodyguard, Citadel Guard and Wall Guard alone will be difficult to defeat, even without the hundreds or even thousands of ordinary warriors he commands.'

'We already know this, Eyota,' Chaytan said.

'We need something special if we are to overcome him. Something that Wamblee and his warriors do not expect, or have never met before.'

Chaytan shook his head. 'We have only ourselves and the scattered tribes who have not yet submitted fully to Wamblee's will.'

Melcorka nodded. 'We may have more than that. I would like to find the warriors whom the Dhegians captured at the same time as me,' Melcorka said. 'I would like the men who were on the great dragon ship, *Sea Serpent*.'

'Wamblee holds them inside the walls of the Citadel,' Chaytan said. 'It will not be easy getting to them.'

'It will be worthwhile,' Melcorka said. 'They are mighty warriors. They will fight the Citadel Guard or the Wall Guard without fear.'

'Without fear?' Chumani repeated. 'We all have fear.'

'The best of the Norsemen do not know fear,' Melcorka said. 'They believe that Fate wrote the span of their life before they were born and nothing they do will change that. If it is their time to die, they will die. If they are destined to live, then they shall live.'

Chaytan considered for a moment. 'Such a belief would benefit a warrior in battle,' he said. 'We'll take you to these Norsemen.'

Sheltered by torrential rain, they moved that night.

'Only three of us,' Chaytan said. 'You, me and Akecheta.'

'It seems a tiny number of men to brave the Citadel of Wamblee,' Melcorka said.

'If I bring more, we might be noticed,' Chaytan pointed out. He had refused permission for Chumani to accompany them; Melcorka guessed that he thought it too dangerous. She wished she had Defender with her. And Bradan.

Wishing solves nothing; her mother had taught her that. *Only deeds matter. Do: don't wish.*

Threading through the now familiar streets of Cahokia, they reached the defending stockade of the Citadel at the darkest point of the night. Rain wept from the walls, causing deep puddles on the ground outside and descending the slope of the mound like waterfalls.

'At least the weather may persuade the Wall Guards to keep under shelter,' Melcorka said.

'Can you climb?' Akecheta asked.

In response, Melcorka lifted herself to the first tiny handhold in the earth wall and hauled upwards. After the ice cliffs of the chasm in Greenland, this wall was simple. She reached the top well ahead of Akecheta, with Chaytan labouring in the rear.

As Melcorka had thought, the Wall Guards were not keen on the rain and had found shelter in an angle of the wall. It was easy to avoid them and drop down to the interior of the Citadel. Now, in this forbidden quarter of the city, Melcorka looked around. With the headband in place, she had an insight into the route and had no difficulty in finding her way through the passageways between the houses.

'I can hear them,' she said, smiling. There was no disguising the distinctive roar of the Norse as they sang their songs of drinking, women, and raiding, praising Odin and Thor through their deeds of bloodshed and slaughter.

'Even when they are prisoners, they can sing.' Melcorka moved toward the longhouse from which all the noise emanated. The outer door was not guarded but was sealed with a heavy bar of wood.

'Wait!' Chaytan's hand was firm on her shoulder. 'This is not where Wamblee holds his prisoners.'

'It's all right. I know these people.' Melcorka shook off Chaytan's hand. She trotted ahead, listened at the door of the house for a few moments and then eased it open. The noise inside did not decrease. Sitting with their backs to the stone walls, the Norse were laughing, passing around drinking horns and swapping tales and jokes. Melcorka smiled at the rough, familiar faces, a reminder of home in this land of contrasts and cruelty. She looked for Erik, but he was not there; neither was Frakkok, so presumably the Dhegians had removed the leaders from the rest. That was a sound practice when taking prisoners.

'Odin!' Arne suddenly shouted and the others laughed, raised their faces and echoed the word.

'Odin!'

'Hello!' Melcorka shouted through the noise. 'It's me!' She stepped in, with Chaytan and Akecheta close behind her.

One by one the Norsemen turned to face her, some looking astonished, others amused. She knew them all, from the young hothead, Arne, to Sigurd who was always smiling, Gunnar of the bad jokes, Knut who could never see a woman without commenting and Vidar, who boasted of the kills he had never made.

'What in Odin's name are you doing here?' Arne sounded surprised. 'We thought you were dead.'

'Not yet,' Melcorka said. 'We've come to rescue you.' She indicated Chaytan and Akecheta, who stood at her back eyeing these strange, bearded men from the north. She took another couple of steps inside the building. Chaytan closed the door.

'Rescue us?' Gunnar repeated the words. 'She's come to rescue us, by Odin! And she's brought along a couple of naked Skraeling savages to help!' His laughter echoed around the room, with the other Norse joining in.

'Rescue us from what, Alban?' Vidar asked. 'Do you think we need an Alban woman and a pair of Skraelings to rescue us?'

They laughed again, just as the door of the house opened and a group of people pushed in. The first was one of Wamblee's bodyguards, with his shoulders taking up nearly the whole width of the doorway. The second was Erik, fully armed with sword and axe and behind him ducked the massive bulk of Wamblee himself, arm in arm with Frakkok. Both were laughing, and Frakkok had Defender slung across her back. The sight made Melcorka feel physically sick.

As soon as they saw Frakkok and Erik, the Norse raised a cheer, chanting 'Odin! Odin!'

'Oh, sweet Jesus,' Melcorka breathed. 'You were right, Chaytan. This is no prison. The Norsemen have joined the Dhegians!'

'Get out! Follow me!' Rather than wait to discuss matters, Chaytan led them in a wild charge that took the incomers by surprise. Despite the bodyguard's bulk, Chaytan knocked him backwards, and the others piled through the door, with Akecheta taking the opportunity to land a shrewd blow with his club on Erik.

'That's the Scottish woman!' Melcorka heard Frakkok's shout as she pushed the staggering Erik out of the way and followed Akecheta into the teeming rain of the night.

'This way!' Akecheta grabbed her shoulder and pushed her in front of him. 'The Wall Guards will be out in force now.'

Akecheta was correct. All along the wall, guards would be seen walking, patrolling, and peering both inside and outside the Citadel.

'You two go that way,' Chaytan said. 'I'll divert the guards.'

'No,' Akecheta said. 'You are the chief. You're too valuable.'

It was the first time Melcorka had heard Chaytan called the chief. 'I'm the stranger here,' she said. 'I caused this. I'll create the diversion.'

'You are Eyota,' Akecheta said. 'You are our only hope.' Without saying more, he ran to the wall, shouting a challenge. The first spear missed him by a fraction. The second grazed his side, and then he was on the parapet, advancing on the Wall Guard with his club, roaring a war cry.

'This way.' Chaytan pushed Melcorka to a different section of the wall. The Wall Guards patrolled above them, their throwing spears and shields held ready.

'We can help Akecheta,' Melcorka said. 'We can't leave him here!'

'He is already a dead man,' Chaytan spoke quietly. 'Don't let his sacrifice be in vain.'

The furthest away of the Wall Guards was looking toward the noise when Chaytan arrived at his feet. He only had time to lift his spear before Chaytan's club crashed onto his knee. His loud yell ended abruptly as Chaytan hauled him to the ground and crushed his skull.

'This way, Eyota.' He vaulted onto the wall, over the other side and rolled on the terrace below, with Melcorka following without thought. They ran through Cahokia, careless of the noise they made, and when a warrior attempted to challenge them, Chaytan killed him without compulsion.

'Stay with me, Eyota,' he said. 'We need you more than ever now.'

Melcorka looked back, thinking of Akecheta. He had been a brave man.

Chapter Seventeen

'It was not your fault,' Chumani said. 'You are not to blame for the actions of others. These Norse warriors have joined Wamblee. Well, they are men, not gods and add only a small number to his forces.'

'We can't forget the prophecy,' Chaytan said. 'The prophecy says that you will return with a band of brave warriors and deliver us from a great evil.'

Melcorka looked around. They were in a small, thatched lodge, with a fire smoking in the centre and the people, men and women, grouped all around. 'That prophecy may well be proved correct,' she said. 'I have returned as Eyota, and I will have a band of brave warriors around me.'

'Where will these warriors come from?' Chaytan asked. 'Will you dream them out of the air? Form them from the ground? Make them from grass, perhaps?'

The Lakota laughed at Chaytan's images.

'I have no need to do such things,' Melcorka said. 'I already have a band of brave warriors who will lead the united tribes against Wamblee and his army.'

'The Norse have turned against you,' Chumani said patiently. 'You cannot rely on them, Eyota.'

'I have better men and better friends than the Norse,' Melcorka said. She felt the power of the headband adding force to her words, making her more loquacious, helping her persuade these people. 'I have the Lakota.'

There was a sudden silence. Melcorka waited until everybody had digested her words. 'The Lakota are every bit as strong as the Norse, they are every bit as brave, they are as skilled in war, and this is their land. They belong in this land. This land is your land!'

There were nods of agreement to that. Melcorka was not sure if it was as herself or as Eyota that she felt the intense attachment of the Lakota to the land, to nature and the world all around them, but it was definite. It was not definable, but there was a connection that was beyond the physical, extending to the spiritual and to the very soul of these people. Melcorka started; perhaps they were correct, and their ancestors did inhabit the spirit world. In that case, Bearnas would be with them, guiding her along whether she wished it or not.

Oh God, I wish that Bradan was here!

'The Lakota shall take Eyota – me– to meet the leaders of the tribes.' Melcorka was standing as she addressed the gathering. She heard the power of her voice and knew it was not her own voice. Eyota was using her as a vessel to talk to these people. Eyota had indeed returned.

'Take me to the tribal chiefs,' Melcorka said, 'and we shall raise all the manpower of these great prairies and the forests, as far as the Great Lakes themselves.' She heard the words tumble from her mouth. She raised her arms. 'We shall cleanse this great evil from the land and bring peace again to the Mississippi and all the lands on either side, across forests and prairies, over mountains and rivers, from sea to sea.'

'Eyota is back!' The words passed from mouth to mouth.

'Eyota,' Chumani said. 'May I come with you?'

'People die when they come with me,' Melcorka said. 'Bearnas, Bradan, Akecheta. They were all good people.' She smiled at Chumani. 'You are also a good person, Chumani. I have no wish for you to die.'

'If it is my time, then I will die, Eyota,' Chumani said.

Melcorka opened her mouth, but it was Eyota who spoke. 'Then you may accompany me, Chumani, and welcome. Chaytan will arrange our visits. His name is known and respected among the tribes.' She thought for a moment. 'At present, we will only contact those tribes who are within a few days walk of Cahokia. The great forest tribes are too far away.'

Chaytan looked into Melcorka's face, saw Eyota's eyes and nodded. 'It shall be as you say, Eyota.'

Some of the tribes were scattered in the lands around Cahokia; others braved the vastness of the prairies to the west of the Mississippi and others were further afield in the eastern forests. The Oglala were nearest. The Oglala were here.

Chaytan was first into the lodge where the Oglala elders met, with Chumani and Melcorka at his back.

'You all know that Eyota will return to remove this great evil that has befallen us,' Chaytan said.

The elders nodded solemnly. They were smoking from a large pipe, passing it from man to man. 'We know the prophecy,' the oldest said. His hair was long and white and his face lined with years, yet his eyes were sharp as any man in his twenties.

'Eyota is back,' Chaytan said directly. 'Here she is.' He indicated Melcorka.

The elders surveyed Melcorka. 'She looks much like any other woman,' they said. 'Except for her paler face and the marking on her cheek.'

Melcorka nodded and slipped on the headband. She saw the elders' expressions alter immediately.

'Welcome back, Eyota,' the man with the long, white hair said. 'What do you wish us to do?'

'Wait,' Melcorka said. 'Wait. Gather your warriors and be ready for my message.'

The elders nodded solemnly and passed over the pipe.

'We will meet again.' Melcorka puffed at the pipe as if she had done it a hundred times before. 'We will let you know when.'

They walked to the chiefs of the Santee and Wahpeon, the Yankton and Creek, Seneca and Mohawk and always the reaction was the same. The elders met them with courteous suspicion until Melcorka donned her headband, and then they asked what they should do. Wise men with steady eyes, they did not question Eyota; they knew and respected the prophecy.

The Oneida and the Pawnees were further out on the prairies, which necessitated a dangerous journey over land where the Dhegian patrols were active and aware that Melcorka was on the loose.

'We're being followed,' Chumani said. 'Three men.' She lay down and pressed her ear to the ground. 'They are two hundred paces away.'

'You two move on,' Chaytan said. 'I will wait here for them.'

Melcorka nodded. By now, she knew that Chaytan was as capable a warrior as any she had ever met. She did not doubt that he could deal with the three men. She trotted on with Chumani at her side. It wasn't long before Chaytan caught up with them, bleeding from his left thigh.

'Two of them were Dhegians,' he said. 'The third was a young man with fair hair.'

'A Norseman,' Melcorka said. 'Did you kill him?'

'I killed them all,' Chaytan said. He showed the long cut along his thigh. 'The Norseman did that with his knife. He fought well.'

'The Norse are exceptional fighters,' Melcorka agreed. 'I would like his knife.' Turning around, she ran back until she found the bodies. It was Sigurd who lay on his face with his head a bloody mess and his sword still held in his hand. Melcorka gently prised it free, unfastened his sword belt and buckled it around her waist. It was certainly not Defender, yet still felt good to have a weapon again.

'You look like a warrior now,' Chaytan approved.

'I fight better with my own sword, not this one,' Melcorka said.

Chaytan looked over the prairie. 'You may have to fight soon,' he said. 'If Wamblee is having us followed, he might know what we are doing.'

'Time to gather the tribes.' Melcorka had an instant flashback to a previous war, when she was calling up the survivors of the Alban clans to fight against the Norse. That had been a precarious time, but then she had Defender on her back and Bradan at her side, as well as a thousand soldiers of Fidach as a backbone. Here, she had a handful of Lakota warriors, an inferior sword and no Bradan, while the enemy was every bit as ruthless as anything to come from the lands of the Norse.

'What are your plans, Eyota?' Chaytan asked.

About to say that he knew the enemy better, Melcorka donned her headband and allowed the power of Eyota to take over.

She closed her eyes. She heard the high piping of an oystercatcher.

'Well, here you are, Melcorka.' Bearnas smiled at her. 'No longer alone, I see, and planning big things.'

'Mother?' Melcorka said. 'How did you get here?'

'You brought me. Or rather, Eyota summoned me.' Bearnas reached out a hand and touched Melcorka's headband. 'You have come far since we last spoke, Melcorka, and you have hardly started.'

'What do you mean, Mother?'

'You are on the first step of your journey,' Bearnas said. 'You will rise further than you ever expected.' She smiled. 'Power and honour and riches can be yours.' Her smile broadened. 'And as many handsome and virile young men as you could wish for. I envy you! Any red-blooded woman would be jealous of the life you could have.'

'*Could* have?' Melcorka asked.

'You will have a choice to make, Melcorka. On the one hand is power and comfort beyond compare. On the other hand is hardship and danger. One you will find fulfilling, the other you will find empty. You will have to make that decision.'

'I made have such a choice already, Mother. I chose between luxury and the way of the warrior.'

'You chose that when you took hold of Defender. Now you have lost her and must make another choice. The road will split, and you will not see the junction until after you have taken your path.' Bearnas shook her head. 'You are losing weight, Melcorka. You have to look after yourself. You will need your stamina for all these men.'

'Mother!'

'It's all right. Nobody else can see me.' Bearnas laughed. 'Only you.'

'Mother, what do I do? These people expect me to lead them in battle.'

'Well, Melcorka, if that is what they expect, then lead them in battle.' Bearnas was still smiling. 'You make quite a formidable pair, you know.'

'I was happier with Bradan and Defender,' Melcorka said.

'I know you were.' Bearnas was no longer smiling.

'Is Bradan still with you?'

'He is with me.'

'Is he happy?' Melcorka thought of her laconic, sensible, enduring man.

Bearnas avoided that question. 'Do you wish him back?'

'Yes.'

Scarcely had that word left her lips than Melcorka found herself in a strange land. She looked around, recognising nothing. There were no landmarks, nothing on which to fix her eyes. There were clouds and serenity such as she had never experienced before. There were people all around her, yet no animosity or any other feelings of negativity. Only favourable emotions were here; a sharing of love and companionship, a desire to help.

Melcorka heard voices calling. She followed the vocal trail and saw Cahokia beneath her, with the slaves toiling under the lash. One young man was appealing to the spirits for strength to bear his load. Aching to help, Melcorka stepped down to him and lifted his burden.

'Eyota?' He breathed her name. His face shone with surprise and hope. 'Are you here to help us?'

With one hand, she lifted his burden.

'Thank you Eyota,' he said.

Melcorka touched him, feeling the strength surge from her into the exhausted slave. 'You will have the strength to bear your torment,' she said.

'Will you be back to save us?' His eyes were ablaze with love.

'I will be back,' she said and stepped into the cloud once more.

Then there was another voice and another. Melcorka knew they were prayers from a thousand different people in a thousand different lands across warm seas and frigid oceans – people with strange languages and unusual clothes, people with a thousand different cultures, yet all sharing the same desires and aspirations and fears. All were human, bound together by common blood, common nature and common suffering. She could not help them all.

'Melcorka?' The voice was distinct. 'Melcorka?'

'Bradan?' She called his name, searching for him among the shadowy figures that floated past her – the hazy, indeterminate faces and half-seen souls; the red haze of pain and the grey weariness of those who had run the race of their existence and wished only for the finishing line and the peace of death. 'Bradan – where are you?'

Then she saw him. He was lying on a litter within a poor lodge with two women caring for him. One placed some poultice on his head where the Dhegian warrior's club had left a fearful indentation. The slash across his chest was red and raised, but healing.

'You are not dead,' Melcorka said, and then Bradan was in front of her, as shady as the others in this spirit world. 'Are you dead?'

'He is with us,' Bearnas said. 'Yet he fights to remain behind in the land of mortals.'

'Can I have him here with me?' Melcorka reached for Bradan, only to see him pull back. The young woman held him close, keeping his soul and body together by the sheer desire not to allow him to die.

'You are not here to have him, Melcorka,' Bearnas said. 'Eyota is guiding you here. You are not of this spirit world. If Bradan came here, you would lose him on the physical plane.'

'I want him!' Melcorka said.

'You can help him live,' Bearnas said, 'if that is what you truly wish. If you do, he will be a different man. You may meet him, you may not. You have choices to make that could keep you apart.'

'I want him alive,' Melcorka said. 'He has too much to discover to die.'

'Are you sure?' Bearnas' voice was gentle.

'I am sure.'

'Even though your paths may not cross again? You have free will. Your choices may lead you apart.' Bearnas was close, her eyes troubled. 'Your gift of life may mean that he is lost to you forever.'

'I want him alive.' Melcorka felt her native stubbornness rise through the spiritual power of Eyota.

'Then grant him life, daughter of mine!' Bearnas altered shape. Now, she was an oystercatcher, flying around this clouded land, taking Melcorka on her wing to deposit her at the side of Bradan's bed.

'Eyota?' The young girl was even lovelier close-to, a plump-faced beauty with tears of compassion in her eyes.

'You are working to save this man,' Melcorka said. Bradan's head was a mess. The war-club had cracked the skull as well as breaking the skin. A purpling bruise spread over the side of his face, closing one eye.

'Yes, Eyota,' the girl agreed.

'Then I will help you.' Bending down, Melcorka put her hand on the ugly, seeping wound on Bradan's head. She felt the heat and the poison and applied gentle pressure. The bones were fragile beneath her fingers, grating together as she pushed. She relaxed slightly, allowing the evil to ease up into her hand. It tingled as it mixed with her love, then shrivelled and died. She shook it off with an exclamation of disgust and returned her hand. She could feel the shattered edges of bone and eased them together, pressing until they fused. The physical, Melcorka knew she could cure; any mental damage, she knew she could not.

'He will live now,' Melcorka said. 'What is your name?'

'I am Ehawee – it means Laughing Maiden.'

'It is a good name, Ehawee.' Melcorka touched her forehead. There was no long future there. Best not say that. 'You will get a good man, Ehawee, and bear many fine babies.'

She touched Bradan again. She did not wish to leave him, knowing that she may never see him again, but she had another life to live apart from her own. Desperately sad, she bent over and kissed him and then she was back in the spirit world, the oystercatcher was piping, and she opened her eyes.

'How long was I away?'

'Away where?' Chaytan asked. 'You have not moved, Eyota. You blinked, and here you are.'

Melcorka nodded. Time in the spirit world, as with the People of Peace in Alba, was different from time in the physical realm. However long she had been with Bearnas, she had returned less than an instant after she left.

'What would you have us do, Eyota?'

The words came unbidden to Melcorka's mouth. 'Gather the tribes,' she said. 'Call the chiefs together. If Wamblee knows what we are doing, then we must act quickly. We will give them war – blood-red war such as they have never seen before!' She saw the delight in Chaytan's face and the anxiety in Chumani's. 'Have faith, Chumani,' she said. 'War is an obscenity, but the result will justify the means.'

Melcorka hoped she was correct. Eyota did not have any doubts.

Chapter Eighteen

They gathered where three white oak trees cast a long shadow over a hollow in the ground. The warriors came in single file, threading through the trees or trotting across the grasslands of the prairie. They came in tens and dozens and scores; the tribes had sent their young men to war.

With painted faces and bodies, with feathers and beads, with loincloths flapping above muscular thighs, and carrying spears, war-clubs or bow and arrows, the fighting men collected around the three white oaks.

Sometimes the young men snarled at each other as the rival tribes squabbled over ancient grievances, but always they looked to the three people who waited under the three white oaks, and they were quietened without bloodshed. On the left was Chumani, serene of face whatever she felt like inside. On the right sat Chaytan, chief of the Lakota, impassive and massive, knowing his tribe was behind him whatever he decided to do. In the centre, Melcorka sat cross-legged and silent, watching Eyota's people gather. *Her* people now. She sat still, unmoving, waiting for her time.

After two days, there were eight hundred warriors crowded around, waiting for her word. And Eyota's word was: 'Wait'.

After three days, there were twelve hundred warriors crowded around, waiting for her word. And Eyota's word was: 'Wait'.

After five days ,there were two thousand warriors crowded around, waiting for her word. And Eyota's word was: 'Wait'.

After seven days, there were three thousand warriors crowded around, waiting for her word. And Eyota's word was: 'Wait'.

And all the time, Chaytan was busy from his seat under the three white oaks, sending out messengers, sending out scouts; gathering information from every town and village in the Dhegian Empire; watching the Mississippi and the other rivers; watching for Wamblee's response, waiting for retaliation, waiting for Eyota's word.

After ten days, the three thousand five hundred warriors crowded around, impatient for Eyota's words. And Eyota's words were: 'Isolate Cahokia.'

The war parties filed out, four companies of three hundred men. One ran to the north of the city, one to the west, one to the east and one to the south. They moved fast, and they moved ruthlessly. They attacked the Dhegian patrols and annihilated all they caught. They wiped out the men in the Border posts. They destroyed the supplies for the outer garrisons and established patrols. Each troop linked together so they knew what was happening and all the information they gathered was passed back to Eyota under her three white oaks.

Melcorka listened to the reports and nodded, allowing Eyota to analyse what was said.

There were casualties. The Dhegian Empire sent out fighting patrols and clashed with the tribal war parties. Sometimes the Dhegians scored successes, but because Eyota had ensured that the tribal patrols were linked, they could offer mutual support and either outnumber the Dhegian patrols, or melt into the terrain if the numbers were against them.

'Many of us are doing nothing,' the remaining warriors said. They crowded around the three white oaks, impatient for Eyota's words.

'Build rafts,' Eyota said. 'And cut smooth logs.'

They built rafts and cut logs as Eyota had ordered. And they waited for her words. And her word was: 'Wait'.

After three weeks, the Dhegians had realised what was happening and had strengthened their own patrols outside the walls of Cahokia. There were more intense and daily clashes between the tribal war parties and the forces of the Empire. Intelligence came to Eyota that Wamblee was gathering his Dhegians. The warriors waited for her word.

'Increase our patrols,' she said. 'Allow the large parties to get through. Destroy those that we can attack without casualties. Bleed their numbers without losing more of our warriors.'

Within two days, the tribes had eased the flow of Dhegians into and out of Cahokia. Only large war parties were getting through. The tribes waited for Eyota's words.

'Cut the crops,' Eyota said. 'Hide the food in caches far from the city. Ensure the Dhegian war parties cannot get food on their way to Cahokia. Make them weak with hunger.'

'Wamblee will be angry,' Chaytan said.

'I am counting on his anger.' Melcorka continued to sit under the three white oaks. 'Anger impairs judgement.'

The warriors crowded around, knowing they were striking at the Empire, wanting to do more. They waited for Eyota's word.

And her words were: 'Use the logs as rollers. Transport the rafts to the river bank upstream of Cahokia. There will be no Dhegians to see you now.'

Nodding at Eyota's wisdom, the tribes did as they were bid. They used the Norse technique of transporting ships across land to bring the rafts to the banks of the Mississippi, and they left them there under cover.

The rain started again, hammering at the land, battering at the lodges and pyramids and mounds within the great city of Cahokia, raising the level of the Mississippi, making the sentries miserable on the walls and ensuring the patrols trudged through ankle-deep mud as they watched for the enemy.

Melcorka remained beneath the three white oaks, listening to every report and allowing Eyota to analyse them and make whatever decision she thought necessary. The rain did not concern her; she was inside her head, so the discomforts of the physical were irrelevant.

Leaving a strong guard around the rafts, the tribal warriors returned to the three white oaks and waited for Eyota's words. She looked upward, where clouds were gathering in a grey premonition of more rain to come. The warriors crowded around, knowing that things were happening and that Eyota had a plan to save their world. They waited for her words, and now Eyota stood up from beneath the shelter of the three white oaks. She stretched herself after so long and looked over her people. They waited for Eyota's words, and she spoke to them in a voice that could have come from the spirit world, it was so cold and hollow.

'One thousand warriors are to board the rafts and sail downstream. You will enter Cahokia by the river's edge, where there are no defences. You will move through the town toward the Citadel. You will keep together and destroy any Dhegian force that is sent against you. You will not attack the Citadel, but you will ensure that nobody from inside it escapes.'

Nodding assent, Chaytan chose the tribes who were to take part in the waterborne assault.

'Five hundred men will remain outside Cahokia. You will ensure no reinforcements come into the city and that nobody leaves to summon help.'

Chaytan chose the tribes for that unpopular task.

'The rest of you will follow Chaytan and me. We will march into the city and take the Citadel. Wamblee will send the best of his army against us. There will be severe fighting.'

The warriors did not look unduly concerned at the prospect of a tough fight. They grinned and nudged each other, raised their stone-headed axes and clubs and boasted of the great deeds that they would do and the Dhegian blood that they would spill.

'When do we go?' Chaytan asked.

'The men of the river assault will leave here when the moon is at its apex. The men on patrols are already there; reinforce them. I will lead the main attack when the moon begins to fade.' Melcorka looked upward. 'This cloud cover will ease tonight and return tomorrow morning. By the time the heavy rains recommence, we will be inside Cahokia and then only God, or the gods, will be able to help us.'

With her orders given, Melcorka retired to her lodge. After so long without food and proper rest, she was exhausted, for although Eyota was immune from human frailties, Melcorka was not. She collapsed without a word and slept, and was only vaguely aware of the handsome, bare-chested man who looked over her.

Chapter Nineteen

'Eyota.' Chumani kept her distance, still treating her with great respect. 'Eyota, it is time.'

Melcorka sat up on the pile of rugs. She looked around, dazed, wishing she could sleep for another hour at least. At this time of the morning she was at her lowest; irritable, tired and more depressed than she had felt for a long time. Why did she not just say that she was Melcorka, not Eyota, and allow these people to fight their own war? After all, she was not much older than Chumani; an island girl caught up in affairs that were well beyond her ken.

'*Because you are needed! Now go and do your duty!*' Bearnas voice was clear and crisp inside her head.

'Yes, Mother,' she replied automatically and rose. If duty meant death, then that was an end to all her troubles.

'Eyota?' Chumani held out a bowl of food and a gourd of milk.

Breakfast always made Melcorka feel better. She ate and drank without relish, fuelling her body more than enjoying the hurried meal. All the same, the fresh energy coursed through her. 'Thank you, Chumani,' she said. 'What would I do without you?'

'I am your servant, Eyota,' Chumani said.

'You are my friend,' Melcorka contradicted her. 'Now, let's get these armies on the move and settle with Wamblee once and for all.'

'The first army is long gone,' Chumani said. 'The river warriors. I thought it best to let you sleep rather than wake you.'

About to say that she would have liked to wish them luck, Melcorka nodded instead. 'Thank you, Chumani. You did well.' There was no point in rebuking the girl for something well-meant that could not be changed.

Stumbling out of the lodge, she reached for the headband and slipped it onto her head. Immediately she did so, her mind cleared, her eyes focussed and this place and these people were alien no longer. She was at home with them.

'Come, warriors!' she heard herself shout. 'This is no time to lie mumbling and snoring within your furs! Arise and take your weapons! Chiefs and war captains, gather your men together. It is time to remove this great evil that has descended on our lands!'

As Melcorka had spoken, she walked forward, confident that the tribes would follow her. Without looking behind her, she altered from a slow walk to a fast march and then to a trot, feeling the ground shake as her army followed, each man in the midst of his tribe and each tribe in the place that Chaytan had allotted it. Eyota may be good at rousing speeches, raising morale and the overall strategy of the war, but Chaytan was the tactician who knew the weaknesses and strengths of each tribe, and how to woo the chiefs into fighting for the cause. He was the glue and the sinews that fused the muscle and bone into a single entity.

The leader of an Oglala patrol stepped aside as Melcorka ran past. She heard him shouting encouragement, with his men joining in, and then she was trotting through the outskirts of Cahokia with some of the inhabitants running before her and others staring or standing to cheer and a few even hurrying to join her.

'To the Citadel!' somebody shouted, and others took up the cry until the entire army was roaring the words.

This is too easy, Melcorka told herself. *Where are the defenders? Where are the Dhegian warriors?*

As if in answer, the first arrow thrummed past her. The second hit the ground at her feet. but at such a low trajectory that it bounced and skiffed harmlessly through the grass. Then came a dozen more and Melcorka saw the small Dhegian force that tried to bar her path. The Dhegian warriors stepped forward bravely and pulled back their bowstrings as a single unit. Each man aimed at Melcorka. She felt vulnerable; never had she missed Defender as much as she did at that moment.

Instead, she increased her pace and shouted, 'I am Eyota of Cahokia!'

She saw two of the bowmen flinch. A third released prematurely so his arrow fell short and a fourth dropped with a Mohawk spear transfixing his chest. The remainder stood their ground, aiming directly at her.

They fired. Melcorka saw the flight of arrows as if in slow motion and increased her speed yet again. One arrow grazed her left arm; another ripped her loin cloth and then she was among them, with the captured Norse sword in her hand. It was no Defender, but she swung it right and left, feeling the jar of contact and hearing the gasp of a brave man in pain. She ran on, only dimly aware of the brief clash of contact and the yells as her army trampled the archers and ran on.

Now the streets were more tightly packed, with alleyways between the houses where Dhegian warriors waited in ambush. Spears and arrows flew in both directions, and the advance slowed as the allied tribes stopped to take revenge, or men dropped, wounded or dead.

'This will take longer than I thought,' Chaytan said.

'We will continue to the Citadel,' Melcorka said. 'Stick to the plan.'

'These are not elite Dhegian warriors,' Chaytan observed, as he casually felled a man with his war club. 'They are ordinary soldiers, armed tribesmen and the like. The real test is ahead.' He glanced over his shoulder. 'Yet we are already bleeding men. By the time we reach the Citadel, there may not be enough of us to defeat the Wall Guard and the Citadel Guard.'

'Eyota knows what she is doing,' Chumani said.

'So does your father.' Melcorka ducked as a spear whistled past her head. 'He is as good a warrior as any I have ever encountered.'

'We can leave the bulk of the warriors to fight their way through the streets,' Chaytan said. 'You and I and my Lakotas will forge ahead and kill Wamblee. Once he is dead, the Dhegians will have no reason to fight.'

'Who will command these warriors?' Melcorka asked.

'Hotah of the Oglala,' Chaytan said at once. 'He is a good man, Eyota.'

'Then that is what we shall do,' Melcorka agreed.

Hotah was quite happy to be in charge of the bulk of the army. He gave his orders. 'Kill the Dhegians! Chase them into extinction and push forward to the Citadel.'

'Come, Chaytan.' Melcorka unfastened her sword belt and let it fall to the ground. 'I have my sword. I have thrown away the scabbard. I will not sheath my sword again until Wamblee is dead, or I am.'

'You cannot die, you are Eyota,' Chumani said.

'Eyota cannot die,' Melcorka agreed. 'Melcorka, the woman whose body she is using, is as mortal as anybody else in this city.'

Chumani frowned. 'I do not understand. Are you Eyota, or are you Melcorka?'

'I am both,' Melcorka said and smiled. 'And I don't understand it, either. Now, come on.'

Holding the Norse sword in her right hand, she ran forward. She could not see the future. She did not think she would survive. It did not matter. Bradan was alive, and her duty was to help these people remove a tyrant. What was death but just another step? She would see her mother again.

A group of Dhegian warriors ran toward them, clubs upraised. Chaytan roared his war cry, and a score of Oglalas charged the Dhegians. Leaving them to fight it out, Melcorka ran on, heading for the Citadel and ignoring anybody who was not directly in her path. She heard the hellish noise of battle behind her, the crack of stone clubs on bone, the groans and screams of the injured and the triumphant yells of the victors.

'There is the Citadel!' Chaytan said.

The great mound dominated the city, with the Wall Guards prominent every few steps along the defending stockade. Their spear-points glinted in the moonlight, a warning that they were alert and waiting for the coming assault.

'We are the Lakota!' Chaytan raised his voice. 'We go right over the wall and into the Citadel. The other tribes will follow soon.'

There was a sudden uproar from the other side of the mound, a rising sound that included war cries and the clamour of battle.

'The river warriors have arrived,' Melcorka said, with satisfaction. 'Now the defenders are split into two sections, and the Wall Guards will have to watch all around.'

'We still have the Citadel Guards to face,' Chaytan reminded her.

'I remember,' Melcorka said quietly. The Norse sword felt very clumsy in her hand.

The Wall Guards were restless, some peering toward the main tribal army and others shifting to look over their shoulders at this new noise behind them.

'The attack from the river has distracted them,' Chaytan said. 'Follow me!'

Rather than run, as Melcorka had expected, Chaytan stepped forward slowly, so he did not attract immediate attention. The Lakota swarmed up the lower slopes of the mound to the first terrace, where they halted for a few moments to gather strength for the next stage.

'This time, we go right over the wall and onto the Citadel,' Chaytan said.

The Lakotas nodded, holding up their clubs and spears. Their war-painted faces were like a hundred hawks and their eyes gleamed with battle lust. Melcorka gripped her sword, felt a mixture of fear and excitement and waited for Chaytan to give the word.

'Follow me and remember that Eyota is with us,' Chaytan said. His sudden grin took Melcorka by surprise. 'Some people would say that this is a good day to die. I think that this is a good day to win!'

The Lakota laughed.

Chaytan rose, took a deep breath and ran up the steep slope as if he was a youth of twenty rather than a man with a daughter of that age. 'Hokahey!'

It was the first time that Melcorka had heard the Lakota war cry. It sounded good to her ears. She repeated it: 'Hokahey!'

Chaytan was already at the base of the stockade, his powerful figure clambering up the log and dirt barrier.

Melcorka followed. She was no longer scared; rather, she felt a sense of elation, as if she were fulfilling her destiny. Was that her own emotion, or that of Eyota? She could not tell. She only knew how she felt as she scrambled up that steep, grassy slope to the base of the palisade.

The last time she had been here, silence was necessary. Now, there was noise and confusion all around, with the Lakota yelling their war-cry and the Wall Guards shouting back. A spear whizzed past her, to transfix a Lakota warrior. The man fell back, plucking at this thing that protruded from his chest. Another spear followed, and another, each one transfixing a Lakota warrior. The ranks of the Lakota were thinning as bodies piled up at the base of the palisade. The assault was already in difficulty.

Chaytan lifted his club. 'With me, Lakotas! Hokahey!'

'Hokahey!' the Lakota yelled in unison and, buttressed by their war cry, they threw themselves at the palisade.

A Wall Guard threw his spear directly at Chaytan, who deflected it with his club, reached up, grabbed the man by the throat and hauled him face down among the Lakota, who finished him off with a flurry of blows. First over the palisade, Chaytan swept aside another of the black-and-white-faced guards and helped Melcorka over. She found she was trembling, yet managed a shaky smile.

'Hokahey,' she said weakly.

'Hokahey,' Chaytan replied with a grin and ran along the parapet to close with the defenders. More of the Lakota swarmed up the wall and fanned out left and right to grapple with the Wall Guard.

'Get close!' Melcorka shouted. 'That way, they can't throw their spears.'

The Citadel lay before them, with its barracks and large buildings, its wide roads and the palace where Wamblee lived.

Melcorka stopped at Chaytan's elbow. 'Leave your Lakota to deal with the Wall Guard. We must go to the head of the snake himself.'

Bathed in Dhegian blood, Chaytan did not hear her. He dodged the thrust of a Wall Guard spear and swung his club underhand, catching the guard a shrewd blow in the groin before finishing him off with a mighty crack to the skull.

'Chaytan! On to Wamblee! Your men can clean up the rubbish!'

Chaytan looked round, bleeding from a cut to his arm and his eyes dazed with the lust for fighting.

'Come on, Chaytan. Hokahey!'

'Hokahey,' Chaytan mouthed, and followed Melcorka down a steep flight of steps that led from the parapet to the interior of the Citadel. Melcorka heard others following her, but did not look round to see who they were.

'Eyota.' Melcorka had not seen Chumani in the assault. She was at her side, pointing forward. 'The Citadel Guard.'

They stood in an oblong block; one hundred of the finest warriors in the continent, with their falcon-feathered headdresses nodding in the faint breeze and their faces set and grim. With spears strapped diagonally across their backs, oblong shields held on left arms and a stone-headed mace in their right hands, they looked as formidable a body of fighting men as any Melcorka had seen.

A captain stepped in front and raised his right hand. Immediately, each man of the Citadel Guard took a single pace to the left and they began to beat their shields with their maces in a rhythmic *thrum-thrum-thrum* that echoed around the Citadel.

'Hokahey!'

The cry came from behind Melcorka. She saw a group of young Lakota braves charge forward, yelling.

'No!' Chaytan's order was disregarded as the young men ran at the Citadel Guard. They may as well have tried to break down a granite cliff. With high courage, they threw themselves forward, only for the guards to raise their shields and block the wild swings of the Lakota clubs. The Lakota tried again and failed again. The Citadel Guard captain gave a single word of command, and the Guard swung their clubs, each man aiming for the Lakota warrior on his right, striking the unguarded side of their opponent. Every Lakota fell, and the second rank of the guard finished them with their spears. The captain gave another single-word order, and the Citadel Guard returned to their original position. They had not lost a man.

'That was impressive,' Melcorka said, inwardly comparing these men with the Picts of Fidach she had fought beside in Alba. 'These Guardsmen are soldiers, not warriors. They fight as a unit.'

'It will be a hard job to get past them,' Chaytan said.

'We need somebody with their level of discipline,' Chumani said.

'How do we find them?' Chaytan ducked as a Wall Guard threw a spear at him. 'Or perhaps we can conjure them out of the ground?' He looked at Melcorka as if expecting her to produce a miracle.

'I might know,' Chumani said.

'You?' Chaytan laughed. 'You are an excellent daughter, but even you cannot create soldiers like the Citadel Guard!'

He was speaking to himself for Chumani had already disappeared.

'We can't stand here watching,' Melcorka said. 'We must do something.' She was not sure what. If she had Bradan here, he would give sage advice. If she had Defender, she would charge forward and slice through the Citadel Guard. As it was, she was alone with five score disciplined warriors barring her path to Wamblee. She took a deep breath and prepared to order her small band to unleash a volley of spears.

'There they are!' That was Chumani's voice. 'There are the men who stole your wives! They are bedding them even now, while the tribes slaughter the Wall Guard and you face the Lakota! See the lust on their bloated faces.'

Melcorka gave a grim smile. Chumani was addressing the Citadel Guard and pointing to the barrack hut that held the Veterans. She had opened the massive front doors so the interior was exposed and the Citadel Guard could see the middle-aged men ignoring the fighting as they concentrated on love-making with the nubile young women they had taken only a few weeks before.

'Chumani has a brain in her head,' Melcorka said. 'Look at the Citadel Guard.'

Trained to fight for Wamblee, the men of the Citadel Guard were still unhappy about losing their women. While most continued to watch the tribes battling with the Wall Guard, a significant number had turned to watch the Veterans.

'Now's our chance,' Melcorka said. 'Chumani has disrupted their ranks.'

'Hokahey!' Chaytan lifted his war-club.

There was an answering yell of 'Hokahey' from behind him and then a greater, less uniform shout from a hundred throats as at last, the united tribes poured over the palisade in the gap the Lakota had made.

Chaytan led the charge, with some of the Lakota joining them and the front runners of the united tribes bunching behind them. Chumani's distraction had given them just enough opportunity for the Citadel Guard to waver and, with the disciplined front disrupted, Chaytan's men crashed into their ranks.

Melcorka thrust forward with her sword, felt the jar as a Guard parried with his shield, hauled it back for a slash and realised that the wickerwork of the Dhegian shield had trapped her blade. The Guard glared in triumph and twisted his shield sideways to try and knock the sword from Melcorka's grasp.

'Oh God for Defender,' Melcorka said. 'Is this where I die?'

The guard pulled his shield down hard to disarm her, lifted his club and shouted some death cry.

'You are a leader, not a warrior, Eyota!' An unknown Oglala warrior pushed past her and stabbed upward with his flint-bladed knife. 'Let us do the fighting!' He yelled his war cry 'Hokahey!' and pushed on.

'He is right, Eyota,' Chaytan said. 'Leave the Guards to the warriors. We have more important people to kill.' Grabbing hold of Melcorka, he pushed her out of the fighting and sideways, toward the palace that glowered down upon the Citadel. 'Here!' He retrieved the Norse sword and threw it to her. 'You may need this.'

Battling warriors filled the streets as the united tribes pushed over the palisade and the Wall Guards and Citadel Guards combined to shove them back. As Melcorka watched, the Veterans filed out of their barracks, no longer interested in carnal pleasures as they formed a third disciplined block and ripped into the tribes. Chumani's ploy had worked to an extent, but now there were another fifty experienced defenders facing them.

'Come on, Eyota.' Chaytan guided her through the streets, felling any Guard who got in his way. 'We cannot linger here.'

There was a flight of stairs to the palace entrance, with statues of various deities at every fourth step and a great, round-headed door at the top, which was firmly shut. Chaytan took the steps three at a time, swinging his club.

The door held under his assault. Roaring in frustration, he tried again, battering at the solid wood without any effect.

'Wamblee will sit inside there in perfect safety,' he said, 'until the fighting is done.'

Melcorka glanced over her shoulder. All three sections of the Guards had merged and were pushing back the tribes. Their line of shields was intact, and their spearmen were stabbing and thrusting, killing and wounding the tribesmen. They had formed a ring around the palace, with the water warriors now joined with the main assault, so the Citadel was a mass of battling men. 'We have to get in,' she said. 'If the tribes are defeated, then Wamblee will take a terrible revenge on them.'

'He will sacrifice all that he captures,' Chaytan said, 'and enslave the world between the Mississippi and the great sea.'

Melcorka glanced upward, where the walls soared toward the sky. 'That's our way,' she said, remembering how she had climbed the outside of the Osprey's broch in Alba, so many months ago. 'Up the wall to the roof.'

'Nobody has ever tried to climb that before,' Chaytan said.

'Then we must be the first.'

Thrusting her sword through the waistband of her linen leine and hoping it would not cut her in half, Melcorka found a handhold and pulled herself up. The wall was so well built that there were only tiny cracks where each solid rectangle of masonry joined the next. However, there was sufficient room for the very tips of Melcorka's fingers or the ends of her toes. Used to climbing the cliffs of her island home for bird's eggs, Melcorka made rapid progress, yet before she was a quarter of the way up, her muscles were begging for relief.

'I can't go on.' Chaytan's voice came from far below. 'I am not built for climbing.'

'Then try the door,' Melcorka shouted. 'I will go alone.'

The wall continued above her, stretching smooth and featureless, without a window to break the monotony. Melcorka forced herself onward and upward, inch by agonising inch as her fingers and calves screamed for rest.

There was a battlement at the top, with an embrasure through which Melcorka almost fell. She lay on a wooden surface, gasping in pain and exhaustion as she sought to regain her breath before her next step, whatever that might be. She had hoped that Eyota would have some idea how to proceed, yet there was no guidance, nothing but the thoughts that raced through her head.

Something sharp prodded her back. Melcorka looked up, reaching for her sword. 'There's no need for that,' a familiar voice said. 'Stand up.'

Erik poked the point of his sword into her back again. 'Somebody wants to see you.' His grin was familiar and unwelcome. 'You may as well see her before you die.'

Chapter Twenty

Rough hands lifted her. Rough Norse voices grated in her ear, laughing as they shoved her towards a small doorway. Unsure what to think, Melcorka could do nothing but obey. Eyota was persuasive among the tribes but her power did not affect these aliens in her land.

Two storeys down, Erik pushed her into a large chamber where half a dozen people sat on large chairs, with the remaining Norse lounging in one corner, joking as they sharpened their swords and axes. At the outside of the main group were Wamblee's two bodyguards, with Wamblee in between them. At his side, smiling softly, sat Frakkok, with Defender strapped diagonally across her back.

'Here she is.' Erik threw Melcorka onto the ground at Wamblee's feet.

'You have caused me some trouble.' Wamblee's voice rumbled like distant thunder. 'You have killed many of my people and caused discontent among the subservient tribes.'

Melcorka rose to her feet. Surrounded by enemies, she had nothing to offer but defiance and courage. 'You are a tyrant, Wamblee, and your rule is coming to an end. Even as we speak, the armies of the allied tribes are destroying your armies in the city. Your Guards are dying in droves, and this palace will soon fall.'

Wamblee shook with laughter. 'You could hardly be more wrong, Melcorka. My men have held the advance of your rebel tribes, my

Guards are clearing the intruders from the Citadel, and you are the only rebel to enter my fortress.' He leaned closer to Melcorka. 'Soon, my priests will be busy sacrificing the leaders of the rebels. All their men will be my slaves and my Guards will have the pick of their women.'

'And this one? Frakkok said. Her gaze was as poisonous as any reptile. 'I want her, Wamblee. I have an old score to settle with Melcorka of the Cenel Bearnas.'

'*You!*' Melcorka lunged at Frakkok, only for Arne to stop her with a brawny right arm. 'How can you join this monster, Frakkok? It was his men who destroyed your settlement in Greenland. He killed your people!'

Frakkok shook her head. 'Oh, you foolish, naïve little girl. How little you know and how little you understand. I came west overseas to seek a man like Wamblee. Do you think I would be content with a puny little village like Frakkoksfjord? I want a man of power – I want a man like Wamblee! It was I who destroyed that insignificant village, so my men had nowhere to return to. They had to go on until I found a man worthy of my first husband.'

Melcorka stared at her. 'You killed your own followers so you could snare a powerful man?'

'I am Frakkok of the Cet. I was queen in Caithness until a bold sea raider took me to wife. He won my body in battle and my heart in bed. He was all man, and all mine until you killed him, Melcorka.'

'If I killed him, it must have been in a fair fight,' Melcorka said. 'And to die in battle is the preferred fate of any true warrior.'

Frakkok stepped closer and spat in Melcorka's face. 'You murdered him by the Standing Stones of Callanish. Now do you remember him?'

The memories surged back like a Hebridean tide. The grand avenue of sacred stones in the island of Lewis; the evil Morrigan with her crows; the death of Hector; the Shining One approaching in his fiery chariot; the battle against the giant Norseman who had killed Bearnas.

'Egil,' Melcorka said softly. 'You are the wife of Egil, who killed my mother and all my people.'

Melcorka stared at her in understanding. No wonder Frakkok had hated her from the onset. As soon as Frakkok heard her name, she would know that she was the one who had killed her husband.

'I am the widow of Egil,' Frakkok said.

'I am the daughter of Bearnas.'

'You may have this woman,' Wamblee said.

Frakkok's smile was not pleasant. 'I thought it was you the moment we met at sea,' she said. 'I waited and listened to everything you said. I saw you with your magic sword,' she touched the hilt of Defender, 'now *my* magic sword, and I knew who you were.'

'Egil deserved to die,' Melcorka said. 'I am not sorry I killed him.'

'I will make you sorry,' Frakkok said. 'I will kill you inch by inch over many days, until you howl and beg for a merciful death.'

Her words gave Melcorka a flicker of hope. 'You wish to kill me in revenge then? You want to kill me to avenge the death of Egil?'

The words were clear in Melcorka's mind, and the voice belonged to Bearnas. '*Defender cannot be used in revenge or for personal gain.*'

She had been warned before. It was unlikely that Frakkok was aware of that restriction in Defender's power.

Frakkok frowned. 'I thought I had made that clear.'

Melcorka heard her mother's voice again.

'*You have three weapons, Melcorka. You have Defender; you have your life experience and skills; and you have your brains. You must choose which one is best suited to which task and utilise it to the full.*'

She no longer had Defender, and her life experience and skills were no use here. It was time to use her brain.

Melcorka straightened her back so she stood erect. She faced Frakkok and laughed loudly. 'What a pathetic old woman you are! You are seeking revenge when you should be thanking me! Did you not know that Egil was sleeping with every woman he came across? Do you not realise that he abandoned your daughter, if she was yours, to be killed by mermaids? Did you not know he was with an ugly old hag when I killed him?' she laughed again. 'A hag even uglier than you, and maybe as old.'

Melcorka saw Frakkok's face darken with anger. That was good. That was the reaction she wished for.

'Did you forget about your daughter Alva, Frakkok? Is she yours, or did she come from another of Egil's many women?' Melcorka could feel the tension in that room as all eyes were on her and Frakkok. They were waiting for a reaction, either physical or verbal.

'I'll have your tongue cut out,' Frakkok said.

'Of course, you will.' Melcorka stepped forward, pushing her face into that of Frakkok. 'You will have somebody fight your battles for you. A man perhaps? That is why you run to a strong man such as Wamblee, isn't it? You need a strong man because you are too weak to fight yourself. Look at you!' Melcorka injected scorn to her voice. 'You are hiding behind a dozen men, afraid to face me even when I am disarmed and alone. You are a coward, Frakkok, not fit to be in the company of real women, and certainly not fit to be Wamblee's wife.'

Melcorka saw a slight change of expression in Wamblee's face. She did not know much about these people yet, but Eyota did. She allowed Eyota to take control of her mind for a moment, probing to discover the best way to achieve her objective.

'You have three weapons, Melcorka. You have Defender; you have your life experience and skills; and you have your brains. You must choose which one is best suited to which task and utilise it to the full.'

Once again, she recalled her mother's words, and then Eyota's insight flooded her. Wamblee was a large man with a hunger for power. He was also vain. Looking at him, Melcorka could see indications of his vanity – the huge chair he sat on, the magnificent falcon's feathers he wore, the splendid jewellery, the tabard which was decorated with thousands of these little shells his people valued so highly. He wore far more valuables than any other man in this city. Not only that, but he was scared, hiding himself away in this magnificent palace set within a Citadel, with hundreds of guards sworn to defend him at all costs and with two huge bodyguards always present.

The impressions raced through Melcorka's mind one after the other, so quickly that she barely had time to analyse one before the next took its place.

'You are a fine figure of a man, Wamblee.' Melcorka injected admiration into her voice. 'I have never met a more manly man.'

She held his gaze, smiling. 'Do you honestly want to be with this woman, who was so poor a wife that her last husband had to find comfort with another woman? Do you honestly wish to be with a woman who is too old to bear you any sons?' Melcorka pointed to Frakkok and laughed. 'Look at her! A dried up old hag!'

One of the bodyguards chuckled as Wamblee smiled.

'Do you think she is better in bed than me?' Melcorka threw out the challenge. 'Or would defend you in battle? She is old and broken and scared. I am young and virile, and I am not afraid of you, or your bodyguards, or of anybody else in your kingdom. Especially not of some haggard old Pictish woman!'

There; she had thrown the dice. Melcorka stepped back, still holding Wamblee's gaze.

'She led the army that attacked you,' Frakkok said. 'Have her killed.'

'It takes skill to raise an army and an enemy one day can be a friend the next.' Wamblee rose from his throne. 'You are indeed a beautiful woman, but too dangerous to live.' He waved his hand in dismissal. 'Kill her, Frakkok, I have given you leave.'

Frakkok's smile was one of pure malice. 'You are wise, Wamblee. You heard the king, Erik. Kill the Alban.'

'Mother...' Erik glanced at Frakkok, over to Melcorka and back.

'Do it!' Frakkok slapped him hard across the face. He flinched.

'Hold!' Wamblee held up a hand. 'I did not tell Erik to kill her. I ordered you to do so, Frakkok. Kill her yourself, here and now.'

Melcorka saw the sudden shock on the face of Frakkok. That was good. 'Come on then, Frakkok,' she challenged. 'Let's see if you can do something yourself, rather than expecting others to do all the work for you.' She stepped back.

'You have three weapons, Melcorka. You have Defender; you have your life experience and skills; and you have your brains.'

Her brains had earned her a quicker death rather than one by torture. That was a definite gain. They had also earned her a slim opportunity of life; she might be able to defeat Frakkok in a straightforward fight, although that was not likely. Frakkok was middle-aged and tough as bull-leather; she had not risen to command a settlement by being nice. She had also been Egil's wife, which must temper any woman to the constitution of iron.

'You are old and slow, Frakkok. I am young and agile. I will kill you before you can even come close.'

Taunt her, mock her. Cause her to lose her temper and her judgement. Melcorka smiled as Frakkok bounced to her feet with Defender still strapped securely to her back.

'I'll tear you apart, Melcorka.'

'Only with your mouth, Frakkok!'

Melcorka landed the first blow, a stinging, open-handed slap that was meant to convey contempt rather than a serious attempt to injure. She heard Frakkok gasp and laughed. 'You are good at hitting your son, but not so good when it is you receiving the blow.' She slapped her again, harder, hoping for a reaction. Both the bodyguards laughed.

'I ordered you to kill her, Frakkok,' Wamblee roared, 'I did not say let her beat you!' His laughter rumbled around the stone chamber.

'Kill her.' Egil appeared, shrouded in dark mist. 'Kill her slowly.' He had the same braided hair, the same tattooed face and the same sword and axe that he had used in life. Except now he was dead and emerging from Helheim, the Norse underworld. Behind him, Melcorka saw a giant female, partly coloured blue, partly the colour of European flesh, with a dour, unhappy face. That was Hel herself, watching over her protégé.

Melcorka stepped back. 'I was never afraid of you in life, Egil, and I am not scared of you in death.'

Egil spat his hatred from Helheim. 'You sent me here. Now you will join me for eternity.' Lifting his arm, he took hold of Frakkok's hand and raked her claws across Melcorka's face, attempting to blind her. Melcorka jerked back as all the audience roared their approval. 'That's better, Frakkok,' Wamblee shouted. 'Rip her eyes out!' Melcorka felt the slow blood drip from her face. She knew that the watchers could not see Egil. To them, this was a straightforward fight between two women and all the more enjoyable for its novelty.

Frakkok raked again, stepping forward, forcing Melcorka to retreat step by stubborn step, knowing that there was a wall behind her and after that there was no more space. The crowd was cheering, demanding Melcorka's blood, encouraging Frakkok to go forward.

Egil was at Frakkok's shoulder, whispering in her ear. Reaching around her, he took hold of both her arms. While Frakkok's right hand formed into raking claws, her left bunched into a fist. She feinted with the right; Melcorka dodged left, and Frakkok's fist smashed into her temple. Stunned, she slumped to the stone-flagged floor as the audience yelled in delight.

'Cripple her, Frakkok!' Wamblee roared. 'Hurt her bad! Make her suffer and squeal.' He leaned forward on his throne, enjoying the fun.

As she stepped on Melcorka's ankle and twisted her heel, Frakkok seemed determined to do as Wamblee wanted. She was smiling now, grinding her heel into Melcorka's flesh, trying to break bones and tear tendons. 'Stay down, Melcorka, so that I can kill you slowly!'

Biting her lip against the pain, Melcorka suddenly jerked her leg clear, rolled over and tried to rise, only for Frakkok to kick her full in the face. Melcorka yelped and fell backwards. Frakkok kicked her again, in the stomach, ribs and groin.

The audience was laughing now, loving Melcorka's pain.

'Get up.' The words were an order. 'Get up and fight back. You are the daughter of Bearnas. You are of warrior blood.'

'Mother?' Melcorka looked up through a film of blood.

'Get up! You don't need a sword to fight!'

That was more a rebuke than an encouragement.

Bearnas stood behind her, dressed in her full regalia of a Celtic warrior, with chain mail armour, a winged helmet, and a long sword. She faced Egil across the width of the chamber. 'Leave my daughter alone!'

Egil laughed. 'I killed you, Bearnas, and I will kill the last of your seed.'

'You struck me from behind when I was fighting two of your men,' Bearnas said. 'You are a coward, Egil.'

'Watch your daughter die,' Egil taunted. 'And then I will welcome her to Helheim, where I will torment her for eternity!' Reaching out, he took hold of Frakkok's leg, lifted it and stomped her foot hard onto Melcorka's chest. 'Watch her suffer, Bearnas! Watch her suffer and die!'

'Fight, Melcorka! Get up and fight!' Stepping forward, Bearnas thrust her fingers hard against Egil's throat. 'Fight!' The Norseman staggered back, leaving Frakkok alone.

Without Egil to guide her, Frakkok was less sure. Her next kick was undirected. It bounced off Melcorka's hip without doing any damage.

'Is that it?' Melcorka forced a laugh, tasting blood in her mouth. Rolling over, she pushed herself upright. Frakkok closed, and her kick missed completely. Taking hold of Frakkok's foot, Melcorka lifted it high and pushed backwards, unbalancing the older woman, so she fell on her back with a resounding thump. The audience roared with glee.

Melcorka realised that they did not hate her, they did not particularly wish to see her die, they just wanted to see a fight, and it did not matter whose blood was spilt, as long as there was blood. They would ridicule the loser, whoever she was, and cheer whoever won the contest.

Encouraged, Melcorka stepped forward once more.

'Remember what Defender cannot do!' Bearnas shouted, as she grappled with Egil.

Defender could not kill in revenge. Defender could only kill if the holder's life were in danger. Melcorka grasped Bearnas's strategy.

Stepping up to Frakkok, she slapped her again. 'I am not going to kill you,' she said. 'Instead, I am going to make you look a fool in front of all these men!'

Using her superior speed, she avoided Frakkok's clumsy rush and kicked her hard on the backside a she staggered past. 'Oops! That was so large a target, I could not miss!' She forced a laugh and gave a genuine smile when the audience joined in.

Frakkok roared in anger and swung a wild punch that missed by a good six inches. Melcorka did not have to dodge. She slapped again. 'Your face is getting quite red now, Frakkok. When you wish to surrender, just let me know. This fighting must be exhausting for an old woman like you!'

'You'll see how old I am!' Frakkok shouted and drew Defender. The great blade, forged by the People of Peace, owned by Calgacus and Arthur, glittered in the rushlight. The watchers roared their approval as Frakkok lifted it high. 'You'll die by your own sword, Melcorka!'

For one brief moment, Melcorka saw the struggle between Bearnas and Egil cease as both turned to watch. Defender's blade poised and swung down as Frakkok put every inch of her strength into the blow. Melcorka saw a smile flick across Egil's face, and a slight shadow of doubt cross the face of Bearnas.

'It's all right, Mother.' Melcorka stood erect, not deigning to flinch or plead for mercy. If the blade was true to her maker, then she was safe. If it was her time, then it would kill her.

'Die!' Egil shouted.

Bearnas instinctively reached out a hand to protect her daughter.

The blade swept downward, aimed at the top of Melcorka's head. Given full force, the blow should have cut her in half. Instead, the blade stopped of its own volition, with the sudden shock jarring Frakkok's arms. She yelled with the pain, dropped the sword and crouched, holding her hands under each armpit. Defender landed on the stone slabs with a metallic clatter that echoed around the chamber.

'Mine, I believe,' Melcorka said and lifted her sword.

Egil's mouth opened in a scream of frustration as Hel extended a mighty arm and hauled him back into her domain. There was a distinct reek of smoke, an instant of darkness so intense that all light was expunged and then normality returned. Bearnas adjusted her mail coat, patted her hair in place and shook an admonitory finger at Melcorka. 'Next time,' she said, 'don't forget you are more than just a sword. You are Melcorka of the Cenel Bearnas.' She leaned closer to Melcorka. 'You are my daughter!'

And then she was also gone, and Melcorka stood in that chamber, alone except for her enemies and with Defender in her hand.

The surge of power and strength was as familiar as it was welcome. Melcorka lifted her sword, exulting.

'I am Melcorka the Swordswoman!' She lifted her voice in a yell. 'Melcorka of the Cenel Bearnas. Melcorka of Alba!'

'Kill that woman!' Wamblee ordered. 'Kill her!'

Arne was first to try. Drawing his sword, he ran forward, roaring. Melcorka decapitated him with a single sweep of Defender. She barely felt the impact. Arne's head spun in the air for a long three seconds before falling to the floor with a hollow thump.

'Who is next?' Melcorka knew she sounded calm. She spun Defender one-handed, glorying in her skill, knowing that now she was a match for any man, or any two men in that room. She did not hear Frakkok approach until the hand grabbed her by the throat and the knife stabbed into the hand that held Defender.

The sudden shock almost made her drop the sword. Melcorka looked round to see Frakkok lunge at her throat with the small blade. Instinctively, she slid to one side and swung Defender. The blade took Frakkok across the face, slicing off the top of her head. The Pict stood for a second with a look of mixed surprise and hatred on her face, and then crumpled to the ground in a puddle of her own blood and brains.

There was a collective gasp from the Norsemen as their leader was killed. Melcorka stepped back, grasping Defender with both hands in anticipation of a concerted attack by Erik and his companions.

Instead, Erik said: 'Oh, thank Odin she is dead.' He looked up. 'Free at last! I am free at last!'

Melcorka narrowed her eyes, expecting some trick as Erik stepped over the dead body of his mother. There were tears in his eyes as he looked down on Frakkok. 'All my life,' he said. 'All my life you have tormented me, bullied me, insulted me, ridiculed me in front of others and told me that I was not the man my father was. Now I am free.' He looked up to Melcorka. 'Thank you, Melcorka. I cannot thank you enough.'

'Kill her!' Wamblee screamed. 'Kill that woman!' He pushed the nearest of his bodyguards forward. 'Kill her now! You Northmen – she killed your leader. Kill her!'

'Kill her yourself,' Erik said. 'If you can.'

'I thought you had joined the Dhegians.' Although Melcorka spoke in a conversational tone, she was ready to fight. Her hands, sticky with blood, gripped Defender and she ensured she had sufficient room to swing her.

'Mother did that. We...' Erik looked round at his men, 'we had no choice.'

'That old hag was a witch indeed,' Melcorka said. 'She was a woman who manipulated solely for her own benefit. You are well rid of her.'

The first bodyguard pushed Knut aside and swung his great club at Melcorka. She parried with Defender, felt her blade cut deep through the handle of the club and withdrew quickly, stepping back. The bodyguard swung again, just as his companion charged at her side.

'Two men attacking one weak woman!' Melcorka said. 'How honourable you both are.' Ducking the swing of the second club, she crouched low, stretched out her arms and swept Defender in a wide circle. The blade cut cleanly through the right leg of the bodyguard on her right and the left leg of the bodyguard on her left. Both fell at once, staring at their foreshortened legs. Leaping over their bleeding bodies, Melcorka ran at Wamblee. 'Fight me, Wamblee.'

Rather than meet her challenge, Wamblee backed away. Melcorka did not see the lever he pulled, but a hole appeared in the wall and

Wamblee disappeared inside; the wall closed again before Melcorka reached it. She clattered Defender harmlessly against the stone.

'He's gone,' she said. The Norsemen were happily disposing of the two dying bodyguards. 'Now, you men have a choice. You may join me and help remove the last of Wamblee's supporters, or you can fight me and die.'

'We're with you, Melcorka,' Erik said at once.

'Come on then.' Melcorka did not relinquish her caution. 'Get me out of this place and into the open air.'

Erik led the way, with Melcorka at his heels and the remaining Norse at her back, in a yelling force suddenly determined to prove their loyalty to the anti-Wamblee coalition. The bottom door was still shut, with a solid wooden bar across it. Without waiting, Melcorka raised Defender and sliced clean through the wood. Erik kicked the broken pieces aside, and they rushed outside, to find a scene of utter carnage.

'Dear God,' Melcorka said. 'Where are my tribesmen?'

Chapter Twenty-One

It seemed that the rising had failed. Everywhere Melcorka looked, the allied tribes had been beaten back and were fighting a desperate rear-guard action, or had been captured and now sat in sullen groups under the spears of the Citadel or Wall Guard. The Dhegian warriors were in the ascendancy, shouting in triumph. She could not see Chaytan or Chumani. Exactly how long had she been in the palace? Melcorka glanced at the sky; a glorious dawn was spreading red across the eastern horizon. She had been away for a few hours and in that time, her rebellion had clearly failed.

Donning the headband of Eyota, Melcorka raised a shout. 'I am Eyota! Follow me!'

With Defender in her hand and the Norse at her back, she led a mad charge into the closest band of Dhegian warriors. Ordinary soldiers, they fought as best they could, but Defender sliced through their clubs and the hafts of their spears and the Norsemen hacked them down without compulsion or mercy.

A huddle of Huron prisoners looked up with hope slowly dawning in their eyes as Melcorka led the Norse in a sword-hewing attack on their captors.

'I am back!' Melcorka was unsure if she meant she was back as Melcorka the Swordswoman, or as Eyota. She did not care. Either would do, just as long as she brought victory to the beleaguered tribes.

Rising, the Huron joined them, grappling the Dhegian warriors bare-handed as Melcorka and the Norse rammed into them from the front. It was a massacre rather than a battle, and then the Huron lifted the Dhegian weapons and joined Melcorka's force.

'What happened?' Melcorka asked the Huron. 'The attack was going well.'

The Huron looked confused. 'The Guards pushed us back,' they said.

'Where are the Guards now?' Melcorka asked.

'At the main gate,' the Huron replied. 'Killing the last of us.'

'Let's kill them instead!' Melcorka led them toward the sound of combat, feeling Eyota's headband tight on her forehead, hearing the solid thump of the Norse feet on the ground contrasting with the patter of the Hurons'.

Formed in three lines, the Guards were pushing the remnants of the allied tribes out of the Citadel. They worked behind a barrier of shields, their spears thrusting and returning as regularly as oarsmen in a Norse dragon ship.

'There is your enemy,' Melcorka said. 'Take the centre and break it, and then fan right and left and roll up the line.'

They hit the Guards from the rear, with Melcorka decapitating the first two Citadel Guards and Erik close at her back. As the Guards tried to close on them, the Norse swung to the right and the Hurons to the left, with the leading warriors of the allied tribes charging forward to help.

The Guards fought well. They reformed as best they could, with their clubs and spears continuing to take their toll of the attackers. Melcorka and Defender crashed into their lines again and again, slicing, thrusting and cutting until the last vestige of Dhegian resistance crumbled. When they finally broke, the allied tribes swarmed right over them.

'I thought you were dead.' Bleeding from half a dozen wounds, Chaytan leaned on his club. 'I saw you reach the top of the palace and disappear.'

Melcorka cleaned the blade of Defender. 'I survived.' She did not go into details. 'Both bodyguards are dead, as well as Frakkok. The Norse are on our side now.'

'I could not get into the palace to help you,' Chaytan said.

'You kept the armies occupied outside. If the Citadel Guards had joined...' Melcorka shrugged. 'I don't know what would have happened. Wamblee escaped. He opened the wall and got away.'

Chaytan nodded; although gasping and wounded, he still retained his massive presence. 'He has lost everything – his bodyguard, his Guards, many of his tribesmen and his prestige.'

'Eyota,' Chumani said, 'how long are you going to stay with us?'

'I have not thought about it,' Melcorka said honestly. She looked at the carnage. 'This place needs to be cleaned up.'

'You have saved us from the tyrant,' Chumani said. 'Are you going back to the spirit world now?'

That question startled Melcorka. She had not thought what to do once Wamblee had been defeated. When she arrived, she had been with Bradan and had a vague idea of helping remove Wamblee. She had not looked beyond that, expecting only that she and Bradan would continue to travel in some way. Now, she did not know. Bradan was alive somewhere, that she knew. She must find him.

'I came here with a man,' she said. 'I would like to look for him.'

'Is he in the spirit world?' Chumani asked.

'No. He is in this world.'

'Then I will pass the word,' Chaytan said. 'Until we find him, are you staying with us? We need your guidance.'

Melcorka considered. 'I will stay until we find Bradan.'

After that? Melcorka shook her head. She could not see anything after that. She felt utterly weary.

Chapter Twenty-Two

It took three days to dispose of the dead bodies that littered the Citadel and the city. There were also hundreds of listless Dhegian prisoners.

'Eyota,' Chumani said, 'how shall we deal with the Dhegians? Shall we kill them all?'

Melcorka shook her head. 'No. If you do that, you will be as bad as Wamblee. You must gather them together and make them swear on their ancestors that they will not cause more trouble. Then you will set them free.'

'It shall be as you wish, Eyota.'

There were other decisions to make, too, such as what to do with the palisade wall around the Citadel.

'Remove it,' Melcorka said at once. 'Nobody should be separate from anybody else. The rulers should not have to be protected from the ruled. All should be together, for the good of the community.'

'It shall be as you wish, Eyota,' Chumani said.

What to do with the slaves was next. Men and women without tribal leaders, they wandered around the city, sleeping where they could and stealing whatever food they could not beg. They were becoming a social menace.

'Divide them into their tribes,' Melcorka said. 'Find out if a near relation to the original tribal chief exists. If he does, then appoint him as the new chief, and he can take them back to their original tribal area. If they cannot find a leader, then each individual will be free to choose which tribe they wish to join. This influx of people will help repair the losses of the war with Wamblee.'

'It shall be as you say, Eyota,' Chumani said.

There was the mess from the battle to repair.

'Select fifty men from each tribe,' Melcorka said. 'They shall work in competition against each other to do the most in setting the city and Citadel to right. There shall be no animosity and no dislike, only healthy competition.'

'It shall be as you say, Eyota,' Chumani said.

There were the inevitable family and tribal disputes to settle. In the past, the priests of the city had arbitrated, but they had fled along with Wamblee. Now, there was no neutral judge to decide on cases so, within a few days, there were arguments and some inter-family and inter-tribal clashes.

'You must do something about this situation, Eyota,' Chumani said. 'If the tribes fall into serious disagreement, there may be open warfare between them.'

'I will judge the urgent cases myself,' Melcorka said, 'to ensure there is peace in the city.'

'It shall be as you say, Eyota,' Chumani said.

For the next few days, Melcorka found herself inundated with disputes old and new. There were cases from many years ago that men and women had refused to take to the priests, and some that had arisen much more recently. Melcorka set up her court within the palace, to find it crowded day after day, with queues of people gathering outside. Some were petitioners, others the accused and many were merely there to watch the proceedings.

There was a case where two families disputed the ownership of a piece of land.

'Our people have farmed this land for three generations,' one man said.

'Then you married into our family and brought no dowry,' said the other.

Melcorka frowned. 'So your families are joined by marriage?'

'Yes, Eyota,' the first man said.

'In that case, there is no dispute. You are now one family and all your lands are owned by all.'

'It shall be as you say, Eyota,' both men agreed.

There was a case where one of the Citadel Guard had taken a young woman, who now wished to return to her family.

'What is the problem?' Melcorka asked.

'She is defiled,' the mother of the woman said.

'Was it her fault that she was defiled?' Melcorka asked, already knowing the answer.

'It was not her fault,' the mother said.

'Then no blame attaches to her, and you shall welcome her back into her own family, where she belongs.' Melcorka raised her voice so it carried around the crowded justice chamber and beyond. 'Henceforth in this city, nobody shall be blamed or punished for actions that were not their fault. No woman shall be blamed if she is violated against her will.'

Some of the faces looked doubtful. For the first time, Melcorka adopted an imperious tone. 'That is my will and my command. Does anybody wish to dispute it with me?'

Immediately she gave her decision, the complaining ended.

'Very well. Let that be the law. And I do not want to hear about any secret attacks on such women. If any of these women who were abducted and abused against their will are harmed in any way, I will not be lenient with their attackers!' Melcorka stood to announce that, feeling all the power of Eyota flow through her and out of her eyes. Clearly, this was a matter about which Eyota felt strongly.

One woman began to cry; her mother held her. Another mouthed her thanks as her father led her away. Melcorka nodded. If she had done nothing else here, that alone was worth her time as law-maker in this city.

'In future,' Melcorka said, 'I shall not be the sole justice of this city. I wish each tribe to appoint a respected elder to a council of elders.

These people, be they men or women, will meet in this chamber as from tomorrow, and they will decide on each case, using their collective wisdom. If they fail to come to a decision, then they may bring the case to me.'

'It shall be as you say, Eyota,' the men and women murmured.

By the end of the third week after the battle, Melcorka was growing into her new role. She lived in the palace, in a set of rooms in which she had windows made to overlook the city. She had the most enormous bed she had ever seen in her life, with fresh water in which to wash and a whole wardrobe of beautiful clothes presented to her by admiring women. Every morning, she would awaken to fresh food and smiling people.

She was the ruler of Cahokia, a city so large she could not see the end, with impressive triangular mounds rising all around, surmounted with tall buildings. Other buildings were smaller, beautifully thatched and neat as anything she had ever seen. Bare-chested people walked all around, bowing when they came to her. There were Lakota warriors with elaborate costumes they had captured from the Guards. Some carried spears, others clubs with heavy stone heads, elaborately carved.

She was in her city. She was wanted here. She was important here.

Melcorka smiled at the memory. That was the vision she had experienced so many months ago, and now it had come true. This city was her home. She belonged here, as she had belonged nowhere else since she left her native island years before. Stepping to the parapet that overlooked her city of Cahokia, she took a deep breath and savoured the wonder and the loveliness of it all.

'I am Eyota,' she said. 'I am Eyota of Cahokia. This is my city, this is my country, and these are my people.'

She looked down on them. All these thousands of people respected and even worshipped her. She was their queen, and perhaps they even considered her divine. It was a strange, heady, intoxicating sensation, to be admired, to have her every whim catered for, her every desire answered immediately, without question. This was power; this was what it felt like to be a ruler.

'I want a bath this morning,' she said quietly, to one of the many people who acted as her servants. The woman bowed and, within a short space of time, a bath of hot water appeared. Melcorka did not have to ask how the water was heated, or what labour had been needed to carry the bath or the water up five flights of stairs. It did not matter. She was Eyota, and her word of command was enough.

She did not need to speak when the bath arrived; she simply stepped toward it and servants came to her, removing her clothes in seconds and easing her into the gentle water. When she asked for music, musicians appeared as if by magic; when she wanted fruit, it would appear. Life was comfortable, life was luxurious, and life was safe.

She appointed Chaytan as the captain of her guard, and he organised a personal fighting force for the Citadel. She had the gates opened so that access was free for all. When a member of her Council of Elders requested that she allow them to build an observatory to watch the stars and the moon, she snapped her fingers and the work started.

A few days later, she watched the line of men and women toiling with baskets of soil to make the new mound that would house the observatory. 'Where are these labourers from?' she asked.

The elder smiled. 'These are the law-breakers,' he replied.

'I see,' Melcorka said and dismissed them from her mind. If they had broken her laws, then they deserved to be punished. She was Eyota of Cahokia, and her word was unchallengeable. Melcorka did not realise how much she was changing; she was not yet twenty-four years old.

After six weeks, Melcorka wished to tour the outlying districts of her empire. She asked for horses and a chariot, only to hear that such novelties were unknown in this land. She realised that she had not seen a single horse since she arrived in Greenland and nobody understood the concept of a wheel. Her laughter came from deep within and ended. For the next few days, she tried to explain what a wheel was for, and then stopped. What was the point of a wheeled carriage when there were no horses to pull it?

Melcorka shook her head and had her servants create a litter and carry her on a week-long tour of the nearest parts of her lands. They did not object; indeed, they seemed excited at the prospect of being so close to the ruler of their world. Her Empire was extensive, with villages scattered over a wide radius from Cahokia, and tribes who seemed happy to have a new regime. Wherever she travelled, Eyota was lauded and feted and treated with adulation.

All the same, Melcorka was always pleased when they returned to her palace. She missed the luxury of her rooms and her daily hot bath, the bustle and the refinements of her home. Life outside the city was cold and airy, while the people undoubtedly lacked the sophistication of urban life.

'Have you not finished repairing all the war damage yet?' Melcorka asked the men working on the wall.

'Not yet, Eyota,' they said.

'Well, get a move on then,' Melcorka said.

It was during the clearing operations that one of the Oglala noticed the staff. He lifted it without comment and threw it in a pile intended for burning. It was there that Melcorka found it.

'Don't burn that!' The very feel of it as she lifted the staff brought back a host of memories. She remembered Fitheach the witch giving this length of wood to Bradan on the islands of the River Ness; she remembered the sound it made, tapping on the ground; she remembered Bradan sitting thinking, with the top of the staff tucked under his chin. Melcorka smiled, running her hand up the length, feeling the smoothness of the rowan wood. She fingered the tip, with its roughly-carved Christian cross. St Columba had carried this staff and with it, Bradan had battled the evil power of the Morrigan. She tapped it on the ground, much as Bradan had done, and smiled at the sound.

God, how she missed that laconic, slow-striding man with his quiet eyes!

She sighed. That was gone now. Bradan and his staff belonged to a different world; a world of toil and trouble, travel and worry. That life was in the past; she had come home and this was her world. She was Eyota of Cahokia now and forever. There was a strange comfort in that, on top of the terrible feeling of loss.

Chapter Twenty-Three

'Eyota.' Chumani approached her as she stood in the pleasure garden the servants were making for her. 'There is talk that you are alone too much.'

'Oh?' Melcorka raised her eyebrows. 'Who is talking about me?'

'The people are,' Chumani said. She stood at a respectful distance, with her head deferentially bowed.

It was some days since Melcorka had last spoken to her. 'What do you think I should do to these people who talk so disrespectfully?'

'That is not what I meant, Eyota,' Chumani said.

'So what did you mean, Chumani?' Melcorka asked. 'Be careful now.'

'I think you need a man,' Chumani said. 'You must be lonely.'

'I am not lonely,' Melcorka insisted. 'I am surrounded by people and if I ever require a man, I can order one of the servants to share my bed. They would not turn me down.' Melcorka had already sought male comfort. It was not something she had done before, but this new presence within her head and body had demanded solace during the long hours of the night.

'I am sure they would not,' Chumani said. 'But you need more than a man to bounce around in bed with. You need a man to share your life.'

Melcorka's face darkened. *How dare this woman tell me what I need and what I should do!* Lifting her hand to slap the insolent Lakota, Melcorka stopped herself. Despite her rise to absolute power, she knew that she was wrong.

'Perhaps you are right, Chumani.' Melcorka dropped her hand. 'I shall see what man is best suitable for me.'

'Do you wish me to assemble the most eligible?' Chumani asked.

'Do that,' Melcorka ordered.

'It shall be as you say, Eyota.' Chumani bowed and withdrew.

When the news spread that Eyota was seeking a husband, men clustered to the Citadel from all across the Empire. They came from Cahokia and the forest tribes, from the vast grass prairies and the bounds of the northern seas; they came with hope and were filled with curiosity. Secure in her rooms, Melcorka stood at her window looking out as they filled the civic area between the Citadel and the priest's temple.

There were young men and old men, men in their prime and men in the full vigour of youth. There were men with broad shoulders and slender hips and men with scrawny shoulders and wide hips. There were boastful men who spoke of the women they had already known and quiet men who started when a woman touched them. There were wild men from the great prairies whose eyes were more used to the far horizons than the confines of a city and there were aesthetic sophisticates who hoped for a serene life in the cloistered palace.

'How many are there?' Melcorka asked.

Chumani shook her head. 'There are many,' she said, 'and many more after that.' Chumani was not good with numbers. She could not count beyond the number of her fingers and toes.

A sense of mischief that she had not felt for many months swept over Melcorka. 'Would you care to help me inspect them, Chumani?'

'I would be honoured, Eyota,' Chumani said.

Melcorka smiled wickedly. 'How shall we do it? Should we have them perform tests of strength and agility to ensure they are fit enough to be a husband? Shall we ask about their treasure and wealth? Or shall we have them all strip naked and examine other parts of them?'

Chumani giggled at the last thought, covering her mouth politely with her hand. 'Oh, Eyota! I did not think you would say such a thing!'

Melcorka stepped closer and whispered so only Chumani could hear. 'Maybe we could test them out one at a time, Chumani. I could have another bed brought into my chambers and we could...' She laughed at the expression on Chumani's face.

'Oh, Eyota!' Chumani was scandalised, yet undoubtedly pleased. 'Oh, I could not do that with you! You are Eyota!'

'And you are my friend,' Melcorka said, laughing. She did not expect Chumani to drop to her knees.

'I am only a woman,' Chumani said.

Stooping, Melcorka raised her to her feet. 'So am I, Chumani. What on earth do you think I am?'

'You are Eyota,' Chumani said. 'You are Eyota.' Backing away, she bowed, turned and fled. Melcorka wondered at the sudden fear in her eyes and then shrugged. It was a pity, but she could not account for the feelings of all her people.

The men lined up in the great rectangular space between the Citadel and the temple, row after row of hopefuls. Melcorka counted them as four hundred strong and walked up and down their ranks, looking at each one individually. They watched her, some smiling, some solemn, some pulling themselves upright, some stepping forward in the hope of instant acceptance.

'I do not know,' she told Chumani. 'I do not know how to choose.'

'What is it you are searching for?' Chumani asked.

'Bradan.' Melcorka answered without thinking, although she knew that Eyota did not approve.

Chumani frowned. 'What is a Bradan?'

Cursing her wayward tongue, Melcorka shook her head. 'I want a search throughout the kingdom and beyond,' she said. 'I am looking for a foreign man, a northerner who journeyed to this land with the Northmen, yet he is different. He is a tall man, with brown hair and hazel-coloured eyes... a man who does not carry a weapon and who

Falcon Warrior

talks slowly and carefully. He is a man of great wisdom.' She frowned. 'I have already given orders for this man to be found.'

Chumani bowed. 'I shall ensure that the search is intensified.'

'Do so!' Melcorka commanded.

'It shall be as you say,' Chumani bowed. 'What shall we do with all these other men, Eyota?'

'Thank them and dismiss them,' Melcorka said. 'My husband is not among them.'

She returned to her quarters, alone, and stared out of the window at the teeming city. Things were not as they should be.

Chapter Twenty~Four

'Are you Eyota or Melcorka today?' The voice was friendly, yet not as deferential as Melcorka now expected.

'Hello, Erik.' She turned to face the Northman. 'What are you doing here?'

'I have come to ask if you have found Bradan yet, or if you have found a suitable husband.'

'I have found neither,' Melcorka said.

Erik sat on a chair, crossed his legs and made himself comfortable. 'These Skraelings think of you as nearly divine,' he said. 'It will be hard to find a man who wishes to treat you as a full-blooded woman rather than as a goddess.'

'I am no goddess,' Melcorka said.

'I know that.' Erik smiled at her. 'We have been through some adventures, you and I. We fought the Ice Giant together, and crossed icy seas and sailed up great rivers.'

'I remember,' Melcorka said.

'Do you remember these long-toothed monsters in the sea?'

'I remember the walruses,' Melcorka said.

'And those dragons in the inland sea?'

'I remember them well,' Melcorka said.

'And that fight with Wamblee's men?'

'I remember,' Melcorka said. 'Do you have a point to make, or are we just swapping memories?'

'You need a man,' Erik said. 'We are connected by experience, and we are both from the same world. We would make a good pairing.'

'Your father killed my mother,' Melcorka reminded him.

'I know,' Erik said. 'And you killed both my parents.'

'That is also true. It is not the best start to any friendship.'

Erik shrugged. 'I hardly knew my father. I never met your mother, and I hated mine. I am grateful to you for killing her.'

'That is still not the best basis for marriage.' Melcorka did not say that she found this man interesting. He was handsome and young and had proved himself in battle. She looked him up and down, wondering what he would be like. No! She killed that thought. She could not trust him. He may be planning revenge for the death of his parents. Chumani was correct, of course; she had the natural urge for a man. Yet she also had that old loyalty to Bradan. If she could find him, she would be happier. She had felt some strange attraction to Erik from the first; he was politer than most Norseman and was certainly not a natural killer. He reminded her of Alva, Egil's little daughter who she had rescued and cared for before she left Scotland. He had something of her allure, allied with definite masculinity.

She took a deep breath. 'Thank you for your offer, Erik,' she said. 'I will not disregard it.'

Erik stood up. 'Will you consider it seriously?' His smile made him look even more handsome; a blond, tall, broad-shouldered man who had travelled halfway around the world with her.

'I will,' Melcorka said. Part of her wanted to invite him to stay. Was that Melcorka or Eyota? She did not know. With a spark of interest in her eyes, Melcorka watched him leave the room. But the next day brought news that put Erik out of her mind, at least for the present.

'Eyota!' Chumani gasped, bowing as Melcorka sat on her favourite chair staring out the window at her city. 'We have news of your foreigner. He is deep in the woods with the Iroquois. Shall we send a party to bring him in?'

'Yes,' Melcorka said at once, and then changed her mind. 'No. No, I shall go to him. I want fifty men as escort, and you as well.'

Chumani bowed again. 'It shall be as you wish, Eyota.'

Melcorka tried to still the hammering of her heart. Here she was, ruler of a vast city and an empire so huge she still did not know its full extent, and yet she was nervous at the thought of seeing a wandering man with neither power nor influence. That was absurd. She could have any man she wished, at any time. What was so special about this one?

'We will leave in two days,' Melcorka said, knowing that the next forty-eight hours would be a torment of doubt and anxiety. She waved her hand to the door. 'Please leave me alone now.' She needed to think. She needed to control these two personalities that struggled for control within her head.

Daylight and night were the same; a mix of worry and torture and power. At some point during the next day, Melcorka used a man. It was a physical thing that dulled one urge without assuaging her need. It was not enough; *he* was not enough. Melcorka dismissed him, watched his naked body without interest and waited for time to pass.

'Are you ready, Eyota?' Chumani asked.

'I am ready,' Melcorka said.

Her people had made a litter in which to carry her if she did not feel like walking, and there were another three litters full of supplies for the journey. Melcorka looked around her apartments in the palace and smiled. Once this trip was over, she would have a more luxurious divan made, and some polished copper mirrors so she could regale herself in them. That was something to look forward to.

'Come, Chumani.' She walked down the stairs and out of the door into the courtyard outside. There must be an easier way to leave her palace, she thought, casually acknowledging the waves and bows of her people.

They moved to the river and boarded a fleet of canoes. Melcorka had considered using *Sea Serpent*, but decided that her people were better suited to paddling canoes than pulling on oars and besides, she was still not certain if she trusted the Norsemen. So she sat in the stern of the largest canoe and watched her kingdom slide past as the paddlers put their muscles to work.

The responsibilities of being queen of Cahokia rested lightly on Eyota's shoulders, while there was great pleasure in enjoying the fruits of her position. She leaned back and enjoyed the journey. Allowing her people to carry the burden of travel, Eyota barely noticed her surroundings, while Melcorka fretted at the thought of seeing Bradan again.

The village was quiet. The collection of lodges was protected by a single slender palisade and a central fire was smoking gently in the light wind.

'Halloa there!' the leader of the guard shouted. 'We have Eyota of Cahokia with us.'

There was a slight pause before a voice sounded. 'You are welcome if you come in peace.'

'We come in peace,' the leader said. 'We are seeking the foreign man known as Bradan.'

They filed through a gate and into the village, where the entire population of the village, less than forty adults and half that number of children and dogs, poured out to stare at them.

'We have nobody of that name,' the Iroquois said.

Melcorka stepped forward. 'I am Eyota,' she said. Rather than instant obedience, the Iroquois merely nodded.

'We heard your name mentioned,' they said. 'You are welcome.'

The villagers grouped themselves around the central fire, staring at these unexpected visitors.

'We have brought gifts.' Melcorka ordered the extra food to be distributed to the Iroquois. She looked around the faces, searching for Bradan.

He sat in the middle of the crowd, dressed as any other of the Iroquois and with Ehawee, the young woman who had tended him, by his side. Even after all these weeks, the side of his head was still swollen, although the bruise had died away. The club had left an ugly scar that was visible underneath the line of his hair. Melcorka felt her heart racing again. Ignoring all the protocol, she walked to him.

'Bradan!' She could not stop smiling.

Bradan and Ehawee looked up at her. Ehawee smiled.

'This is Eyota, Capa. She is the lady who came from the spirit world to save you.'

Bradan smiled without recognition. 'Thank you, Eyota.'

Melcorka felt a sudden surge of nausea. 'Bradan – don't you recognise me?'

'Ehawee told me that you saved me, Eyota,' Bradan said. 'I cannot remember your visit.' His smile was quicker than usual, and his eyes not as focussed.

'You are Bradan the Wanderer,' Melcorka said.

'I am Capa of the Iroquois.' Bradan sounded confused but not unfriendly. 'I don't know this Bradan at all.'

Melcorka closed her eyes. Bearnas had warned her that Bradan would not be the same man, but she had not expected him to have forgotten her completely. For one moment, she considered using the power of Eyota to send warriors to wipe this village off the earth, take Bradan to Cahokia and make him her man. But she would not. She could not. Melcorka would not do that and Eyota did not have the same feelings for Bradan as she had. Ehawee smiled at her in complete trust with her arm intertwined with Bradan's. They were man and maid together. Bradan had a new life.

'I am glad that Capa is well,' Melcorka said. She allowed Eyota to take over, so there were no tears as she left that village. They would come later when she lay in her bed at night.

Melcorka looked back at the Iroquois village. 'Goodbye, Bradan,' she said softly. 'Goodbye, my love.' She did not weep. How could she, when all the time Eyota was celebrating that she was free of that link to an unwanted past?

Chapter Twenty-Five

'You did not find your man,' Chumani said.

'The man we thought was Bradan was named Capa.' Melcorka did not elaborate. She forced a smile.

'Do you wish to search again for a suitable man?' Chumani asked.

Melcorka thought of Bradan. She would not find another like him. However, Eyota did not want Bradan. Without further thought, Melcorka slipped Eyota's headband over her forehead.

'I do.' She heard the deeper timbre of her voice. 'I do wish to find another man, one suitable to rule Cahokia with me. Bring me men.'

'It shall be as you say, Eyota.' Chumani bowed low.

Once again, the call went out for men for Eyota, and once again they gathered. This time, Melcorka examined them through Eyota's eyes, looking for a man suitable to control her realm. Rejecting men who were too old, or striplings with no experience of life, she looked for men in their late twenties, virile men she could mould and control. Their appearance was less important than their potential.

'Bring them to me,' Melcorka ordered, 'so I may examine them.'

They came in a steady flow, singly and in small groups and she had them line up outside the palace so she could scrutinise them before inviting them in. It became a daily occurrence, with crowds gathering to watch Eyota of Cahokia standing at her window, goblet in hand, examining the morning's parade of men before she crooked her finger at one, or two, or three and gestured for them to enter the palace.

They would enter in mixed hope and trepidation, and she would interview them about their past and their dreams. Some, she would reject within minutes, and the unwanted would face the humiliation of a long walk home, knowing that his dreams of power and wealth were forever shattered. Others would pass the initial examination and would enter her private quarters. The fortunate would progress further and would provide entertainment in her bed for a day, or a day and a night, or occasionally more. Very few lasted longer than that, for Melcorka discovered that Eyota had an insatiable carnal appetite and she wore men out. Melcorka did not care; the physical activity was pleasing, and she had no emotional attachment to any of them. They were bodies for her use and nothing else.

'Bring me more,' Melcorka would say. 'More men!'

After the initial surge, the flow became a trickle and then only a dribble as the word spread that nobody suitable was being found. At length, after some weeks, Melcorka donned Eyota's headband and walked to her window to see the usual crowd outside but not a single man hopeful of her company.

'Where are the men?' She shouted.

'There are none, Eyota,' Chumani answered.

'What do you mean, there are none?' Melcorka asked.

'You have tested and rejected so many, Eyota, that others are discouraged,' Chumani said.

'Find me more!' Melcorka ordered. 'Drag them to me in chains if need be!' Stepping away from the window, she threw her goblet at Chumani. It missed, bounced off the far wall and rolled on the floor. 'Do you hear me?'

Chumani bowed, stepping back. 'It shall be as you say, Eyota.'

Next morning, four men were waiting outside Melcorka's window. One was tall, bare-chested and handsome. Two looked as if they had been dredged from some backwater hovel and the fourth was Erik.

Beckoning for the bare-chested man and Erik to enter, Melcorka dismissed the other two.

'That's better, Chumani,' she approved.

Bowing, Chumani ushered in the two men.

Leaning back on her couch, Melcorka surveyed them both. 'Now, that is much better. What are your names?'

'I am Enapay,' the bare-chested man said. 'Of the Lakota.'

'You already know my name,' Erik said.

Melcorka felt her anger rising. 'I did not ask you what I knew or did not know,' she said. 'I asked for your name.'

'I am Erik,' Erik's smile taunted her. 'As you well know.'

Stepping forward, Melcorka aimed a slap at Erik, which he blocked with a simple movement of his arm.

'I am not here to be a target of your temper,' he said. 'I had enough of that with my loving mother.'

Melcorka stepped back. 'I am Eyota!' she said. 'I will not be treated in such a manner!' She pointed to Enapay. 'You! Kill this man!'

Enapay looked at Erik and shook his head. 'No, Eyota, I will not. He has done nothing to warrant death.'

Melcorka felt the struggle within her. Part of her wished to dominate, to control, and part of her wanted to praise these men for standing up to her. Which was Eyota and which Melcorka? More importantly for the future well-being of these two men, which was the more powerful? She opened her mouth to shout to Chaytan to take them away.

'Then you must both stay,' she surprised herself by saying. She pointed to Enapay. 'I do not know you, yet you are very familiar,' she said.

'I have been watching you since you returned, Eyota.' Enapay had the deep voice and graceful movements that seemed to belong to this part of the world.

Melcorka gasped with sudden insight. She did know this man; she knew him well. Enapay was the man from her visions. Enapay was the man who was at her side when she was the ruler of this empire; when she was Queen.

'That must be it,' she said. 'I must have seen you in the crowd.' She eyed him up, her heart beating faster as her visions became a reality. It was an instinct that made her hold out her hand to him. Enapay accepted it as if it was his right, and moved so close that his hip brushed against hers. The sensation sent a tingle through her that none of her many bed partners – they had never reached the status of lovers – had been able to achieve.

'You know me.' Erik stepped forward. 'I am Erik Farseeker.'

'I know you well, Erik,' Melcorka agreed. She did not relinquish hold of Enapay's hand. 'Come!'

With his characteristic smile back in place, Erik stepped to Melcorka's left side. He smelled different from Enapay; an alien, northern scent in her city of Cahokia.

'Now I have two men.' Melcorka heard the words come from her lips, mused over them and was satisfied. 'Now I am complete. Now I can rule my city and my lands without fear. I have Chaytan as my guard commander, Erik and his Norsemen will become my bodyguard and Enapay will be my chief advisor.'

She waited for the inevitable reaction.

'Who will keep you company in bed?' Erik pressed closer to her. He was all muscle, as hard and active as any Norseman.

'Whoever I choose,' Melcorka said. 'I am Eyota, Queen of Cahokia.' The words sounded pleasant to her ears, as if she had said them before. She knew she would say them many times in the months, years and decades to come. She was where she belonged; she was home. That thought was immensely pleasing.

The streets of Cahokia emptied before her as the people stepped aside to allow her passage. They bowed as she walked by, or held up their children for the blessing of her touch. Eyota-Melcorka luxuriated in the reverence in which she was held, accepting gifts from her subjects as her right and smiling as she was daily complimented.

'I am Eyota, Queen of Cahokia,' she announced, as she stood on the topmost terrace of the Citadel with her subjects gathered below. She smiled fondly upon them, bestowing her goodwill as she lifted her right hand in greeting.

'There will be no more human sacrifices,' she announced, to the cheers and adulation of her crowd. 'All the tribes will be equal in my city.'

Nobody objected. Even when the erstwhile oppressors were allowed back into society, they accepted her word, for she was Eyota, the Promised One, for whom they had been waiting for many years. They took her word as they would accept the laws of a divine being and Melcorka blossomed in their praise and expected her whims to be obeyed instantly and her subjects to accord her respect without limits.

'There shall be no more slavery,' Melcorka decreed. 'Every man and every woman shall be free in my city.'

There was great cheering at that.

'The compound shall be used to hold grain in case of future drought,' Melcorka decreed.

'There shall be no guards patrolling my city,' she said. 'Only Chaytan and the palace guards will be armed, and Erik and his Norseman will carry weapons as my bodyguards.'

She expected the approval. Living in the royal palace high on the Citadel pyramid, she did not know of the slow surge of crime in her city as the unhappy and discontented, and those from broken tribes who had not found a home, stalked the unguarded night-time streets. She did not notice the lack of work on public buildings or the basic public sewage systems. Without slaves, and with no monetary system to give rewards, people did not wish to labour on such menial tasks. They much preferred to attend to their crops and ignore the good of the city and the community.

Knowing nothing of such matters, Melcorka lost herself in the smiles and compliments and allowed the adulation to carry her away to places she had never dreamed existed. Except when she passed casual judgement on various legal cases or proclaimed her wishes to her people, her days were filled with pleasure and Erik, or Enapay, or some other man kept her company at night. Deep within her, there was disquiet; but Eyota had taken charge, and Melcorka had nearly forgotten her old self. Alba and Bradan were memories and Defender sat quietly on the wall of her bedchamber, unused and disregarded.

'Eyota.' Enapay smiled at her from their pillow. 'You are safe in this bedroom, are you not?'

Melcorka stretched out beneath her furs and breathed deeply. 'I am safer than I have ever been,' she said.

'Do you still need that foreign weapon to decorate our bedroom?' Enapay pointed to Defender. 'When I wake up in the morning I want only to see you, not a metal device for killing.'

Melcorka pushed back the covers, so she lay naked to his gaze, then did the same for him, and smiled at the sight. 'You are all man,' she said approvingly. 'All man.'

'And you are all woman.' Enapay smoothed his head over her body, from the crown of her head to her shins and back.

'I am also a Queen,' Melcorka said.

'You are my Queen.' Enapay allowed his hand to dally a little.

'I am everybody's Queen,' Melcorka said lazily, rising to meet his hand.

'Everybody loves you,' Enapay agreed.

She giggled softly. 'I may love them all,' she said, 'or at least all the men.' Her laugh gurgled in her throat. 'But only one at a time. Or perhaps two at a time, if I am impatient.'

They laughed together.

'That would be one way of cementing the bond between the people and their Queen,' Enapay said, with his hands doing wonderful things to her.

'Don't you mind?' Melcorka sat up suddenly, holding his hand in place. 'No, don't stop!'

'I won't stop until you wish me to, Eyota,' Enapay said.

'Answer my question!' Melcorka heard the regal snap in her voice. 'Don't you mind that I pleasure myself with other men apart from you?'

'You are Eyota,' Enapay said. 'You are free to do as you wish in your own city and your own country. You are Queen.'

'That is true.' Melcorka lay back down again. 'But aren't you just a teeny bit jealous that I share my favours with other men?' She smiled at a hidden memory. 'With many other men, some of whom are very…' She shook her head. 'Perhaps I had better not say more.'

Enapay looked down at her, smiling. 'Naturally, I would prefer to have you all to myself for always, Eyota. Any man would. I am only happy that you honour me with so much of your time and your presence.'

'That is a good answer,' Melcorka said, as other matters began to divert her attention. 'It was a diplomatic answer from a diplomatic man.'

'Not only a diplomatic man, I hope.' Enapay was busily engaged now, yet still held her gaze.

'Oh, absolutely not,' Melcorka agreed, gasping slightly. 'Erik is very jealous,' she said. 'He wants a larger share of my body.'

'Any man would wish that,' Enapay said.

'He is very young,' Melcorka gasped, a few moments later. She giggled again and lowered her voice. 'He rushes things.'

Enapay slowed down, as Melcorka had intended. 'Young men can sometimes be too energetic for their own good,' he said.

Later, when Melcorka lay panting and satisfied, Enapay reached across and stroked her stomach. 'You have a very firm body,' he said. 'You are beautiful. Even if you were not a Queen, you would be beautiful.'

Melcorka closed her eyes, savouring his adulation. 'I used to be leaner and firmer.' She looked down at her sleek stomach with its layer of prosperous fat. 'Before I was a Queen.' She shook her head at the memories. 'That seems so long ago, before we met. You are all man.'

She used her favourite phrase of praise. One that was already well-worn in this room that was now dedicated entirely to her pleasure.

Sometimes, it was difficult for her to remember life before she became Eyota. Had she really wandered the world with some laconic man with a stick? Had she honestly spent so much time in wind-battered islands and fought ice-bears? It seemed unbelievable that she, Queen of Cahokia, should have done such things.

'You are very noisy at the crucial time,' she said, smiling and returning Enapay's caresses. 'People must hear you.'

'I'll have some servants strengthen the walls,' Enapay said, 'so the sound is deadened.'

'Do so,' Melcorka said drowsily, 'and make sure they are quick about it. I want it done today, so I am not disturbed by their banging.'

'They might not manage it in one day,' Enapay said.

'Then make them,' imperious Eyota-Melcorka ordered. 'I order it.'

'It shall be as you say, Eyota.' Enapay half rose and bowed. 'And the sword?'

'Oh, move that damned thing away as well,' Melcorka said. 'I no longer need it, and it spoils the symmetry of the room.'

'It shall be as you say, Eyota.' Enapay bowed again.

'Good. Now get back in here.' Melcorka patted the furs, smiling. 'You didn't think I was finished with you yet, did you? We're not half done yet!'

One day every week, Melcorka listened to the report from the Council of Elders and passed judgement on those cases that they could not reach a decision on.

Grave-faced and wise, the Council elders filed into the room that Melcorka had ordered to be kept for their deliberations. There were fifteen men present, as dignified as any that she had ever seen. With Erik at her side, she greeted them formally and accepted their respect.

'We have had a busy week, Eyota.' The Council's spokesman was of the Iroquois, a serene-eyed man who must have been approaching his seventieth winter. 'There have been many cases to listen to.'

Melcorka sat on her chair with the headband around her forehead and her newly-made robe draped from her shoulders. She had specifically demanded the image of a falcon picked out in white shells and had the dress-maker hang her trinkets from the sleeves. These small falcon models she had rescued from the woman in the ice added an excellent decorative touch, she thought, and they rattled nicely as she walked. They acted like small bells, drawing attention to her royal status.

'Did you resolve all the cases?' Melcorka asked. She knew that such small affairs mattered to her subjects. Family matters and such like were vital to the little people who made up the bulk of Cahokia's population, and if the people were happy, then they would adore her all the more.

'Not all, Eyota.' The Elder said. 'There are many cases of theft and of...' he stuttered over the words, 'attacks of an indecent nature.'

'Rape?' Melcorka felt a surge of anger that such things should happen in her Cahokia. 'Did we find the culprit?'

'Culprits,' the Elder said. 'There were many cases.'

Instinctively, Melcorka stood up. 'I can't allow that,' she said. 'What is the usual penalty for such things?'

'When the soldiers were patrolling the streets,' the elder said, 'such things were a rarity. If the guards caught anybody, they put him in the compound as a slave.'

'And quite right, too,' Melcorka said. 'We shall do that again.'

The Elder bowed his head. 'Eyota,' he hesitated over the words, 'you have ended all slavery in Cahokia and destroyed the compound.'

Melcorka considered for only a minute. 'Very well. I order that any man found guilty of rape shall be enslaved by the family of the victim.' She enjoyed the collective gasp from the Elders, knowing she had just given the rapist a life that would be worse than death.

'There is also the case of the petty thieving,' The Elder said. 'We had nothing of the sort before.'

'Then why is it happening now?' Melcorka asked.

'The problem came from the released slaves.' The Elder said. 'Those who belonged to tribes could move in with their kin. Those from broken tribes – that is, where the chief has been sacrificed – had nothing, not even clothes. They wander the streets stealing food and clothing.'

Melcorka felt the disapproval of the Elders at this plague she had brought to her city. She thought quickly. 'There is empty land on the fringes of our Empire. Give these people clothes and food and grant them that land.'

'As you wish, Eyota,' the Elders said.

'And reinstate the guard patrols,' Melcorka said. 'The Elders shall appoint warriors from every tribe to patrol one area of the city and keep down theft and rape.'

'It shall be as you say, Eyota,' the Elders said. 'What shall the elders do when they catch anybody?'

Melcorka thought for a moment, without inspiration striking. 'What would be normal?' she temporised.

'Death or slavery,' the Elders replied.

Melcorka frowned; death seemed too severe, and she did not approve of slavery. 'Limited slavery,' she decided. 'If the patrols catch anybody, they shall be enslaved to the patrol's tribe for one year.'

'It shall be as you say, Eyota,' the Elders agreed.

'Is there anything else?' Melcorka asked.

The Elders glanced at Erik. Their spokesman faced Melcorka.

'The Council of Elders has heard many people asking why Eyota of Cahokia has a bodyguard of foreigners. Does she not trust her own people?'

Melcorka raised her eyebrows. 'Do you dare criticise me?' She felt anger mounting within her.

The Elder straightened and held her gaze. 'I am merely repeating what the people are saying, Eyota. You arrived here with the pale foreigners, and you have appointed them to positions of authority. The people of Cahokia wonder if you trust these unnaturally pale foreigners more than you trust them.'

Opening her mouth to blast this impudent old man back to silence, Melcorka paused. How would the Picts of Fidach or the Gaels of the Isles have felt, if some foreign potentate had arrived as their king and brought a bodyguard of Norse, or Cahokians? They would have felt deeply insulted, and within a few weeks, some of the young warriors would undoubtedly have challenged or at least provoked the bodyguard.

'You are right, Spokesman,' Melcorka allowed graciously, after a pause. 'I apologise for my behaviour.'

The Spokesman looked embarrassed at this magnanimity from a woman he considered nearly divine. 'No, Eyota, there is no need to apologise.'

'There is every need,' Melcorka said. She turned to her smiling bodyguard. 'Erik, I want your Norsemen to help Chaytan.'

'Help Chaytan?' Erik frowned. 'We are Norsemen. We are not here to be ordered around by some naked Skraeling.'

Melcorka was thankful that he spoke in Norse and not in a language that the Cahokians could understand. Even so, it was evident by his tone that he was displeased. The Elders watched without expression. Melcorka knew she had to be as authoritarian with Erik as she would be with any Cahokian in a similar situation.

'I am Queen!' she snapped, wondering if she sounded anything like Frakkok. She hoped so. 'You will obey me or suffer the consequences.' She saw Erik's face darken with rage and his hand stray to his sword hilt. She moderated her tone. 'Think of the Varangian Guard,' she said. 'They are noble Norsemen, and they are proud to serve as bodyguards to the Byzantine Emperor.'

Erik dropped his hand a second before Melcorka called for Chaytan. 'These people are Skraelings, not civilised Greeks.'

'These are my people.' Melcorka dropped her voice to a menacing hiss. 'You will treat them with respect.' She held his gaze until Erik looked away.

The Elders watched, seeing all and saying nothing.

'Now, bow to your Queen.' Melcorka sharpened her tone. 'Bow! Or by the sun I will bring in the guard and force you to your knees!'

Erik took a deep breath and bowed.

'Thank you.' Melcorka faced the Elders. 'Thank you for your time, help and advice,' she said. 'You may now leave to attend to your own business.'

The Elders left in a solemn row, unsmiling and dignified as befitted their position and ages.

'Now, Erik,' Melcorka said. 'Don't forget that I am Queen here. I am Eyota to these people.'

'I remember you as Melcorka of Alba,' Erik said, 'not Eyota the Skraeling.'

'You know that I am no Skraeling.' Melcorka removed Eyota's headband and smiled. 'And sometimes I wonder what we are sitting on out here. There is a handful of us and many hundreds of these very courageous and skilled men. We have already lost Bradan and many fine warriors.' Melcorka shook away the pang that mention of Bradan brought to her heart. 'If these people ever find out that I am not Eyota, God only knows what they will do.'

'My Norsemen would take care of them,' Erik said.

'All of them?' Melcorka raised her eyebrows. 'The Norse are doughty warriors, but so are these men. Chaytan is as bold and tough a fighting man as any I have met.'

'They are Skraelings with stone hammers,' Erik scoffed.

'Thor has a stone hammer,' Melcorka reminded him softly, 'and he is said to be a bit of a warrior.'

Erik shook his head. 'You are too clever with words for me,' he admitted, as his good nature returned.

Melcorka laughed, remembering her previous thoughts about this man. He was so different from Enapay. Indeed, he was so different from every man she had ever met and a complete contrast to the typical Norse warrior that he tried hard to emulate. The impulse to put out her hand and take hold of his arm was too strong to resist. His bicep was hard enough for any fighting man. 'More importantly, I wish your company tonight.'

Erik looked confused and pleased simultaneously. 'What about the Skraeling that keeps your bed warm? Are you not his woman?'

'Tonight, I want you,' Melcorka said. 'Enapay will have to look elsewhere for a woman.'

'He can have one of mine,' Erik said carelessly. 'I have plenty.'

'I'm glad to hear you are so generous with your women,' Melcorka said dryly. She knew that Erik slept alone. She hid her smile. Erik reminded her of a young teenager, eager to impress a female with his warrior skills and sexual prowess.

Erik's smile was a reminder of the youngster Melcorka had met in mid-ocean. She shook her head. 'You are some man, Erik.' The idea came to her as quickly as her passion rose. Taking hold of his arm, she pulled him close and kissed him full on the mouth.

'Oh!' Erik pulled away.

'Erik!' Melcorka could not help her exclamation of surprise. She knew then that he had no experience of women. She remembered his discomfort in Greenland with the Skraeling women and her smile was entirely genuine. 'It's all right, Erik. You can trust me.'

'You caught me by surprise...'

Melcorka ended his bluster with another kiss. 'I know,' she whispered.

'You know...?'

'I will be your first woman.' She spoke the words softly as her attraction to this nervous, handsome and unique young Norseman increased. 'We will make it memorable, you and I. Come with me.' She led him by the hand into her bedchamber and closed the door.

Chapter Twenty-Six

Erik smiled at her across the table, looked away and returned his gaze, still smiling.

'You look happy.' Melcorka gestured to a servant to refill her goblet, tutting when the girl nearly spilt a drop.

'I've never felt happier.' Erik looked stunned. 'Thank you.'

'For what?' Melcorka shook her head. 'Oh, for that! Don't be silly.' She watched the delicate manner in which he ate. 'You had better go and ensure your men are all right,' she said.

'I'd prefer to be here with you,' Erik told her.

'Off with you!' She shooed him away. 'Go on.' She pushed him out of the room, watched as he walked away and returned to her breakfast.

Erik was the most unusual Norseman Melcorka had ever met. Polite, diffident and usually happy, he was handsome as sin and surprisingly clean. Melcorka had not had to pressurise him to wash the previous night and had watched him wash again in the morning. She sat back on her couch, wondering. While Enapay was all-man, tough, masculine and as confident as a warrior should be, Erik was... She searched for a word. What was he? Vulnerable, perhaps. Melcorka stood up. She felt as responsible for him as she had for his sister.

That was the truth. Melcorka was acutely aware that she had killed Erik's father and caused the death of his mother, yet still Erik liked her; more than liked her, if his behaviour of the previous night was any indication. She smiled at a sudden recollection of their activities, shook her head, smiled again and took a deep breath. Erik... She ran the name through her mind, pondering the simple double syllables and the hard ending: Er-ik. He was the very opposite of his father and nothing like his mother. He was handsome and kind and gentle in a way she had never experienced in a Norseman before. For a second, she compared him to Bradan and then shook that thought away; that was unfair to him. It was unfair to both of them. It was unfair to all three of them. He would make a fully trained husband in time.

That thought slid through her subconscious and into her conscious mind before she was aware of its existence. Melcorka shivered. Ever since Greenland, she had thought of Erik. He had infiltrated her mind in a way she had never expected and now that Bradan was lost, Erik was available. A gentle, amenable man such as he was would be a fitting partner for Eyota. He would do her bidding without demur, as any Queen's consort should.

Melcorka began to pace the width of the room; eight steps forward, turn and eight steps back, with her short tunic snapping against her thighs and her sandals padding on the stone-flagged floor. She had been Melcorka; now she was Eyota. She was Queen of Cahokia with servants rushing to do her bidding, armed bodyguards to protect her, a palace in which to live, enough clothes and food to last forever, prestige, a huge city and prosperous country to rule and a whole host of handsome men gasping to share her bed. And now she had a willing, semi-deferential man who would be an excellent partner for life.

Melcorka continued to pace as the thoughts crammed and battered through her head. She could settle here. She could leave her life as Melcorka entirely behind and become Eyota, Queen of Cahokia, forever.

Melcorka closed her eyes as a future of luxury and power beckoned. *Why not?*

Melcorka shivered; why not indeed? She was wanted here, she belonged here and she was needed here. She smiled. She should not indulge in such thoughts when she had her duty to perform.

Reaching for the headband, she placed it on her forehead.

'Chaytan!' she shouted. 'I wish to tour the city.'

Chaytan was there within a minute, stone mace balanced across his shoulder and two sturdy Lakota warriors at his back.

'As you wish, Eyota.'

The city was quiet without the teams of slaves working on the pyramids. In their place were groups of idle men and women dressed in rags, or less than rags.

'Are these the people who have been causing trouble in my city?' Melcorka asked.

'Yes, Eyota.' Chaytan kept close by her, with his mace held ready. The other two Lakotas watched the ex-slaves through hard, watchful eyes.

'I have given the Elders instructions to remove the problem,' Eyota said.

On every previous occasion when she had walked the streets of Cahokia, Melcorka had been greeted with smiles and near-adulation. This time, the people remained politely respectful but no more. Remembering the problems that the Elders had brought to her attention, Melcorka nodded. She would cure this city of all its ills. She was Eyota, Queen of Cahokia.

The man bowed low as he approached. Tall and copper-skinned, his teeth flashed white as he smiled and explained his problems with noisy neighbours.

Melcorka paused to listen to his words while her eyes were busy with his body. Truly, there were many advantages to being a Queen. All she had to do was rid Cahokia of these pestilential ex-slaves... That man was extremely impressive. Eyota crooked her finger to him.

Chapter Twenty-Seven

'You look a bit concerned, Enapay.' Melcorka turned away from the view. She liked to stand on the parapet looking down on her city.

'I am worried for you, Eyota,' Enapay said.

'For me?' Melcorka did not hide her smile. 'You do not need to worry about me.' Stretching out, she touched his arm.

Enapay pressed closer. 'I have news that you will not like, Eyota.'

Melcorka felt her smile freeze. 'Tell me, Enapay.'

'I hope you do not think I am causing trouble...'

'I have no reason to think that, Enapay.' Melcorka defended him stoutly. 'Please tell me what you have to say.'

'May I show you, Eyota? It means leaving the palace.'

'I am sure I remember how to walk,' Melcorka said. 'Do we need Chaytan?'

'No, Eyota, unless you wish to have somebody killed.' He hesitated for a moment. 'It is better that you do not have an escort or anybody that could draw attention to you.'

'As you wish, Enapay,' Melcorka said.

Stopping only to pick up Eyota's headband, they left the palace and the Citadel, walking quickly down the stairs that descended the great pyramid. As always, Melcorka was impressed by the skill of the builders. There had been nothing on this scale when she lived in Alba. Indeed, she would have been surprised if there was anything as large as this anywhere on the European continent, although she had heard that Rome was quite large.

Not that it mattered. Cahokia was her home now.

Enapay slipped through the gate and trotted westward through the city, with Melcorka following without thought or worry. For the last few weeks, she had been used to moving at a more sedate, regal pace, so it was refreshing to stretch her legs and use her muscles again.

'Where are you taking me?' Melcorka gasped slightly with effort.

'Here, Eyota.' Enapay guided her up a small, partially completed pyramid that overlooked the Mississippi. 'I don't like to show you this,' he said, 'but it would not be right that you did not know.' He pointed toward the river.

Melcorka started as she saw *Catriona* lying on her side on the bank. She had almost forgotten what the ship looked like after so long. Melcorka shook her head; she had left that life behind long ago. She may decide to keep *Catriona* as a reminder, or just have her burned. But that was not what Enapay had brought her to see.

Attached by two mooring ropes and floating in the river, *Sea Serpent* was river-worthy in every way. Her mast thrust skyward with the sail furled to the spars; her forestay and backstay had been recently repaired and replaced, and some of her planking renewed. Skilled hands had repainted the dragon figurehead so the eyes gleamed and the teeth were sharp and white.

Erik stood in the stern. He was giving sharp orders to his crew in between enjoying caresses from the group of shapely women who were around him. Not only *Sea Serpent* had altered. Erik's hair hung around his face in neat braids, in a style similar to that which his father had adopted. One of the women slipped her arms around his waist, and he laughed.

Melcorka felt the lurch of betrayal. *Erik was her man. Was he not?*

'Thank you, Enapay.' She forced the words out. She was not sure what to say. 'It seems that Erik Farseeker and the Norsemen are planning to leave us.'

'I know you are friendly with Erik,' Enapay said.

'Come with me,' Melcorka said.

'Be careful Eyota,' Enapay warned. 'The Norsemen can be dangerous. I could fetch some warriors if you wish to challenge them.'

'There is no need.' Melcorka was already walking down the steps of the pyramid, careless of her safety and dignity. She stalked to the riverside in time to see Erik engaged in a passionate kiss with a young woman.

'Lend me your knife.' Melcorka took Enapay's knife and cut through *Sea Serpent's* mooring cables. The flint blade was sharper than she had expected and it parted the cable without effort.

'Hey!' It was Knut who first noticed that *Sea Serpent* was drifting with the current. 'Who did that?'

'I did!' Melcorka shouted. 'I see you are planning to leave.'

Erik disentangled himself from the woman and stepped forward. His smile was as fixed as ever. 'Farewell, Melcorka.' He lifted a hand. 'Enjoy your exile with the Skraelings.'

'What?' Melcorka stared at him. 'Erik! What are you doing?'

'We are going home,' Erik said. His laugh was mocking. For the first time, he looked and sounded very much like his father. 'Did you think I would stay as your pet? I am a Norseman! We are bred for the open sea, not to be stuck hundreds of miles inland with naked savages!'

Melcorka felt Enapay stiffen at her side.

'I am Eyota of Cahokia!' Melcorka said the first thing that came into her mind. 'I order you to return!'

Erik laughed again, with the other Norsemen joining in. Knut spat his contempt into the river.

'Oars!' Erik ordered, and the Norsemen took their places on the rowing benches as if they had never been away. 'Sail!'

They hoisted the great striped sail, and it rippled and then bellied in the breeze. *Sea Serpent* eased slowly into the deepwater channel in mid-river. For a moment, Melcorka considered calling out the guard and following her in canoes, or racing upstream to replace the boom at the frontier. She did neither. What would be the point in forcing reluctant foreigners to remain in her kingdom?

Melcorka watched *Sea Serpent* take Erik away from her life, with the dragon-head pointing the way back to the north. Suddenly, she felt very lonely in this foreign land so far from everything she knew and understood.

'Eyota?' Enapay's voice was deep. 'Have I offended you?'

Melcorka touched her headband. 'You have not offended me, Enapay.' The dragon ship was well upriver now, with the ripples from her wake breaking creamy-brown on the bank of the river.

'I never trusted these foreigners,' Enapay said.

Melcorka did not smile. 'I rather liked Erik Farseeker,' she said. 'He was...' She searched for a word she had once used. 'He was cute.'

'He is gone now,' Enapay said.

Sea Serpent was out of sight around a bend in the river now, with a copse of overhanging trees blocking Melcorka's view. Melcorka was entirely alone, while Eyota was Queen of this vast empire.

'Come, Enapay,' Melcorka said. 'We have a city and a nation to rule.' She placed her hand on his naked thigh, enjoying the rubbery feel of hard muscle. The last wave of *Sea Serpent's* wake broke on the Cahokian shore of the Mississippi.

Eyota smiled and slid her hand upward.

Chapter Twenty-Eight

Melcorka heard the slight sound. She turned over in her bed, pulled the furs over her face and closed her eyes. It did not matter what the noise was. She was safe in her own rooms in her own palace and, with Chaytan commanding the guards, she had nothing to fear.

She felt the man beside her stir. 'Keep still,' she ordered. He moved again, so she pushed him away and said, 'Get out.' She watched him rise and stumble around naked in the dark. He turned once, opened the door and left. The door closed. Melcorka turned around again and closed her eyes.

That noise came a second time.

Melcorka grunted and sat up. She contemplated shouting for a servant, decided not to, threw back the covers and stood up. 'Is somebody there?' She should have kept that man with her after all. What was his name again? She shrugged; she could not remember. It did not matter, There were always more, and then there was Enapay when she wanted him.

The sudden flare of light temporarily blinded her. Throwing up her hand to shield her eyes, she stepped back. 'Who's there?'

'Your death is here.'

The voice was deep and harsh and terribly familiar.

'Wamblee?' Melcorka reached for Defender, cursing in sudden panic when she remembered she had hung it on the wall of another room rather than have it spoil the luxury of her sleeping room. She looked around as the light subsided to a dull glow. The wall gaped open at her side and men stepped into her room from some secret passageway.

'Wamblee indeed,' Wamblee said. 'You will know these people.'

Enapay was next, followed by three feather-bedecked priests. They all crowded into Melcorka's room, pushing her against the wall.

'What's this?' Melcorka stalled for time, reaching for her headband.

Enapay was faster, grabbing the band and holding it tight. 'I know that you are not Eyota,' he said. 'Only this thing gives you power and authority over our people.'

'Enapay?' Melcorka said. 'You are my man! We have shared my bed!'

'Many men have shared your bed,' Enapay said caustically, pushing her away.

Melcorka looked behind her, calculating the distance to her living quarters where Defender was, but Wamblee casually knocked her to the ground with a backswing of his hand.

'How does it feel, Eyota of Cahokia as you call yourself?' he asked. 'How does it feel to know you are going to die?'

'Chaytan!' Melcorka shouted as loudly as she could. 'Chaytan! I need you!'

'He can't hear you,' Enapay said. 'Nobody can. You strengthened the wall, remember?' His smile contained no humour at all. 'I think your pet Lakota will have troubles enough without considering some foreign woman.'

'That was your idea to strengthen the wall.' The realisation bit Melcorka. 'You planned this!'

Enapay laughed. 'You're correct. Did you think that you, a foreigner, could replace the king and remain in power, pretending to be Eyota? A long-dead woman?' He laughed.

'You fooled me,' Melcorka said.

'It was not hard to fool you,' Enapay said. 'You thought your subjects worshipped your every word!' He looked up at Wamblee. 'Shall I kill her now?'

'No,' Wamblee said. 'That would be far too easy. The people must see their ruler humiliated. They must see how foolish it is to try and take my place. Hold her.'

'I won't go so easily!' Melcorka kicked out, catching Enapay a shrewd blow in the groin. She grunted in satisfaction, ducked under Wamblee's clumsy grab, pushed one of the priests away and dived for the door to her living quarters. The other two priests stepped in her way, both holding great, stone-headed maces. Melcorka tried to jink past, realised that there was no room and returned to the room. Reaching under her pillow, she grabbed at her clothes. If she were to be displayed to her people, at least she would be decent.

That small delay cost her dear, as one of the priests took hold of her tunic and held on tight. Melcorka pulled away; the tunic ripped, leaving her with only the hem and one of the small copper falcons. She swore, slipped the falcon in her mouth for safe-keeping and turned away.

The only escape was the hole in the wall through which Wamblee had entered. Melcorka dived for it and found herself in a narrow passage that spiralled both up and down. She headed downward, saw a stone lever in the wall and pushed it hopefully. The door into her room groaned shut, and she was left in darkness so complete that it pressed down upon her.

With her footsteps sounding hollow in the passage, Melcorka followed the stairs, hoping they led to safety. They continued downward into stinking darkness, step after steep step. Listening to the sound of her breathing, feeling the thunder of her heartbeat, she tried to think of some way out. There were only two possibilities: find Chaytan and Chumani, or retrieve Defender. She shook her head at the ease with which she had been deceived. Enapay must have pretended friendship purely to bring in Wamblee. This had been planned for weeks.

If she could not trust Enapay, how could she trust Chaytan?

The stairs ended in a long passage that stretched left and right, and one way seemed as dark as the other. Melcorka moved left, hoping for an exit, hoping for help, hoping for some escape from this strange world where luxury and absolute power was intertwined with extreme danger and where someone who was a friend one minute could be a deadly enemy the next.

There was the sound of voices ahead. Melcorka hurried forward. She saw a slender shaft of light emanating from the wall and a slight draught of air. She stopped and pressed her face to what was a finger-wide gap. She was looking into a chamber in the lower reaches of the palace, where the servants lived.

They were packed into a tiny room, with bare stone walls and stone floors, sharing a filthy rug for a bed. A single rush lamp gave out a feeble light as three women struggled to their feet. The women in the bed were in rags; it was evident that the one set of decent clothes was shared between them and used only when they were on duty.

I did not know, Melcorka thought, ruefully. She had been so intent on her own position that she had never considered that of others. *When I get back into power, I will change things. I swear I will.* She considered shouting, realised that the servants probably did not know about the passageway or the spyhole and moved on.

There were more spyholes looking into other rooms; more servants, or stores, or empty rooms, and no way of escape that Melcorka could see. She moved on, not giving up as the passage dipped down and thrust onward through deeper darkness, with dampness dripping on her from above and the sinister rustle of many tiny feet on the ground. Melcorka did not know what type of insect would live here and she did not wish to find out.

The passage ended at a single stone slab. Melcorka stopped, running her hand over it, desperate for an exit. She found a circular stone handle, tugged and pushed, and then turned it anti-clockwise. The slab turned on a central axis, rotating a full one hundred and eighty degrees. Melcorka peered into a room that seemed even more luxurious than her quarters in the palace. She stepped forward, and the door swung shut behind her.

'I thought you would end up here,' Wamblee said. 'We've been waiting for you.' His laugh was full of genuine humour. Stepping forward, the priests on either side of him took hold of Melcorka's arms and held them tightly. 'We'll keep you secure until the time comes to execute you.' He patted her face. 'Your sacrifice will be a fitting example to my people of the futility of rebellion.'

'The people won't accept you as their king,' Melcorka said. 'Your tyranny has alienated you.'

Wamblee laughed again. 'Were you any better? All you did was increase rapes and robbery and hunt for men to pleasure you. You had no interest in the people, only in your personal enjoyment.' He jerked a thumb to the priests. 'Take her away and keep her safe. If she escapes, I will have both of you on the altar.'

With her hands twisted behind her back, Melcorka was pushed through a labyrinth of corridors to a dungeon comprised entirely of stone flags, with no windows and a stone door sealed by an immense stone bar. She was thrown onto her back, and her wrists and ankles tied securely to four stone posts in the ground.

'Nobody has ever escaped from here,' the taller of the two priests said, 'and nobody ever shall escape from here.'

Looking around, Melcorka could see why. She was surrounded by nothing but stone and, when the stone door slammed shut and the stone bar ground into place, there was not even a glimmer of light. Lying in the immense darkness, Melcorka had only her thoughts as uneasy companions.

Wamblee was partially correct. She had concentrated on her physical pleasures. But why? She was not by nature an overly sensual woman. What has caused the change? Was it because she had lost Bradan? Partly, Melcorka acknowledged. Yet there were other reasons. Every time she wore that headband, Eyota took over, and she lost something of herself. The sensuality was undoubtedly from Eyota; with the headband, she adopted more of Eyota's personality, yet without it, the Cahokian people would never have accepted her. Melcorka swore; she could not think of a way out.

After only half an hour, she began to suffer from cramp. Her arms and legs ached abominably, and her back was stretched to its limit. She was hungry, thirsty and cold, yet all that did not matter beside the fact that she had let so many people down. She had removed a tyrant, only to prove herself as a weak and ineffectual leader. She was Melcorka the Swordswoman, not Eyota of Cahokia. This city had never been her place. It was too late now; Cahokia looked like being her final adventure. Melcorka closed her eyes; her mother would welcome her into the next world.

She did not know how long she had lain there. It may have been hours, it may have been days, it may have been weeks. It seemed like an eternity. She was not sure if she wanted her physical, emotional and mental agony to end, or if she wished it to continue, knowing that the eventual relief would only end with her death.

There was a tiny sound in that place. An insect of some sort was trapped with her inside that stone tomb. She twisted her head, looking for the culprit but seeing only darkness. Nothing else. It was some time later, hours or days, that she saw it. A small, long-legged lizard that searched for food in the minuscule cracks where the stone slabs had been laid in the unimaginable past.

Stretched out and securely tied, Melcorka tested her bonds for the hundredth time. They were so tight that they cut into her ankles and wrists, and any movement merely added to her pain. She felt her feet and hands swell until she realised that the only thing she could do was lie still and hope the swelling would die down.

Melcorka formulated a plan. The second she was untied, she would launch herself at the nearest priest and knock him down. Even without Defender, she should be a match for a priest. She had worked and lived with fighting men long enough to have picked up moves and tricks; she knew how to fight, even though she lacked the muscles of a warrior and months of easy living had made her soft. She could fight, and she would win, Melcorka told herself. That thought gave her strength as she lay there, prone and scared in the dark.

As time passed, Melcorka became quite friendly with that solitary lizard that was sentenced to imprisonment just as much as she was. She named it Erik after the Norseman and spoke to it as a companion. Erik the lizard appeared to listen to her, turning its head this way and that as she spoke. Sometimes it came up to her and pressed its body against hers, and once or twice it ate the tiny but disgusting six-legged things that crawled over her as she lay there, too helpless to brush them off.

Erik never replied, but his presence helped keep her sane when her mind threatened to explode with a mixture of despair and disappointment that she had let so many of the Cahokian people down. Now it was too late. Now she had no future. Her release from here would end only in her death.

Death. That word was so final. She would enter the spirit world with Bearnas and her own people. That could not be a bad thing. Yet she was not ready.

'I am not yet ready!' she called out. 'I am not ready!'

The priests stood over her. 'That is a shame,' one said, 'for this is the day that you will be sacrificed to Wi.'

'She stinks,' the other priest said.

'I can smell that! She has been lying in her sweat and filth since we tied her here.'

Melcorka cringed at the sound of people again after so many days of solitary silence. The priests seemed to be shouting at the top of their voices, and their presence filled the nearly empty space that she had come to think of as home.

'I can't leave Erik behind,' she said, with her mind confused.

'You'll never see the Norseman again.' The priests said.

As soon as they untied her, Melcorka remembered her plan. She tried to rise, to throw herself at the nearest priest, but the agony of circulation returning to her swollen hands and feet made her cry out in pain and writhe on the filthy stone slabs. With much experience of handling such prisoners, the priests had expected no less and watched dispassionately. They did not care about her suffering. They were about to inflict immeasurably more.

'Wash her,' the first priest called over his shoulder, and a slave lifted a bucket of Mississippi water and threw it over Melcorka. A second slave added another bucket, and then a third, until Melcorka cringed and writhed under the deluge. She looked up through a curtain of wet hair.

'I'm not defeated yet,' she said, with the sharp beak of her falcon jabbing painfully into the roof of her mouth.

'Prepare her,' the priests said. They had heard such promises of defiance before, from brave and proud chiefs of once powerful tribes. Their words had not helped them, and they had all died under the flint knives in unbearable agony.

The slaves moved forward. Now was Melcorka's time. Fighting her pain, she rose and grappled with the first, throwing him in the move she had learned from Erik. The second slave was stronger than the first; she thrust her straight fingers into his throat and sent him gasping back against the wall. The third lifted a short mace and crashed it against the back of her head. Melcorka winced and staggered.

The slight delay was sufficient for the slaves to recover. They, too, were used to dealing with reluctant prisoners and threw themselves on Melcorka. One held her arms, another her legs and a third attached hobbles to ankles as if she was a horse to be tethered, so it could walk but not stray.

'Get her up,' the priests ordered, and a slave grabbed a handful of Melcorka's hair, dragged her unceremoniously to her feet and pushed toward that great stone door. Unable to walk properly because of the hobbles, Melcorka took tiny baby-steps with the slaves pushing her along, taunting her, poking at her with sharp sticks, mocking her nudity and generally doing their job of ridiculing her.

Melcorka did not know what to expect when she left her dungeon. She remembered the execution of the two tribal chiefs, yet was unprepared for the explosion of noise and colour that greeted her. After so long in the dark, she was disorientated, confused and blinded. She blinked and turned her head from the light, stumbled from the hobbles and nearly fell, which gave the slaves more opportunity to prod and beat her.

It seemed that every person in Cahokia was present. Men, women, children and dogs bayed and jeered as she was pushed along the broad thoroughfare between her dungeon and the sacrificial pyramid.

Another prisoner was pushed toward her. It was Chumani, with a swelling bruise on her right eye and a bloody cut on her right arm. She looked up at Melcorka.

'You tried, Eyota,' Chumani said. 'Thank you for trying.'

'I failed,' Melcorka said. 'I was a very poor Queen.' She staggered as one of the slaves pushed her from behind. Turning, she tried to kick, swore as her hobbles held her feet together; swung a punch that missed and gasped as one of the other slaves thrust his sharpened stick into her ribs. Melcorka closed her eyes. She knew that she was fighting the wrong battle. The slaves were under orders to torment her; if they failed, they, too, would doubtless be horribly tortured to death.

There were guards around, the rump of the Wall Guard and the remains of the Citadel Guard, glaring at her in utter hatred as she walked to her execution. Melcorka stared back. She was going to die. She did not care about their hatred; they were her enemy. She should have killed them all when she had the chance, rather than allowing them back into society. It was too late now.

'Get your head up, woman!' Bearnas snapped. 'You are Melcorka of the Cenel Bearnas! Act like it!'

'I let you down, Mother,' Melcorka said. 'I let everybody down.'

'You have never let me down, Melcorka. Walk erect and proud!'

For one moment, Melcorka heard the piping call of an oystercatcher, guiding her on her last walk in this realm before she joined her mother in the spirit world, or Tir-nan-Og, or heaven, or whatever name was given to the place she would go to after death. She watched that black-and-white bird disappear toward the fatal pyramid, straightened her back and walked on as best she could.

The crowd watched her, some curious, some sympathetic, some gloating, some afraid. Bradan stood among them with that young woman, Ehawee at his side. Melcorka smiled at them. She was glad that Bradan had found a good woman. Ehawee would look after him.

They were at the base of the pyramid now and the steps stretched ahead, leading up to the altar where the priests and Wamblee waited.

The crowd was hushed. As Melcorka mounted the steps one at a time, moving sideways because of her hobble, there was a collective groan, instantly hushed by the guards. Somebody cried out, 'They can't sacrifice Eyota!' The words were no sooner spoken than a Guardsman stepped forward and clubbed the speaker to death.

'Murder!' somebody else called, and the Guards moved toward the speaker.

'Hurry up, the rabble is getting restless,' one of the priests said. 'The sooner we sacrifice this one, the better I'll like it. That's the only thing that'll settle them down. Push her up the stairs!'

Taking hold of Melcorka's hair, one of the slaves hauled her up the next step, with the other two alternatively shoving at her and thrusting their pointed sticks into her backside.

'If I survive this,' Melcorka said, 'I'll teach you how to treat a lady!'

'Hurry it up!' the priests said. 'Get that sacrifice up to the altar.'

There was another voice raised in protest and another crunching blow from a stone mace, and then Melcorka stood on the summit of the pyramid with a group of priests around her and Wamblee in front, grinning, with Defender in his hand and triumph bright in his eyes.

'There is nobody to save you now,' he gloated. 'Your Norsemen have fled, your Lakota warriors are dead or vanished, and your friend Chumani will be sacrificed at your back.' Reaching forward, he smoothed his hand across her face. 'You will die screaming in front of those people who looked to you for leadership, Melcorka of Alba.'

'I am never alone.' Melcorka had expected to be afraid, but she was not. She stood erect, facing Wamblee eye to eye.

Wamblee looked away. 'Are you ready, priests?'

'We are ready,' they said.

'Then put her on the altar,' Wamblee ordered.

Before Melcorka could say another word, four priests took hold of her and held her across that altar. She felt the pressure of cold stone pressing against her spine and the pain of grown men pushing down on her limbs. The sky above looked very clear and blue; it was a good thing to look on as she died. She raised her chin in stubborn defiance. She would die in silence, she decided; Wamblee would not have the satisfaction of hearing her scream.

'Hold her there,' Wamblee said. He stepped past her. 'I will address my people.' He looked down upon the assembly in the arena between the pyramid and the Citadel and raised his voice.

'I am Wamblee,' he said. 'I am the ruler of Cahokia and the Dhegian Empire!' He raised his arms, holding them wide in unconscious imitation of a crucifix. 'Lately, there was an attempt to usurp me.' He pointed to Melcorka, lying naked on the sacrificial altar. 'There is the usurper now, waiting to greet Wi. Waiting to feed me with her heart.' His laugh boomed out across the arena. Some people joined in, others did not.

'She can wait,' Wamblee shouted. 'I am sure she is comfortable as we slowly break her back.'

There was another shout from the crowd, and another ugly crunch as the guards crushed a skull with their maces.

'Here!' Wamblee held up Defender. 'Here is her sword of power.' Lifting it high, he tossed it down the stairs. It landed with a clatter and slithered slowly, step by step until it came to rest on the middle terrace. 'You see how useless it is!'

'And here is a stick that she valued.' Wamblee lifted Bradan's staff and threw it high, like a spear. It soared over the stairs, reached its apex and whistled downward to land a foot away from Bradan. He looked at it without interest, put an arm around Ehawee and returned his gaze to Wamblee.

'And now, Melcorka, you have nothing – no friends, no weapons, not even a stick,' Wamblee declared in triumph.

'I have my soul,' Melcorka said. 'And that is more than you have.'

Wamblee lifted the headband of Eyota. 'Perhaps I have no soul,' he said with a leer. 'Yet I have this.' He held it up for the crowd to see. 'I hold the power of Eyota as well as of Wamblee. Is there anybody who dares to challenge me?'

Chumani had been standing erect, waiting her turn to be executed. Now, she took a step forward and reached for the headband as if hoping to grab it from Wamblee. He held it out of her reach. 'Would you not like to?' he said, taunting her. 'Do you not crave the power of Eyota?'

Pushing her away, Wamblee removed his falcon headgear and slipped on the band, stretching it so it clamped onto his larger head. 'Now I have the power of Eyota as well as my own! My victory is complete!'

'Not quite!' Melcorka had waited until all eyes were on Wamblee. Now, she had one single, slender chance. All this time, she had held the falcon trinket at the back of her mouth. Now, she pushed it to the front, used her tongue to manoeuvre the sharp beak forward, held it momentarily between her teeth and spat it with all the force she could at the priest who held her right arm. The falcon's sharp beak landed full in the priest's left eye. The man screamed and jerked away, loosening his grip on Melcorka's wrist. She pulled her arm free and pushed the priest back, so he collided with Wamblee.

'Fight them, Chumani!'

Seeing the priests in temporary disarray, Chumani banged into the closest, providentially freeing Melcorka's right leg. She swung it in a kick that caught the priest's companion full on the chest and sent him staggering backwards.

'Fight them!' Melcorka yelled and saw a disturbance in the crowd below her. Ehawee had slipped away from Bradan and was running forward. 'Save Eyota!' Ehawee shouted, until a guard lifted his mace and swung it at her.

'No!' Bradan's voice was distinct even above the turmoil. He pushed forward to help Ehawee, but too late. The mace landed a glancing blow, sending Ehawee to the ground. She yelled and held her head.

Pushing at the guard, Bradan lifted Ehawee, holding her close as the guard swung again. Even from her lofty position, Melcorka heard the crunch of contact. She saw Bradan's expression alter, saw his mouth open in a shout of grief and saw him throw himself at the guard.

Bradan was no fighting man. He carried no weapon and had never learned even the most elementary of defensive or offensive techniques. The Citadel Guard tossed him aside without effort and lifted his mace to finish him off.

'Bradan!' Melcorka screamed. She was aware that Wamblee was beside her and that the priests were recovering, but all her attention was on Bradan. Nothing else mattered.

Bradan lay sprawled on the ground and the Dhegians and others were backing away, watching the Guardsman raise his mace to kill this impudent rebel.

Melcorka dived for the head of the stairs, hoping to reach Bradan before the Dhegians killed him. A priest blocked her path, and then another, so a knot of muscular men submerged her, each one intent on putting her back on the altar. She looked sideways, watching the drama unfold so far beneath her.

Knowing he was outmatched, Bradan scrabbled for a weapon. His fingers closed around his own staff that lay untended on the ground. Melcorka saw something change as he grasped the length of rowan wood. He looked up, and for a moment he stared straight into Melcorka's desperate eyes.

'Bradan!' Melcorka shouted. 'Run!'

Bradan was not a fighter, yet, when he looked at the crumpled body of Ehawee, he rammed his staff into the Guardsman's face.

'Bradan!' Melcorka screamed. 'Run! Please run!'

And then she could see no more as the priests struggled to lift her back onto the altar. She fought back, desperate to help Bradan before the Guards bludgeoned him to death with their massive stone maces.

'Kill them!' Wamblee put his hands to the headband, pulling it further down. 'Kill them all!'

Grabbing the flint knife from the careless hand of a priest, Melcorka bent low and sliced through Chumani's hobbles. 'Run, Chumani,' she said. 'Run for your life!'

'No, Eyota!' Chumani said. 'I will not leave you.'

'Run when I say!' Melcorka pushed her toward the steps. 'Save yourself!' Gripping the flint knife, Melcorka wriggled free of the priests and threw herself at Wamblee.

'Now my Melcorka is back!' Bearnas was at her side, a misty figure with an oystercatcher flying at her shoulder. 'Now you are my warrior daughter!' She was laughing, wearing her full chain mail and holding a shining sword.

'Out of my way, Mother,' Melcorka yelled, slashing at Wamblee with the small flint blade. 'This is my fight!' She felt the thrill of contact as the sharp blade sliced a deep cut in Wamblee's face.

Wamblee flinched and put a hand on the wound, from which a ruby of blood seeped and began to flow down his chin. He swung an arm to deflect Melcorka and caught Chumani on the back.

Melcorka saw Chumani stagger under the blow, trip, and fall. She fell onto the top stair, scraping the skin from her cheek, reached out for balance and fell further, rolling down the stairs. Melcorka saw her vanish and nodded; Chumani was out of harm's way. Now, Melcorka was alone on the summit of the sacrificial pyramid, with five priests and Wamblee. She slashed again with the flint dagger, ripping a priest's tunic and cutting into his shoulder.

'I am Melcorka!' she shouted. 'Melcorka of the Cenel Bearnas! Come and face me!'

As one priest reeled away, two others took his place, thrusting with their knives. Laughing, knowing she was about to die, Melcorka accepted the pain of the first cut and slashed at the priest's throat with her dagger. 'I am a warrior woman!' she shouted. 'I am Melcorka the Swordswoman!'

She felt the sting of another wound across her hip, turned abruptly and kicked at a priest before stabbing upward with her dagger. There was an immediate rush of blood, and a squeal as the man clutched at the new wound in his stomach.

And then there were three priests facing her, three knives stabbing and Wamblee grasping her by the hair.

'I have her,' Wamblee roared. 'Take her to the altar!'

Wamblee's strength was immense. His arms were as thick as most men's thighs and rippled with supple muscle. Melcorka struggled in vain. She kicked backwards in the hope of catching his shin. She threw her head back, hoping to crack his chin, mouth or nose. She reversed the knife in her hand and jabbed into his flesh, but he seemed immune to the pain.

'I have her safe.' Wamblee lifted Melcorka clean off the ground, so her feet and legs kicked uselessly into the air. 'Take her to the altar!'

Dishevelled and angry now, the priests grabbed hold of her arms and legs and helped Wamblee carry her back to the altar. They banged her down so hard that Melcorka thought her back was broken and they hauled brutally on her limbs, so she was once again spread-eagled, face-up.

'This time there will be no mistake.' Wamblee was gasping with effort, bleeding where Melcorka's knife had rammed into his side. 'Rip her open!'

Four priests hauled at Melcorka's limbs, as the fifth placed the tip of his knife on top of her pubic bone.

It had taken that long for Chumani to return. 'Leave Eyota alone!' Her leap was perfectly timed. She landed on Wamblee's chest, unbalancing him, so he staggered backwards. One of his feet made contact with a priest, and Melcorka again jerked free her arm, pushing at the priest with the knife.

'Melcorka!' That was Bradan's voice, strong and very welcome. 'Take this!' He threw Defender across to her. Sunlight glinted on the silver blade as the sword seemed to hang in the air. Still lying on the altar, Melcorka grabbed at the sword but missed. It fell with a loud clatter.

'Eyota!' Chumani shouted. Pushing herself away from Wamblee, she scooped Defender from the ground and passed it to Melcorka.

As soon as she grasped her sword, Melcorka felt that welcome surge of strength and power. There was no time to enjoy the sensation. Slicing sideways, she killed the priest with the sacrificial knife and cut the arm off another. The remaining priests recoiled, shrieking in horror. Melcorka swung left and right, killing two more and watching the sole survivor run.

He did not get far. A surge of men and woman had followed Bradan up the stairs, and they grabbed the priest. Melcorka did not watch the resulting slaughter.

Wamblee's deep voice roared out, calling for his guards. Throwing Chumani off, he reached for his mace and laid around him, with every swing knocking down one or more of the crowd.

'I am Wamblee!' he shouted.

The people pulled back. After years of fear, they were still apprehensive of this giant of a man. Melcorka stepped forward with Defender balanced across her shoulder.

'We shall fight,' Melcorka said. 'Or I can give you to your subjects so they can sacrifice you to whichever god they please.'

Rather than replying, Wamblee swung his mace at Melcorka's head. She blocked it with Defender. Wamblee was a head and shoulders taller than she was, and as broad as two ordinary men; every swing on his mace sounded like the ripping of cloth and when he missed, the mace cracked the stone flags on which it landed.

Holding Defender in front of her, Melcorka backed away, parrying, blocking and dodging. A crowd formed around her, men and women with anxious faces and worried eyes. Chumani was there, with Bradan at her side.

'Are you Bradan or Capa?' Melcorka asked.

Bradan tapped his staff on the flags. 'I am Bradan the Wanderer,' he said.

'When did you get back?' Melcorka parried another colossal swing of the mace.

'When I lifted my staff.'

'It is good to have you where you belong.' Melcorka caught the mace on Defender's blade, twisted and pushed back. She saw the confusion on Wamblee's face as a mere woman managed to rock his balance.

'I have the power of Eyota!' Wamblee shouted. 'I wear her headband!'

Melcorka stepped back and rested the point of Defender on the ground. 'It does not suit you,' she said. 'It was made for a woman, and you are a man. Or so I have been told.' She raised her voice. 'I have yet to meet the woman who can prove that particular claim.'

Wamblee's yell was of fury mixed with frustration. Lifting his mace, he charged at her. Melcorka waited until he was close and then crouched down with Defender held before her like a lance. Unable to stop himself, Wamblee ran straight onto the point of the sword. The impetus of his own lunge drove Defender right through his body and out the other side.

Wamblee grunted. He looked down at the gleaming steel blade that protruded from his belly, in something like disbelief. 'You have killed me,' he said, sounding completely astonished.

'I know,' Melcorka said and ripped the sword sideways and out.

Wamblee stared at his blood as it poured from him like a waterfall. Then he crumpled to the ground. He kicked once, twice, stiffened and died. Melcorka knelt beside him and closed his eyes.

All around, the crowd fell silent. They were not sure what this death signified, but they knew it was important, a landmark in the history of their city.

'He was a cruel man,' Melcorka said, 'but he died bravely and honourably. He shall be buried as the king and mighty warrior that he was.' Removing Eyota's headband from the dead despot's, she lifted it high in the air. Despite all the slaughter and killing, not a single drop of blood stained the immaculate beadwork.

'You are indeed Eyota,' Chumani said.

'No. I am Melcorka of Alba. I only borrowed some of Eyota's powers.' Melcorka stepped over to Chumani. 'When all was lost, Chumani, it was you who enabled me to fight. It was you who turned the tide of battle.' She slipped the headband over Chumani's black hair and eased it down to her forehead.

Blood from the scrape on Chumani's cheek had congealed to form a pattern very like a pouncing falcon. Melcorka nodded: the prophecy had spoken of a woman with a patterned cheek coming from the north. Chumani had come to the altar from the northern side, and warriors of Cahokia surrounded them.

Chumani gasped. 'Eyota...' Her eyes widened. 'Eyota...' Placing both hands on her head, she reeled backwards.

Melcorka reached out. 'Chumani? Are you all right?'

'Leave her.' Bradan placed a firm hand on Melcorka's arm. 'Let her adapt to the power of Eyota.'

Melcorka looked into his eyes, seeing the wisdom that she had missed so badly these past few months. 'What is happening?'

'Eyota's power is happening,' Bradan said. The scar on his left temple was very visible. 'It is a positive power.'

'It was not always good with me,' Melcorka said, as Chumani crumpled to the ground.

'You had three forces working within you,' Bradan explained. 'You had the stubborn, wilful woman that is Melcorka, the passionate goodness of Eyota and the strength and skill of Defender. The combination of all three came out as a strongly passionate leader, with two powers competing. Chumani does not have Defender's influence to deflect Eyota's goodness.' He patted Melcorka on the arm. 'Give her a few moments.'

'I do not need a few moments.' Chumani rose to her feet. Although she had Chumani's face and body, there was something fundamentally different about her. The spirit that glowed within her was stronger, brighter and more powerful than anything Melcorka had ever seen before.

'You are Eyota.' Melcorka leaned on Defender.

'I am Eyota,' Chumani said.

Melcorka understood at last. 'I never was Eyota, I was only a messenger for her. You are Eyota, and I was one of your warriors who overturned the evil one.'

Chumani lifted her arms and the whole of her people fell silent. 'I am Eyota,' she said. 'I am returned to herald a new period of prosperity and peace. From this day on, there will be no human sacrifice, there will be no slavery and there will be peace in the lands. The great river Mississippi will be open for navigation and trade north and south, and there will be trade east to the great sea, north to the vast inland seas and west across the great empty lands, as far as they stretch and further.'

The people listened. They did not cheer; they bowed before her.

'Rise,' Chumani said. 'Rise and stand proud. I am proud of you.' She gazed over her people with such an expression of love that Melcorka knew things would be well in Cahokia for as long as Eyota was in charge.

They buried Wamblee near his Citadel, with tens of thousands of shell-beads beneath him, fashioned into the shape of a falcon. There were those who mourned his death and those who said he would be discovered in the unimaginable future, and that people would wonder at this great king who ruled Cahokia.

Bradan and Melcorka were present as Wamblee was laid to rest, and they watched as Eyota took control of her land.

'I think it is time for us to leave now,' Melcorka said softly. 'Our duty is done here.'

'I think it is,' Bradan agreed.

'Where shall we go?'

'We were heading south down the Mississippi,' Bradan said. 'We have *Catriona,* and we have Defender and my staff. I am sure that these good people will supply us with food and water.'

Melcorka nodded as Bradan tapped his staff on the stone flags. 'On to new adventures,' she said.

Dear reader,

We hope you enjoyed reading *Falcon Warrior*. If you have a moment, please leave us a review – even if it's a short one. We want to hear from you.

The story continues in *Melcorka of Alba*

Want to get notified when one of Creativia's books is free to download? Join our spam-free newsletter at http://www.creativia.org/.

Best regards,
Malcolm Archibald and the Creativia Team

Author's Note

Many centuries before the present United States of America was founded, Cahokia existed. It sat beside the Mississippi River, dominating the surrounding countryside, the largest urban centre north of Mexico and larger than most contemporary cities in Europe. It was founded sometime after 700 AD and flourished from around 1000 to sometime before 1500 AD, vanishing not long before European explorers and adventurers probed into this beautiful corner of the New World.

Nobody knows what it was called, or who lived there, but the site is known, and the great earthen mounds mark what was undoubtedly a remarkable example of the skill and ingenuity of the indigenous peoples of North America. There were at least 120 of the mysterious earthen mounds in and around the city. Similar in shape to the pyramids of Egypt or Central America, these square-based mounds would have been topped with a building in which the leaders of the community lived. In the city centre was a large plaza, where the most sizeable mound of all rose. The mound is today known as Monks Mound.

Cahokia – or whatever it was called – was surrounded by fertile fields where food was grown. There was trade across much of North America, while the city held priests and skilled workers as well as astronomers who built wooden henges, possibly to predict the movement of the sun. This society had not yet discovered steel, so all working was completed with tools of stone or wood. The city manufactured hoes with flint blades and stone-headed axes.

There were no horses or other beasts of burden, so the building work was carried out by men or women, presumably slaves. One major piece of construction was the high palisade built around the city, which argues for some external threat. At two miles long and with towers at regular intervals, this wall was an impressive piece of work; one wonders what sort of enemy the city faced and what happened to them. The first wall was built around 1100 AD, with more walls later. It seems that the citizens of this particular Mississippian Camelot had to look over their shoulder at less than friendly neighbours. Within the walls dwelled the elite and presumably the artisans and astronomers. Outside it, in single-storey houses and neat streets with alleys, paths, and courtyards, was the bulk of the population, not important enough to be protected but necessary for the continuation of the city.

Cahokia was not a monetary-based society, so presumably, trade was by barter, with the surrounding cornfields possibly providing a staple commodity. In return, Cahokia imported shells, copper, salt and mica.

When European pioneers reached this area in the 17th and 18th centuries, they questioned the local Illini tribe, who did not know who had been the builders. The name Cahokia was taken from a small group of the Illini who moved to the area from further east over a century after it was abandoned.

Dedicated work by archaeologists has unearthed (literally) many facts about Cahokia. There was an upper class controlling the city, retaining power and influence by giving away gifts. They seemed to favour ornamentation, with sea-shell beads particularly popular. The elite was born into their position, much like royalty in Europe, and passed on their power to their children in a society where caste seems to have been highly important.

There are also traces of a coppersmith's workshop, games, much skilful building and rebuilding and possible religious ceremonies. All in all, Cahokia was an impressive place with a population of perhaps fifteen thousand souls. One grave site held a man who was interred about the middle of the eleventh century, around the time of Macbeth in Scotland and before the Norman conquest of England. He was tall and obviously important as he was accompanied by some twenty thousand shells and hundreds of arrowheads, perhaps for his use in the next world. The shells were arranged in the shape of a falcon, which gave the idea for the falcon warriors and copper objects. Over fifty women and four men had been executed to keep him company. Other bodies have been found, killed by arrows, clubbed to death or beheaded.

Despite the many discoveries, archaeologists have much work to do before all the secrets of the city are laid bare. So far (2017) only a couple of dozen of the surviving 80 mounds have been excavated.

So why did this great and intricate civilisation die? Did the external enemies breach the defensive palisades and slaughter all the inhabitants? Unlikely: there has been no evidence of a general slaughter. It is much more likely that a rise in the Mississippi flooded their agricultural land, or the Little Ice Age that started in the middle of the 13th century made the land less productive. With a large population, the nearby hunting would have been poor, and the temptation of crossing the Mississippi to hunt the prolific herds of buffalo may have been too much to resist. The people certainly left and never returned.

The city of mounds, abandoned by its people, was forgotten. It is not mentioned in folklore, myth or legend, which is a mystery in itself. In British legend, Camelot and King Arthur's battles against the invading Saxons loom large, yet this city did not give rise to any story. Perhaps the human sacrifices were so shocking that the inhabitants blocked the memory from their history?

Whatever the truth, each year the indigenous peoples of the United States gather here for dancing and music. In some way, it is a part of their heritage, although they do not know quite how or why.

Today, the city is best known as the Cahokia Mounds State Historic Site in Illinois. Some archaeologists think the Dhegihan-Siouan speaking tribes were related to the city, which was something I took advantage of and twisted to meet the ends of the story. One thing is certain: this site is well worth visiting and reveals much about the pre-Columbian history of the area. The mighty Mississippi still flows, and the mounds remain, but all else has changed.

Let the dead rest in peace, from the falcon warrior to the sacrificed women. They have had their day; life moves on.

Malcolm Archibald.
Moray, Scotland, 2017

About the Author

Born and raised in Edinburgh, the sternly-romantic capital of Scotland, I grew up with a father and other male relatives imbued with the military, a Jacobite grandmother who collected books and ran her own business and a grandfather from the legend-crammed island of Arran. With such varied geographical and emotional influences, it was natural that I should write.

Edinburgh's Old Town is crammed with stories and legends, ghosts and murders. I spent a great deal of my childhood walking the dark streets and exploring the hidden closes and wynds. In Arran, I wandered the shrouded hills where druids, heroes, smugglers and the spirits of ancient warriors abound, mixed with great herds of deer and the rising call of eagles through the mist.

Work followed, with many jobs that took me to an intimate knowledge of the Border hill farms, to Edinburgh's financial sector and other occupations that are best forgotten. In between, I met my wife. Engaged within five weeks, we married the following year and that was the best decision of my life, bar none.

At 40, the University of Dundee took me under their friendly wing for four of the best years I have ever experienced. I emerged with a degree in history, and I wrote.

Malcolm Archibald

Printed in Great Britain
by Amazon

75544735R00168